I0685073

Mother of Shadows
Volume Three in the Shadow God Trilogy
By Kathe Todd

Chapter 1

The ogre was tall, reaching up almost to the ceiling in the sitting room where Miri and her brother shared a divan – squeezing together for comfort as they confronted the horrific apparition. It wore nothing but a poorly-tanned fur loincloth, and its skin was a pebbly gray-green color. Its eyes were yellow, the size of saucers, and enormous tusks protruded from its slobbery mouth as it roared, "The penalty for trespass in this forest is death!"

Gauging her audience's reaction, Leila became once again ten-year-old, fiery-haired Pippa Farstrider, the tales of whose adventures had filled more than one book on the shelves of her bookcase during her early girlhood in Marsine's House of the Golden Fish. The girl was lanky, her dark red hair in a long braid down her back, and she was dressed in the muted green and brown leathers of a forester, with a silver bow slung across her back and an enchanted black dagger at her belt. She was carrying a large burlap sack.

"But sir!" Pippa said, not flinching though the ogre stood nearly twice her height, "I meant no trespass. I am here as an emissary of the Elven Queen, bearing a gift for King Sendgar of the Trolls!" She proffered the sack. Now Leila extended her abilities to create the illusion of both the girl adventurer and her antagonist. Miri and Gabriel were both grinning, now, their eyes wide with anticipation.

The ogre's eyes took on a sly look. If this girl were really sent by the Elven Queen, it would be unwise to kill her out of hand. But he must see what she carried. He opened the sack, and at once an enormous black snake struck out and sank its fangs into his face. He dropped the sack and screamed, as the rest of the snake came free of the sack and began wrapping its coils around his body. It was improbably large to have fit in that sack.

Pippa stood there with her hands on her hips and a smile on her face, as the ogre collapsed to the ground and gradually ceased its thrashings. The snake uncoiled itself from his body and she held out the sack so it could return to its snug home. "Good job, Yggi," she said. The ogre's flesh had turned nearly black and was beginning to bubble and melt away, so strong was the snake's venom. Setting the sack on the room's carpet, which seemed unaffected by the melting ogre, the girl dipped a gloved hand into the puddle of ooze that had formed.

She rose to her feet clutching an enormous red gem, shaped roughly like an apple but larger – the ogre's heart! "With this I can penetrate the Troll King's defenses, and free Prince Morningstar!" Pippa declared, smiling brilliantly. Then she, the gem, the ex-ogre, and the sack full of snake all vanished and it was only the children's mother standing there.

"More, more!" cried five-year-old Miri, clapping her hands and bouncing up and down on the divan.

"Yes, Mama, please?" Gabriel begged. He was two years older and far too reserved to try the tricks his adorable younger sister used to get her way. Leila knelt on the thick carpet before the divan and threw her arms around both of them, her dark beauties.

She gave them a squeeze and rose again, saying "That's it for this afternoon. You both have chores to do, if I'm not mistaken?" They both nodded guiltily. "If you're good and eat all your supper tonight," their mother promised, "I'll read you both a story before bedtime. One that's not quite so exciting. I don't want to give you nightmares!"

After Miri had tidied her room and collected eggs from the henhouse Leila took a little time off from her duties as arch-priestess of Betsalel to sit quietly with her little girl. Kathal, now getting up there in years, was curled up on the sofa between them and purring as the little girl stroked her smooth fur.

"Mama, when will Kathal have babies again?" Miri asked. She dimly remembered how much fun it had been to have pard kittens in the house, back when she'd been no more than three. Their other pard, a two-year-old boy named Chavo, had been given to them at age one – already past the cute stage.

Leila ran her hand down Kathal's back, eliciting a deeper purr. The pard had bonded to her when she was only a half-grown kitten, even though Leila – then fourteen – had been disguised as a boy. "Sorry Miri," she told her daughter, "Kathal's getting to be too old to have babies." Pards could live up into their early twenties, but producing litter after litter was hard on the females. The Nima used a contraceptive tea to halt their pards' heat cycles – but Kathal had gotten far too good at avoiding it. She'd had five litters of two cubs each during the past eight years.

"I asked Mulia to make it so Kathal won't have babies anymore," Leila explained. She saw no reason to hide the facts of life from her daughter. The Eight knew, nobody had ever hidden them from *her* at that age. Miri gazed at her mother, owl-eyed. Her skin was lighter than Leila's, black hair wavy rather than curly; but her eyes were Tevo's dark brown.

The wheels were turning. "Is that why *you* don't have any more babies?" Miri asked, and Leila flushed.

"That's right," she admitted. "Your papa and I are very busy bringing the worship of Betsalel back to the Dominion," she said – though truthfully that was just an excuse. She and Tevo had agreed that two children was plenty. It wasn't like they were trying to found a dynasty. Miri sighed. She knew full well how busy her parents were. Mama mostly worked at home, but Papa was often gone for days at a time traveling all over the place, organizing the rebuilding of the hundreds of temples that had been destroyed.

"I wish I had a baby sister," she remarked pensively, and Leila smiled and ruffled her hair.

"Babies are cute," she admitted, "but they are a lot of work, too. If we had another baby in our family it would mean I had less time to spend with you and Gabriel."

Miri sighed again, still stroking the purring cat. Then Leila had a thought. "Your uncle Vandasi is a baby. Maybe we could invite nana Busara to visit with us from Iskand and bring the children, just for the summer. Would you like that?" None of the Karmarzin family had yet met Vandao and his wife's youngest child, the first son. Busara was ten years younger than Leila's father, but she had already been in her middle twenties when they wed seven years previously. It was uncertain whether there would be any more children for them. Vandao, though many wives were the norm for the kings of Palambo, had so far shown no sign he planned to add to his harem.

"If Vandasi is my uncle, why is he younger than me?" Miri wanted to know. Busara and Vandao also had two girls, the younger of whom was a little bit younger than Miri. But she was probably only now reaching the level of mental development to be wondering about such things.

"Bapa Vandao and my mother had me when they were very young," Leila explained. She hadn't shared the details of that tragic match with her children, and didn't plan to do so anytime soon. "My mother died a long time ago, but after Bapa Vandao became king he needed to get married because people in Palambo expect that their king will have lots of children. So because Zurishi and Keisha and Vandasi all have the same father as me, they are my half-sisters and half-brother – even though I'm twenty years older than Zurishi. And my sisters and brother are your aunts and uncle. Do you understand?"

Miri furrowed her brow, trying to wrap her mind around the concept. Finally she nodded. "I think so," she said airily. She had already flitted on to the next concern. "Can we go riding tomorrow?" she asked. Leila and Tevo had sold the original Shadow Manor soon after Gabriel had been born, swapping it for much larger, grander house a few blocks away. This house had real stables at the back and was not far from one of Parat's magnificent public parks – where they could ride Nimble and Milacek, the mare they'd bought for Tevo, and go ice-skating on its frozen pond in the wintertime.

That evening Elyzia Petrowski, a grandmotherly woman in her fifties, deposited tonight's supper on the sideboard in the dining room and then retreated to the kitchen. She and her husband Adalbert constituted the entire servant staff at the new Shadow Manor. Leila loaded plates for the children and herself and they all sat down to eat near one end of the magnificent dining table. It was carved of Palamban bloodwood and could seat sixteen at a pinch, but the Karmarzins rarely entertained.

"How was your trip to Londres?" Leila asked Tevo, as she tucked into the delicious food. Elyzia was every bit as good a cook as Marcelina Walesa had been, the single mother who'd served her and Tevo as a housekeeper for several years before leaving their service to marry a widower. She kept her own house now, and had grown plump and satisfied. They still saw her occasionally, as her son Maksim had decided to go into the priesthood. Now at age twenty he was a lower-level priest of Betsalel in Parat's temple to the Shadow God.

"Chilly," Tevo replied with a grin. Though he was twenty-seven now and had spent much of the past decade as a high official of the church of Betsalel, he hadn't lost the boyish charm that had won Leila's heart. And the former thief had maintained his slim, muscular build.

"What did you do in Londres, Papa?" Gabriel asked. Leila's late first husband Imbaso might have fathered him, but Tevo was the only papa he had ever known. Nor had his parents yet told him anything about his birth father, who had died long before Gabriel was born.

"I brought them an idol for the dedication of the new Temple of Betsalel," Tevo explained after swallowing his mouthful of food.

The fact that the Eight's true idols were created by the gods and goddesses themselves, taken from the "flesh" of an existing idol, was not widely known in today's world. Most of the Eight had been worshiped continually for thousands of years, and generations of their priesthoods had come and gone since there had last been need to acquire new idols. But nearly every idol of Betsalel in the Dominion had been destroyed in Emperor Fernand IV's pogrom against the Shadow God's church centuries ago. Only in the past decade had it once again become legal to worship the dark one.

After consulting with Betsalel on the subject, Leila and Tevo had decided to keep the secret of the idols to themselves and not teach it to the priests and priestesses they were training. The god himself was free to reveal this fact to any he chose, but it seemed best that it remain secret knowledge. Had the late Mauaji, father and murderer of Imbaso, known about it he might have spawned dozens more idols for his djinn Kivuli to manifest in – and they might still have been fighting that evil cult eight years later.

"You know, Leila," Tevo said after taking a drink of wine to wash down a mouthful of beef, "the kids are getting big enough now. I was thinking maybe they could come along on some of these expeditions. We could make a family trip of it, leave the cats and horses for Elyzia and Adalbert to care for. It would be a great educational opportunity, to see new places."

With Leila either pregnant or caring for young children all of the time since they'd been reunited, it had fallen to Tevo to travel all over the Dominion – carrying seed idols to the Temples of the Eight that were scattered throughout the land, rebuilding the priesthood, setting up church finances and collecting donations so that the temples could be rebuilt. But now that Betsalel's idols were once again in every Temple of the Eight, traveling had become much less burdensome. The Shadow God could carry them to anywhere he had an active idol, in the blink of an eye.

"That might be fun," Leila replied. They had used Betsalel's services to carry them (Gabriel just a babe in arms, at that time) to Palambo for the royal wedding of Vandao and Busara, and had been back a couple of times since. But Palambo held unhappy memories for Leila – and anyway, the climate was too bloody hot a lot of the time. "Maybe later this year, a trip to one of the Center Sea ports would be good. But I was thinking I'd like to invite Busara to bring the children and come to stay with us in Parat for the summer."

Tevo cocked an eyebrow. He liked his stepmother-in-law. A devotee of Deline, she had been a scholar and had spent years traveling around Palambo exploring ancient ruins before returning to the palace in Iskand where she'd grown up. "Miri wants to see Vandasi while he's still a baby," Leila pointed out. Of course, she herself would *also* like that.

"Me, too!" Gabriel chimed in. He was tickled by the idea of having relatives even darker than he was, and Palamban royalty at that.

"Sure, why not?" Tevo said. "I don't have that many trips on the schedule for the next couple of months, anyway. And we've certainly got the room." There were six bedrooms in Shadow Manor, only four of them occupied. Leila reached across and squeezed his hand, grinning.

"Great!" she said. "I'll nip down to the palace and invite them in person after supper." It had been awhile since she'd seen her father, anyhow, and she didn't mind a *short* trip to Palambo.

After cleaning her plate Leila kissed her children and husband, then took herself to the room that had once been the house's ballroom. It was tiny by the standards of the imperial palace – or some of the mansions of the wealthy that lined the slopes below it – but it had the house's highest ceilings, and they had wanted a family shrine where the idol of Betsalel could become large enough to carry multiple people without shrinking them first.

The Shadow God was busy these days. His worship and priesthood had been restored throughout the kingdom of Palambo eight years before, and he had worshipers all over the Dominion as well though the work of rebuilding his temples would yet take decades to complete. But he still found time to visit with his arch-priest and arch-priestess in their home, and had been introduced to their children while they were still in the womb.

"All is well, beloved?" Betsalel asked when he had manifested in his idol, coming to Leila's call. It had been only a couple of hours since he had last manifested here, returning Tevo from his journey thousands of miles to the west.

"Sorry to bother you, master," Leila said with an impish smile. She had gotten used to prevailing on her mighty god for trivial favors, but it still amused her that he was so willing to grant them. She didn't truly realize how much he owed her. "I'd like to be taken to the palace in Iskand, please," she told the Shadow God. "I'm just going for an hour or so, then coming back home. If you wouldn't mind?"

He smiled at her, ruby eyes glistening in the late light coming in through the windows to the south. This far north, there was another hour or more of daylight remaining. But it would already be dark in Iskand. He bent his knees, crouching like a loving father bending to receive his little daughter, and opened his arms.

Chapter 2

In his palace within Ashbat, capital of the Gholim Khanate, Oghul Khan sat his wooden throne with a scowl on his face. He was not a happy man. Though Simdal Tzurkano was his oldest and most trusted advisor, a man who had served Oghul's father before he himself had been born, the old man's face was ashen with fear at the news he had to impart.

Oghul required all who came before him to kneel. He had not united the disparate and warring Gholim tribes in the arid lands just east of the Pahadai (what the soft foreigners in the Dominion, on the mountains' western side, called the "Killtops") by being a kindly gentleman. But in token of his lifelong friend's age and stiff knees, he had provided him with a cushion.

"I negotiated with him at length, Great Khan," he was saying, "returning three times and waiting for more than a week between visits to allow him time to communicate with his emperor. But he was adamant. Emperor Ostden is firmly against permitting the Khanate to have an enclave within Miradil."

"This is an outrage!" Oghul fumed, bringing his fist down on the arm of the throne. It was nothing more than an oversized wooden armchair, ornamented with some gold leaf and inset with polished horse bone; but among the Gholim tribes, most of whom led a nomadic lifestyle, any chair at all was a luxury. "The Palambans maintain a trading enclave within Miradil, do they not?"

Miradil was the world's foremost trade center, through which goods from all over the continent were bought and sold. That it (and the mouth of the Huang River, along which most of the goods from the nations east of the Pahadai passed) was controlled by the Gaspari Dominion was a source of frustration for more than one ruler within what Gasparis mistakenly called "the realms of the Hando."

True, the Hando nation of Hanshu was the eastern part of the continent's largest political entity, and the Hando tongue was spoken everywhere as a trade language; but at least three-fifths of the people in the heavily-populated region that made up a major part of the earth's only land mass were Dravim or Gholim, not Hando. It was insulting!

As for the issue of the Gasparis permitting the Khanate a trading enclave within Miradil's high walls, it was admittedly true that Oghul Khan had intended to use this concession as a foothold. Once inside, his warriors would overrun the defenses from behind and take over the city, putting a stranglehold on all foreign trade – and eventually spreading out to turn the poorly-defended Dominion into a slave state.

There had been no war in the Dominion in dozens of generations, while the Gholim tribes had been battling each other, and anyone else inclined to pick a fight, since time immemorial. The rich lands of the Dominion would fall like a ripe plum, providing food and luxury goods to the Gholim. And Oghul Khan, who would be known ever after as "The Great," would be the one to bring this about.

Yet it was almost as if Emperor Ostden had somehow guessed his plans. Not only the kingdom of Palambo but Hanshu, Indaya, and several smaller states east of the Pahadai had been granted space within Miradil's walls. Yet over and over again, Oghul's overtures to be granted equal treatment had been turned aside. The Gholim were a fierce, contentious people and no matter how great his strength he would not be able to hold them together forever without an outside enemy to fight. He *needed* to get that foothold in Miradil, and soon!

The Khan rose from his throne, and extended a hand to Simdal. "Rise, Uncle," he said, granting the old man the term of endearment by which he'd called him when he was a boy. "I am sure that you did everything you could. We need to find another way to convince this Gaspari emperor to give us what we want."

They retired to a small chamber off of the throne room, and servants brought hot, heavily-sweetened tea and little date pastries for them. "Might we perhaps blockade the Ivory Road?" Simdal asked. The foremost highway east of the Pahadai ran along at a distance of about a mile north of the Huang's northern bank, paved all in stone and broad enough for two caravans to pass at once. Most goods traveling from the Dominion and Palambo went by caravan along this road, whereas goods coming from Hanshu, Indaya, and other eastern lands traveled by boat on the mighty river.

"This could be done, but it would not be long before the war bands would demand to be moving again," Oghul admitted. He knew his people well. And while it might well inconvenience some Gaspari exporters, this would not likely be enough leverage to make the Gaspari emperor relent and let the Gholim into Miradil. Nor could they simply storm the city. Unlike nearly every other city in the Dominion, Miradil was heavily fortified.

"I think we need to consult with the Black Witch," Simdal said regretfully. He misliked the woman, but there was no denying she had mysterious powers. Oghul sighed. The women of the Gholim were famed throughout the world for their ferocity, but decisions of war – and the ruling of nations – were supposed to be man's work. Yet he knew Simdal was right. All he had worked for over the past dozen years would come crashing down, if he did not act soon.

"She's staying in the palace at the moment," he told his advisor. "I'll have her sent for." While they waited for the sorceress to arrive they continued to take their ease, drinking tea and talking of old times. When the woman who had been summoned walked into the room, it was as if it were she who was the ruler, not Oghul Khan, and the two men had been caught out like little boys engaged in some mischief.

"I have come," Rajani said coldly, taking the third seat at the small table without being asked. At the court of the Great Khan she was known as the "Black Witch," partly because of her complexion. The tribes of the Gholim ranged in hue from mahogany brown to as pale as any Gaspari; but Rajani's father, the man who had inducted her into the mysteries of Danava, had been of the Dravim. Before it began to turn silver her hair had been a deep black, lightly waving; and her eyes were black as coal. Her skin, now lined from decades in the sun, was the color of strong kaf with only a little milk added.

Nor was Rajani the name her long-dead Gholim mother had given her. It was a name of power in Indaya, a name to strike dread in the hearts of those who recognized it. And it suited her well enough. The other reason for her sobriquet was the black arts she practiced. She had found no friends here at the court of the khan, but he and his subordinates valued her services. They had given her wealth and power, and that would have to do.

The sorceress was dressed in rich robes in the Gholim style, loose trousers of fine wool tucked into polished leather boots, and a heavily-embroidered coat of the same material. Even as summer was coming on, the weather near the eastern foothills of the Pahadai was cool. She slipped one hand into her pocket to touch the small idol there, and spoke in her mind to her goddess: "Danava, come to me."

Rajani's black eyes bored into the khan's gray ones. He was of the Azherbim, one of the lightest of the Gholim tribes. His unkempt mop of hair and shaggy, short beard were a medium brown in color, now in his fifty-fifth year becoming streaked with gray. She was a decade older than he was, and showed no signs of fear in his presence though his feat of uniting the Gholim tribes had only been accomplished twice before in all of recorded history.

Finally it was Oghul Khan who broke. "Thank you for coming, Rajani," he said politely. He might be a bloodthirsty warlord, but he was also a consummate politician. Listening to the whisperings of her goddess, the sorceress replied, "The Count of Miradil has denied your request to allow Khanate troops within the city," she said matter-of-factly. The faces of Oghul and Simdal froze as they struggled not to reveal their shock at this demonstration of the Black Witch's powers.

"Emperor Ostden is no more a fool than his father was," Rajani went on. "The tribes have little to offer the Dominion in trade, nor do they offer much of a market for the Dominion's goods. There can be no reason but the most obvious one for you to seek a foothold in Miradil." After killing her father Rajani had sought out her mother's people, only to find that the mother she could not recall had died years before. Nor had there been any welcome among the Kazhakim for this strange young half-breed foreigner and her black goddess. To her, the tribes of the Gholim would forever be "they" and not "us."

"I must have that foothold in Miradil," Oghul Khan pronounced. "I need a way to force Emperor Ostden to grant it to us, before the Khanate dissolves into chaos and infighting once more." Danava, whose worship dated back more than two thousand years, was known as the Destroyer of Illusions. Her purported powers included clairvoyance and the ability to read the future. But in working with Danava almost her entire life Rajani had noted that the goddess' vision could be curiously blind at times – and as for the future, was not knowing it just the first step in changing it? With every decision taken, a thousand new futures might open up.

But while Danava might be the source of most of her powers, the sorceress had other tools at her disposal. She was a canny survivor, literate and well-read, and she kept abreast of world events. Pretending to go into a trance for a moment, her black eyes unfocused, Rajani abruptly sat stiffly upright and stared into the Khan's eyes once again.

"The Gaspari emperor and his bride have two children," she said portentously, as if this knowledge were mystically derived and not common knowledge. "Take them, or one of them at least, hostage, and you may obtain what you need. Perhaps, even, it might be that they were abducted by someone unconnected with you. You managed to rescue them from their captors, and are returning them to the emperor as a gesture of good will – and all you ask is this small concession, the opportunity to enjoy the same benefits a presence in Miradil offers to so many other rulers. How could he refuse?"

The khan's gray eyes darkened as excitement seized him. A brilliant plan, and it could work! But… "Surely the children of the emperor, especially the heir to the Gaspari throne, must be heavily guarded day and night? How could they be taken, there in the midst of the Dominion's strength?"

Rajani lowered her eyelids, dark eyes glinting in the torchlight. "My arts will find a way," she said. "But if I achieve this for you, the payment I claim will be high. Are you prepared to meet my price?" Oghul Khan looked stunned. She was just a little old woman, but somehow Rajani scared the crap out of him – he, a man who had taken more than a dozen heads before his eighteenth birthday. "If you bring me a child of the Gaspari emperor, alive and well," he said solemnly, "I will grant you anything you wish."

Chapter 3

The city of Parat often got rain in the spring and summertime. It was what made it such an attractive place, gardens blooming lushly and hills glowing emerald green on either side of the Vizha. But so far the month of Sunheight had been absolutely lovely – day after day of clear blue skies and warm sunshine, light breezes off the river keeping it from becoming too hot.

Emperor Aleksander III, who had ruled for most of Leila's life, had died suddenly of a stroke three years earlier and put his son Ostden (twenty-fourth of his name) on the throne at the tender age of twenty-seven. The young emperor and his beautiful wife were the darlings of the Dominion at large and Parat society in particular. They had two young children, and enjoyed hosting celebrations. Some of these were festivals where any member of the public could attend, others by invitation only to the imperial capital's elite.

Empress Lisabet had prevailed on her husband, who could deny her nothing, to take advantage of the fine weather by staging a garden party on the palace grounds – a family event with games for the little ones, and a chance to get to know some of Parat's more prominent citizens who were also parents of young children. So invitations were engraved, and sent out on fairly short notice.

The guest list of course included Tevo and Leila Karmarzin and their son and daughter, along with other prominent members of Parat's clergy as well as the relations of counts and the scions of wealthy merchant clans with their broods. Leila immediately sent a messenger back thanking Lisabet and informing her that the queen of Palambo, her stepmother, was visiting in Parat for the summer with her three young children and would love to be included.

Leila had met Lisabet a couple of times before she and Ostden had taken up residence in the Imperial Palace. He of course had been born and raised there, but had set up his household in Andarria. Both their daughter Berta and son Aleksei had been born there, but brought to Parat to be introduced to the gods at the Temple of the Eight when they had reached the age of one month.

The new emperor and his wife had had to relocate to Parat on his accession to the throne, and she missed the circle of friends they'd had in Andarria. Maybe this party would be the start of some new friendships, ones that would enrich their children's lives.

The Karmarzins, along with Busara and her three children, arrived at the palace with their invitations and were admitted inside, then shown by a smiling servant to the little private park the emperors of the Dominion had kept for their own pleasure for generations.

Busara had visited them in Parat twice before, though never for so long – and never had she brought all three children with her. She loved visiting the Dominion in the summer, when temperatures in Iskand soared so high you could scarcely leave the cool confines of the royal palace without perishing in the heat. The much greater humidity was better for the complexion, she felt, as well. Though prejudice against dark-skinned Palambans was still widespread in the Dominion, especially among the lower classes, the emperor and empress welcomed Busara and her beautiful black children warmly – and the other upper-class citizens of Parat took their cue from the royal couple.

The royal palace in Iskand had many lovely gardens too, of course, but Busara found herself dazzled by the many varieties of plant she'd never seen before. While Palamban history and pre-history had been her primarily fields of study, she was interested in everything in the world around her. As the older children were taken in hand by servants who were supervising the games, Leila volunteered to watch little Vandasi so that her stepmother could go exploring. She'd met a young scholar from the Archives who knew all the plants and trees, and was ecstatic to have an enthusiastic audience as he led the tall, graceful queen of Palambo around the grounds pointing out this or that cultivar.

Vandasi was an adorable baby. Both of his parents were very dark-skinned, tall and lean – like nearly all members of the Palamban royal family. But at this stage of his life, a little short of fourteen months, he was a chubby-cheeked toddler with laughing black eyes who found delight everywhere he looked. Of course he wanted to get down and go exploring, but he didn't mind being held and cuddled either. Miri had been very much enjoying his visit.

Ostden and Lisabet, as the hosts of this party, were circulating among the crowds and welcoming their guests personally. It was not a huge gathering, perhaps fifty couples and their children ranging in age from babies like Vandasi to teenagers.

Lisabet came up to Tevo and Leila where they were standing near one of the refreshment tables sipping chilled lemonade. Luncheon would be served at dozens of round tables set up on the lawn later, but for the moment it was time for the children to play organized games while their parents socialized.

"Leila, is it?" the empress asked. She was slightly younger than her husband, around Tevo's age; of medium height with a slender but curvy figure, creamy skin, green eyes, and flaming red hair. A stunning beauty, but managing to look like a cheerful housewife at this casual event. She was wearing a pretty frock but without much ornamentation – and no jewelry.

Lisabet offered her hand, and Leila took it with the one that was free. Vandasi was tucked into the crook of her other arm, grinning from ear to ear as the pretty lady came up to say hello. Are you here to shower me with love, perhaps? "We met most recently at young Aleksei's Godsight ceremony," Leila reminded her.

"I remember!" the empress dimpled. "I believe you had a baby in your arms then, too. A little girl?" Leila smiled back.

"Our daughter Miriam," she confirmed. "She's five now and off playing with the other kids." She gestured in the direction where the games were being held. "This is my baby brother Vandasi." Lisabet chucked him under the chin, and he broke into giggles.

"What a cutie!" she exclaimed. "But you said he's your baby brother?"

Leila really didn't want to go into all the gory details, but she felt she owed the empress at least a token explanation. After nearly a decade as Betsalel's arch-priestess she'd become much more comfortable moving in the circles of the elite than she once had been – but it wasn't every day she was actually hobnobbing with the empress of the entire Dominion.

"My father is King Vandao of Palambo," Leila said. "My mother was of the Dominion, and I grew up here. But I became close with my father years ago. You know I used to be queen of

17

Palambo?" She grinned. Lisabet looked her up and down, green eyes widening.

"I…" she said, then trailed off. "I seem to recall hearing something about the priestess who restored Betsalel to the pantheon here in Parat having become queen there, but I didn't realize… that was you?"

Leila smiled again. She could hardly believe it herself. The deadly fight against the Kivuli cult, falling in love with Imbaso, their months of dodging assassins – all ending in his tragic death, followed by public demands that Palambo's first and only queen regnant abdicate her throne. Eight years later, those events sometimes seemed as if they had happened to someone else.

"My lord Betsalel requested my help in overcoming an evil djinn that was being worshipped in his name there," Leila explained. "One thing led to another. My first husband and I managed to eradicate the djinn, but after an assassin killed him I abdicated the throne. As you probably know, the rulers of Palambo are elected by a council of arch-priests from among the qualified members of the royal family. My father had been doing much of the work of running the country for years, under his late uncle King Omali, in any case. I think they made the best possible choice."

Lisabet twinkled at her. "Yes," she said, "Your father has been making some startling reforms there. At the rate he's going, Palambo might be rivaling the Dominion in another few years." Vandao had taken steps to institute universal education as a first step toward democratization of the kingdom's government, and had begun working on a constitution – something Palambo had never had before. The days of the king ruling by decree, with the power to execute anyone on a whim, were drawing to a close.

"Your story sounds fascinating, Leila," the empress went on, "and I hope I'll get a chance to hear more of it later. For now, though, I have many more guests to greet. See you soon!" She squeezed Tevo's offered hand and murmured a few words, then drifted off to another little knot of guests.

"Let's stroll, shall we?" Tevo suggested. He'd been amused by the exchange. He took Vandasi from her, the boy growing heavy, and put him up on his shoulders. They knew many of the people here, at least casually, but had not formed any really close friendships. The pair had first arrived in the imperial capital in disguise, plotting to free Betsalel's idol from its imprisonment in the imperial Treasure House. After that success, they had found themselves too busy for much socializing – the more so for Tevo when Leila had left him behind to travel to Palambo on the god's mission.

Still, many sought their acquaintance. They were foremost in the favor of the Shadow God, after all, and though it had been nearly a decade since the laws banning Betsalel's worship in the Dominion had been rescinded there was still an aura of mystery, of danger about the Dark One that appealed to the younger generation. They ambled through the beautiful gardens, going out to watch the children at their games, greeting people they knew. Vandasi spotted his mother inspecting a tall flowering shrub in company with her archivist, and demanded to be let down to run to her on his stumpy little legs.

Whooping, laughing children came streaming back from the enormous lawn where the games had been held, and a servant asked people to please take seats as luncheon was about to be served. Though this was an informal party tables had been reserved, and as Tevo, Leila, Busara, and Vandasi found their way to the one with their names on it Gabriel came running up to them, a huge white grin on his dark face, hand in hand with a girl who looked to be close to his own age though she was inches shorter.

"We won the three-legged race, Mama!" he cried excitedly. The boy was tall for his age and athletic, having been trained in gymnastics since he was just past toddlerhood. Busy as she was, Leila loved moving her body and had taken a lot of trouble these last few years to keep herself in shape – while playing with her children.

The girl was pretty, and would someday be a rare beauty, Leila guessed. Though at the moment there was a gap where her front teeth should have been, and her face was covered in freckles. Her flaming red hair left little doubt who her mother must be. "Introduce us to your new friend, please," she asked her son. Along with his physical training he'd been well-schooled in the courtesies.

"Berta," he said formally (though the irrepressible grin had not left his face), "This is my mother and father, Leila and Tevo

19

Karmarzin, the arch-priestess and arch-priest of Betsalel in the Dominion. And my grandmother Busara of Iskand, queen of Palambo, with her son Vandasi – who's my uncle! Mama and Papa, this is Berta of house Piastin, daughter of Emperor Ostden and Empress Lisabet."

Berta curtseyed. "Pleased to meet you," she said politely, grinning just as broadly as Gabriel.

"Where's your sister, Gabe?" his mother asked him, concerned. She'd expected him to be looking out for Miri.

"With my brother!" Berta said. She looked around, then pointed and waved. "There they are!" To the audience of adults she added, "They were in a different race than we were, the under-six group. We beat some kids who were nine or ten!"

"And Zurishi and Keisha?" Busara asked. Now it was Gabriel's turn to peer around. His aunts, far darker than nearly anyone else here, were easy to spot.

"Here they come," he assured his grandmother. "Zurishi was in the race with us, but Keisha had to be in the later race. Zurishi was waiting for her."

The girls came up together laughing, moments after Miri arrived still holding hands with a boy who had hair of a medium auburn color and green eyes. Aleksei, heir to the throne of the Gaspari Dominion. He was taller than she was already, though several months younger – of an age with Keisha, Leila believed. The emperors of the Piastin dynasty had been breeding themselves for beauty for many generations, and she could see the boy would be a heartbreaker when he grew up. Couple that with the likelihood he would become ruler over nearly a third of the world's population, and maidens all over the Dominion would be falling at his feet. She hoped Miri would have better sense than to be one of them.

But for now, they were just a couple of cute, innocent little kids. They had not been the winners in their race, but had enjoyed Berta and Gabriel's victory vicariously and had fun trying. The games had been configured so that everyone who participated won a prize – though the winners, obviously, got bigger and better ones. Berta donated her prize to Miri, announcing that it did not seem fair for her to win one since her family were the party's hosts.

The Karmarzin children and their new-found friends would have liked to eat lunch together, but there weren't enough chairs at the table. After a little while, as lunch service was getting underway, a couple of servants tracked down the emperor's wayward two and they were herded back to eat with their family at the table assigned to them.

The luncheon was a delight worthy of the royal palace at Iskand, a series of light, delicious little treats that together managed to comprise a meal. And if some of the children ate rather more of the candied fruits and less of the spinach salad with nuts and raisins, that was surely a matter for their parents to decide.

Busara's children, even little Vandasi, had been accustomed to a dazzling array of exotic delights from a young age, and eagerly ate of everything that was put in front of them. They'd worked up good appetites running and playing earlier. For those who grew up in Palambo's royal palace, there was nothing you could really call "comfort food." Children there would be exposed to twenty different dishes nightly, and while each of them had their favorites it was hard to wind up as a picky eater coming from that background.

After lunch was finished there was more play, supervised but not formalized. The emperor and empress had hoped that the children would have gotten acquainted with each other during the pre-lunch games, and would now be free to enjoy playing in whatever way their imaginations took them. A full-size pirate ship had been erected in a corner of the garden, along with a miniature replica of Mad Count Oester's castle and some other play structures.

Berta and Aleksei were back at the Karmarzins' table as soon as lunch was over, and Gabriel and Miri (along with Zurishi and Keisha, whom the Piastin children found entrancingly exotic) had soon run off with them to explore the pirate ship. Mama had told them the tale of the dread pirate Mgondi, about whom the captain of the ship she'd taken to Palambo nine years ago had warned his passengers. Her stories tended to be heavily embellished, and of course dramatized using her power of illusion; so they were filled with excitement at the romance of it all.

Following along in their children's footsteps, the emperor and empress came by and invited themselves to sit down. "Berta and

Aleksei have really hit it off with Gabriel and Miri," Lisabet said with a smile. "She couldn't stop talking about how wonderful your Gabe is!" Leila grinned. Her boy had a lot of his father's inborn charm – and some of his papa's as well.

"She's a doll," the arch-priestess replied. "Quite a handful, I'm guessing?" Lisabet rolled her eyes. As the wife of the heir to the Gaspari Dominion her responsibilities as a mother might well have ended after the midwife's exclamation of "it's a girl!" But she loved her children dearly, and wanted to be a much bigger part of their lives than was common among women of her class. She had nursed them herself until weaning, and though they did have a governess and various tutors, a large part of her time was spent caring for them.

"They say the red hair is a sign," the empress replied. "I can't think what they mean by that," she added with a slight smile, "but it's true that Berta can be quite forthright about expressing her desires. And disinclined to take 'no' for an answer. I'm trying to work with her on that."

"And Aleksei?" Tevo asked, not wanting to let the women completely dominate the conversation.

"A complete angel," the boy's mother assured them with a wink. "His sister has hardly managed to corrupt him at all." Ostden proved to be a little more reserved than his charming wife, but nearly as personable once you drew him out. The parents sat around the table for half an hour, talking of this and that, and passing Vandasi around so that he could be cuddled, tickled, and played with. He *was* an awfully cute baby.

By the time the gathering was winding down, as the dinner hour was approaching, the Karmarzin kids were begging to be allowed to stay at the palace for a sleepover. Empress Lisabet's garden party had been a huge success. And her children had acquired some fast friends.

Chapter 4

As full summer came on, the friendship between the Karmarzins and the Piastins deepened. It was hard for the emperor and empress to have intimate friends – their station in life meant that every social interaction was fraught with political considerations. Should it be seen that Leila and Tevo had the ear of the emperor, they would be besieged with people seeking to become their friends for the sake of political advantage. So the families kept their gatherings quiet, for the most part. Part of the reason Ostden and Lisabet liked the Karmarzins so much was that they *had* no political agenda. They were in no need of positions at court or financial favors, they just wanted to enjoy their friends' company.

A very small guard force accompanied the imperial family in their private carriage (the one *not* covered in gold leaf and imperial seals) for an intimate dinner party at Shadow Manor. Elyzia, whose name was a variation of Lisabet's, outdid herself to produce a meal that was exquisitely prepared without being elaborate, and everyone loved it.

After supper Leila extended the Piastins the rare privilege of letting them in on one of her secrets, as she entertained them all with storytelling acted out by illusions. Very few people knew she had this ability, and she really wanted to keep it that way. Though she had lived the past eight years of her life without any peril whatsoever (beyond the perils of childbearing, from which she had been protected by both Betsalel and Mulia), the Shadow God had given her these gifts and she treasured them.

Later, as the children played a simple game in the ballroom at the feet of Betsalel (who was not present in his idol at the moment), Busara and Lisabet chatted with Leila as Tevo traded stories with the emperor. "Oh Leila," the empress said sincerely, "that is the most *wonderful* ability! I would so like to be wearing my soft robe and slippers while appearing to be dressed in a jewel-encrusted ball gown. It would make life so much more comfortable!"

Leila grinned at her. Her danger-free life had long since gotten her away from the practice of dressing in assassin's garb laden with weaponry, beneath the illusion of normal clothing. She was genuinely dressed in a soft cotton skirt, silk blouse, and velvet slippers. Comfortable, but dressy enough for a quiet evening among friends.

But while motherhood and a quiet life as a respectable member of Parat society had mellowed her, the former gutter rat/thief/assassin still had a streak of mischief. In an instant she was dressed in a gown so absurdly covered in gems and gold, that had it been real it would have weighed too much for her to be able to stand upright while wearing it. "Ooh, I like the emeralds!" Lisabet laughed. "They set off your eyes so well. Come to think of it, they'd set off my *own* eyes quite nicely…" Leila reached out a hand toward the empress, and she looked down to find she was clad in an identical gown.

Busara gazed at them in delight, clapping her hands. "You ladies are magnificent!" she said, in her lovely Palamban drawl. She and Vandao had made sure that their two older children were fluent in Gasparto as well as their native Kiswa, and Vandasi was already beginning to speak in both languages. "Join us," Leila insisted, and putting out another hand she clad her stepmother in a similar costume. But in place of the emeralds, Busara's gown was encrusted in black diamonds and rubies – better suited to her ebon complexion.

Taking the other two women by the elbows, Leila led them into the study where Tevo and Ostden were conversing over brandy. "What do you think, gentlemen?" Leila asked. "Is this too much for the next imperial ball?" The men looked up and goggled in disbelief. Leila had demonstrated the ability to appear as mythical beasts, men at arms, and tiny children – but neither of them had completely realized what she could do for the appearance of others.

"Do you have to touch the other person to do that?" the emperor asked. Like most of his line he was no dummy, and his inquiring mind always wanted to know and understand more. "I've been practicing this for nearly nine years," Leila explained, "and I can cast the illusion up to around five feet away now. But it's a strain to maintain. If I'm in physical contact with the person, it's a lot easier." She released the illusion, and the three women's clothing reverted to normal.

Elyzia had volunteered to ride herd on the seven children, who were enjoying themselves in the ballroom, so the adults had leisure to stay in the study talking. "The biggest Nima gathering of the year is coming next week," Leila mentioned. The gathering grounds east of the river in Parat were the largest in the Dominion, and drew Nima bands from all over the eastern part of the country plus occasional visitors from as far away as the realms of the Hando.

There were gatherings every couple of months from Pluvius through Frostmoon, but the one at the beginning of Ettas, in early summer, was the largest and longest. For a week a festival atmosphere would take hold, and visitors from the nearby city would come to see the horse races and games, admire the nomads' colorful garb and wagons, sample their foods and buy their handicrafts. To the average stay-put citizen of Parat, the Nima and their lifestyle seemed romantic and exciting – if a little untrustworthy.

"You are friends with the Nima?" the emperor asked Leila, and she smiled and nodded.

"I traveled with a band of them in the western Dominion during my misspent youth," she remarked casually. Just how very misspent that youth had been was something she had not discussed with their new friends. "I've never met any of the people I knew then here in Parat, though," she went on. "Most bands will follow the same circuit each year, and those who travel in the west would never come this far east. But I've found new friends among those who make Parat a regular stop."

"That explains the pards, then," Ostden said. The visitors had been entranced by the personable cats, who'd greeted them politely at the door and permitted the children to make much of them.

"I got Kathal from the people I traveled with in the west," Leila explained. "She's eleven now, but she was a valiant companion to me back when my life was more exciting."

"Then the younger cat is her son?" Lisabet asked.

"No, he's not related. Somewhere in this city is someone with an adult male pard. The females come into heat in the late winter, and Kathal kept getting out before I realized what was going on – and returning pregnant. She's had babies six times since we took up residence here, until I got Mulia to put a stop to it. It wasn't long before we ran out of friends and acquaintances in the city to give kittens to – pards are not really all that well suited to city life – so

I've been giving them to Nima families at the gatherings. Chavo was an in-kind gift, a thank-you from one of the families who'd gotten kittens from us in the past."

The emperor and his wife chuckled at the tale. The cats were amazing, but they could well imagine how an animal forty-fifty pounds in size might not be the ideal house pet. They had a few regular cats around the palace, good for keeping down the mice; and of course the palace also kept a large pack of dogs for hunting. But those had kennels to live in, and a kennelmaster to look after them.

"Anyhow," Leila went on – having gotten thoroughly sidetracked on what she was going to say – "I was thinking that it might be fun to have a family expedition to the gathering one day when the weather's nice. I can introduce you to some of my Nima friends, and I know the children would enjoy it." Beloved as the imperial couple were, they didn't fear going out in public among their subjects. And the Nima *were* their subjects, even if they lived their lives apart from the rest of Dominion society. "That sounds wonderful," Lisabet said enthusiastically. "Let's do it!"

Chapter 5

It rained off and on during the first two days of the Nima High Summer Gathering, but the third day dawned clear and bright. An Imperial Messenger appeared at the door of Shadow Manor as the Karmarzins, augmented by Busara and her three children, were seated at the dining table eating breakfast. The message read, "Shall we come and collect you in our carriage so we can all go together to the gathering?"

Five adults and seven children, plus presumably at least a coachman and footman, and maybe a few guards, were a lot to cram into a carriage – even one as large as that belonging to the imperial family. But the weather was fine, and there should be plenty of room up top for the older kids. Leila scrawled a reply and handed it to the messenger, who dashed off back up the hill to the palace.

At around ten in the morning they were all ready to go, as the carriage pulled up outside. It was accompanied by a couple of Imperial Guards on horseback. The imperial family could hardly just go out into a crowded gathering without at least a little protection. In token of this Leila armed herself with a couple of the daggers she'd owned for more than half her life, and let illusion provide her costume. Ladies' clothing, at least the respectable sort, tended not to include secret scabbards for knives.

The children were bouncing off the walls with excitement. Neither Berta and Aleksei nor Zurishi and Keisha had ever seen a Nima gathering. Though the traveling folk had supposedly originated in northern Palambo at around the time that the ancestors of the Daregs were building Iskand, their migration had taken them north. They were widespread in the Dominion, less so east of the Killtops, but not to be found in Palambo any more at all.

Berta, Zurishi, and Gabriel rode on top of the carriage with Tevo, feeling as if they were on top of the world as it rolled along the streets of Palambo heading down to the river and the nearer of the two large bridges that now spanned it. Much of Parat's more recent development had taken place in the less hilly area east of the river, and they had to travel for more than a mile before the industrial buildings began to thin out and they found themselves approaching the Nima Gathering Ground.

This flat field, some fifty acres in size, had been granted to the Nima in perpetuity by some long-dead emperor, in token of a service the so-called "King of the Nima" had provided. This title was one that was often claimed by multiple people at any one time. The Nima were united by culture and lifestyle, and to some extent by blood; but they were not a political entity – more like a very scattered tribe. But they had often found that they could get more respect from the rest of Gaspari society if they were believed to have a king.

The grass had been thoroughly trampled down and the entire area was a riot of color, as brightly-dressed Nima walked around among the brightly-painted caravans that were their homes. The new arrivals parked their carriage over near one side of the Gathering Ground, and everyone piled out. The guards left their horses hitched to the carriage, and joined them on the ground while the carriage driver remained with it to guard it from the depredations of the thieving Nima.

Leila took Miri in hand, while Lisabet had Aleksei in tow and Busara held onto Zurishi and Keisha. She'd put Vandasi into a backpack that somewhat resembled a miniature camel saddle, letting him ride high up with a great view of his surroundings. He seemed pretty content. Tevo and Ostden immediately made for the race track, where they would no doubt be placing bets. Over the years Tevo had developed a good eye for horseflesh, and he'd found a fellow enthusiast in the emperor.

Gabriel and Berta were holding hands. A bit of a pre-adolescent romance going on there, Leila thought. With his height and dark good looks coupled with his charm and sweet disposition, Gabe had swept the little red-headed princess off her feet. She sighed. She still loved Tevo with all her heart, but she remembered with fondness how passionate and exciting it had been when they first fell in love – the aching desire, the wonder of it all. Things had gotten awfully routine, eight years into their marriage and with two underage roommates around the house.

The kids of course wanted to be allowed to run loose around the gathering together, but that couldn't be permitted. One of the guards had accompanied the men to the racetrack, acting as body servant to the emperor. Ostden and Lisabet were not precisely in disguise here at this huge public event, but they were definitely trying to avoid notice and just enjoy the day the same as any of their subjects might. The other guard volunteered to stay with the two oldest children, after Leila assured her friend that she was armed – and pointed out she could frighten off anyone who menaced them with her illusion power. Even the guards were out of uniform, wearing casual clothing – though there was no mistaking them for anything but what they were, if you had eyes to see.

While Leila, Lisabet, and Busara watched in amusement, Gabriel began dragging Berta and their unwanted chaperone off in the direction of one of the Nima band enclaves. Those who traveled together in a band tended to camp together at gatherings, too – setting up a little temporary village that would, for the duration of the gathering, be known as "Nicolae's encampment" or "Tobor's encampment" – whoever was the leader of the band. Nima band leaders were like tribal chieftains, in many respects. Often everyone in the band was related, and the leader might be the patriarch of the clan; or it might just be someone, man or woman, who was well-respected. But the Nima, always, were ruled by consent.

"I'll bet Gabe's going to see if his friend Yanko is here," Leila explained. "Yanko's about a year older than Gabe and Berta, and his family are the ones who gave us Chavo. We visit with them almost every year when they're in Parat."

"I think this is a good experience for Berta," Lisabet replied. "It's good to meet people who are different from you, and to experience other cultures." She smiled at Busara, letting her know that she appreciated getting to spend time with her and her children too.

Lisabet was dressed in modest riding clothes, and had covered her fiery red hair with a kerchief. She was still stunningly beautiful, and got many admiring looks from Nima and Gaspari men alike; but so far it seemed, nobody had recognized her. They passed unmolested through the crowds, stopping occasionally to buy little treats from food vendors. Lisabet bought brightly colored scarves for Miri, Zurishi, and Keisha, and a fourth one for her own daughter to be given to her after she got back from wherever Gabriel was taking her.

They all took seats on benches that had been set up under a colorful pavilion, to watch a puppet show. It didn't offer quite the immediacy of one of Leila's storytelling sessions, but it was funny and entertaining and the children all loved it. Vandasi was whooping with glee as the brightly colored puppets interacted on stage, even if he didn't really understand what was happening in the play. Everyone was having a wonderful time.

Over near the southern edge of the gathering ground, not far from the road that led south and east, Rajani stood inside her brightly-painted Nima caravan and called her goddess. In her long life she had had frequent dealings with the Nima who traveled the byways of the lands east of the Pahadai. With her medium-dark skin, black hair, and dark eyes she looked enough like them to pass among them. She knew their language and customs, and had journeyed here to the gathering ground in Parat twice before – many years ago. It had not been hard, even in Ashbat, to acquire a caravan and join with a band who were traveling into the Dominion.

"Danava, come to me," she said quietly – speaking aloud, though at this close proximity to the goddess' idol she could have done so silently. This idol was the same one she had carried in her pocket during her conference with the khan, though it now stood some three feet high and was set on a slab of black stone atop a cabinet built into the caravan.

The goddess was all black, as jet black as Betsalel, slim and graceful with full, round breasts. In addition to a simple loincloth she wore a necklace of skulls, and in two of her four hands were knives – tokens of her aspect as The Destroyer. The other two held a sheaf of wheat and a glowing orb – indicative of her benign attributes and her claimed ability to see all. She was posed as if caught in the middle of a dance, two arms up and two down – her legs apart with knees bent, one foot raised. At her feet lay the bloody corpse of a pigeon, Rajani's offering to coax Danava's aid.

The sorceress had worshiped Danava since she had been old enough to speak, guided by her father in the black arts. Her mistress had begun life millennia before as a daemon, of course, a belief construct given life by focusing worship on an idol and providing it with a human soul. But she was generally accounted to be a true goddess in the lands east of the Pahadai, worshiped by thousands and possessed of powers the equal to those of the Eight – at least there, in her stronghold of power.

Here in Parat, with only Rajani to worship her, Danava's powers were restricted. Three days ago they had arrived at the gathering with the band Rajani (pretending to be a half-Nima widow who had chosen to return to her father's people after the death of her Gholim husband) had joined, and the search had begun. The goddess had glimpsed the future, and had told the sorceress that beyond a doubt one or both of the emperor's children would come within range of her power sometime during the week. But each day, they had not been found.

After Danava had absorbed the blood sacrifice, inhaling its essence and boosting her powers, Rajani addressed her. "Mistress, the gathering now has only a few more days to run. Do you yet have sight of our quarry?"

"Yes," the dark voice of the goddess hissed in the Hindai tongue, the one shared by most of her worshipers. "They are here, not more than a quarter mile away!"

"Together?" Rajani asked hopefully. If she could capture both children, including the young heir to the Gaspari throne, the emperor would do anything to get them back. "The boy is with a large party of people. His mother, and some other women and children," Danava replied, able to encompass the entire gathering with her sight thanks to the power granted her by the sacrifice.

"No imperial guards?" the sorceress asked. With the powers supplied to her by Rajani, a few women and children would be nothing to get past. She might just blind their sight and pluck the boy from their midst.

"No," the goddess replied. "But one of the women is armed, and possesses dark powers of her own. She is protected by Betsalel, strong protection. I do not think you could get past her."

"What about the girl, then?" Rajani asked, disappointed. Females were not held in much greater regard here in the Dominion than they were in most other parts of the world in this age, but little girls could be dear to their fathers' hearts. Probably dear enough that she would make an acceptable hostage for the khan's purposes.

"She is in company with a dark boy, and an imperial guard, eating with a family of Nima on the far side of the gathering ground," Danava said, bringing the child she sought into focus in her mind's eye. A lone guard might be easier to get past than a group of women, Rajani thought.

"Can you send him into confusion, mistress?" she asked.

"Yesss," the dark goddess hissed. "He will fail to notice when his charges slip away. I will call the girl to you."

"And the boy?" One of the arms holding a knife waved angrily. "He is the son of the woman protected by Betsalel!" the goddess cried in annoyance. "He too bears the Shadow God's protection, though it is not so strong on him. I may be able to lure him, but I will not be able to control him or cause him harm."

"The girl and boy are friends?" Rajani asked. She was thinking about how she was to get her hostage back along the road to Miradil and beyond, into the khan's custody. If the boy were the son of an important priestess, he might be a valuable hostage as well – and kidnaping the two children together would help to keep them calmer, less afraid. "I cannot see into the boy's mind," Danava replied. "But the girl is very fond of him. And from physical appearances, he cares for her as well."

"Very well," Rajani said. "Call the children to me, subtly so they won't sense what is being done. When they and their minder have left the encampment of their Nima friends, confuse the guard so that he will lose track of them. Once they have arrived here, I will take care of the rest."

Berta burped politely, grinning at her new friend Yanko and his family. "Thank you so much for the delicious lunch," she said, and they all smiled back at her. "I think that we should be going, though," she added, standing up and taking Gabriel's hand. "There is so much to see, but I don't want to be gone from Mama and Papa and Lexi for too long."

The Nima all squeezed her hands and bid her farewell, making her promise to visit them next year. Gabriel hadn't told them she was the daughter of the emperor, but the presence of Jurig (their guard) was something of a tip-off. She was right, though. All the sights and sounds of the gathering seemed to be calling to him, somehow.

"I want to get my fortune told by a real Nima fortune teller!" Berta declared, leading the way as if she knew where she was going.

"Uh, you know that's mostly just nonsense, don't you?" Gabriel asked her. He didn't want to burst her balloon, but Mama's stories of life among the Nima had made it clear that most "seers" were just charlatans – telling the marks what they wanted to hear and taking their gold.

She gave him a brilliant, gap-toothed grin. "Of course I know, silly! But it will be fun – and kind of spooky too, don't you think?" Having grown up in the bosom of the dark god Betsalel, Gabriel and his sister had a somewhat eccentric view of what counted as spooky. But he was happy to go along with her. She was bossy as hell, and he didn't mind a bit.

Berta was rushing ahead, and Gabriel assumed that she had seen a sign marking the caravan of a Nima seer as they'd been wandering among the encampments before lunch. With his long legs it was easy for him to keep up with her, and he was caught up in her excitement and the fun of running through the crowds. It didn't occur to him to check that Jurig was still dogging their footsteps, until they arrived at a brightly-painted wagon near the southern edge of the gathering ground and came to a halt.

A woman dressed in typical Nima garb – layers of cotton skirts, blouses, vests, and sashes, all in contrasting colors and laden with gold jewelry – stood outside it. She was old, way past fifty at least, and had a rather grandmotherly appearance. Her coloring was closer to Gabe's than to the average Nima of the Dominion, but he had seen Nima from the realms of the Hando before and they were often darker – intermingling with the black people of Indaya and elsewhere in the southern part of the region.

She smiled warmly at them as they came up. There was no sign offering fortune-telling on her wagon (usually it would be a picture of the Mystic Eye, sometimes with "Past – Present – Future" written beneath), yet she seemed to have some true mystic powers for she addressed Berta as "princess."

Suddenly shy, Berta goggled at her. "How did you know I'm a princess?" she asked. She'd been expecting some fun fakery, not a person with unknown powers. But having now been exposed to Gabriel's mama's powers, such things were not as frightening to her as they had been a year before.

"Rajani sees all and tells all," the woman replied with a kindly grin. "Come inside, child, and I will tell your cards. And you, too, child of shadows."

How did she know *that*? Gabriel wondered. Or was she just referring to his dark complexion? He was far darker than almost anyone here, darker than either of his parents, though he didn't know why. Growing up in the white world of the Dominion as the beloved son of a wealthy and prominent family had made all the difference to him. He had never faced the obstacles his mother had.

He glanced behind him and was surprised to see that they were alone. "What happened to Jurig?" he asked aloud, and Berta turned to find their constant companion nowhere to be seen.

"He must have gotten tangled in the crowds," she said dismissively. "I'm sure he'll catch up with us soon. Come on, let's get our fortunes told!" Rajani grinned broadly at her.

"Please come in," she said, holding open the door to the caravan. "I have tea and cookies, as well!"

It was more than two hours past lunchtime, and the women and younger children had joined the men at the racetrack. Tevo and Ostden were jubilant, having won big on two of the races. The Karmarzins were comfortable, the Piastins wealthy beyond most people's dreams of avarice – but it still felt good to bet and win!

"Where are Gabe and Berta?" Tevo asked, relaxed and smiling.

"Jurig is with them," Lisabet said. There were thousands of men in the Imperial Guard, but the two they'd brought with them were the family's own personal guards and almost considered part of the family. Leila smiled.

"Yanko's probably leading them all over the gathering," she said. While Gabriel (and to a lesser extent, Miri) was far more familiar with the Nima and their ways than most ordinary citizens of the Dominion, there was nothing like having a native guide.

They all stood among the crowd beside the track, far enough back to avoid being splattered with mud as the horses ran past. Three races along, they were surprised when Jurig came up behind them and addressed the emperor. "Princess Berta!" he cried anxiously. "She's not here?"

The children didn't understand what was going on, but the adults all took on looks of concern. "Let's move away from the track," Ostden commanded. He was the ruler of nearly a third of the world's population, after all. They moved out into an area where the occupants of an encampment had recently pulled out. Not everyone who came to the gathering stayed for the whole time.

"Tell me what happened!" the emperor demanded of his house guard. Jurig, who had another two inches on his tall sovereign, hung his head – his face a mask of frustration and shame.

"We had lunch with some Nima friends of the Karmarzin boy," he said. "Then after we'd finished eating Princess Berta suddenly got it into her head that she wanted to go exploring. She dashed off, with young Gabriel behind her, and I was right on their heels. Then suddenly, I don't know… one minute they were right in front of me in the crowds, and the next they had just vanished. I've been searching for them for hours now, and I haven't been able to find them. Nobody I've talked to has seen them, either. It's as if they became invisible!"

Lisabet's eyes were wide with fear. She had been so enjoying this time spent just being part of a crowd of happy people, and now this! She would never forgive herself if anything had happened to her beloved Berta. Clutching Aleksei's hand all the tighter, she said "We need more guards. I want every person here interviewed, every caravan searched."

"Tevo and I have quite a few friends among the Nima here," Leila volunteered. "We can get them to search. You'd be more likely to get information if it's being asked by Nima rather than Imperial Guards in any case." Lisabet nodded. What her friend said made sense. The Nima could be friendly and hospitable to outsiders, on occasion; but they tended to keep to themselves and were unlikely to trust government officials.

"Tevo, please go talk with Nicolae," Leila added in a tone that was not quite a request. "He should be able to organize everyone in his band to help with the search." He hurried off, and she turned to Busara. "Can you please watch Miri for me?" she asked, and the taller woman nodded silently. She was thanking all the Eight that it was not *her* children who were missing, and feeling guilty for it.

"I don't usually carry Betsalel around with me in my pocket anymore," Leila told the emperor and empress. "I need to get to the Temple of Betsalel and find out if my master can locate Gabe. It's a pretty good bet that the kids are still together. Can I borrow one of your guards' horses?"

"Yes, go ahead," Ostden said distractedly. "Perhaps it would be best if we all went back to the carriage. The women and children can stay there, safe inside the carriage, while the guards and I search."

Lisabet gave him a look that suggested she didn't like the idea of remaining safe in the carriage, waiting anxiously, while her husband actually *did* something about finding their daughter. But on the other hand, she must keep Aleksei safe at any cost. If Berta had been abducted by someone who knew she was the emperor's daughter, it was a sure bet they'd have been even happier to lay their hands on the young heir to the throne.

Leila kissed Miri and Busara, and squeezed her young sisters before hopping up onto the back of a tall sorrel gelding. "Thank you, Jurig," she said as she reined him away in the direction of the bridge. "I'll bring him back as soon as I've consulted with Betsalel."

Chapter 6

Gabriel awoke to an aching head, and a creaking sound accompanied by swaying and jouncing. Where was he? The last thing he remembered, he'd been enjoying some delicious tea well-sweetened with honey, washing down crispy little cookies with hazelnuts in them. He and Berta had both been enjoying them, and the fortune-teller lady – what was her name, Rajari? Rajani? – had been dealing out cards from a deck with amazing pictures on them. Then he had suddenly felt sleepy, too sleepy to keep his eyes open.

He realized that he was bound head and foot, and lying on what felt like a hard pallet. His hands were tied in front of him, though, and in moments he reached up to find a cloth had been tied over his eyes, another wrapped around his face to gag his mouth. He ripped them loose, and gazed around him in the dim light coming in through some tiny colored-glass windows. They were still in the Nima caravan!

Gabriel rolled onto his side and saw Berta lying on a pallet across the aisle, similarly gagged and bound. "Berta!" he hissed. From the movement he felt, the caravan must be underway – and unless the Nima woman had an accomplice, she would be out on the driver's box holding the reins. The tea, or maybe the cookies, must have been drugged, he realized. Mama had told them tales where the bad guys drugged the good guys in order to take them captive. Then when they awoke, of course, they used their hidden daggers or their magic powers to escape. Except, Gabriel didn't have any hidden daggers or magic powers. Not like Mama did.

"Berta!" he called again, a little louder. She moaned and rolled over on the pallet, but did not wake. She must have gotten a bigger dose of the sleeping potion, or maybe it hit her harder because she was smaller than he was. It was no use, it was up to him to do something before that old witch and her creepy-looking black goddess (if that's what the thing was, and not just a statue) took them too far away from home. Berta's papa would surely have the entire Imperial Guard on their trail before long, but they needed to know where to look.

"Hey!" Gabriel yelled at the top of his lungs, "Help! Help! We're in here!" The caravan lurched to a halt, and in moments Rajani came up the steps and into the caravan. She gave Gabriel an evil glare.

"Shut your mouth!" she snapped, and the boy faltered. It had suddenly occurred to him that it was Berta, not him, whom the old woman had intended to kidnap. If he didn't do what she said, might she not just dump him out beside the road, bound, to die of exposure or be eaten by wolves?

"Where are you taking us?" he asked, in a considerably quieter tone.

"You'll find out when we get there," Rajani replied. "Don't worry, no harm will come to you," she continued in almost kindly tones. "Provided you don't cause any trouble!" He just looked at her with his dark brown eyes, only a little lighter than her own. There was anxiety there, and question, but not the terror she might have expected from a seven-year-old who'd been taken away from everything and everyone he had ever known.

"You, the little princess, and I are going on a nice trip together in my caravan," Rajani said, trying to sooth him. "We'll be visiting a friend of mine, a sort of king like Berta's father is, and then you'll be going home to your mothers and fathers. It will be like a fun adventure!"

"I don't want to go on a trip with you," Gabriel murmured. The thought of being tossed out beside the road was making him afraid to say anything that would make her mad.

"You're free to leave, if you want," the woman said, as if she'd read his thoughts. She *had* seemed to have mystical powers, when they first met her at the gathering. "I'll just drop you off right here, and you can walk home – if you can find it!"

"And Berta too?" he asked. No way he was leaving his friend in the power of this evil woman. Rajani's face took on an expression of regret.

"I'm so sorry, but that won't be happening," she said. "My goddess Danava has the power to make Berta forget that she ever knew her mother and father. If I want, she can be made to believe that I am her mother. And she will certainly not agree to leave with you."

She walked over to the creepy black statue of the woman with all the arms, and called her goddess. "You have done well, Rajani," Danava's voice said. It was cold and low, and sent a chill through Gabriel as he lay there bound on his pallet.

"Please, mistress, tell our young shadow child what you will do if he causes a fuss or brings the Imperial Guard down on us."

To Gabriel's horror, the now-live idol hopped nimbly down off of the platform on which it had been resting and grew to six feet in height – about as tall as a person could be and stand upright within the caravan. She looked down at him, her jet eyes glittering in a face as black as Betsalel's.

"Your Shadow God grants you protection from my supernatural powers," the goddess said, "but while I am manifest I have two sharp knives to hand. It would be no problem at all to slit your throat. I would be happy to drink your blood, a sacrifice the richer for having stolen it from my brother Betsalel."

"Betsalel doesn't drink blood!" Gabriel protested, so outraged he forgot to be terrified.

"I need not use knives to harm your little princess, however," Danava continued – ignoring what he'd said. "I can stop her heart with a thought, or hold her mind in my thrall so that she will do, will believe, anything I tell her."

The goddess seemed as if music was playing silently in her head, for she was constantly moving in a slow, sinuous dance. Even while her feet were planted, standing still on the wooden floor of the caravan. "I'll be good," he promised, eyes wide. Danava was the scariest thing he had ever seen, in his short and sheltered life. "Will Berta wake up soon?" He was concerned that she remained unresponsive. What if Rajani had given her too much, and the princess never woke up at all?

"Soon enough," Rajani said. "What I gave you is safe enough. You may have a headache, and feel a little tired. But the effects will soon fade. But now, we have to get on our way again. Must I gag you again, and tie your hands behind your back, which I fear will be very uncomfortable – or will you remain silent?"

Gabriel looked at Berta, an expression of sorrow on his face. "Can I talk to Berta, when she wakes up?" he asked meekly. Rajani's expression softened.

"Certainly," she said. "Explain to her that we're going on an adventure, and that we must be very, very, quiet. Soothe her fears. I promise, if you and she both behave you will be treated kindly and no one will hurt you. All right?"

She *smiled* at him! First the death threats from the goddess, who had returned to her smaller size and hopped back up atop the cabinet where she'd been riding, and now Rajani was expecting him to treat her as if she were just a kindly old babushka? Gabriel smiled back. "Whatever you say," he replied.

Chapter 7

"I cannot see him, he is gone!" Betsalel said in alarm. When his beloved arch-priestess had called him to his idol in the Temple of Betsalel (miles closer to the Nima gathering ground than was Shadow Manor) he had immediately known what was in her heart. Even before she had called him, he had sensed her anxiety and anger. She still bore, nestled beneath her heart, a fragment of his idol from the long-burned monastery in the Blackwald.

"How can that be, master?" Leila asked in disbelief. Betsalel had been a literal godfather to both her children, and he had a bond with them that permitted him to reach out and find them anywhere – as long as they were within a reasonable distance of one of his true idols.

"Another deity is involved in this, I think," he said solemnly. "One of the Eight?" Leila asked, horrified at the thought. At the back of her mind, she had always considered the possibility that Lucia might someday seek her revenge for what Leila had done to balk her nearly ten years before. Yet so far, the Goddess of Light seemed to have moved on. She and Betsalel were even civil to one another when they were both manifested at the same time within the Temple of the Eight, as happened a few times a year.

"Not one of my siblings, no," he said. "One of our bastard offspring, I think." She looked at him blankly. "A daemon," he explained. A wash of terror passed over Leila as she remembered Kivuli. "In the lands east of what the Gasparis call the Killtops there are many ancient daemons who have been worshiped for centuries or even millennia. The human imagination is a powerful thing, and those in the east are more imaginative than most. I think it likely that one these daemons with powers to rival any of the Eight is working with whoever took the children. This daemon would be unable to harm Gabriel supernaturally, but could cast a circle of illusion, of darkness around them that might hide them from my sight."

"So the children's abductor must be a worshiper of this eastern daemon, else surely he or she could not enlist its help," Leila said. Betsalel nodded.

"Deities do little without reward, for our powers come only from the psychic energy of human worship. This person who took the children must be high up in the cult of whichever daemon it is, to have obtained assistance with a crime of this magnitude."

"But aren't some daemons evil?" she asked. Kivuli had certainly been.

"True," the dark god responded. "But most are a mixture. Still, I can think of a dozen daemons at least who would not hesitate to help their worshipers to kill – let alone abduct a couple of children."

"And are any of these daemons worshiped here in the Dominion?" Leila asked. She was an arch-priestess, and had been one for nearly a decade; but she was not a religious scholar.

"Not in any great numbers, no," Betsalel replied. "Your kidnaper is almost certainly from the east, though they might have lived in the Dominion, worshiping their daemon in secret."

"There are a few Nima from beyond the Killtops at the gathering every year," Leila said hurriedly. "We must talk to them, find out if any they know were cultists!" She turned as if to hurry off, then turned back. "Master, please give me another idol so I can take you with me!"

The Shadow God pulled off a small amount of "flesh" from his side, which immediately formed itself into a miniature idol little more than an inch high. Leila took it from him eagerly, saying "Thank you! I will talk with you soon!" as she ran out the door. His mind filled with concern, Betsalel returned to the eight foot height that was standard for his altar in this place and climbed back up onto his pedestal before leaving the idol behind.

Some half hour later Leila arrived on Jurig's lathered horse beside the Piastin family's carriage where it was parked near the western edge of the gathering ground. It was high summer, and there were still hours of daylight left in which to search the milling crowds. Surely whoever took the children could not have gotten far!

"Mama!" Miri cried when Leila appeared, and jumped down into her arms. The adults' fear had been transmitted to the children, and they were all becoming as anxious as their parents. Aleksei was whimpering and demanding his papa, and Busara informed her stepdaughter that Vandasi had been screaming his head off before

42

collapsing into an exhausted sleep. Zurishi was worried too, but she had been trying to keep the younger kids entertained by singing Palamban songs for them.

"Have you seen the men since I left?" Leila asked Lisabet.

"Tevo came by to tell us that Nicolae had pressed his entire band into service, searching for the children or word of them," the empress replied. "Then he went out again. So far, they hadn't found anyone who remembered them."

How very strange, Leila thought. There were thousands of people on the gathering ground, it was true, and many of them were children. But she doubted any of those children looked anything like Gabriel and Berta together. The boy, nearly as dark as any Palamban, and the girl with her fiery red hair made a striking pair that should stick in people's minds. Unless maybe the abductor's daemon had clouded their memories somehow? If it were possible to hide Gabriel from the god who had known the boy almost from the moment he was conceived, it might be possible to do anything.

"I need to find them!" Leila said anxiously. "I have more information to impart."

"Did Betsalel find the children?" Lisabet asked, hope shining in her emerald eyes.

"I'm sorry, Lisabet," Leila replied. "The children have been shielded from his sight somehow. He suspects that a powerful eastern daemon is involved." The empress stared at her wordlessly, pale skin gone paler.

"Oh wait, I know how to find them," Leila said. She was so upset by the situation that she wasn't thinking straight. Putting her hand in her pocket she murmured "Betsalel, come to me."

"I am here," the god spoke in her mind. They hadn't interacted like this in years, and it was a strange sensation. "Please find Tevo for me," she requested silently, and he began leading her through the crowds.

If anything the crowds were thicker now than they had been earlier in the day. The partying would culminate with a feast of spit-roasted goat and traditional Nima dishes (plates of which would be available to paying customers), and go on into the night with dancing, music, and storytelling. It was the most exotic entertainment most citizens of Parat would ever have the opportunity to enjoy. And Leila *really* hoped they would find the children before it got dark. If the eastern daemon was blinding people's eyes and confusing them, it would at least be unable to work those effects on Leila and Tevo.

After slithering through the crowd of tourists and revelers for more than twenty minutes Leila finally found Tevo on the far side of the gathering ground. He was speaking with the leader of another band, a man they'd met on a few occasions though he was not as good a friend as Nicolae was.

Leila hurried up to them. "Greetings, Stevo," Leila said, inclining her head respectfully.

"Little Leila!" he smiled, embracing her and kissing her on both cheeks. Oh right, in her anxiety over Gabriel and Berta she'd forgotten why Stevo was not a closer friend. The man was an unrepentant letch. Tevo eyed him tensely, and Stevo released the arch-priest's wife. There was a gleam in his dark eyes, though.

"I am sorry, Leila," he said sympathetically. "Your husband was just telling me that your son is missing?"

"That's right," she said. "I have been talking to Betsalel about it, and he says that an eastern daemon is involved. He was not able to find Gabe, and that can be only because he was cloaked by supernatural powers. Are there some *Estikano* here at the gathering?

The word meant "eastern" in the Nima tongue, and was used by the Nima on this side of the Killtops to refer to their cousins living east of the range. It was usually only at gatherings like this one that the two groups ever got a chance to meet and mingle.

Stevo looked sorry and shrugged. "There are so many people here," he said. "I have been busy catching up with old friends, and I don't personally know any of the *Estikano*. Any who came here would likely have come up the south road from Miradil, though. Perhaps you should try on that side of the gathering grounds."

"We'll do that," Tevo replied. "But please, ask all of your people if they've seen our dark boy in company with a little red-haired girl. And ask them to keep their eyes open. Any information can be brought to us at our carriage, parked over near the west road. And there'll be gold aplenty for anyone who can help us find the kids!" At that Stevo's dark eyes glittered again.

"I will do as you ask!" he promised, as the young couple plunged back into the crowds.

It was another half hour before Leila and Tevo reached the part of the gathering ground nearest to the road that led off south and east toward Miradil. The countryside on this bank of the river was considerably flatter than on the west, a gently rolling floodplain that gave the eastern Dominion some of its most fertile farmlands – though this far north, the growing season was short. The road that eventually connected with the main highway to Miradil was lost around a bend no more than a mile to the south.

They found themselves in a busy encampment, the style of the wagons here subtly different from that to be found on most Nima caravans they had seen. They were about the same shape, configured to be hauled by one or two cart horses, and as gaudy as peacocks. But there were little architectural fillips applied to the corners, small carved peaks covered in gold leaf and some with unfamiliar writing on the sides.

Leila wondered how to approach these people. Would they even speak Gasparto? Surely they must have a little of the tongue, or why bother to come all this long way for the gathering? A small family group was sitting beside one of the caravans at a campfire, over which a teakettle was heating. An old woman, seventy if she was a day, peered at the strangers questioningly.

Leila came up to the fire and nodded her head politely. "Greetings, grandmother," she said. "I am Leila Karmarzin, *te' sorthene* of the western Nima, and this is my husband Tevo. May we speak with you?"

"Sit, have some tea," the old woman commanded them. A *te' sorthene* was an outsider the Nima had named friend, and one could usually count on receiving at least some degree of welcome from Nima anywhere.

The old man sitting beside the woman stood and beckoned Leila to take his seat. Tevo sat beside her, and the oldster gave him a toothless grin and moved around to take a stool on the other side of the fire. He was as dark as any of the western Nima, but his eyes were slanted and almond-shaped – more like the Hando. Leila had seen sailors from those far-off realms aboard ships in the harbor at

Marsine when she'd been a child living on the streets along the waterfront.

"You are from the realms of the Hando, grandmother?" Leila asked, as she took a sip of the tea. It was surprisingly delicate, and seemed to have been brewed with some kind of fragrant dried flowers among other ingredients.

"Oh, the Hando are much farther east, dear," the crone replied in clear but accented Gasparto. So ignorant, these foreigners! "Our band moves in a circle through northern Indaya and parts of the territories of the Gholim. Once every few years we come through at Miradil and travel to Parat for the summer gathering. The weather here is much nicer at this season than in Indaya, and I have a granddaughter who married into one of your western bands. It is good to see her, and my great-grandbabies."

Leila smiled at her. She enjoyed traveling, had loved her time spent traveling with the band of Nima through parts of Spania and the west-central Dominion. But she had also grown to love her home and the comforts it offered. There certainly weren't many hot baths or flush toilets to be found on the road with the Nima! "It is about children that I wish to speak," she told the old woman. "Our son Gabriel is seven years old, tall for his age and slender, and very dark. Darker than me. He and his little friend, a red-haired girl a few inches shorter than he is, have gone missing at the gathering. Have you seen them?"

The old woman took a sip of her tea and looked over at her husband. His grin had changed to a frown, and he was shaking his head. "Nobody like that, just the children of the band around here today," he said. His wife agreed.

"I've been in and out of the caravan and I had a little lie-down after lunch. And I'm afraid my eyesight's not what it used to be. But I think I would have noticed a red-head!"

Leila sighed and took another sip of her tea. Divine obfuscation might not have been necessary with these two. Eyeglasses had been invented in the Dominion centuries ago, but the Nima would be unlikely to be able to acquire them. The old folks probably didn't notice anything that happened further away than a hundred feet from their caravan.

"I have reason to believe that my son and his friend were abducted by a member of the eastern Nima, a worshiper of one of the eastern gods," Leila said. "Do you have such a person in your band?" The old woman looked at her speculatively.

"There are three bands here," she said. "We met up with each other at the gathering ground near Khirzai, and traveled together for safety. The Gholim have all been united under that khan of theirs, but some of the tribes are still raiding the Ivory Road. Not that we Nima have all that much worth stealing, but sometimes the young bucks will sweep in and steal a few horses, rape a few women, and so forth."

"So you don't know if any of them might worship one of the eastern gods?" Leila asked. It was usually considered rude, in whatever society, to pry into a person's relationship with their god or gods.

"Not that I heard," the old one admitted. "I've met most of these people before, of course, known some of them for years even though they're not of our band. We run into them once or twice every year at the gatherings east of the Pahadai."

At Leila's blank look she added, "What you call the Killtops. Anyway, most everyone who came with us is still here and will be camped here until the end of the gathering. You can talk to them about your missing children." She gestured to the caravans parked around them.

"Most?" Tevo asked.

"All the members of the three bands," the woman replied. "But there was this one woman, looked more Indayan than Nima really. We picked her up near Ghezh, not that far from Miradil. She said she'd gotten delayed and separated from her band, and wanted to join us going to Parat. So we invited her along."

Leila and Tevo exchanged a look. "Where is she camped?" Leila demanded excitedly.

"Well that's what I was trying to tell you," the crone said patiently. "She's the one who left, I'm not sure when. I'm pretty sure she was here when I went to lie down for my nap after lunch, but when I got up again she was gone. Rajani, her name was."

47

Tevo was sure this Rajani must have been the one who had taken the kids – why else, as a lone woman described as middle-aged, would she have left the protection of the combined Nima bands and struck out on the road alone? But Leila wanted more confirmation. An hour or two's delay wouldn't make all that much difference. A Nima wagon moved little faster than a trading caravan, after all. If she was the one who had abducted the children, they could take a couple of fast horses and catch her in a few hours – but they needed to know where she was going, first. She might have left by the south road, but this part of the Dominion was honeycombed with roads and country lanes.

Thanking the old woman for the tea and the information, Leila took Tevo by the hand and they went to speak with the leaders of the three eastern bands who were encamped in the area. They all agreed, the woman Rajani had joined them on the Ivory Road no more than a hundred miles from Miradil. She had claimed to be one of the Nima, and had the knowledge to back up that claim – but none of them had ever met her before.

No, she had not spoken of any goddess. Most of the Nima Leila had met worshipped Mulia and Andros, paying devotion to them when the opportunity arose. But they were not a devout tribe. None of the people in the joined bands had been invited into her caravan, though they had shared her fire a few times. She had seemed a nice enough woman, and they had seen nothing amiss.

Huh, Leila thought. Just like Zurina was a "nice girl," eight years ago in Iskand. That lovely, innocent maiden had led one suitor to throw himself from the top of a sixty foot tower, and later that same night had cut the throats of two of his friends as they lay unconscious. Of all the scoundrels she had met in her life, it seemed to her that the women among them had been the cruelest – and the most devious. And that bitch had her boy!

Time was burning. "It has to be her," Leila said. It was what Tevo had been trying to tell her for the last half hour. "But in case it's not, Emperor Ostden had better get some guards down here for a caravan-by-caravan search. It's not going to endear him to the Nima, but I hope people will understand how desperate he is to find his daughter."

"What do we do, then?" Tevo asked. "We ride!" she said, breaking into a trot as they jinked and dodged through the crowds between them and the west side of the gathering ground. "We'll borrow those guards' horses and try to catch them. Unless her daemon has lent wings to her caravan horse, it's a sure bet they won't have gotten many miles down the road in the few hours since they left Parat."

Tevo worried at that one. Betsalel had, in a sense, lent wings to both Leila's horse Nimble and his own Milacek, granting them the power of tirelessness that had been such a help to him in the earlier days when he was forced to travel thousands of miles per year re-establishing temples for the Shadow God. Could this ancient and powerful daemon have done something of the kind for Rajani's cart horse?

"But are we sure we'll find her on the south road?" Tevo asked, as they trotted on their way.

"Nothing is certain," she replied. "But she joined the Nima only a hundred miles east of Miradil, so she probably came from somewhere north of there (south of the Huang, the area east of the Talj Jabal was a scrub desert waste with few inhabitants) and will be taking the children back to her home base to sell them to whoever hired her. I seriously doubt she's just an old lunatic who suddenly decided she needed children in her life."

"The daemon's screening tells us that can't be the case," Tevo panted as they ran. "Children are a dime a dozen out there, I'm afraid. She could have picked up a couple of street urchins without going to any trouble at all. But she took the emperor's daughter, and I'm guessing she took Gabe along with her to help keep Berta pacified. She and whomever she's working with must mean to use the kids for hostages."

Neither he nor Leila mentioned the possibility that, had Rajani not cared about using Gabe to keep Berta sweet, they might well have found his bleeding body lying under one of the caravans in the encampment. Their son meant the world to them, but in the larger scheme of world politics he was worth less than nothing. Leila pressed down hard, crushing her mounting panic, and put on a burst of speed as they spied the carriage ahead.

49

Its occupants had climbed down and were milling around, Ostden and his two imperial guards joining the women and children who'd been waiting anxiously for their return. They all turned as Leila and Tevo came running up. "What word?" Ostden asked. He was a handsome man, tall for a Gaspari at over six feet and with bright blue eyes beneath a shock of sandy hair. So far ruling the vast Gaspari Dominion had been something of a lark for him, and he now looked more drawn and worried than Leila (or Lisabet) had ever seen him.

Lisabet and Busara had already informed him that the Shadow God had been unable to find the children. Now he looked hopefully to Leila. Her demonstration of the powers Betsalel had granted to her gave him hope that she would somehow magically pull Berta and Gabriel out of an inner pocket of her skirt – or at least point the way to where they were hidden.

Leila came up to him and seized him by the forearms, looking up into his face with as much reassurance as she could muster. She was certain that no harm would befall Berta – the girl was far more valuable alive. But might Gabriel be cast aside as dead weight, as soon as the going got tough? He was all she had left of Imbaso, the man she had loved and lost. But more, she loved him beyond life for himself, for the boy he was and the man he would – he must – someday become.

"We believe that we know who took the children," Leila told her emperor. "A woman named Rajani, who may or may not be of the Nima. She joined a group of the eastern Nima traveling to the gathering east of Miradil, and was camped with them here since they arrived but left this afternoon not long after Jurig lost track of the kids. We believe that this woman worships one of the eastern daemons, ancient artificial beings with godlike powers, and that daemon has not only cloaked her from Betsalel's sight but clouded the eyes and memories of the people here at the gathering – including Jurig."

The emperor glanced at his man, and they exchanged a look. The relief on Jurig's face was plain. He had been a loyal and faithful servant of the Piastin family since before Ostden had married Lisabet and left home, and he loved their children as if they were his own.

The idea that a divine agency might have robbed him of the ability to look after his charge was the first ray of hope he had seen since he had lost sight of her hours before.

"She left?" Ostden asked, cutting to the heart of the matter. "When, and in what direction?"

"Probably around five hours ago, now," Leila said. "But she's traveling in a Nima caravan, which cannot have gone much above forty miles in that time. Let Tevo and me have your guards' horses, and we will go after them."

"You know which way they went?" the emperor asked.

"She must be making for Miradil and the border," Leila replied. That was hundreds of miles away, though. "We'll take the south road, and see if we can catch her. If she's somehow escaped, taken some other road, you can mobilize the imperial guards to search every highway and byway until she and the children are found. But I hope that we may be able to catch them in no more than an hour or two, if we get on the road now."

Ostden, Lisabet, and Busara looked concerned. "But my guards..." the emperor said. Leila pulled a dagger out of one of the many hidden pockets in the outfit she wore beneath the seeming of a summer dress.

"I am as skilled at dealing death as they are," she said darkly – showing him a side of her he had never imagined. Then the dagger disappeared and the spell was broken. She grinned at him fiercely, a look that gave him a shiver. "Let us have the horses. It's just one old woman, and I have a god in my pocket."

Chapter 8

The sorrel gelding had had more than an hour to recover from his quick gallop back and forth from the Temple of Betsalel. His companion, a dark bay gelding with white socks, had been taking his ease since the group had arrived at the gathering ground this morning. So both horses were happy to make good time as Lela and Tevo urged them along the road to the south.

The Dominion's marvelous system of well-built, well-maintained highways had been a huge boon to the nation's economic well-being, facilitating the movement of goods and allowing even ordinary citizens an extraordinary amount of mobility. But as they galloped along the broad, stone-paved road, Leila could almost have wished it were a dirt track instead. For one thing, a softer surface would have been easier on the horses' feet; and for another, they might well see the tracks of Rajani's caravan to tell them they were following the right path.

She also wished they'd had the time to get Nimble and Milacek from the stables behind Shadow Manor. The tireless horses could have run at top speed for as long as it took to catch up with the mysterious woman who had taken the children. And assuming they caught her and recovered Gabe and Berta, those same tireless horses would have had no problem returning with the kids riding double, at a somewhat slower pace.

I'll worry about that problem when I come to it, Leila thought to herself; and dismissed her concerns as she concentrated on getting the unfamiliar mount to maintain his pace. She glanced over at Tevo and he looked up and grinned at her. He, too, missed those exciting days when it had seemed it was just the two of them against the world, performing bold deeds on behalf of Betsalel as they traveled in disguise to Parat to carry out the god's mission.

And he, like most people, was guilty of painting the past with a golden brush. He had forgotten how scared and unsure of himself he'd been then, a teenage orphan learning that his skills as a thief were not as great as he'd believed them to be. He'd nearly wet himself the night he and Leila met, when he'd broken into the inn room he believed to be occupied by a helpless crone and found

Kathal snarling at him from the bed while Leila threatened to skewer him in the kidneys with her dagger. Ah, the good old days...

They passed numerous side roads – some paved, some heavily rutted dirt tracks leading off into the countryside. Would Rajani be canny enough to get off of the main road, even if it meant that the trip to Miradil took longer? Surely, she could not be going anywhere but there – Leila fervently hoped.

The main highway passed through a small farming village some ten miles south of the gathering ground, and Leila spied a middle-aged man tending a fruit and vegetable stall set twenty feet back from the road. He must sell a lot of his produce to travelers, she thought.

He was in the process of boxing up the unsold goods and closing the stand for the evening, as it was now past six and time to be heading home for dinner. "Good evening sir," she called as she and Tevo walked up to him. He looked up and smiled at them.

"I'm just closing up," he said, "but I've some nice ripe plums. I'll sell them to you cheap if you take the lot."

"Thank you," she said, "but it's not fruit we mean to buy. We're looking for information." The implication that she would pay for such information didn't go unnoticed. "You've been out here selling your fruit all afternoon?" Leila asked, and the fruit-seller nodded. "I'm trying to catch a friend of mine," she explained, "a Nima woman in her sixties driving a brightly-colored caravan. She left the gathering in Parat earlier today and forgot some of her belongings. Did you see her pass this way?"

The man stood lost in thought for a moment, then shook his head. "Saw a whole lot of Nima coming through here from the south in those wagons of theirs a week or so ago," he said. "They were coming up the highway in groups for days, and some of 'em stopped and bought fruit or vegetables from me. But there's been none today." Seeing her questioning look, he assured her "I would have noticed, believe me. I haven't left the stand since lunch, and it hasn't been all that busy today."

Damn, damn! Leila slipped the man a couple of shillings for his trouble, and wheeled her horse. "She must have turned off somewhere between the gathering ground and here!" she told Tevo, and they returned the way they had come. Now, though, they were moving more slowly – something the horses were thankful for. The horses in the Imperial Stables rarely traveled very far from the palace, and usually at the sedate pace appropriate for moving through crowded city streets.

The road was paved with stone, but it was not scoured clean. Here and there it was possible to make out hoofprints in the dust that had formed since the rains earlier in the week. But this was a major highway, the road most traffic took moving between Parat and Miradil. Which hoofprints, which wheel tracks, might belong to Rajani's wagon?

A little more than half of the way back to Parat they came to one of the paved side roads. This one traveled due east toward Biala, a small city at the feet of the Killtops, connecting with another good road running more or less straight south along the mountains' western edge to Miradil. It was a longer way than taking the south road they'd been on, which led east as much as south; but it was a viable route.

Looking at the signpost to Biala, Leila reined in her horse and got down. She left him with his reins hanging down. Like most horses throughout the Dominion, he'd been trained to stand still and wait in that situation; but he did move a little further off the pavement to nibble at some shoots of grass. Tevo stayed mounted, watching as Leila carefully examined the road surface.

Yes, definitely, the tracks on the road's eastern side had been cut across by a pair of broad wheel tracks. In the Dominion it was customary for traffic to keep right, so these tracks would have been made by a good-sized wagon coming south and then executing a sweeping left turn onto the road headed east.

Despair nibbling around the edges of her resolve, Leila mounted up again. She had so hoped that Rajani would continue south, counting on her daemon's occult power to screen her, not guessing that mounted pursuit was so close behind. Well, if those tracks were hers, they would catch her soon enough. Heavy wagons needed to stay on the paved roads, or they might find themselves mired when the frequent rains came again.

"I think she must have gone that way," Leila said, and urged the sorrel gelding down the road to the east. They cantered along slowly, resting the horses and keeping their eyes peeled for anything that might guide them. Sunset was still almost two hours away, but traffic was already light. Other than Imperial messengers, few people would be traveling this highway at the dinner hour.

Leila had stuffed a couple of cold piroshky she'd bought at the gathering into one of the pockets of her clothing, wrapped in waxed paper. They were somewhat the worse for wear, but still edible and she passed one of them to Tevo. They ate their calorie-laden snacks as they rode, eyes searching the roadsides but seeing nothing.

She had just finished licking the grease off her fingers and cursing herself for failing to bring along a bottle of water, when her eyes caught something up again. Along a flat, straight stretch of the road with nothing but pastureland on either side, an area of bare muddy ground marked where the wagon tracks they were following had pulled off the road.

"Tevo, look!" Leila called, reining up. The wagon had been pulled completely off the road, as if for the driver to relieve himself. The tracks were deep and unmistakable – exactly the right size for a Nima caravan. And other tracks as well could be seen in the drying mud: hoofprints of a single cart horse, and small bootprints which from the pointed toes must be those of a woman! "We've got 'er!" Leila cried exultantly, putting her heels into the sorrel's flanks to speed him on his way. "They're just ahead of us! Let's go!"

Chapter 9

Danava was not happy about remaining manifested in her idol during the long hours as Rajani fled slowly along the road toward Biala. But she saw the sense of it. The sorceress sacrificed another pigeon, which ritual Gabriel watched in wide-eyed horror, and as they continued on their way the goddess divided her attention between the interior of the caravan and the petitions of her other worshipers scattered around the realms east of the Pahadai.

The sacrifice had given her power enough to continue to screen the entire caravan, including the shadow child, from the probing eye of Betsalel. And though it was annoying and difficult, she was able to commune with those other worshipers while simultaneously talking with Rajani where she sat the driver's box outside, urging her cart horse along at its greatest pace.

"The red-haired child is awake," Danava informed the sorceress. Rajani's sacrifice of her own father, the man who had inducted her into The Destroyer's mysteries in the first place, had cemented her place as Danava's foremost priestess alive on earth. There was powerful magic in blood, and the blood of one's close kin held the greatest power of all. By accepting that sacrifice, the goddess had bound herself to Rajani and all her enterprises.

"Does she cry out?" Rajani asked silently, hands on the reins. She had not heard any clamor such as the boy had made when he awoke.

"A little whimpering," the goddess replied in her mind. "I spoke to the boy and reminded him of what was promised, and he has been comforting her. I believe that his presence will keep her quiet and calm"

Good, Rajani thought to herself. She had had reason aplenty to kill her father, the man who had stolen her from her mother and the life that she might have had among the Gholim. And she had killed others in her time. But she had no real desire to murder a child.

The sorceress knew it was difficult for her goddess to remain a presence in the physical plane in multiple locations, and she did not tax her with idle chatter. She was alone with her thoughts as she pushed the horse on down the road. The goddess had gifted the animal with strength and speed far beyond that of the ordinary Nima cart horse it had been before she acquired it. But it would still need to rest and eat before too many more hours had gone by.

Rajani had one eye out for any side roads, perhaps leading to a copse of trees where she might camp for the night. She had planned to care for two children on the trip back to the Khanate; and if the two she had captured were not the two she had hoped for, at least she had gotten one good hostage. And she was prepared for the several days' journey east and south.

She was amusing herself fantasizing about the reward she would claim from Oghul Khan. Should she ask for gold and jewels, a palace? Perhaps he would build her a magnificent temple to Danava in Ashbat, bringing the worship of The Destroyer to the benighted Gholim at last. The personal idol the goddess had given her, which she carried with her always, had been the only one in the entire Khanate so far as she knew. Danava's worship was much more prevalent within Indaya and some of the small southern nations around it than it was elsewhere.

Dusk was descending on the land and Rajani had still not spotted a safe place to camp for the night, when her reverie was shattered by the voice of Danava speaking in her mind. "Rajani, we are pursued!" the goddess said suddenly. "Two come on horseback, bearing the protection of Betsalel. Their horses are tiring, but they will catch us in less than a quarter of an hour."

Shit! That this situation might occur was something Rajani had considered, and she knew what to do about it. But she had been really, really hoping it would not come to this. Their pursuers must surely be the boy's parents, or perhaps some other members of Betsalel's priesthood in Parat. She could, she supposed, just leave the boy here for them to find. But she needed to flee, anyway, so she might as well take him along. Leaving him behind would not stop the pursuit, she knew.

Pulling the wagon off the road, she reined the horse to a halt and set the brake. Then she climbed down and hurried around to the side, climbing up into the caravan once again. There was almost no light inside, and she took out a Lucifer match and lit a kerosene lantern attached to the wall.

The children lay on their pallets atop built-in cabinets on either side of a narrow center aisle. Berta had also freed herself of her blindfold and gag, and was staring at her wide-eyed and pale. "It's all right, Berta," the boy said, hoping to quiet her fears. He was pretty sure Rajani didn't mean to kill them, no matter what that creepy goddess of hers had said.

Danava tore her attention away from her other worshipers across the continent and hopped down off of her platform. "Where do you wish to go?" she asked, and Rajani (who was rummaging in the caravan's cabinets for some items she needed to take with her) turned and said "Delai, I think. That's the closest temple by road to where we need to be."

The goddess had grown to her maximum height for the cramped confines of the little cabin on wheels. "I will need to shrink you all in order to carry you," she said, and Rajani nodded. She had been through this many times.

"It won't hurt you, I promise," she told the children. "My mistress will take us to a very big temple, and you will be back to your normal size in no time."

Gabriel cried out in horror as the goddess touched Berta and she began to shrink in the bed, including her clothing and the ropes binding her hands and feet, until she was the size of a kitten. But when the goddess touched him (the items she had been holding in her four hands had vanished) she recoiled. "I cannot take you," she said. "I can work none of my supernatural powers on you unless you grant consent."

Rajani pulled a dagger from her sleeve. "It would be shame for poor little Berta," she remarked casually, "if she were to be all by herself in a strange land, surrounded by strangers. Very sad, very distressing. Who knows, she might lose her mind. Or she might cry out at the wrong time and I would, so regretfully, have to cut her throat. Wouldn't you like to come along and keep her company?"

His dark face ashen, eyes wide, Gabriel said "All right. All right! I give you my permission. Shrink me and take me with you to Delai! But I do *not* give my consent for you to do anything else to me, understand?" He hadn't even been aware of the mystical protection Betsalel had placed on him, let alone how it worked. But he didn't want the black goddess to get any more power over him than necessary.

In an instant Gabriel found the interior of the caravan, and the pallet on which he lay, growing bigger and bigger. Soon Rajani could have plucked him up and held him in the palm of her hand. But then she, too, began to shrink and it was the now-enormous black goddess who scooped them up, in three of her four jet-black hands. The next thing he knew he was looking down from a long way up at the interior of a black stone temple that reminded him of the one at home. But this was no temple of Betsalel.

Chapter 10

In the gloaming up ahead, as the day's last light glowed in the sky behind them, Leila spotted a large object pulled onto the dirt beside the road. The caravan! It must be! "Hiya!" she yelled, pounding her heels into the sorrel's flanks. But he had had enough of running, and all of her urging only got him up into a slow canter.

"It's all right, Leila!" Tevo called behind her. "Another few seconds won't matter!" His own horse had fallen from a trot to a walk, head hanging.

There was a warm light glowing through the caravan's small windows as she approached and leaped down to the ground. Putting her hand in her pocket, Leila called Betsalel. "Is this it, master?" she asked silently.

"I cannot be sure," he replied. "There is no protection on this caravan, and no one is inside it." *What?!*

The door to the caravan was ajar, and despite what the god had told her Leila had a dagger drawn as she climbed the steps and went inside. Tevo was right behind her. They found a single lamp burning, and on the floor between two wall-hung pallets stood a grotesque-looking black idol six feet tall.

Leila set her own idol on the floor, backing off to give Betsalel room, and in moments the six-foot Shadow God stood confronting the four-armed female idol that looked to have been carved from black stone. "Danava!" he said, sounding surprised. "A true idol, but she is not within it. She must have carried Rajani and the children to one of her temples on the far side of the Killtops."

Leila flopped down on the pallet. There was a small indentation in it, and still some residual warmth. Gabriel! She put her head in her hands and squeezed her eyes shut as she tried to fight back tears. Her baby, and Lisabet's, were thousands of miles away – and they had no way of knowing where. How were they ever to find them, now?

Tevo sat beside her and put his arm around her, squeezing her tight. "Be strong, love!" he murmured in her ear. "We'll find them!" Leila turned and buried her face in his chest, arms wrapped tight around him. Then, with a shudder, she pulled herself together again.

"The kings of Indaya and Hanshu have no trade disputes with the Dominion," she said quietly, and Tevo nodded. "But one of those Gholim tribal leaders has been uniting the tribes just east of the Killtops for the past few years. And I know that he's been rebuffed in his efforts to get his 'kingdom,' what he's calling 'The Gholim Khanate,' recognized as a nation."

"Ostden was talking about that while we were watching the horse races," Tevo replied. "He's convinced the Gholim tribes are nothing but a bunch of nomadic savages, and that granting them the privileges of a diplomatic relationship with the Dominion could only lead to trouble. But he didn't seem to think they were that much of a threat, as long as they're contained beyond the pass at Miradil."

"I'll bet anything it was this 'kahn' that Rajani stole the children for, then," Leila said. "The Nima we talked to said they had picked her up not that far from Miradil, and that's Gholim territory. Betsalel, does this Danava have any worshipers among the tribes?"

The Shadow God, who was inspecting the details of the idol, turned to her and said "I would be very surprised to learn of it. The tribespeople are strong adherents of my brother Belantos, as they greatly value the virtues of the warrior. Mulia and Andros are honored as well, though they have few permanent settlements and still fewer temples. There are probably not two dozen true idols of any kind within the Gholim lands."

"And none of yours, I suppose?" Leila asked. Betsalel shook his head.

"I have never had many followers in those lands. Partly, I suppose, it is because they worship so many daemons there. For whatever reason, the One created us in Parat. But the human need for worship is at least as strong in the east, and they made their own gods thousands of years ago."

"So it's pretty likely, then," she mused, "that Danava carried Rajani and the children to someplace where there's a temple to her. One big enough that she could expand to the size needed to restore her passengers to the size they started out at.

"Yes," the god replied. "She will have taken them to somewhere in Indaya, probably. It is likely that she grew up there and will have friends or some kind of power structure that she can tap. To have her own personal idol, and for the daemon to be at her beck and call, she would be accounted a mighty sorceress among the Dravim or the Gholim."

"Then she'll probably be trying to get back to the Khanate with the kids by surface means, if her daemon can't carry her there," Tevo said.

"Probably by taking horses or a hired coach to the Huang, then riding a riverboat downstream before going overland again to the khan's capital," Leila added. "We can go there and intercept them, if we move swiftly enough."

"I can take you to Miradil," Betsalel said. "That is far closer to the lands of the Gholim than any of my temples in the Hando realms."

"That will have to do," Leila replied. "But first, we need to go home."

Chapter 11

It would have been convenient if Betsalel could just have carried them all back to the Temple of the Eight in Parat. But that would have left the caravan and its horse, the large idol of Danava, and Leila's own idol of the Shadow God standing forlorn in the middle of nowhere beside the great east road; so they hitched their tired horses to the rear of the caravan, made a broad circle, and drove the caravan back the way it had come.

Leila leaned into Tevo as he drove, sighing. She still possessed the power of tirelessness Betsalel had bestowed on her in Iskand eight years before, and it had been a great help to her as the mother of young children. But she was emotionally exhausted.

They turned north toward Parat and pulled into the gathering ground late in the evening. Many people had already gone to bed, but the space was alight with torches and there were uniformed imperial guards to be seen walking around and talking with people. Leila hopped down and went to speak with one of them.

He recognized her. The friendship between the imperial family and the high officials of the church of Betsalel had not gone unnoticed by the men who were tasked with keeping order in the city. "Good evening, uh… Lieutenant, is it?" she said, and the man stood at attention.

"Your holiness!" he said stiffly. "We were advised to watch for your return. Please follow me, so you can speak to my commanding officer."

The commanding officer proved to be none other than Pyotr Drovski, who had been a lieutenant and commanding officer of the night shift guards on the night when Leila and Tevo had broken into the Imperial Treasure House and freed the Shadow God's long-lost original idol from its confinement. The guards under his command had fired crossbows at the retreating god and hit Tevo, killing him. But Tevo had long since forgiven them. After all it had been an accident, he and Leila being invisible at the time. And besides, Betsalel had restored him to life.

"Major Drovski," Leila said, holding out a hand. "Good to see you again." Young Drovski's career in the guards had not been harmed by his activities on that fateful night. "Your holiness," he responded, eyes eager. "You have returned already! What did you find?"

"Is the emperor, or any of my family, still here?" she asked.

"The queen of Palambo and her children, along with your daughter, were returned to your home some hours ago," he assured her. "Likewise, the emperor, empress, and their son are now back at the palace under enhanced guard. My company of guards has been conducting a thorough search of the gathering as you suggested, in case your theory that the children were taken by that Nima woman proved wrong. We have found nothing."

Leila sighed. She had so hoped to return triumphant with the children – Rajani locked in a cage or dead by the side of the road, it made no matter to her. "You can call off your search and let people get to sleep, Major," she said. "My husband and I have returned with the caravan and the woman Rajani's heathen idol. I do not believe that she is truly Nima, though she masqueraded as such. Her 'goddess' has taken her and the children to somewhere east of the Killtops, I'm afraid. They are out of our reach for the time being."

Major Drovski's youthful face (at less than forty, he was one of the youngest of the Imperial Guard ever to achieve the rank of major without having been involved in combat) fell at her words. The empress had been devastated, nearly hysterical, and desperate for the return of her little girl.

Leila and Tevo turned the caravan over to the guards. It was to be searched top to bottom for any evidence that would help them to learn more about Rajani. The evil-looking idol was to be crated up and locked into one of the rooms in the Imperial Treasure House. They hoped this would make it impossible for the daemon to manifest here in Parat, kept away from the presence of any of her believers.

Everyone had gone to bed by the time they had returned to Shadow Manor, dropped off by an escort of imperial guards. They took hot showers, then fell into the downy softness of their huge bed in the house's master bedroom. They slept for a few hours wrapped in each other's arms, then awakened as soon as they heard Elyzia stirring downstairs.

Drinking strong kaf and munching on warm pastries, Leila and Tevo sat at one end of the dining table and plotted their strategy. "Ostden's going to want to send a company of Imperial Guards to track down Rajani and take back the kids," he pointed out.

"And the khan isn't going to let that happen," Leila replied. "Even if it *wasn't* him who got Rajani to steal the emperor's daughter, it's a sure bet he would see a military force, even a police force like the Imperial Guard, going into his territory as an act of war. Those people will fight anyone at the drop of a hat."

"You're right," Tevo said, swallowing more kaf. "We need to infiltrate the Khanate in secret, somehow." Leila smiled grimly at him.

"Secret infiltrations are my specialty," she reminded him. "Oh, no!" he said. "You are not going anywhere without me. Not this time."

Nine years ago, as the rebuilding of Betsalel's church in the Dominion was only barely underway, the Shadow God had needed an agent to penetrate his temples in Palambo and discover a way to free them from the evil djinn who had taken them over. He had called on Leila, leaving the church in Tevo's increasingly capable hands, and the young once-thief had performed admirably. But meanwhile the love of his life had been torn from his arms for weeks that became months, and eventually she had fallen in love with someone else. He thought he had lost her forever, and had only gotten her back by chance. He didn't truly bear Imbaso, Gabriel's biological father, any ill-will. But he was not sorry the man had died.

Leila rose from her seat at the table and touched Tevo on the shoulder. "You're right," she said. "Come on, let's go talk with Betsalel." She had the little idol he'd made for her yesterday in her pocket, but it was more convenient to stroll into the nearby ballroom and speak with the god in his larger manifestation.

As soon as they had called him he shrank to the height of six feet, his preferred size for conferring with his worshipers. Especially those he loved as much as he did these two. "Master," Leila said, "I think it is time for Tevo to share my powers – shadows, illusion, tirelessness, and the bubble of silence. He will need them if we are to find our son, and the emperor's daughter."

Betsalel gazed down at her thoughtfully, not exactly reading her mind but sensing her soul. Though his beloved little priestess had truly loved her Imbaso, as had he (the young man had served him wholeheartedly during the cleansing of the Palamban temples), he knew that she harbored an unending guilt for having turned away from Tevo to be with him. Though there was good and practical need for Tevo to have these powers now, he thought it likely that she saw them as a way of evening things up between them. She would no longer be the one more favored by their god, and they would be truly equal partners.

"You wish this, Tevo?" Betsalel asked. He rarely did anything to anyone without their consent, his sinister reputation as the God of Death aside.

"Yes, please," his arch-priest responded, deeply touched at this gesture of Leila's. He knew she truly loved him, had loved him still even when she wed another – and had been his loving wife for eight years now, borne his child. But though he was the older, there had always been an imbalance between them – her powers, her wit, eclipsing his own.

Resting his hands gently on Tevo's shoulders, the Shadow God (who overtopped him by nearly half a foot, even at this reduced size), kissed him tenderly on the brow. As she watched, it almost seemed to Leila that she could see the god's gifts, the god's love, fall over Tevo like an invisible cloak. She had witnessed Betsalel conferring the power of the bubble of silence on Imbaso, and he had seemed exalted by the experience. But that had been just a faint shadow of what happened now.

When he stood back again, Tevo took a deep breath and shook himself. "Wow," he said in hushed tones. Then he vanished, reappearing a moment later as the image of Leila. Nine years ago he had been discomfited when she had appeared as a lovely young blonde in his bed. But from the look he gave her, he was now getting some ideas of his own of the fun he could have with this new ability. Leila was suddenly glad that he had never met Imbaso.

"Thank you, master!" Tevo cried, returning to himself. Testing the powers of tirelessness and the bubble of silence would have to wait. "I think we should gather our things and tell Busara what we plan, then take the horses to the palace," Leila told him. There had been no opportunity yesterday to discuss things with Busara, as she had gone to bed by the time they returned home. They hoped she would be all right staying here in Parat alone and looking after Miri while they were gone.

Her stepmother looked worried when Leila told her they planned to travel east of the Killtops to bring the children back themselves. "Will you be safe?" she asked worriedly.

"Did Father tell you all I did during the time when Imbaso and I were ruling?" Leila replied. She had gone, undercover and alone, to Namei and later to Dikka on Palambo's west coast, there to root out the deadly Makucha Nyeusi assassins who were working hand in hand with the cult of Kivuli. She might have gotten a little rusty these past few years, true; but the continent boasted few women deadlier or more competent.

"You're right, I shouldn't worry," Busara said.

"Betsalel has granted all my powers to Tevo as well, so the two of us will be unbeatable," Leila assured her with more confidence than she truly felt. Plans had a way of going awry, she had lately been reminded. "All we have to do is lurk along the Ivory Road and wait for Rajani to bring Gabe and Berta to us. Then we'll scoop them up and have them back in Parat in an eyeblink!"

Busara smiled, that warm smile that lit her whole beautiful face. She was as beautiful inside as out, and Leila felt a happy satisfaction that Vandao had been able to claim such a woman for his wife. She doubted that, had he been able to marry her mother, *that* relationship would ever have worked out so well. Miriam had been gorgeous, and she had loved her little Leila with all her heart; but she had had a restricted, loveless upbringing and it had ruined her chances for happiness.

"Just a few weeks, do you think?" the older woman asked. Elyzia was feeding the children in the house's enormous kitchen, keeping them out of the adults' hair for the time being. "I hope, but I can't promise anything. You were planning to stay with us through the end of Canis, weren't you?"

"Yes," Busara admitted. That was more than a month away.

"We should be able to send word through Betsalel the whole time we're on the road, even stop back for a brief visit if we get to where there's a temple," Leila promised her. "I'm sure that Ostden and Lisabet will still want you to visit with them at the palace, and Adalbert and Elyzia will be here all the time. You should be all right."

Busara squeezed her stepdaughter's hands. She was very nearly in awe of Leila and the things she had done, and proud to be related to her. Tevo came in, carrying a couple of packs loaded down with spare clothing, weapons, and supplies. "I've got Adalbert saddling the horses," he said. "Are we good to go?"

"Yes, everything's fine," Busara told him, rising. "Come and kiss the children goodbye, and we'll see you off." They went into the kitchen and found the girls and Vandasi grinning and giggling around the table as they stuffed their faces with strudel and fresh fruit, washed down with copious amounts of sweetened tea. The baby boy was sitting in a wooden high chair at the kitchen table, and appeared to be happy as a clam. He was so chubby at this stage of his existence it was hard to imagine that in just a few years he'd be getting as tall and lean as his mother and father.

"Your papa and I are going on a trip to get Gabe and Berta back," Leila told her daughter. Miri's happy smile dissolved as she suddenly remembered the trouble from yesterday. She would go through periods of remembering and get sad and fearful; but she was a naturally joyful person and it wouldn't be long before the memories would be driven from her mind by some new delight. When you are five, the world is full of such delights.

"Nana Busara will be here while we're gone, looking after you," Leila promised. "You'll have Zurishi and Keisha and Vandasi to play with, and you can visit with Aleksei at the palace, too. And of course Elyzia and Adalbert will be here, and Lord Betsalel will be watching over you. We'll be back as soon as we can."

The thought of how much fun that might be made Miri decide not to cry and whine after all. All of them, including Elyzia and Adalbert, gathered at curbside to deliver goodbye hugs and kisses before Leila and Tevo mounted their tireless horses and set off at a trot for the palace on the hill above them.

Chapter 12

"But I can't just sit here and do nothing!" Ostden cried. While he was a constitutional monarch rather than an absolute ruler he still held more power than any other individual within the Gaspari Dominion; and he longed to just reach out his powerful fist and take his daughter back from the demon-worshiping harridan who had stolen her. He had gotten a good look at the idol of Danava before it was crated for storage.

"You'll just be playing into the khan's hands if you try to send guards into his territory," Tevo assured him. The short, slim and muscular priest might be three years his junior, but the emperor had come to respect his judgment. He had access to arcane knowledge others did not.

"We can go in disguised as tribesmen, or Hando traders, and pass unnoticed among the traffic along the Ivory Road," Leila assured him. "We'll ambush Rajani before she can reach him with her prize, and the moment the children are in our hands we can whisk them right back to Parat. We're both carrying idols of Betsalel with us, in case we get separated, and with those we can call the god to our aid whenever we need him. We *will* get them back, I promise you!"

"Listen to her, Osti," Lisabet put in. "She's right – it's the only way! Even if a troop, or a company, or a regiment of guards could be sent to capture Rajani, what would stop her from slitting the children's throats? But Leila and Tevo can take her unawares!"

They were conferring in the Piastin family's private sitting room, and the emperor slumped down in his comfortable chair with a sigh. "I give up. But isn't there something I can do?" Leila hesitated, thinking through the consequences. She and Tevo were convinced they were right, that Oghul Khan (as they had learned the Gholim's ruling warlord was calling himself) was the one who had sought to take the emperor's daughter hostage. But it wasn't as if the two of them had never been wrong about something – even just recently.

"There is something you should probably do," she admitted. "Issue a proclamation, in Gasparto and Hando and maybe some of the other languages of the realms east of the Killtops, offering a whopping big reward for the capture of Rajani – but only if the children are recovered, safe. Your garrison at Miradil can make sure that it is distributed to every traveler heading east, and in time traders on the Ivory Road will have reached nearly every corner of the realms. In case we are wrong about where she was taking them, or in case she decides that her plan to sell them to the khan will no longer work, we need people to be on the lookout for them everywhere."

Ostden looked nonplussed. "Good idea," he said. "I'll send for a scribe immediately. But Hando and other languages? How am I to do that?" Leila slapped her forehead. In Miradil, of course, there would be many people fluent in all of the more commonly used tongues of the east. But how did she and Tevo think they were going to move along the Ivory Road, when he knew only Gasparto and she only the language of her birth plus Kiswa?

"Go ahead and send for your scribe," Leila said, giving the emperor an embarrassed smile. "I kind of forgot something, and we need to have a conference with Betsalel." The Piastins had only met the Shadow God a few times in the years since his worship had returned to their realm. The imperial family's shrine to Lucia had been quietly removed from the palace after the revelations nine years before, and currently there were no true idols of any of the gods to be found within the palace compound – not counting the idol of Danava recently ensconced in the Treasure House. The imperial family frequently worshiped in public at the Temple of the Eight, but they were not particularly devout. In their world the people most interested in worshiping the gods were those most in need of assistance – and people of the Piastins' standing lacked for scarcely anything.

Ostden got up and went to the door to send a servant for a scribe, and Leila looked to Lisabet, holding her small idol in her hand. "Do you mind?" she asked, and Lisabet shook her head with a smile. She was actually fascinated, and eager to see what would happen next. Leila set the idol on the floor and called to Betsalel, "Master, may we speak with you? There is something I forgot!"

Immediately the tiny idol began to grow, and as Ostden returned to his seat he gaped to see the Shadow God, six feet tall, standing on the elegant thick-pile Hando carpet. "Dark one," he said politely, inclining his head.

"Your Imperial Highness," Betsalel replied, with an air of sardonic humor. In a way both gods and emperors derived their powers from ordinary humans. Who held precedence?

"What is it that you need, Leila?" Betsalel asked.

"More languages!" she blurted. "We're going into the realms east of the Killtops, and we need to be able to pass as natives! Can you give us Hando, both speaking and writing?" He smiled at her. Of course, how could he have overlooked it?

"If you wish to pass as natives in that broad land, you will need more than Hando. It is the *lingua franca* of that region, the traders' tongue, and is widely known. But if you hope to move among the Gholim you will need the language used by the tribes to communicate with one another. And the Dravim use another tongue, and a completely different system of writing."

Oh *why*, Leila thought despairingly, had she so blithely ignored the opportunities she'd had to learn more about the world? The Sisters of Deline might regard her as a dilettante, but among most of the women in the Dominion she was considered well-read and well-educated. Yet it had never occurred to her to spend more time learning about that huge area of the continent east of the Killtops, from which so much of modern technology had flowed. Well, if a god-given instant learning course could repair the deficit, she stood ready to embrace it!

"You know this language of the Gholim, master?" Leila asked. She'd gotten the idea from their recent discussion that he had no worshipers among the horse tribes. And she'd often noted how ignorant the Eight could be, in areas where their human worshipers seemed to know far more than they did.

"The tribes were not always as they are now," Betsalel replied gently. "I have had my adherents among them, and once they had great cities. I can give you their tongue, and their writing as well. Though few of the tribesmen today can read and write."

Leila had come to think of the Shadow God as a trusted friend, a beloved father. Knowing his limitations, it was hard for her to recall that he was an immortal god who had been in existence since her remotest ancestors were living in caves and had only recently mastered the art of making fire. His occasional ignorance about current events was eclipsed by his long, deep knowledge of humanity.

Leila and Tevo stood before him as he granted each of them the gift of the tongues spoken and written to the east of the continental divide. The common tongue of the Gholim was known as *Rusich*, that of the Dravim (most of whom lived in Indaya or the dozen small countries that surrounded it) *Hindai*. Those languages, and Hando, all used writing systems drastically different from the characters employed in writing Gasparto – or Kiswa, for that matter. Those Palambans who could read and write (and in another generation, if Vandao's reforms held sway, that might be most of them), used the beautiful, sweeping characters developed by the Daregs to render their own tongue – though it bore little resemblance to Kiswa.

Betsalel made ready to shrink his idol, so that Leila might return it to her pocket. "Wait, dark one!" Lisabet cried out. "I would that we had a true idol of you here, so that we might get news of Leila and Tevo as they seek the children. Can that be done?" Betsalel looked to his arch- priest for guidance. It had been Tevo's request that the secret of the idols' proliferation not be made public.

He took a chance. Tevo had truly come to think of the imperial couple as their friends, had been through some tough situations with them and seen that they had mettle. When he'd been a kid growing up on in the mean streets of Buda, he would never have dreamed that nobles could be so... noble. Ostden and Lisabet really were good people, and he felt he must trust them.

He turned to the emperor and empress. "Betsalel is going to reveal to you something that is considered to be a secret of his church. I would appreciate it if you would never tell anyone about it." They both nodded eagerly, promising to remain silent. Smiling at him, the Shadow God pulled a pinch of substance from his side and passed the tiny idol to Tevo, who handed it over to Lisabet. "Were you to open your heart and mind to my lord," he told her, "he could grant you his protection from supernatural harm. Uh, assuming it won't conflict with your duties as empress..."

Lisabet smilingly accepted the idol, holding it up to examine it and marveling at the detail. It had been clear to her and her husband that Leila and Tevo were not "their sort of people" – not hereditary aristocrats – but they cared more for a person's character and personal attributes than they did for their pedigree and upbringing. As the rulers of this land, they didn't have to follow social trends – they made them.

Betsalel shrank until he was small enough for Leila to pick him up and put him in her pocket. Then she told Lisabet, "Place your idol on the floor, so that the god can manifest at a reasonable size."

"Can he manifest smaller?" the empress asked, intrigued.

"Even at a size too small to be seen," Leila admitted, "though that is not something generally known and we'd like to keep it that way. Once you have opened yourself to him, you can speak with him mind to mind while he is manifest in an idol."

The empress looked astonished. Like most people of her class within the Dominion, she had scarcely ever done more than pay lip service to the Eight. The idea that one might have a deep personal relationship with one of them, might carry one's god around in one's pocket, was a startling thought. She gingerly set the new idol on the carpet, where it immediately fell over. The nap was too thick to support such a tiny statue. But before she could right it again, Betsalel began to grow and climb to his feet.

He reached a height of six feet and bowed slightly to the empress, who was staring at him wide-eyed. "If you will give me a place in your home, and in your heart, Lisabet," he said in his deep dark voice, "I will come to you when you call and let you know what Leila and Tevo are doing."

Lisabet smiled brilliantly, her green eyes huge. "Yes!" she said, "Yes I will! What do I need to do?"

"Just remain calm," the Shadow God told her, "and open your heart." Leila and Tevo watched fondly, Ostden with a hint of apprehension, as his wife opened herself to the dark god who, when they had both been teenagers, had been regarded as the epitome of evil.

After a few moments the empress opened her eyes. "Wonderful!" she breathed. She had never had a true religious experience before. "Will you grant me safety from bad dreams, master?" she added. "Last night I could scarcely sleep for the horrors I was imagining my little girl was enduring." Betsalel laid a gentle hand on her arm.

"You will sleep soundly, and have only the best of dreams, empress," he promised her.

The Shadow God had established close personal bonds with millions of individual humans over his millennia of existence, but it still gave him profound satisfaction to reach another. He hoped that Ostden might eventually join his wife and become a worshiper. But in the meantime...

"I should deliver you and Tevo to Miradil," Betsalel told Leila.

"We will need the horses," she reminded him. Nimble (at that time going under the name of Wapesi) had been returned to Parat by Betsalel when he brought Vandao to attend Tevo and Leila's wedding. He had had to send the horse to sleep, to prevent him from panicking at the strange sensations. "Also," Leila added, "we need to translate Emperor Ostden's offer of a reward for return of the children into the languages of the eastern realms so we can take them with us when we go."

Just then the scribe who'd been sent for arrived, and Ostden and Lisabet were dictating to him as he sat a nearby writing desk. "I can handle that for you," the Shadow God pointed out. When King Imbaso and Queen Leila had been fighting to bring down the cult of Kivuli, the gods and goddesses had produced many copies of their proclamation and delivered them into the hands of their priesthoods all over the kingdom.

"Great idea," Tevo said. He hadn't been there when all that was going on in Palambo, but it should have occurred to Leila. As soon as the scribe had written the proclamation to the satisfaction of the emperor and empress, Ostden affixed his seal to the document. Then Leila took it from him and handed it to the god, who promptly produced three identical documents in Gasparto – and another handful, all apparently bearing the official seal, in the three major languages of the eastern realms.

Ostden was looking seriously impressed, now. Printing presses abounded in the Dominion, but it would have taken days to have the proclamation translated and many copies run off before signing and sealing each of them. "I will produce more as needed by the authorities in Miradil," Betsalel told them. "Tevo, I don't think you and Leila should be handing any out yourselves, as this would certainly cast your disguises into question."

"You're right," he said. "But I think we can carry some with us. If we're posing as Hando traders or whatever, we can always say the proclamations were given to us at the border."

"All right," the god replied. "Are we ready?" Leila and Tevo exchanged glances, then nodded.

"We left the horses hitched out in front of the palace entrance," she told him.

"Lisabet, can I prevail on you to carry this idol out there?" Betsalel asked.

"Of course!" she said, and as the idol shrank to palm size she picked it up and studied it. The god was still manifest in it, but now only a couple of inches high. So odd!

The emperor, empress, and a small contingent of palace guards escorted Leila and Tevo back to where they'd left their horses. Then Lisabet set the tiny idol down on the stones of the courtyard, and it immediately grew to ten feet. "My idol at the Temple of the Eight in Miradil is large," Betsalel said, "but there is not room for me to manifest there carrying two horses and two people. I will have to shrink you all."

"Why don't you take us first, then the horses?" Leila suggested, and he nodded. He touched his arch-priest and arch-priestess on the shoulders, and they shrank to the size of toddlers. Then he scooped them up, one in each arm, and a second later the people had vanished and the idol had assumed the standard posture. Ostden put his arm around his wife and squeezed her to him, both giving and getting comfort as they confronted the strange experience. Not a minute later the statue came alive again.

"Leila and Tevo are back to full size again and awaiting their horses' arrival in the temple at Miradil," the god assured them. "Lisabet, after I have delivered the horses I will manifest here again so I can shrink this idol for you. I think it would be best if you carried it with you, or kept it in your personal quarters so we can communicate at need."

"All right," she said softly, eyes shining in wonder.

The black god sent Nimble and Milacek to sleep, then the guards holding their reins released them as the horses shrank to the size of lap-dogs. Once again the idol became just a statue, and all gathered there stood watching it until it moved again. "They are on their way," Betsalel announced. "May they find success."

Chapter 13

The Temple of Danava in Delai was huge by that dark goddess' standards, one of her largest in the world. But to the eyes of Gabriel and Berta, residents of Parat who had often gone to the Temple of the Eight there, it seemed modest in size. After the goddess (for both children were willing to accept the status claimed for the daemon by her priestess) had deposited them on the temple's stone floor and restored them to their normal size, she addressed Rajani in Hindai – the tongue in which the woman had first done her worship. "I must go elsewhere," she said shortly. "Do you need anything else?"

"A new idol, mistress," Rajani said. She was sad to have left her personal idol of the goddess behind in the caravan – one that she had carried with her for many years. But there had been no help for it. The goddess nodded curtly and broke the tip off of one of the jet black curved knives that had reappeared in two of her hands as soon as she had offloaded her passengers. As she handed it to the sorceress, it immediately writhed and became a tiny idol of the four-armed goddess. Then the ten-foot idol before them froze in the dancing position that was its standard pose, and the goddess was gone.

Both children were wide-eyed. Gabriel no more than Berta knew that deities – whether one of the Eight or any of the myriad living daemons – possessed the ability to spawn new true idols for themselves. It was an ability as intrinsic to their nature as the ability of humans and other natural creatures to reproduce themselves sexually, or by budding. But few humans knew of it in this day and age, and Gabriel's parents had not told him about it yet. They took it for a sign of some powerful sorcery.

Rajani tucked the new little idol into a pocket in her voluminous Nima skirt and turned to her charges, pasting a smile on her face. "Well," she said in cheerful tones, "here we are in Delai, in the kingdom of Indaya. We will be here for a few days, getting ready to travel north by horseback to the great Huang river. Then we'll be taking a riverboat to the west, in the direction of your homes. Won't that be fun?"

They looked at her as if she were mad, but fear was showing in their faces. After witnessing her interactions with the extremely scary-looking goddess, they didn't want to do anything at all to make her mad at them. Danava had said Gabriel was protected from her by Betsalel, but was he protected from Rajani as well? Berta had hold of his hand and was clutching it so hard that her knuckles were white.

It had been near dusk when they had fled the caravan. Here, thousands of miles to the east, it was the middle of the night and they were the only people inside the temple except for one old man, a priest clad in blood red robes, who was dozing in a chair near the door behind the idol. He had not stirred when they had arrived.

Rajani had hastily packed a duffle bag before they left, and she now rummaged in it. She didn't want them to stand out too much, didn't want them to fall under the eye of anyone who might want to take advantage of the curiously-garbed strangers.

The boy was as dark as she was, might easily pass for her own grandson. But the girl, the important hostage! With that creamy, freckled skin and fire-red hair she would stand out like a beacon – here in Delai, especially, where nearly the entire populace was Dravim. And all along their journey to the Huang, and downriver to the confluence of the Tekushi where they would turn north for Ashbat, her looks would be a liability.

Well, once they were traveling maybe she could have Danava hold a glamour on the girl, one that would make her appear to be a sister to the boy. With appropriate clothing, they would just be a half-Gholim woman and her grandchildren, returning to the tribal lands for a visit. In the meantime, she could at least make them less conspicuous.

From her bag, Rajani pulled out several lengths of dark red cloth. She worked first on Berta, telling her "We're going to play dress-up, now, and pretend that we're citizens of Delai. You and your friend should not speak while we're out in public, since you don't speak the language." She wrapped the red-headed girl in the cloth from head to food, hiding her hair and most of her face as well as the clothing she was wearing. Then she did the same for the boy, before wrapping a much larger length of cloth over the top of her Nima garb.

The Nima were found in most parts of the realms east of the Pahadai, but seldom to be seen wandering around on foot. It would be better not to attract any notice at all, which Rajani hoped could be achieved at this late hour. They had more than two miles to cover to reach the apartment where they would take shelter for the night.

Now that they were attired in local dress, Rajani slung the duffle on its strap up over her back and took each of the children by a hand. "What's your name, boy?" it finally occurred to her to ask as she led them out the temple's front doors. The night was warm and steamy, and a light rain was falling.

"I'm Gabriel Karmarzin," Gabe said, standing up straight. "My parents are the arch-priest and arch-priestess of Betsalel for the whole entire Dominion, and my grandfather is the king of Palambo. You had better take us home, or Betsalel will kill you. Or Papa and Mama will. I think they might be worse."

"Bold talk, boy," Rajani said scornfully, as she hurried them along the narrow streets. At this hour there were few people stirring, and it was possible to make good speed. Shops were boarded up for the night, filth littering the streets, and the children's overall first impression of Delai was miserable.

"Your Shadow God can't harm me," the sorceress went on, maintaining a fast walking pace that had the children trotting to keep from being dragged along. "I have the protection of Danava, and should your parents find me I will call her to this idol in my pocket and she will cut their heads off with her *kukrisi*. Then you'll be an orphan like me, and I don't think you'd like that much. But all they have to do is relax and wait, and you and Berta will be going home again safe and sound. Right after we visit with my friend the king."

That took the wind out of Gabriel's sails. He knew that his mama had the power to create illusions, and he suspected that one of her illusions was to become invisible – there was no other way to explain how she knew about things that had happened, or been talked about, when she was not there. He had no idea whatsoever that both of his parents had once been highly skilled thieves, or that his mama was a full member of the (now, presumably, completely disbanded) Makucha Nyeusi cult of Palamban assassins. Which was just as well, else he might have bragged of it to Rajani and put her on her guard.

The children had had hours in which to rest on the pallets in Rajani's Nima wagon, but the stresses of the day were beginning to take their toll as the woman hustled them through the wet, filthy streets of Delai in the darkness. It was clear she knew this city well, but they were hopelessly lost.

"My feet hurt!" Berta wailed, digging in her heels. She was used to getting her way. "And I'm tired, and hungry!" she added for emphasis, as Rajani didn't immediately drag her onward.

"So am I, child," the woman replied not unkindly. "But you don't hear me whining about it." She unslung the duffle bag for a moment, releasing their hands. There was nowhere for them to run, no people on the street to call to, none who spoke their language even if there had been anyone about.

Rajani pulled a couple of waxed paper-wrapped bars out of her bag, and handed one to each of the children. Gabriel peeled it open and sniffed it suspiciously. The last time he'd taken food from this woman, he'd woken up hours later tied and gagged, with a headache. But he was so *hungry*! It had been hours and hours since he'd eaten lunch, and he theorized that if she wanted him dead she could have just killed him with that dagger she'd been waving around earlier. And he couldn't imagine why she would want him unconscious – that would just mean she had to carry him. So he took a big bite.

Oh, it was wonderful! It must have been some confection they were selling at the Nima gathering, Gabriel thought. It was loaded with dried fruits and crunchy nuts, and covered with something like powdered sugar. He devoured it in a few bites and stood there licking his fingers and grinning as the rain poured down around them.

"Thank you, Rajani!" he said. His parents and Elyzia had worked to teach him manners, and he saw no reason to be unpleasant. Maybe if he got into the old woman's good graces she would start to trust him and there might be a chance for him and Berta to get away.

Surprised at the boy's about-face, Rajani patted him on the shoulder. Berta, too, had eaten up the snack bar and was looking happier for it – though her feet did still hurt. "Come on you two, let's get out of this rain, shall we?" the sorceress said, taking their hands again after returning the duffle to her back. They hurried onward.

80

In less than half an hour more they arrived at a three-story building that appeared to be masonry overlain with crumbling stucco. There were ornamental but effective iron grates over the ground-floor windows and the painted wooden door, but Rajani produced a key from somewhere on her person and ushered her dripping-wet, exhausted charges into the building. She led them to an apartment on the second floor rear, and unlocked the door.

The hall and stairwell were dimly lit with kerosene lamps, else it would have been pitch dark within. Rajani lit some candles after they came inside, standing on a thin woven cotton rug set inside the door. On one side of the room where they stood was a counter and some kitchen facilities. On the other, some large cushions had been put on the floor. Gruesome wall hangings depicted Danava trampling her foes, slaughtering her enemies, and fighting with some even more hideous-looking demons. The colors were very bright.

Gabriel looked at Berta, and saw her stiff with fear – and standing cross-legged, hands to her crotch. Yet she had not mentioned this complaint to Rajani earlier, and seemed too afraid to do so now. "Rajani," he spoke up, "Where is the privy, please?"

The old woman barked a short laugh. She strode through an open doorway to a room beyond and returned in a moment with a ceramic chamberpot. He thanked her, then offered it to Berta. "Ladies first," he said gallantly. A look of relief and gratitude flooded her face as she snatched the pot from his hands and dashed to what he assumed was the bedroom, slamming the door behind her. Rajani's eyes followed her with an amused expression.

Berta had been born and raised in a palace, but Gabriel's short life had been spent in surroundings scarcely less palatial when compared with this rude dwelling. Lord Betsalel had become quite used to Leila's requests for improvements in climate control and plumbing, and the current Shadow Manor had hot and cold running water and flush toilets throughout. Yet the idea of staying in a dingy apartment and using a chamberpot didn't bother Gabe. It was sort of like an adventure, like camping out. For a moment, he almost forgot their circumstances.

Berta emerged in a couple of minutes, saying shyly "I left the pot in there for you, Gabe. Sorry, I don't know where to dump it out."

"It's all right," he assured her, with a grin dazzling white in his dark, handsome face.

Taking a cue from her friend, while Gabriel relieved himself Berta asked Rajani, "Is this your home?"

"One of them," the sorceress replied. "I have homes of a sort all over the eastern realms. One of them is even in a king's palace! But I grew up in Delai, and it was here that I first knew my goddess. So perhaps this is more truly my home than some of the others. I doubt it's up to *your* standards, princess."

"Oh no, really, it's quite all right," Berta said, remembering her manners. The courtesies were drummed into girls of her class from the time they began to walk and talk. "I'm very glad to get out of that rain!"

Rajani snorted. "If you thought that was rain, pray you never see the monsoon!" Berta looked at her speculatively. The children of the emperor were expected to be well-educated, and she had been tutored by the best since she was a little older than Aleksei was now. But from what she recalled of her studies of Indaya, a monsoon was a furry little creature like a weasel that liked to prey on big poisonous snakes.

"The monsoon...?" she asked, as if they were making small talk.

"Later this month, and through the month of Canis and into Breeze, rain falls almost continually. In some ways it is a blessing, for the city is washed clean. But it is not a good time to be in Delai." She saw the girl's look, and assured her, "We will be gone from here within two days, going north and returning west to take you and Gabriel back home."

Berta came from a long line of people sharp enough to hold together a vast empire, without resorting to war, for dozens of generations. Them, and the people who were smart enough – or admittedly, beautiful enough – to marry them. This woman who had drugged and captured her and Gabe clearly wanted them to forget that anything was amiss, and just go along meekly with her while she carried out her plans.

Though she was only seven, Berta had already received schooling in history and politics. She guessed that she had become a hostage against her father, and that Gabe had just gotten caught up in plans that had nothing to do with him. But she was determined to keep him safe. For now at least, she would play along with Rajani and try to convince her she truly thought they were on their way home. And if any suggestion arose that Gabe was expendable, she planned to raise a storm that would make Rajani's monsoon look like a light drizzle.

Chapter 14

After the horses, once again at their full sizes, had been awakened, Leila and Tevo made their first stop the headquarters of Miradil's imperial garrison. This was one of the largest forces of the Imperial Guards within the Dominion, and the one that most resembled an army. They decided to become Imperial Messengers, since that was, in a way, what they were. It would save a lot of time in explanations.

Tevo, new to his powers of illusion, was having almost too much fun with them. When he assumed the aspect of a black-haired, black-bearded man nearly seven feet tall, Leila tactfully pointed out that nearly all of the Messenger Corps were no bigger than he truly was. Had he not been raised as a thief, and had he been given some instruction in riding earlier in life, Tevo would have made an ideal messenger. Like the assassins of the Makucha Nyeusi, most of them were small and wiry.

The pair of Imperial Messengers who delivered the sheaf of papers – in several languages, comprising Emperor Ostden's proclamation of reward for the safe return of a red-haired girl, age seven (and her dark male companion, of the same age) – looked as though they might have been brothers. They were prepared to answer questions, but the proclamation did not reveal the identities of the missing children. Leila feared that anyone who paid any attention whatsoever to world events would know in a moment who the red-haired girl would be; but what else could Ostden do?"

After they'd parted company with the garrison commander, a competent-seeming man in his early fifties, the pair went back down to the stables to retrieve their horses. "What do you think?" Leila asked, as they mounted and rode out through the gates of the compound to the city below. "Should we get onto the Ivory Road immediately? And what guise should we take?"

Of the two of them, Leila was far more skilled at intrigue and deception. But she had no experience of the lands east of the Killtops, nor any idea of what to expect when they got there. "Let's tie the horses up down by the docks," she suggested, "and present ourselves as Miradil merchants' agents while we look around and try to get a handle on things."

"Good idea," Tevo said sagely. He really, really wanted to take the lead, to be the man. But this was his first covert assignment in nine years and he had to face the facts. He had no idea what he was doing. They went down to the river docks. The mouth of the Huang was far narrower than that of the Azraq to the south, having broken through the rocky rampart of the Killtops where it gave way to the gentler slopes of the Talj Jabal hundreds of millennia in the past.

Before that, there had been an enormous inland sea covering much of the land to the east of the mountains, north and south. But that was long before humans had inhabited the land. Now the Huang, which east of Miradil was more than a mile wide, constricted slightly as it flowed into the Center Sea and found itself corralled by the ancient harbor of Miradil. The city itself clustered mostly on the rocky promontory of the north bank, but there were fortifications to the south as well. And the Dominion's fleet patrolled the waters day and night to make sure that all traffic coming down the Huang was regulated and accounted for, and that all tariffs had been paid.

The river's flow near the mouth was so strong that no vessel, under sail or oar, could traverse it upstream for nearly a hundred and fifty miles to the east – beyond where the Tekushi, which drained the eastern slopes of the Killtops, joined it. So most of the river traffic was east to west. Despite its name, the Ivory Road was more likely to carry goods from the Dominion and Palambo than the ivory, silks, and spices of the east.

Leila and Tevo, appearing to be a pair of middle-aged Gasparis clad as second-rank traders of Miradil, strolled along the waterfront. The Ivory Road was blocked right down to the riverside by the walls of Miradil, its gates heavily guarded and controlled. But the road continued within the city, still following the river as it opened out into the Bay of Miradil – a half-round indentation in the eastern shore of the Center Sea.

Both of the travelers from Parat were dazzled by the activity along the waterfront, Leila in particular. She had thought that her home town of Marsine had been a bustling port – but it seemed like a small fishing village compared with the miles of jetties, wharfs, and more advanced port facilities to be found here. Miradil was truly the gateway between east and west, and the level of commerce was beyond anything she had dreamed.

They saw no signs of caravans forming up for the journey east up the Ivory Road, however. Tevo spotted a sign saying "Shipping Office" and nudged Leila. "Let's consult the locals, shall we?" he suggested, and they went inside. The place was like an overgrown version of the Municipal Shipping Office the middle-aged traders' agent from Miradil, Suleiman Abaza, had patronized in Jena nine years earlier. More than a dozen windows, each attended by a clerk, offered anyone who came in the chance to book passage to a destination on the Center Sea, arrange for shipment of cargo, or register one's vessel as one that could supply those needs.

The elder of the two Gaspari traders approached the young clerk at one of the windows after waiting in line for perhaps five minutes. "I have a cargo I wish to send to Hanshu," he said, and the clerk looked at him in bafflement.

"There is no sea trade east," he said, as if pointing out that men do not fly. "You must seek a caravan going to Hanshu in the Mustering Ground outside the city gates."

Leila turned away embarrassed. They should have realized that there would be no need to assemble caravans here inside the city walls, where space was at a premium. Miradil was one of fewer than a handful of the Dominion's cities that still boasted the high stone walls, the defenses, that all of them had had before Ostden the First had united the realm. And the longer the wall around a city, the more troops (or imperial guards, in this case) would be required to defend it. Of course caravans would muster outside the eastern gate.

"Are you ready to get started?" Leila asked, as they walked away.

"Might as well," Tevo replied. "Who should we be?" They walked back toward where their horses were tied, watched over by a boy to whom they'd given a couple of silver shillings. That question was another poser. They intended to go no further than Ghezh, the port a little more than a hundred miles upstream. There, the Tekushi joined its waters to the Huang and it was there, likely, that Rajani would disembark to travel north – assuming she intended to sell the children to Oghul Khan. But they needed to gather information in the meantime.

"Let's be Gholim," Leila said, after considering for a time. "But Gholim women, I think. We had some reason to go into Miradil, but are now returning to the tribal lands. And away from our tribe, we will join a caravan for the short trip to Ghezh. There we will await our son, who will collect us for the journey north with other members of the tribe."

Tevo looked at her askance, as they guided the horses along the western spur of the Ivory Road toward Miradil's east gate. "*Our* son?" he asked. Leila had been reading up on the subject.

"Among the tribes, men – especially the more powerful warlords – often take more than one wife. All of his children are considered to belong to the family, rather than to the husband and the wife who bore them."

He mused on that as they rode along, picking their way around dockside traffic. Well, he considered Gabriel to be *his* son as well as Leila's, though he had not actually engendered the boy. Why not the other way around? The city's east gate was open this afternoon, and already it was clear that the guards were on higher alert. Normally they were concerned only with who was coming *in* to the city; but now they were scanning everyone going out as well, on the hunt for the missing children. They paid the two middle-aged traders scant attention, however.

"How are we to change our appearance in the midst of these crowds?" Tevo asked. He was very new to this business of being able to adopt a new disguise with a thought, and beginning to realize that the ability carried its own unique problems. Leila looked around, and spotted a wooded area some hundred feet off the road, up against a weathered cliff. When the Huang had broken through to join the Center Sea, what had once been a mountain pass had become a fractured chasm. Caravans mustering to begin the journey east along the Ivory Road used the area along the cliffs as a camping ground, pitching their tents and letting their animals graze. But at the moment, a stretch of those woods stood empty.

The two middle-aged Gaspari traders ambled their mounts over toward the cliff, and in among the trees. A couple of minutes later the same horses came out, this time ridden by a pair of very similar-looking women in their sixties. From their weathered bronze skin, black hair gone gray, and slightly slanting brown eyes, they were of the Monazhim: one of the most numerous of the Gholim tribes.

They spoke to each other in Rusich, which came as easily to them as breathing thanks to the god's gift. Both were lean and wrinkled, clad in the traveling clothes favored by the horse tribes: leather breeches, thick wool tunics slit up the side for riding and heavily embroidered in colored wool, and soft leather boots that were wrapped to mid-calf in strips of dyed leather. They wore square wool felt hats on their heads, also ornamented with embroidery.

Tevo had had to see Leila's take on what their appearance should be before crafting his own illusion. They had glimpsed a few of the Gholim outside the city gate, but Leila was also recalling illustrations she'd seen in books. She hoped they were not too far out of date, but she'd be willing to bet that styles among the nomadic horse tribes of the steppes did not change with the same lightning fluidity they did among the upper classes in Parat. For a young matron of the Gaspari capital, being caught at a formal ball wearing last year's gown would be a humiliation. For a wizened Gholim grandmother, she thought it likely there would be no notice taken even if her garb had gone out of fashion a generation before. She hoped!

Given that Tevo had used Leila as a model for his own appearance, the two old women looked like sisters. Which, she assured him, was fine. It was not uncommon for sister wives to be sisters in fact, and only helped to strengthen the family's blood bonds. They continued walking their horses east along the strip of land between the road and the cliffs, which rose ever steeper on their left. On their right, across the broad river, the water lapped up against a somewhat lower escarpment that marked the beginning of the range the Palambans called the Talj Jabal.

The pair came upon a caravan that appeared close to leaving, wagons packed with trade goods from the Dominion. It was unlikely it would be on the move before tomorrow morning, however. Most of the amenities to be found along the road were spaced at a distance that would allow travelers to go from one camping spot or town to the next in a full day's travel. If you hadn't left by around nine in the morning, you would find yourself benighted on the road without even a wide spot to pull off and camp.

The two old Gholim women approached a man who looked to be a functionary for the caravan's management, a young fellow in his early twenties. From his features he was clearly of the Hando, but he was clad in garb not dissimilar from their own. After all, he would be riding a horse for thousands of miles before the caravan once again reached Hanshu.

Switching to accented Hando, Leila asked the young man "You are leaving tomorrow, yes?" The horse tribes were famously truculent with outsiders – or among themselves, for that matter. The youngster looked up. He had a sheaf of papers with him, clipped to thin, flat board. "That is correct, grandmother," he replied respectfully.

"We wish to accompany you as far as Ghezh, and eat at your fires." The good-sized river port at the confluence of the Huang and its mighty tributary the Tekushi was the caravan's planned third stop, out of the dozens it would be making as it made its slow way across the eastern half of the continent. "Do you wish fodder for your horses, as well?" he asked.

The sisters switched to Rusich, as they discussed the question. "How much is this going to cost us?" the younger asked. "Don't forget, we may be days at the inn in Ghezh before Koblin comes to collect us."

"Don't worry about it," the elder replied. "We got good money for the colt, and Zhara at the inn is a friend of mine. She'll let us stay for half price. Likely there won't be much grazing along the way – you saw how sparse the grass was."

"Very well, then," the younger woman replied, and the elder turned back to the youngster with the paperwork.

"You can feed us and our horses as well. How much?"

Hiding a smile, the man said "Six shillings all found, and you can share our tents." The grandmother fixed him with a gimlet eye.

"Four, and we'll sleep in our own tent."

"Five," he countered, and she grudgingly handed over the silver. "You can camp over there in among the trees tonight," the lad said after tallying their names and information on his log. "Dinner is an hour before sundown, and if you want breakfast before we get underway you should be up by 6:30 tomorrow morning."

The sisters nodded to him curtly, and went on their way. Leila was beginning to regret her decision to take this part of their journey as grumpy old tribeswomen. The whole point of traveling with the caravan was to pick up information about the area and its people, and maybe some rumors about the children, the khan, or anything else helpful. But it would seem odd if the notoriously stand-offish Monazhi grandmothers were to be effusively friendly and anxious to engage others in conversation. Likewise, it might be hard to hold up their disguises if they began talking with fellow members of the horse tribes.

Well, perhaps after they pitched their tent (Tevo had packed the one he had taken with him during the early years of spreading Betsalel's church, a snug fit for the two of them but that was all right), the sisters could go to bed early and then emerge, invisible, to eavesdrop on what was being said around the caravan camp. With all the languages they had now, there'd likely be few conversations they wouldn't be able to understand.

Leila and Tevo pitched the tent with the entrance flap near the cliff, then walked the horses back to where the caravan's animals were being fed and watered. They removed the horses' tack and carried it back to the tent for safekeeping, rubbing the animals down though they'd scarcely walked twenty miles today. Then they just wandered around the gathering, observing. They spotted a couple of imperial guards talking to the caravan clerk, and handing him copies of what they guessed would be the proclamation they brought earlier today. The caravans that left here for the east every day or two would spread the word far and wide.

The two Gholim grandmothers kept to themselves as they sat on folding stools around the fire eating a mutton and vegetable stew with flatbread, washed down with spring water. The caravan management evidently had no intention of providing ale or wine to its paying customers.

There were few of the Gholim around the fire, and none who made any attempt to engage them in conversation. The prickly nature of the tribes' culture worked in their favor there, and though they said little as they ate their ears were pricked to hear the conversations of those around them.

The group consisted mostly of Hando traders, as the caravan had been mounted by Honorable Liang Tai, a gentleman in his middle fifties. Liang Wei, the young man who had signed them up to travel with the caravan, was his nephew it seemed – presumably the son of his brother since they shared the same family name. The caravan employed nearly a dozen people, most of whom Leila suspected were also members of the Liang family, and another twenty hired guards.

If you were fit and skilled with weapons, signing on as a caravan guard was not a bad way to travel east, with your bed and meals covered and cash at the end of the journey. Though of course there was always the prospect of getting killed by bandits to sour the deal.

While Tai was the owner of most of the horses, oxen, and wagons, and the organizer of the caravan, there seemed to be three additional parties of his countrymen who had joined the caravan to shepherd the trade goods they had bought in the Dominion back east to Indaya and Hanshu.

There was little cash within the economy of the Gholim, though they did make marvelous woolen goods, exquisitely embroidered garments, and some of the finest carpets to be found anywhere in the world. Likely the caravan would stay a day or two in Ghezh, to take on some of these in exchange for the cotton and linen fabrics made by the factories of the Dominion, mechanical devices like clocks, and the good quality, inexpensive pottery the Dominion had become famous for.

When they'd cleaned their bowls, wiping up the last of the juices with the last of the flatbread, the two grandmothers turned the bowls over to the women in charge of cleaning up after the meal. Then, yawning – though the sun had not yet gone down below the horizon – the two retreated to their tent. They'd pitched it as far as they could get from any others, wanting their privacy.

They crawled inside and pulled down the flap, shedding their illusions as they did so. Tevo was grinning from ear to ear. "I can't believe I've gone nine years without asking for this power until now!" he said. "Remember what you had to go through to become, what was her name? That old half-Nima woman."

"Halima!" Leila said with an answering grin. "To tell you the truth, the only reason I recruited you to help me instead of skewering you in the kidneys was I was *so* anxious not to have to continue with that disguise! Plus," she added after a moment, with a sly look, "you were so damn cute…"

For a moment Leila recreated the appearance of the fat old woman she'd posed as while she was moving toward Parat at Betsalel's behest, with Count Wilhelm's guardsmen and thief-takers hot on her heels. "Lovely lady!" Tevo exclaimed, scooping her into his arms and planting a deep kiss on where he hoped to find her mouth. It was strange embracing someone who was not nearly as rotund as they appeared. At least the original Halima had been built from spare clothing and cushions, more substantial than air and illusion.

Leila transformed herself back to herself – but herself as she'd been ten years ago, a tough little maid of sixteen. Tevo responded by becoming himself as a hapless seventeen-year-old thief, so shy and ignorant by comparison with the worldly-wise arch-priest of Betsalel. They fell into each other's arms, then down upon the bedrolls they'd spread to cover the floor of the tent.

An hour or so later, as darkness was beginning to cover the land, they emerged from the tent again. The Gholim sisters would not be joining the campfire for socializing tonight, but others would be there conversing for at least another couple of hours.

They were alone in the woods, and it was dim in among the trees. Once again Leila wished she'd thought to ask Betsalel for the ability to see in the dark. She didn't want to bother him with such an arbitrary request, though, so she let it pass. Casting a bubble of silence around them as a precaution, she asked Tevo "Have you tried your silence power yet?"

"No," he replied. "The invisibility and illusion are just a matter of thought. I assume silence is the same?"

"Yes," she replied. "But it can be hard to realize that it's in effect. It creates a bubble ten feet in diameter centered on your belly."

"Stay there," Leila commanded her husband, and stepped away from him until he fell outside the bubble. He could see her mouth moving, and walked toward her until suddenly he could hear her again. But there was no other indication of bypassing the invisible barrier, no tingling on the skin or anything like that.

"Weird!" Tevo declared. "And it works both ways?"

"That's right," she said. "When you're inside your bubble, you won't hear anything that's happening more than five feet away from you. That's why it's best only to use the bubble when you absolutely need to. Well, are you ready to go hear the latest gossip?"

Tevo grinned at her nervously. He'd been on a career path that would have led to him possessing all the skills of stealth nine years ago; but the abrupt transition from thief to priest had short-circuited his education. He hoped he was up to the task of sneaking near enough to those gathered around the fire to hear what they talking about, without being detected. With a thought, he vanished from sight – and Leila did the same.

Chapter 15

Gabriel awoke hungry. It appeared that no one had been living in this squalid apartment for months, and there had been no food in the kitchen when they'd arrived. The art of preserving food in jars for long-term storage in the absence of ice boxes (which modern conveniences were notably lacking in the tropics, Mama had told him) did not appear to have reached Delai – or at any rate, it had not reached Rajani's Spartan kitchen.

She had brought along quite a few small, non-perishable foodstuffs from her wagon, though; and the three of them had made a very odd meal of Nima fruit and nut bars, apples, and a sort of cracker-like flatbread washed down with water. Rajani had locked her charges inside the apartment while she carried away the chamberpot to dump in the first-floor privy hole and fetched a large pitcher of water from the pump in the bathroom on that same level. There was one bathroom, with cold water only, for the entire building. But in Delai in the summertime, cold water was fine.

While she was gone Gabriel and Berta had scurried to explore their surroundings. Might they be able to slip out the back and run for safety? But they soon discovered that the apartment's lone window, which looked out over a narrow alley and another building behind this one, also had a security grate over it. In any case it was the middle of the night and raining out there.

There was a sharp knife in the kitchen, and Gabriel toyed with the idea of using it to overpower Rajani. But he could imagine how well *that* would work out, with the sorceress having an idol of her black goddess in the pocket of her tunic. In Mama's stories the heroes always did bold deeds, defeating the evil villains with their swords (or more often, by Leila's preference, their wits).

Papa knew how to use a sword, and how to throw daggers too. But Gabe had never been allowed to play with one that wasn't made out of wood. Maybe the time for bold deeds would come later, after they had come to know Rajani better – and after their continued good behavior had lulled her into thinking that they were cowed and would not cause her any trouble.

By the time the sorceress had returned to the apartment with the water and the cleaned chamber pot, he and Berta had struck a pact. They wouldn't whine, they would pretend that they believed everything Rajani told them; and they would bide their time while they waited for an opportunity to escape. But when the opportunity came, it must be one that both of them could take.

After the filth they had seen (though it had been dark) as they traveled here from the temple, Gabriel was worried about drinking the water. Even in the Dominion, people had been known to get sick from drinking out of the river near cities. But Rajani assured them that the pump downstairs drew water up from a deep well, and that she'd been drinking it for years without any ill effects.

He'd made it through the night without getting diarrhea, so it must have been all right. As Gabriel sat up on the thin pad Rajani had provided (she'd laid two of these on the floor for the children, while taking the narrow bed herself), his stomach growled loudly. He looked up and realized that somehow the sorceress had risen and left the bedroom without disturbing him.

The night had been very warm despite the rain, and he could already feel the steamy heat of the day beginning to develop. He went to the barred window and looked out, seeing a patch of gray sky overhead. From the pink light beyond, this window must face east. And it was still pretty early in the morning. He thought he could have slept several more hours if he weren't so hungry.

On the far side of the bed, Berta stood up and looked over at him. They had slept in their underwear, and neither of them was sure whether they should put their clothes back on. If Rajani didn't want them to stand out in their western garb, there was likely no point in putting it back on. Besides, it was probably still damp from last night.

She came and stood beside him, and he put his arm around her for comfort. "I'm hungry, Gabe," she murmured quietly.

"Me too," he replied as softly. "But we'll probably have to go shopping before there will be any food." She nodded, recalling that the three of them had eaten nearly everything that was edible from Rajani's duffle bag last night. After another few moments, during which they stared out at the bleak dawn sky, Gabriel suggested "I'll go see what Rajani's up to, and find out if she wants us to wear those things we had on last night."

He found the bedroom door unlocked, and stepped out into the apartment's only other room. He was surprised to see Rajani working at the kitchen sink. Was he wrong, had there been some food in the apartment he didn't know about? As if she had eyes in the back of her head, the sorceress turned as quickly as a snake to see him staring at her. "Oh good, you're up," she said almost cheerfully. It was hard for him to go along with her pretense of normalcy, but he gave it his best shot.

"Good morning, Rajani," Gabriel said politely. "Are you making breakfast?" The old woman laughed at his hopeful expression.

"If only I were!" she replied. "I'm as hungry as you are, no doubt. But what I'm doing will make it possible for us all to go out and get some breakfast soon enough. Is Berta stirring?"

"Yes, she's up," he answered her. "Shall we get dressed?"

Rajani considered for a moment. Outfitting these two in appropriate garb was on her to-do list, but there was no way these ignorant westerners could be expected to know how to wrap a *siri*. "You're fine as you are for now," she told him. "Bring the girl. I'll get you both dressed later on."

Berta emerged from the bedroom shyly, dressed in her camisole and drawers. "Come here, girl," Rajani beckoned. The princess walked barefoot over to where the sorceress stood near the sink. She observed that there was a medium-sized mixing bowl on the counter, full of some mix of powdered herbs and water that had started green and was beginning to turn almost black. It smelled funny.

Like most Dominion females, especially those of high birth, Berta's hair had been growing throughout most of her life and now hung down past her waist. She kept it coiled around and pinned up most of the time, though when she'd had it braided down her back one time Gabriel had told her she looked exactly like Pippa Farstrider. It was now hanging around her shoulders, making her (in Gabriel's opinion) look absolutely lovely.

Rajani produced a comb and began running it through those long, glistening red locks. Unlike Gabe's hair, which was curly bordering on kinky, hers was straight with only a hint of a wave –

closer to Papa's. He often wondered why his hair was so much curlier than that of either of his parents – it was a nuisance to comb.

When the sorceress had pulled out the tangles caused by Berta's hours spent sleeping on the hard pallet – a far cry from the featherbed the princess slept on at home – she produced a pair of scissors and the girl's eyes got wide with fear. "Don't fret, girl," Rajani said impatiently. "It's impractically long for traveling, and after you're back home it will grow back again in no time." As Berta stood there rigid, trying to be brave, the old woman snipped away at that magnificent fiery cascade until it barely reached her shoulders – a little shorter than the length at which Rajani kept her own hair.

I will not cry, I will not cry, Berta thought, lower lip trembling. Her hair was her glory, an important part of her self – and having it callously shorn away to fall on the kitchen's dirty wooden floor was a personal violation worse than any she had experienced in her short, pampered life. There was no room for Gabe to stand beside her and take her hand, but he hovered close and his dark eyes spoke his love and support.

But the worst was yet to come. Setting down the scissors and slipping on a pair of gloves that appeared to be made from rubber, Rajani dipped a hand into the bowl with the strange-looking paste and began applying it to Berta's head. She worked it into all of the hair that remained, until it was piled atop her head like a bizarre-looking mud pie.

Both children wanted to scream at her, "What are you doing?" but fear kept them silent. Rajani rinsed the gloves off in a basin of water, then reached for another bowl Gabriel hadn't noticed before. Its contents were more wholesome looking, a smooth creamy substance in a deep brown color. As Berta stood there trembling, the sorceress began rubbing it into her skin, starting with her legs below the drawers and then working upward. In a few minutes, Berta was nearly as brown as he was.

Rajani had Berta stand on a stool at the sink and began rinsing the paste from her hair. The old woman must have been busy fetching water from below since before the sun had come up, Gabriel realized. When she had finished toweling the girl's hair dry she stood back, surveying the effect. "Those green eyes of yours look a little out of place," Rajani said. "But the skin dye will fade quickly so you'll look more Gholim, and many of those people have light eyes. I think you'll do." She looked at Gabriel, and addressed both of them. "You are my grandchildren," she said. "You, boy, will be Aadi. You and your twin sister Alisha were born deaf and dumb, unable to hear or speak. Alas, my dear daughter has died, leaving you orphaned, and I am taking you from your former home in Delai to live with my people in the tribal lands to the west. Do you understand?"

"Can we speak if nobody else is around?" Gabriel asked. He thought there were some obvious flaws in Rajani's plan. What if there was a loud noise, and he couldn't help reacting to it? But with he and Berta knowing no words of the languages spoken east of the Killtops, she could hardly pass them off as her grandchildren otherwise. "When we are in public, school yourselves to neither speak nor react to being spoken to," the sorceress told him. "As soon as we have reached the tribal lands, I can tell people that you speak only Hindai. But until then, deaf and dumb. Or else…"

Rajani wrapped the children in the makeshift *siris* she had put on over their Dominion clothing yesterday. They were to be buying new clothes in the market today, and boots appropriate for riding; but for today, they'd be going barefoot. Once she had recovered from the shock of her transformation, Berta found herself delighted. She was all dark and exotic, just like her friend!

When they stepped out onto the street both children were overwhelmed. What had been dark, wet, and dismal the night before was now a riot of colors, of people and animals, the babble of voices talking, the smells of food cooking. Many people in Delai had little or no cooking facilities in their homes, and street vendors were everywhere.

Those smells soon had all of them salivating, and they had not gone a block before the sorceress stopped at a stand and bought a paper sack full of pastries. These were not the delicate, flaky confections of the Dominion, but a more solid and substantial sweet dough wrapped around fillings of fruit preserves or caked poppy seeds. Rajani got no complaints as Gabriel and Berta stuffed their faces with the unfamiliar foods.

The streets were packed with people going about their business early. Come mid-afternoon, they would be nearly deserted again as everyone sought shelter from the oppressive heat. Rajani knew exactly where she was going, and led the kids by a zig-zagging path through the narrow (but at least, stone-paved) streets. Berta supposed that if it rained here as much as Rajani had claimed, the streets would become impassable had they not been paved.

They had imagined that the apartment building where they'd spent the night was in one of the worst sections of the city – it was as squalid as anything you would find in Parat's poorest quarters. But they passed through areas worse still, where the buildings were crumbling and families lived twenty people to a room, where people pitched tents in alleyways and cooked food over campfires laid on the cobblestones. Forbidden to speak or react to sounds, the children held hands and stayed silent as they were led along by their guide.

Gabriel was burning to ask why, in the midst of these slums, there were no feral cats, packs of mongrel dogs, or at least rats in evidence. All of those could be found down along the riverfront in Parat. Then he spotted a small corpse roasting on a spit over one of those alleyway campfires, and he knew.

They left the worst of the slums behind and came to a fringe area – halfway between there and the areas of town occupied by respectable tradesmen. A two-block stretch of the main street here was lined with tables on which used clothing was offered for sale, and Rajani headed for one on the end of the row staffed by a man in his fifties who looked out of place among the mostly dark-skinned people they'd seen in Delai so far.

He's lighter than Mama, Gabriel thought, almost as light as Papa. The man had gray eyes and coarse medium brown hair that was going grizzled. His short, unkempt beard was even grayer, and he was dressed in clothing that seemed far too warm for this climate. It was made of cotton not wool, true, but the cut and style looked more like a picture Gabriel had seen of some Gholim tribesmen. The pants were simple, the tunic covered in colorful yarn embroidery. He grinned as Rajani came up, a gold tooth flashing.

The two spoke in Rusich, and the "deaf and dumb" children were left out of the conversation. "Rajani!" he said, as if greeting an old friend. The two were not truly friends – the half-Gholim sorceress had none of those. But they had known each other for decades. "I haven't seen you in years," he went on. "Are you back in Delai?"

"You're looking well, Ferid," the sorceress said ingratiatingly. "I'm afraid I'm only here for a couple of days, picking up these two." She gestured at the silent children.

"Relatives of yours?" he asked. They didn't really look Dravim, though they were dark.

"My late daughter's children," Rajani lied. "They're orphaned now, so I'm taking them back to the Kazhakim to live with their uncle's family."

The street vendor eyed them, but made no effort to engage the children in conversation – a fact for which they were both grateful. Flies were everywhere in the streets of Delai. But there were no *figurative* ones on Ferid. "You'll be needing some traveling clothes for them," he said.

"That's right," she replied. "We'll be riding, so I want pants, tunics, vests, riding boots, and some warm coats. Oh, and a couple of changes of underwear."

The entire area where the horse tribes made their home was elevated, a long slope falling east from the foothills of the Pahadai. Even in the summertime it got cold there at night, and Rajani couldn't be sure what weather they might encounter. But they had days of riding to reach the Huang, and more days riding a riverboat west before they would be free of the heat of Indaya.

Rajani began pawing through the piles of clothing on Ferid's table, as Gabriel and Berta looked idly around them. They gathered that their captor was negotiating to improve their disguises by putting them into the kind of clothing the Gholim tribespeople wore. That must be where she was taking them, the tribal lands just east of the Killtops. Last night Gabriel had hoped that they might have a chance to get away from Rajani once they were out in the city – but now he realized that Danava could find them before they could get more than a block away – and she had said she could kill Berta with a thought. So there they stood.

Gabriel's eyes kept going back to Berta, staring at her in her dyed hair and darkened skin. It was so strange to see her thus! Just as she'd been drawn to him by his exotic good looks, he'd been entranced by her fiery hair and beautiful green eyes. But though he was having a hard time getting used to her new appearance, he realized she was just as beautiful now.

Finding the clothes and boots Rajani wanted for them seemed to go on forever. Even after everything had been selected, she and the man Gabriel assumed must be a Gholim tribesman were gabbling on in that unfamiliar language for nearly half an hour – haggling over the price, he thought, for the tone of their discussion didn't suggest an exchange of pleasantries.

Finally they were finished. Coins had exchanged hands, strange foreign coins with designs on them the children had never seen before. The clothing and boots had been bundled into Rajani's duffle bag, and they set off in a new direction. She halted at another street vendor's booth, where they got flavorful rice with vegetables in a richly seasoned sauce, wrapped up in soft, puffy pieces of flatbread. They ate it as they continued walking down the street, going only Rajani knew where.

The flavor was like nothing the children had ever tasted, and Berta found it too spicy. Food in the northern Dominion was heavy, rich, and bland. But Gabriel had been to Palambo a few times and his ancestors – some of them at least – had come from that hot land. Somehow, even though the food was unfamiliar, he found he liked it. Berta slipped him the rest of hers to finish, and he ate it up.

This city was not as big as Parat, probably. But it *seemed* bigger, to two small children walking barefoot through its stone-paved streets. Finally they reached an area that was less built-up, down alongside a medium-sized river. It was narrower than the one that ran through their home city, running slowly and clogged with sewage and debris. As Gabriel and Berta watched in horror, the body of a man came floating lazily downstream. The corpse was lying face down, thank the Eight, but carrion birds were perched on it pecking at it for morsels of food. Gabriel put his arm around his "twin sister" and squeezed her tight.

They looked away when they realized Rajani was glaring at them. No doubt two children born and raised in Delai would have taken no notice. "Oh, just another rotting corpse…" They realized that they had apparently come to a commercial stable. They'd seen relatively few people riding in the streets, most going afoot. But this place had a large fenced paddock and a long, low wooden barn. Three or four horses were tied up at a hitching rail out front.

Once again Rajani, who appeared neither Gholim nor Dravim but more like the latter than the former, sought out a middle-aged man who had the look of a Gholim tribesman. This man's eyes were brown and slightly slanted, his hair black; but his skin was only a medium bronze color. He, too, seemed to know Rajani from years past.

"Tzarakh, how fare you?" the sorceress asked politely in Rusich. Among the tribes, one could not simply leap to doing business without at least minimal attention to the courtesies. The fellow, who was scarcely taller than Rajani but twice as wide, gave her a smile that did not reach his eyes. "I am well, Mistress Rajani," he replied. "And you?"

"Alas," the sorceress said – without looking particularly tragic about it – "it is a sad errand that brings me back to my childhood home of Delai." She gestured slightly to the two dark, *siri*-wrapped children who huddled together behind her. "My grandchildren here have become orphans," she explained, "and since I cannot care for them myself I must take them back with me to the Khanate, as they're calling it these days." Her expression showed how little faith she had that the constantly-warring tribes would be held together into a cohesive political entity for long. It was an opinion shared by the majority of Gholim women, especially those old enough to remember the past decades of history.

Tzarakh's impassive face took on a hint of what might have been sympathy. "My condolences, Rajani," he said. "Have you come to buy mounts for the trip north and west, then?"

"Indeed," she replied, "though I think that two should suffice. The children are small." He eyed them skeptically. From the darkness of their skin, they must surely have little Gholim blood. And what she'd said suggested they had grown up here in Delai, as

Rajani herself had done – before *he* was born, to be sure. He had first met her in the tribal lands some fifteen years earlier, when he was just taking over the horse-trading business from his father.

"These grandchildren of yours, can they ride?" the horse dealer asked. Rajani considered. She herself had never been on a horse until after she'd left Delai – after killing her father. Only the elite of Indaya, or those who were in their service as soldiers, ever went mounted on horses. Children in the tribal lands learned to ride almost before they could walk. But these two? She didn't know that much about them.

"Better give me something gentle," Rajani said. "Do you have any Gaspari or Hanshu stock?" The horses of the tribespeople resembled the Hisan of Palambo but were rangier and shaggier, bred to withstand the cold. Those favored by the Indayan nobility were taller, but still thinner and less robust than those of the Dominion. In Hanshu, the Hando people preferred tall, sturdy animals closer in configuration to the Gaspari breed from which they'd originated.

The two children didn't weigh all that much, but if they were to ride double it would still be quite a burden for the typical horse of Indaya or the tribal lands. "Come with me and see if there is anything you like," Tzarakh suggested, and Rajani motioned to Aadi and Alisha to follow her.

"They're deaf and dumb," she explained quietly to the horse trader. "Most sad."

The children followed along, holding hands. In fact both of them had been in the saddle from an age almost as young as any child of the tribes; but the riding they'd learned in Parat had been a pale, civilized activity compared with the hell-bent-for-leather horsemanship expected of any young tribesman or woman.

Gabriel and Berta had been bosom friends since they day they met, only a few weeks before; but they had not yet been riding together. Between the stench from the river and the rank odor of manure and decomposing urine from the stables, it did not seem out of place for him to draw a dangling end of his *siri* up over his nose and mouth. He spoke so quietly only Berta could hear, "Cover your nose and mouth against the stink, Berta, and we can talk."

The two stood side by side, staring at the horses in front of them with cloth drawn over their faces, conversing in low murmurs. "You can ride, Berta?" Gabriel asked.

"Of course I can," she replied. At her age it was hard for her to envision the very different circumstances under which others lived.

"Me too," he replied. "But I think it would be a good idea if we pretend that we're not very good at it. Maybe it will make Rajani less careful, once we're underway."

"Good idea," she murmured back. If they had a horse under them, the chances of getting far enough away, fast enough, that Danava could not reach out to them by supernatural means were greatly increased. Gabriel understood something of the way the gods' powers worked, being the son of two top-ranking members of Betsalel's clergy.

He had never heard of Danava until yesterday; but from the size of her idol in the temple where they'd been taken, her power hereabouts must be strong. But, he reasoned, surely Rajani would have taken them to the tribal lands in the first place if there had been any temples closer to where this "king" she wanted them to meet was staying. So when they got closer to there, the black goddess' powers would be reduced. Maybe then, they could make their move.

Chapter 16

The caravan had at last reached Ghezh, and had pulled off the Ivory Road to camp and hold market for a couple of days. Leila and Tevo, as the two unfriendly Gholim grandmothers, took their leave and were not seen again – at least not in that disguise. They took rooms in one of the small city's dozen inns, now disguised as a young Gholim couple, and hunkered down to wait.

"We need to give Rajani a couple of weeks to get here," Leila said with a sigh as she and Tevo sat together on the room's double bed within a bubble of silence. The only thing that had made the slow, creeping progress from Miradil to Khirzai bearable was the knowledge that once they arrived in that hub of commerce they would be stuck waiting for many more days.

"Two weeks from the time of the abduction," Tevo suggested. "That would be eleven days from now. If she has not brought the children to Ghezh by then, we have to conclude that we were completely wrong about her being in the pay of the khan." Leila didn't even want to consider that possibility. If they were wrong, then they were lost in a vast region with no idea whatsoever where to search for their son and his friend. As it was, she expected she would be going insane with anxiety as they lingered here for the next week and a half, waiting and watching.

But she had to say it. "What if she has not come within the time limit, what do we do then?" He considered. Over his years as Betsalel's arch-priest, he had become adept at solving problems – especially logistical and political ones. When you got right down to it, two-thirds of running a church was politics. Their god needed worshipers in order to remain strong, and it was up to his priesthood to acquire them – though the god himself had his own role to fulfill.

Finally he spoke, squeezing his wife's hand. He could sense the pit of despair that yawned before them, if they were not able to recover the children. "We go east on the Ivory Road, asking everyone we meet if they have seen Rajani or the kids. We'll pass out copies of the reward proclamation, and grease palms. No caravans this time, just us on the horses but maybe looking like mercenary soldiers or something. If we get attacked by bandits, we and the horses can always just fade from view."

Leila squeezed his hand back, then threw her arms around his neck and kissed him. Their sex life had gotten a lot more active on this trip, with no children around. When they were home, Miri especially was always wanting to come and get into bed with Mama and Papa. "It just has to be the khan," she said, reassuring herself as well as him. "Just about every other nation east of the Killtops has established diplomatic relations with the Dominion, and been allowed to come inside Miradil to trade. But Ostden has refused to recognize the Khanate as a nation, so the khan has a reason to want leverage. Nothing else makes sense, unless maybe Rajani is working on her own in order to be paid a big ransom. And if that were the case, she would have sent a demand for money by now." With idols of Betsalel in both their pockets, any information that needed to be relayed from the Dominion would have reached them in far less time than it would take to send a messenger across the city of Parat.

For three nights the two of them, silent and invisible, had hovered near the caravan's campfire after supper to listen to the conversations going around the circle. They had learned of the prices of ivory and porcelain, tiger skins and turnips. They had heard gossip that the king of Hanshu's mistress had been banished from the royal palace after it was rumored she had been dallying with the chamberlain. And they learned that Emperor Ostden's proclamation had reached at least some of the people traveling with the caravan.

Furthermore, it appeared that the wording of the proclamation had not fooled anybody. Two middle-aged merchants from Hanshu, speaking in Hando, were discussing it with relish. "A red-haired girl!" one said disbelievingly, and the other nodded and smiled.

"It can only be the emperor's own daughter who has been taken," he said firmly. "No other child would have caused him to post such a large reward."

"You are undoubtedly right," the first man replied. "I suppose he does not state that it's his own daughter because he knows that the ransom for such a child would far exceed the reward he's offering. Though I can't imagine who he thinks he is fooling. Should anyone manage to take her from the woman who stole her away, there will be far more to pay."

"I'll wager it was the khan who arranged the kidnaping," the second man mused. "Old Oghul must have decided that diplomatic solutions weren't working, and he needed to speed things along."

"I should say he does," his colleague replied. "Things have been relatively settled in the tribal lands for over a year now, thank the Eight for the effect that's had on trade. But you know those Gholim barbarians. They won't remain quiet for long. Oghul probably wants to get his foot in the door at Miradil and then send his hordes raiding in the Dominion. Those people haven't had to fight a war in so many generations they'd probably just throw up their hands and surrender at the first sign of an armed invasion."

The other chuckled. The Dominion's centuries of peace had made it rich, money spent enhancing its roads and farmlands instead of building fortresses and buying arms. But now it was a sitting duck for anybody with an army and ambitions. Were not Hanshu so far from the Dominion, and with so much potentially hostile territory in between, King Wang Qian might well be intrigued by the idea of carving off a little of the Dominion for Hanshu – including Miradil, the gateway between east and west and also the source of enormous tax revenues.

Leila and Tevo had not liked the tone of this conversation. These two traders, who traveled broadly in the world, were undoubtedly more savvy about international affairs than the average citizen – especially the average citizen of the Dominion, for whom the rest of the world was something they'd read about in books if they paid any attention to it at all. They were busy leading their peaceful, usually prosperous lives, with no concern about what was going on in the lands east of the continental divide.

But in three nights of eavesdropping, there had been no mention from anyone of knowing Rajani, or of seeing either of the children. No other suspects beyond the khan had been suggested for commissioning the abduction, and evidently anyone who had seen the proclamation was quite sure that the red-haired girl could be none other than the elder child of the emperor and empress.

There was some speculation as to who the dark boy could be – perhaps some prince of Palambo? Actually, under the new rules of succession initiated using bribes and threats by Gabriel's late grandfather Mauaji, Gabe *was* a prince of Palambo. He was descended through the female line from the current king, his other grandfather. It amused Leila to imagine her boy being elected by the Council of Eight to rule over a land he had scarcely even visited, let alone lived in. But she herself, with Gabe's father Imbaso, had ruled over that country for a period of months – despite having been born and raised in the Dominion.

So now here they were, in the city through which Rajani must surely pass if she were taking the children north to Ashbat to deliver them to the khan. Leila supposed it was possible that she might exit the road east of the city and cut around it to reach the road heading north; but it seemed much more likely she would be bringing the children down river from the area north of Indaya, and using the Ghezh docks.

So, each morning after breakfast the young Gholim couple, who were waiting here for the arrival of some relatives (quite true, that), would leave the inn and subsequently vanish. In various guises, rarely the same twice, they would split up to cover the riverfront, watching for the arrivals of boats from upstream. The Huang was broad enough here, only a hundred miles or so from its mouth, that small sailing craft or oared galleys could travel upstream as well as down. But it was more practical to ship goods east along the Ivory Road.

Ghezh had over a mile of docks along the mighty river's north bank, many of them in use by local craft that rowed or sailed both up and down the stream. Fishing in the area of the confluence a few miles to the west, where the swifter-running Tekushi (which drained most of the dryer eastern side of the Pahadai) joined it from the north, was superb. River fish formed an important part of the diet for residents of the city.

Betsalel had discovered a new ability, not the first that had come to him since he had first taken Leila for a priestess. If called to the idol in Leila's pocket, he could then manifest simultaneously in the idol in Tevo's – and the three of them could carry on an unspoken conversation. The god found it unsettling being in two places at once, but it was a great way for him to assist them as they fought to bring back their child. Leila and Tevo both had done so much for him. He was determined to help them in any way he could.

So the two of them, half a mile apart, would haunt the docks and talk with each other from time to time. At lunchtime they would return to the semblance of the Gholim couple and eat in one of the inns, usually not the one they were staying in. They didn't want to become too familiar to the locals, who might start to wonder about them.

After eating they would resume their vigil, watching both the docks and the road that ran inland of them by less than a quarter of a mile. Both of them wished they had some idea of what Rajani looked like beyond the vague description they'd received from the Estikano at the Parat Nima gathering; but Betsalel assured them that if she bore the supernatural protection of Danava he would be able to detect it. The daemon-turned-goddess was known to him from of old.

The work they were engaged in was important, crucial – their one best chance to intercept the children and their abductor before she spirited them off into the hands of the khan. From what the Hando traders had said around the caravan campfire, for Ostden to accede to the khan's expected demands in exchange for the children's lives might bring disaster on the Dominion. Yet the consequences if the emperor did *not* scarcely bore thinking about. They needed to get Gabriel and Berta back before he got his hands on them!

But as crucial as the work was, it was also tedious. Day after day, they watched the docks and the road and saw hundreds of people – but not the ones they sought. And night after night, usually in the guise of the young Gholim couple, they would frequent the inns and taverns. Ghezh sprawled north for quite a way, up along the road to Ashbat. But all dozen of its inns were located in an area around a mile wide and a quarter of a mile, a few blocks, deep.

They would appear to eat and drink, letting Betsalel search the inn for any bearing the protection of Danava. Then they would move on to the next. Quite a lot of bar-hopping for a couple of tribespeople, who were reputed to prefer hanging around a firepit in a skin yurt while drinking fermented mare's milk. But then they were young, and the young were always defying tradition. Yet it was all to no avail. Day after day went by, and their quarry did not appear.

Chapter 17

Gabriel drew a hand across his brow, wiping away perspiration. They had been on the road leading north from Delai for no more than two hours, and the sun was not yet high; but already it was hotter than blazes. Unlike the dry heat he'd experienced visiting with his grandparents in the royal palace in Iskand, the hot air of Indaya was so humid that perspiration did little to cool you.

He and Berta were mounted on a tall, well-muscled Hando horse Rajani had told them was called a Shuang. The sorceress had made sure it was outfitted with the kind of saddle that was nearly impossible to fall out of. The children had told her neither of them had ridden more than once or twice before, and she had swallowed the tale. After all, she herself had never been on a horse at their age. And she was most anxious to deliver the emperor's daughter to the khan in perfect condition!

They shared the saddle, Gabe pressed up against Berta's back. Their clothing was soaked with perspiration where they touched. The extra-long reins attached to the bridle, which was fitted with a curb bit, ran forward and were secured to the rear of Rajani's own saddle. She'd chosen one of the smaller, rangier horses of Indaya for her own mount, as they could survive on less food and water than larger animals and she was not a large person. Both horses were laden with packs containing changes of clothing and other supplies. The weight of those would decline as their journey went on.

All three riders were wearing lightweight straw hats, shaped like low conical bowls, to keep the sun's heat from beating down on the top of their heads. They would also serve to keep off the frequent (and growing more so) rains, to some extent.

Since they were riding behind their abductor and she rarely turned to look at them, Gabriel and Berta were able to abandon the "sack of flour" posture they'd first assumed on being helped up onto the horse's back and sit up straight like proper riders. His name was Bai Shu, the Gholim horse trader had told them, which meant "sweet potato" in the Hando tongue. Berta had been enthusiastic about the name, and about the horse himself – though for Gabe's money, the big animal couldn't hold a candle to the sweetness of his own family's Nimble. Mama had had that chestnut gelding since long before he was born, and he had only gotten more sweet-natured and biddable with age (he was now fifteen, but seemed as tireless as ever).

The oppressive heat aside, both children were fascinated by the countryside around them. This close to Delai the road ran along beside the river, which was much cleaner here than it had been in the city itself. Little farms were scattered through the low hills, everything brilliant green from the frequent rains. People cut the hillsides into terraces to prevent erosion, and grew rice as well as other grains, a wealth of vegetables, livestock such as water buffalo, goats, chickens and ducks, and tropical spices.

The road was a major artery between Delai and the Huang river, where some of those spices would eventually find their way onto river traders heading west. Rajani had told them they and the horses would be riding on one of those river craft (similar, the kids gathered, to the boats that plied the river in Parat) all the way down almost to the Pahadai – which they learned was what people on this side of the mountains called the Killtops – before riding north again.

They passed a lumber mill, off to the east side of the road, and the children were so thrilled to see gigantic gray beasts carrying logs on their enormous ivory tusks, held in place by their long snake-like noses, that they forgot to be deaf and dump. "Oliphants!" Gabriel squealed, pointing. Both of them had seen pictures in books, and he'd been told that one kind of oliphant lived in Palambo; but this was the first time he'd seen one in the flesh.

Fortunately there was no one around to hear. Rajani turned in her saddle and fixed the children with a glare. "They're called hathi, and shut up! Don't forget your tragic condition, or I'll give you a worse one!" The woman seemed to vacillate between trying to emulate a kindly aunt and threatening them with bodily harm, but didn't appear to realize that she was doing it. Gabriel grinned at her, his dark eyes sparkling, and held his hands up to squeeze his lips, showing they were sealed.

As the hottest part of the day approached they walked their horses off the edge of the road and into a grove of trees where they dismounted for a picnic. The terrain had become hillier, the river left behind, and there were fewer farms in this region.

Gabriel and Berta were glad to be helped down off of Bai Shu. They might be much better riders than they were letting on, but they had rarely ridden for more than a couple of hours at a time and they were both beginning to feel stiff and sore.

They sank gratefully onto the grass in the shade of some tall broad-leafed trees of a type neither had seen in the Dominion. Likely anything that thrived here would be killed by the icy winters of Parat. The three of them lunched on baked rolls that were stuffed with minced seasoned meat and vegetables. As the days went on the food would become less appealing.

Gabriel had a thought. His mama had told him that Betsalel had given her the Kiswa tongue spoken throughout Palambo years ago. He was really tired of pretending to be deaf and dumb, which seemed like a feeble ploy anyhow. "Rajani," he asked sweetly, "Betsalel can teach people the languages used by his worshipers. Do you think maybe Danava could teach me and Berta to talk like they do in Delai, or maybe whatever language you were speaking with the horse trader? I'd give her permission, and it would help our disguises a lot."

"Huh," the woman said, wiping her mouth after downing a swallow of warm water from one of their skins. It had never occurred to her that Danava might have this ability. Rajani had had to learn Gasparto the hard way, as Danava had no worshipers west of the Pahadai. And while Danava undoubtedly knew Hando, her arch-priestess had never had occasion to need the language.

"I'll ask her," she said, taking the idol out of a pocket of her tunic. She was dressed as they were, in lightweight cotton versions of Gholim traveling garb. In moments the idol had grown to a height similar to the first one Gabriel had seen, when he'd awakened in Rajani's wagon. "Mistress," the sorceress said formally, "can you teach these two to speak and understand Hindai?"

"Read and write it as well, if you wish," the black goddess replied. "To the girl, at least. The boy must grant me permission to work any supernatural powers upon him." "I'll let you teach me," Gabriel spoke up, eager to learn. For one thing, knowing what was said around him would be useful if they hoped to escape. "What about that other language, though?" Gabriel asked Rajani.

"If you are traveling as my grandchildren, born and raised in Delai, I see no reason for you to know Rusich. The people I am taking you to see speak and understand Gasparto, and that will serve well enough," she replied shortly. Rats, Gabriel thought. The old witch was too smart. If they'd known the language of the tribespeople, or maybe even Hando (which he'd read was spoken as a trade language almost everywhere in this part of the world), they could have gotten away and made their way back to Miradil on Bai Shu's back, being able to speak with people they met and offer them a reward for helping them.

Still, the Hindai language offered was better than nothing. Gabriel was glad to find that the black goddess had no need to touch them in order to confer her gift, his mind suddenly opening to an understanding of the tongue Rajani had been speaking with the street vendors and sellers of supplies in Delai. "Thank you, honored Danava," Gabriel said politely in that tongue. He was mighty glad that Betsalel's protection sheltered him from the four-armed one's wrath, but pleased enough with her boon.

Thereafter their ride was more entertaining. The children were able to ask Rajani to tell them about the country where she'd grown up, about its people and history. And she didn't mind answering them, for the most part. She was glad that they were acting as if they truly were on a fun adventure together, rather than crying and sniveling – fear-filled captives ready to bolt at the first opportunity. She deeply regretted the necessity that had added hundreds of miles to her journey back to the khan's palace – but at least that journey need not be as unpleasant as she'd feared it might be.

They spent the night in an inn, and the children happily chattered away in the local tongue. Gabriel and Berta could now exchange words in private, speaking in low tones, whenever Rajani was out of earshot. It would not have done, before, for the deaf and dumb twins to be seen whispering to each other.

"Do you think we could creep out of our room tonight while Rajani sleeps, and get away on the horses?" Berta asked.

"Possibly," Gabe murmured in reply as he considered the idea. Taking both horses might make it harder for Rajani to give chase. "But how would we get Bai Shu saddled?" The Shuang stood seventeen hands high, and even with both of them lifting it would be hard to get the heavy saddle up over his back.

"The thing I'm really worried about," he added, keeping an eye on Rajani as she stood at the bar ordering food for them, "is Danava. Indaya is where most of her worshipers are. The more worshipers she has close by, the more power and range she has. You remember what she said. It might be better to wait until we're away from here, up on the Huang and in the Gholim lands."

"Maybe when we get on that boat she was talking about, we can push her overboard!" Berta suggested. She was doing her best to convince Rajani that there were no hard feelings, but deep inside she was furious – at the assault on her person, at the death threats, at the harm done to her family. She spent a lot of her time plotting revenge.

"Yes, let's do that if we can," Gabriel replied. Then the two of them fell silent as Rajani returned to the table. Shortly warm bowls of a lentil dish and steaming slabs of flatbread fresh from the griddle came to the table. There was even some fresh goat's milk for the children, and they dug in with good appetite.

Four days later, the little party reached the south bank of the mighty Huang. Over their days of travel Gabriel had become still darker – tanning from the tropical sun. Meanwhile Berta had become lighter. The frequent rains, as the monsoon season approached, had washed a lot of the dye from her skin and hair. I'll need to redo that, Rajani thought. But there had been no opportunities for a touch-up during their journey. Perhaps once they were on the river boat and under way she would have the opportunity to re-apply the hair dye, at least – in the privacy of their cabin.

The road from Delai terminated at the small city of Purah, a major trading hub. Here, where the Huang was not nearly as broad as it was further downstream, one of the river's few bridges stood – allowing wheeled and foot traffic to pass from the Ivory Road south into Indaya, or the other way around.

There was a large caravan camping ground on the north side of the road across the river, but most of Purah itself was spread out along the south bank – and south from there by a mile or more. Here, Rajani planned to book passage for herself and her two grandchildren, and their horses, on one of the river traders heading downstream. She was quite unaware that her "grandchildren" were plotting to throw her overboard.

Gabriel and Berta were still riding together on Bai Shu's broad back, but now Berta held his reins and they walked along the road beside Rajani and her nameless mount. She had convinced the sorceress that she was beginning to get the hang of riding on the horse's back, and now wanted to try guiding him with the reins herself instead of being towed along behind. The children had plotted this move, wanting to be ready to flee on horseback if an opportunity came up.

Rajani was a little leery about letting her prizes ride free, but on the other hand what did she have to worry about? They were lost thousands of miles from their home and would soon be entering territory where hardly anyone would be able to speak with or understand them. And she was mounted herself – as long as they didn't get too far away from her, she could have Danava send the child into a deep sleep – or infect her with an unreasoning panic that would send her fleeing back the way she had come.

Purah was a major stop for most of the river traffic coming from Hanshu, picking up goods from Indaya to add to those they were carrying to sell in the Gholim lands or the Dominion, dropping off goods to be sold in Indaya. So it was no problem for them to find a boat.

The typical Huang river boat was not all that big a vessel. They were usually broad and shallow of draft, but rarely more than a hundred feet in length. Those that went past the mouth of the Huang to unload cargo in Miradil would have to be towed upstream by teams of oxen on the towpath that ran along the river's southern shore, for a hundred miles and more until they had gotten past the mountain range and the confluence with the Tekushi. Only then was the Huang's current gentle enough to permit sailing or rowing upstream.

Rajani was able to book passage for them on the Yunqishi without too much difficulty. The horses were stabled with other livestock, some of which had been brought along to provide fresh meat on the voyage, in a sheltered area on deck. On the level below, they had a cabin about half the size of one of the walk-in closets in Parat's royal palace. It contained two narrow cots mounted on the wall, one above the other, and a little wooden cabinet built into the opposite wall where they could stow their belongings. No table, no chairs, no basin.

Nor had the price been cheap, Rajani thought sourly. She had plenty of gold back in Ashbat, thanks to years of proving invaluable to Oghul Khan. But she had not brought that much money with her on this trip, had never anticipated she would be going thousands of miles out of her way and needing to buy clothing, horses, and other items. Her price to the khan for the delivery of the Gaspari emperor's daughter would go up accordingly.

At least, the exorbitant price of the Spartan accommodations included meals in the galley with the boat's crew. For the week-plus they would be sailing down the river, she could sit on her butt and do pretty much nothing at all – a welcome change from the days spent on horseback coming up from Delai. She had been surprised to find the children's company welcome during those long hours. Rajani had had lovers in her younger life, but had never married nor borne any children. The way in which they saw the world through fresh eyes, she'd found, helped to give new savor to old sights of which she'd long since tired. She certainly hoped she wouldn't have to kill them.

Chapter 18

Gabriel and Berta had both ridden on river boats in the past. The city where they'd been born and raised had a major river running through it, after all. The Vizha ran beyond Parat to the Northern Ocean, its mouth clogged with ice in the wintertime. But in the summer, the northern shore was clear and a welcome relief from the heat of the city. Families who could afford it would take boats north, spend a week or two or perhaps an entire month at the shore, then ride or take a carriage down the highway south to return home.

But the Huang was a far cry from the Vizha. Here, a thousand miles from where it spilled into the Center Sea at Miradil, it was broad and murky and slow. The Yunqishi mounted sails fore and aft, and had rowing ports as well so that the boat could move enough faster than the current to be steered. The river was hazardous, with shallows and snags to beware of, and the crewmen warned the travelers that there were river pirates as well.

These, they told the wide-eyed children, would lurk in the hidden channels of tributary streams and come out in small boats to swarm aboard hapless trading vessels – killing any who opposed them and taking captives for ransom, before stealing the cargo and setting the boats afire.

This far east, they were also told, there were frequent towns along both banks of the river; but as they traveled west those on the south bank would become fewer and fewer. A low mountain range ran along a few hundred miles west of the western border of Indaya, and between that and the Talj Jabal was a desert wasteland where even the Gholim horse tribes could not find sustenance. It was inhabited by cousins of the Daregs of northern Palambo, fierce nomads who took small herds of goats, camels, and sheep from oasis to oasis, and slew any strangers they found.

Gabriel was beginning to wonder if Dzengi, one of the few crewmen who spoke Hindai (from the look of him, he had both Dravim and Hando ancestry) was amusing himself by striking terror in the children's hearts with tales of the perils to be found while journeying down the Huang.

"Could we really be captured by pirates, Rajani?" he asked their abductor when they were alone in their tiny cabin. He and Berta, being far smaller and more agile than the old woman, were sharing the upper bunk.

"I very much doubt it," she said sourly. She was annoyed at Dzengi for filling the kids' ears with such stories. There was truth to those tales, she knew, but she didn't need her captives plagued with irrational fears about things that were unlikely to happen.

"There are pirates along the river, to be sure," Rajani explained. "But they seldom bother to attack a boat that is underway. They would come in the night, as the boat is moored, and the captain will have plenty of guards posted. And should we find ourselves under attack, I will call Danava to deal with the pirates. One sight of her in the night, blades swinging, and they will be tripping over one another for the chance to jump into the river and drown."

Gabriel and Berta found this information less comforting than perhaps Rajani had intended. Being reminded of the fearsome black goddess, so different in character from the black god Gabe's family served, was enough to give them nightmares.

By mid-morning on their third day traveling downriver, they need not have jumped into the river in order to drown. Monsoon rain had come, pounding down so fiercely one might drown merely lying face up on the deck. They retreated to the galley, by no means a large room but bigger than their cabin by far, and sat playing a card game Rajani knew. The deck of cards was the same one she'd used to lure them into her caravan, Berta realized. They had been in the midst of getting their fortunes told when the drug the old woman had put into the tea had sent them both to sleep.

That experience had been unpleasant, but the cards were beautiful and fascinating – hand painted, the old woman claimed, some fifty years before. Obviously they had been well cared for over the years, as the cards showed no sign of crumbling around the edges and the colors were still bright. Berta tired of the game, which she had lost twice, and instead asked Rajani, "Can you show us how to read fortunes from the cards?"

The old woman felt a thrill of warmth pass through her, as she realized how pleasing it was to have a young person at her feet asking her to pass along wisdom. She supposed it was another reason people had children, aside from wanting somebody to will their property to. It was far too late for her to birth any children of her own, but perhaps after she had disposed of these two, and the superb temple to Danava had been built in Ashbat, she would take in some acolytes to train. Her own training would be far less cruel than that her father had given to her.

Rajani laid the cards out face up on the table, which would not be needed for lunch until an hour from now, showing the fascinated children what each was and what they symbolized. Reading the cards was an elaborate and complicated art, dating back for hundreds of years; but when it came down to it, the skill of the reader and any psychic abilities she might possess was far more important than the cards themselves.

The Yunqishi was riding down the river through the storm with sails furled, half a dozen oarsmen below helping to keep her in the center of the channel. The river had risen three feet in the past hour, and the usually placid surface of the Huang was roiled as water pouring in from its many tributaries sped the current. The captain was peering through the sheets of rainwater, searching the shore for a dock or anyplace the boat might tie up, when there came a shuddering crash from astern.

Everyone standing on deck was shaken, several including the captain knocked off their feet. "What in the seven hells?" he cried in Hando, getting quickly to his feet again and hurrying across the lurching deck toward the rear of the boat. The Yunqishi was already beginning to ride lower at the back, the prow rising and the deck slanting. From the boat's squared-off stern the captain gaped in horror to see an enormous hardwood tree, a dead snag from the lack of leaves, thrashing in the boat's wake. The sudden fierce, prolonged downpour must have washed the tree from the bank where it had once grown and sent it hurtling down the river!

Many of its branches were riding below the surface of the water, and one of them appeared to have punched a hole in the rear of the Yunqishi. Water was pouring into the cargo hold below decks – a disaster! And one that might drown them all, if something wasn't done quickly. "Bring poles!" he shouted to a nearby crewman. And to another he commanded, "Tell the rowers to head to port! We need to get to the shallows near the bank before we sink!"

In the galley, Rajani and the children were on their feet in a moment. "Can you two swim?" she asked, and they admitted that they could. Gabriel and his mother had learned to swim together, in fact, when he was no more than two or three. "Stay here with the cook!" she commanded, and dashed out into the storm and down a gangway to their cabin. There was a little bit of water at the far end of the corridor, toward the rear of the boat.

Once in the cabin Rajani pulled her idol from her pocket and called her goddess. As soon as Danava had manifested, she knew what was troubling her priestess. "Can you repair the hole and refloat the ship?" Rajani asked anxiously. "The snag has been pushed away by the crew using poles," the black goddess replied coolly. "And the crew below are rowing toward shallow water on the south shore. Shall I speed their progress?"

Rajani took that to be an oblique way of saying ship repair was not within Danava's powers. None knew better than those who served them, how limited the gods' abilities could be. "Yes, mistress, please!" she implored. This trip seemed to have been cursed, almost from its beginning. Ever since she'd snatched the kids... Could Betsalel somehow be influencing everything that had gone wrong?

The sorceress had never worshiped Betsalel, preferring her own dark deity. But she doubted his powers in this land, many miles away from his centers of power, would be up to the task of arranging to sink the boat she was on. Probably, it was just a run of bad luck.

A short time later the Yunqishi was grounded in shallow water near the southern bank of the raging Huang, and her crew had gotten lines tied from the boat to some trees growing a few yards up a low embankment. No lunch would be served in the galley, but the cook passed out flatbread and dried beef to everyone to tide them over as the work of evacuating the boat and rescuing its cargo began.

They ran a gangplank from the deck to the embankment, and Rajani and the children (along with their horses and belongings) were able to walk ashore. By then the rain had subsided from a deluge to a light, steady downpour. They had no rain gear, and all of them were soaked to the skin. The captain, who had his own worries, had told them that there was a town ten miles back where they could take a ferry to the north bank. From there, along the Ivory Road, it would be no more than two days' journey to reach Khirzai, the easternmost river port in the tribal lands.

He was reluctant to refund any of the steep passage she had paid, considering all the money he would be out getting his boat repaired and dealing with damages to its cargo. But there was something about the old woman's aura of menace that made him reach into his pocket and give her back all but a few silvers' worth. Then he turned his back on her and returned to directing the efforts of his crew. What a disaster!

Two hours later the small, sodden party arrived in Zaneesh, what passed for a small city in this part of the world. Miraculously the rain had stopped, and everything was steaming in the heat of the afternoon sun. Here, though, they were a long way north of Delai and that heat was not so oppressive.

"Are we still in Indaya?" Gabriel asked.

Rajani told him, "No. We are in the neighboring nation of Myangosh. They have no king, being ruled by a council of arch-priests."

"Oh, like the Council of Eight in Palambo?" he asked, having been told about that body and its role in the government of his grandfather's kingdom during his last visit there. The old woman gave a grim smile.

"Try the Council of One Hundred," she replied. In response to his questioning look she said only, "We in what you call 'the realms of the Hando' are rich in gods."

They decided to spend the night in an inn, giving them a chance to dry out before what would likely be two full days spent traveling the Ivory Road before they reached a city big enough that another river boat would be stopping and allowing them to book passage. Dry clothes, a decent bed, and a hot meal soon had all three of them feeling a lot better. As Gabriel drifted off to sleep, sharing the second bed in their room with Berta, it occurred to him that adventures were better in the telling than they were in the living. He could not recall any of Mama's tales in which Pippa Farstrider came out looking like a drowned rat.

Chapter 19

The morning dawned dry and sunny, though dew sparkled everywhere as Rajani and the two children, on their horses, made their way from the inn to the ferry landing. An immense cable had been strung across the stream between towers on either bank, high enough that even the tallest of river craft could pass beneath it. Not that river craft were ever tall – with wide bottoms and shallow keels, their masts rarely exceeded twenty feet.

The ferry was a sort of raft, squared off on either end, with ramps that flipped up when the boat was in motion. It ran along its cable, winched from either bank, and Rajani's ire mounted at the fare charged for the transport. But it was the north bank where she needed to be, and there were no more bridges to the west. Nor would the charge for a ferry crossing be any less in that direction.

They led the horses onto the swaying platform, then off again on the north side before mounting up again. Now it was Gabriel who was holding Bai Shu's reins and had his feet in the stirrups, with Berta clinging to him from behind. They climbed the embankment and found themselves on the Ivory Road, broad and stone-paved. But there was no traffic on it at the moment. They had been the only passengers on the ferry.

As they set off heading west Rajani told them, "We'll be on the Ivory Road for a couple of days to get to Khirzai, which is the first river port within the Gholim Khanate. At least there's a pretty good chance it won't rain while we're on the road, and I hope we'll be able to camp tonight at one of the caravan campgrounds."

"There aren't any ports east of here?" Gabriel asked. He and Berta had been focused on the boat, and hadn't paid all that much attention to their surroundings as they'd been floating downstream.

"There's another port city behind us," the old woman explained, "but it's nearly two hundred miles away. It'll be faster for us to catch another boat in Khirzai." She was thinking, but did not say aloud, that should anything happen to their next river transport she would not have the money to hire a third. And she would know for sure that some supernatural force was working against her.

They mostly walked their horses along the road through that day, which remained dry though gray clouds covered the sky. They were passed by other westward traffic, groups of riders on horseback; and encountered a small convoy of wagons heading east accompanied by a large group of armed guards.

They had refilled their water skins and bought more food supplies before leaving the inn this morning, and that proved a good thing. It seemed there were no settlements here, just undulating plains rising toward low hills on the northern horizon. There were frequent small watercourses coming down out of the hills, running through pipes that had been set beneath the road as they deposited their water (when there was any) into the Huang. Without the smooth paved road, it would have been impossible for wheeled transports to move between Hanshu and the Dominion, and most west-east trade would have been impossible.

The little group camped for the night in a copse of trees that sat some fifty yards from the road. The air had become cooler and dryer as they rode west, but it was still warm enough overnight that they had no need to make a fire. Rajani seemed reluctant to do so, concerned about drawing unwanted attention.

As darkness closed in and they sat on their sleeping pads eating hard bread, dried meat, and fruit, Berta looked around anxiously. "Are there wild animals here?" she asked Rajani.

"Oh yes," the old woman replied. "Wolves, bears, the occasional wildcat. And elk can be a problem during the rut, but that's not for another couple of months." The girl looked at her owl-eyed, and the sorceress snorted a laugh.

"Fear not, little one!" she said. "Have you forgotten we have a goddess with us? We need no fire to keep animals away, for Danava can cast an aura that will cause any who come here to be filled with fear."

"Oh," Berta said, eyes downcast. She wished that grown-ups were not always trying to frighten her. She thought of herself as a brave girl, a veritable Pippa Farstrider – in addition to being a princess. But this trip had not been good for her self-image in that regard.

Gabriel, too, was tired of adults trying to frighten him for their own amusement. As the eldest child of two of the Shadow God's top clergy in the Dominion he was less easily frightened than some children – though his life so far had been far more sheltered than those of his mother or the man he knew as a father. Betsalel was supposed to be the god of death, after all, and many who did not know him feared him. Yet the dark one had been a literal godfather to both of the Karmarzin children.

Darkness was closing in, but he was not yet ready to sleep. "Rajani," he said, "might you tell us of your goddess? We had never heard of her before we met her in your caravan." Where she threatened us both with horrible death, he did not add. He had spent a lot of his life around priests and priestesses, and he knew it was easy to get them talking about their favorite deities. His namesake, the High Archon, could talk for hours about them – every story a personal anecdote.

He had definitely pressed Rajani's button, and she was happy to open up on the subject. Her early indoctrination in the goddess' mysteries might have been unpleasant, but for more than forty years she had enjoyed Danava's favor. She was genuinely eager to spread the black goddess' worship far and wide.

The sorceress, now high priestess, began in a voice that was quiet but carried easily to the ears of her two young listeners. "Mother Danava, as she is known, is the daughter of the gods that came before her – all of them, the Eight included."

Gabriel wondered at that, though Berta accepted it without comment. His religious education had of course been much greater, and he had never heard of the Eight producing any offspring. It was said that Dionos coupled with his worshipers as men did with women, but there was nothing in the Temple of the Eight's archives to indicate that any of these unions had borne fruit. When he'd asked about it, Mama had been embarrassed and had just said that the bodies that came into being when the gods manifested in their idols were not the same as human bodies even though they looked very much like them.

He didn't speak any of his questions, but waited for Rajani to continue. "At a time long ago, many thousands of years in the past, there had come onto the earth a horrible demon called Blood-seed. He attacked men and gods alike, and when he was attacked each drop of blood that fell from him would create a new demon when it hit the ground. So it was that the earth was becoming overrun with demons."

The children remained silent, and she could not see their faces. But Rajani sensed their rapt interest, and continued. "All of the gods gathered together in the Celestial City, far to the east in the kingdom of Hanshu; though at that time the land had another name. They vowed to defeat Blood-seed by combining all of their divine energies into one being, a being so powerful that it would be able to destroy the demon."

"And that was Danava?" Berta asked shyly out of the darkness.

"That is right," Rajani replied. "She had been given all of the weapons of the gods, and with these she sought all of the lesser demons that had been spawned by Blood-seed. When she found them she swallowed them whole, so that no more blood would be spilled, until all of them had been destroyed. At the last, she met with Blood-seed in battle and cut off his head with one swipe of her *kukrisi*, the sacred blades she wields."

"Wouldn't that just make more demons?" Gabriel asked, caught up in the story and forgetting himself. Rajani smiled, though they could not see it in the dark.

"Before a single drop could fall," she said triumphantly, "Danava drank it all – every last bit of Blood-seed's blood did she consume, so that none touched the earth."

The children digested the tale for a moment. Clearly, Danava was younger than the Eight, younger than some other gods that were worshiped in this strange eastern land. Mama had told Gabriel that only the Eight were truly gods, created by the One in the time when humans had first begun to yearn for gods. And that all other beings that people called gods had been created by humans themselves, built by their imaginations and given life by human souls. But he hadn't really understood all she'd told him.

It seemed to him that it didn't make a lot of difference whether a god or goddess was one of the Eight or not – when you were in a place where many people worshiped them, they were as powerful as any true god or goddess. And at this very time and place, it seemed there was no deity more powerful than Danava. "Thank you, Rajani," Gabriel said. "I hope you can tell us some more about Danava tomorrow as we ride toward Khirzai. But for now I suppose we had better get to sleep."

Chapter 20

They passed the night unmolested, and in the morning it did not take the three travelers long to eat some breakfast from their packs and get on their way. Once again, Gabriel rode Bai Shu while Berta sat behind him on the saddle, holding onto his waist. The morning air was chillier than they had experienced since their arrival in Delai, and the children were glad of the pocket of warmth between them.

After fewer than ten days in the saddle the two were riding far better than Rajani had expected. Was it just that children were agile, and quick to learn? Several things about them had surprised her. Her thoughts were all on reaching Khirzai, which she hoped they would be able to do before dark today. She wasn't looking forward to paying another fare for river passage, and their recent experience had anxiety gnawing at her.

So she was not paying all that much attention to their surroundings as they rode along the broad, paved road – now traveling through a stretch where a low, hilly woodland flanked it on either side. The Huang was a mile away to the south, and there was no other traffic on the road so early. Rajani was not sure what nation claimed the lands to the north. Was it Jhirga? Or perhaps Urkhrian? The land here was better for agriculture than the steppes to the west, and the people led more settled lifestyles than did the Gholim tribes – though racially, there was not a lot of difference between them.

Suddenly her horse screamed and reared, throwing Rajani from the saddle. An arrow had sprouted in its shoulder. Cursing his missed shot, a Gholim bandit came running out of the trees to their north and took aim at Gabriel where he sat high atop the Shuang gelding. Berta cried out, and Gabriel reined Bai Shu hard to the right and charged toward the archer.

Half a dozen more bandits came swarming out of the trees, trying to surround the party who had seemed like such easy pickings. An old woman and two children? It didn't matter whether they had anything of value in their packs, they had horses – and the gang desperately needed horses. Perhaps the one that idiot Zirghei had shot, aiming for its rider, was not too seriously injured?

As soon as Rajani had recovered from her fall she had called Danava to the idol in her pocket. "Mistress, they mean to kill me!" she cried silently. "Can you slay them as they stand?" Among other aspects, Danava's worshipers believed her to be the Goddess of Death – and like Betsalel, she had the ability to kill with a thought if the individual in question wore no protection from another deity.

"I cannot," the goddess answered in her mind, "these bear the protection of Belantos. Get me out!" I should have known, Rajani thought. They might be on the wrong side of the border, but these bandits had the look of Gholim tribesmen. And a dedication to the God of War was almost universal among them. She dropped the idol gently to the stones of the road – her goddess was not completely immune to harm, and were the idol to be broken she would be unable to remain manifested in it.

On an instant the idol grew until black Danava, all four arms now bearing *kukrisi*, stood eight feet tall beside her arch-priestess. The archer, who had narrowly avoided being ridden down by the children on the enormous horse he'd been so anxious *not* to shoot, shot an arrow at her. But it bounced off an invisible shield the goddess had erected around herself. So did the blades of tulwars wielded by the other members of the outlaw band.

Rajani was not a helpless old woman, and she was armed. But the outlaws stood nearly a foot taller than she was, and the blades of their tulwars were thrice the length of her daggers. She stood with her back to the goddess, and when one of the bandits attempted to get at her from in front she threw a dagger into his throat. The highwaymen were not armored, their horsehide jerkins providing only scant protection.

How desperate *were* these men? Rajani wondered. Most people, suddenly confronted with an eight-foot figure out of nightmare, would have turned tail and fled. Yet Danava found herself in a serious fight as more than one of the bandits got through her guard only to find their blades bouncing harmlessly off the invisible shield. She gutted one of them with the *kukris* in her lower right hand, slashed the throat of another with the one in the upper left; then kicked a third one away. He flew through the air for a couple of yards and landed hard on the paving stones with a grunt.

As he was recovering from that fall and retrieving his tulwar, which had fallen from his hand when he landed, Danava whirled to find another of the band dead a few feet away with a dagger in his throat, while one was sweeping in with his tulwar aimed at Rajani's head. The goddess bent protectively over her arch-priestess, the blow glancing off her shield, and a return stroke with her upper right arm took the bandit's head off. Those *kukrisi* were razor-sharp.

Meanwhile the archer Zirghei, frozen in horror as the black apparition swept through his companions like a scythe through ripe wheat, kept firing arrows in the vain hope that one would get through. Had his earlier shots perhaps struck an unseen piece of armor, black against black?

He did not recognize Danava, knowing no gods but Belantos, Andros, Mulia, and Roschig – the Gholim God of Horses. But she certainly did not appear to be wearing much. Her round breasts (which, under other circumstances, he might have admired) were bare, a necklace of small skulls around her neck. Her crotch was covered by a black loincloth, but the foot with which she'd kicked his companion halfway across the road was bare.

It was the four arms, each bearing a wicked curved blade, that captured Zirghei's attention the most. They were waving hypnotically, almost as if she were doing some sort of eastern dance. In a single long stride she reached the bandit she'd kicked as he scrambled to his feet, stooping to thrust the blade in her lower right hand into his belly and ripping upward through his torso until it came out above the collarbone, splitting him open in a welter of blood. As the dead man collapsed to the stones of the road again, she turned her attention to the last of the band.

Zirghei's bowels and bladder let loose, and the bow dropped from his fingers as he fell to his knees. His dark eyes were wide with terror as the eight-foot monstrosity closed on him. "Please, mistress! Do not harm me! I will serve you!" he cried in Rusich. The knives in Danava's hands vanished and for a moment Zirghei though he would be spared. Then she reached down and picked him up in all four hands, snapping his neck before throwing his lifeless corpse down again.

Danava put her lower hands on her hips and surveyed the carnage. Only she and Rajani stood on the road, six of the bandits lying in pools of blood while the seventh, the inept archer, sprawled like a broken doll. The arch-priestess' wounded horse had bolted thirty feet away and was now standing with eyes rolling in fear but unable to run any farther with the arrow lodged in her breast.

Rajani was breathing hard, eyes wild as she looked around. Where were the children? Had there been more bandits in the woods, ones who had not come out of hiding to attack her? "Mistress, where is the girl?" she asked. Gabriel had proven to be good to have along, but Berta was the important one. The goddess concentrated, closing her eyes. But the child, and her companion bearing the protection of Betsalel, had slipped beyond her range during the battle.

"I am sorry, Rajani," the goddess replied. "They have gone beyond my sight." The sorceress cursed silently. She was happy to be alive and unharmed after the bandit attack, but why in all the hells had the children fled so far? They were in the middle of nowhere, miles from any town and lacking the ability to speak Rusich or Hando.

"We had been talking of Khirzai for days," Rajani mused out loud. "They must surely be making for it, heading in the direction of home. Mayhap they hope to contact city authorities and ask for help in being returned to their parents. We must catch them as quickly as possible, before another outlaw band or an opportunist in Khirzai itself decides to claim them for the ransom they'll bring." She had learned in Purah that the Gaspari Emperor was offering a huge reward for the return of the children.

"Can you heal my horse, mistress?" the sorceress asked. Healing was not one of the Destroyer's usual attributes, but Danava had done many unusual things at the behest of her foremost priestess in the past. As they approached the animal, the goddess shrank to the same height as Rajani and cast a spell of calm over the creature. It stood with the right forefoot lifted slightly, but ceased its eye-rolling and cries of distress.

The goddess seized the shaft of the arrow, which appeared to be buried in the muscle and cartilage above the front leg's ball joint, and destroyed it with a thought. It vanished, returned to its component atoms, and blood gushed from the wound. The horse quivered slightly but did not move. Danava now put a hand on the wounded shoulder and concentrated. She did not know exactly how to do this. The widely-believed story of her birth, which Rajani had told the children the night before, was apocryphal of course. She had been sculpted in her present form by a man with a goal, worshiped as a goddess for generations, and at last infused with the soul of a human woman – a sorceress who had taken her own life in order to achieve godhood.

Eventually the tissues began to knit, and the wound stopped bleeding. It looked as if it had been healing cleanly for a week or so, still raw and red – but at least the horse was no longer in danger of bleeding to death. The goddess seemed exhausted by her unaccustomed efforts, and stopped. "I must rest," she told her priestess shortly, and shrank to less than two inches tall before departing her idol.

Damn, Rajani thought. She wondered whether the story she'd told the children was really true. Killing half a dozen bandits and healing one horse didn't seem like all that much work for a goddess who'd defeated the mighty Blood Seed and his spawn. But on the other hand, Danava had been called into existence to kill, not heal. Probably she could have killed many times that number of bandits with no difficulty. It was being asked to stray beyond her area of power that had tired her.

The sorceress took the horse by the reins and led it forward. As she'd feared, the arrow wound had not healed completely and the animal was limping. It should be able to walk, carrying the packs, for the miles it would take to reach Khirzai. But it would be slow going, and likely she would not arrive there until after dark.

The packs contained all of her extra clothing and other belongings, as well as all of their food and four of the six water skins. Another reason the children had been foolish to run off – what were they going to do for food out here? If they had any sense at all, and if they didn't run into more bandits, they would probably get to Khirzai before her. As soon as they were back within the range of Danava's psychic powers, she would have them under her control again.

Chapter 21

It was Leila and Tevo's eighth night in Ghezh, with three more to go before their self-imposed deadline would force them to begin moving again. She snuggled into his embrace, feeling his morning hardness pressing against her belly beneath the thin nightdress she wore. Mmm.

Being alone with her husband of eight years, with no church duties and no small children for distractions, had been an unlooked-for benefit of their frightening situation. But all these days without her Gabriel, so bright and sweet, without Miri in her arms, were beginning to eat at Leila. She thought that maybe today, after they'd called the god, she would ask him to take them home. Just for an hour or two, a quick visit to let Busara know how things were going, to kiss their beloved daughter. Then maybe they could report to Ostden and Lisabet in person before returning to their inn room. The idol they left behind would be safe enough while they were gone.

They made love quietly and sleepily, then arose from the bed. "Three more days," Tevo said with a hint of anxiety. Both of them had been praying that Rajani would walk into their grasp before the deadline, that Betsalel would have them all back in Parat a heartbeat later and all would be well. But with each day that passed, their hopes receded.

Slipping into her underclothes, Leila said "I want to have Betsalel take us back to Parat today. Just for a quick visit. But I miss Miri so much, and I'm sure Busara would appreciate a little support." He stepped forward to enfold her in his arms. She appreciated the firm embrace. So much of her life had been spent fending for herself in a hostile world, hiding behind one mask or another. Now she had her lover, her friend, her strong companion by her side and it made all the difference.

They broke apart and finished getting dressed, then went downstairs to breakfast in the inn's common room. Inns here in the east, they had found, were not all that different from those in the Dominion. But this one boasted a pair of communal bathhouses on the ground floor – men's and women's – and they'd been able to enjoy hot baths much more often than they'd feared would be the case. At home, of course, hot baths and hot showers were enjoyed daily.

Breakfast consisted of a dense, grainy bread, warm from the oven, with fresh yak butter and river fish that had been pickled. It was sweet and sour all at once, and had taken some getting used to. As they were supposedly a man and woman of the Gholim tribes, it would have been suspicious for them to request something else.

After the meal, washed down with hot tea, the two returned to their upstairs room and barred the door. Tevo removed his idol of Betsalel from the pocket of his trousers and set it on the floor, then called the god. The Shadow God rose quickly before them to a height of six feet. "Still no success?" he asked his priest and priestess, and they shook their heads sadly. As he did each time he was manifest in an idol on this side of the continental divide, he reached out for Gabriel. His range was not good here, in an area full of people who neither knew nor worshiped him; but Leila and Tevo gave him strength – more strength than Danava had so far from her own centers of power, certainly. And this time, he felt the boy – the barrier was gone!

"Leila, Tevo," Betsalel said excitedly, "I sense your son." They looked at him in astonishment. "Is he near here?" Leila asked, a grin spreading over her face. "Is he coming closer?" The Shadow God concentrated, closing his two "normal" eyes (as red and glittering as the third one, that stood always open on his forehead).

"No…" he said after a moment. The child seemed to be near the limit of his ability to sense him, and that only because he had bonded with the boy when he was a baby. He could not sense Berta at all. Might the two have become separated?

Finally he spoke again. "The blinding of my sight, the barrier erected around the children by Danava, has been removed. They must have parted company with the sorceress and her daemon. But they are, or at any rate Gabriel is, now many miles to the east of here, days of travel on horseback. And he is moving away from us. In another few hours, I think he may be out of my range."

"Let's get going!" Tevo cried. Betsalel shrank again and was returned to his pocket, as Leila began gathering up all their belongings and stuffing them into packs. Since the clothing they

134

wore was illusory, they had not needed to bring much. Hurrying downstairs, they got filled water skins and some non-perishable foodstuffs from the innkeeper before paying what they owed and making their way to the stable. In less than half an hour from the time Leila and Tevo called the god, two fierce-looking Gholim riders mounted on curiously out-of-place Gaspari horses were hurrying east along the Ivory Road at a gallop.

Chapter 22

"I don't think anyone is following us," Berta panted into Gabriel's back, and he let Bai Shu subside from the full gallop he'd been carrying them at to a gentle canter, then to a walk. The horse was big, and reasonably young, and he'd delivered an astonishing turn of speed during their panicked flight from the bandit ambush; but now he was lathered, lungs heaving like a bellows.

"We'd better keep moving," Gabriel said. "Are you all right back there, Berta?"

"Okay," she replied. She'd been terrified that they had been about to be killed, too frightened to pay much attention to their surroundings. But now she'd recovered her wits and was considering what had just happened.

"I think we must have gotten out of Danava's range," she said thoughtfully. "If we weren't, she would have done something to me – made me want to turn back maybe, or made Bai Shu stop dead. I don't think horses have any protection from gods."

"You're right," Gabriel replied, turning in the saddle to look at her. "Do you think Rajani's dead? It looked like there were a whole bunch of those bandits."

"I can't believe that," Berta replied. "Wouldn't Danava just manifest in her idol and kill them all? She might not even have to get big and use her knives, if they didn't have supernatural protection." Gabriel had imparted some of the religious lore he'd learned from his parents to his friend, and she was coming to have a better understanding of the subject than even most adults in the Dominion.

"So…" Gabriel said, urging the horse to continue walking at a comfortable pace along the game trail they'd found when they'd dashed into the woods, "Assuming Rajani's alive, she probably can't chase us because they shot her horse. She might expect us to come back after the bandits were defeated, and if we didn't she'd think that we'd continue west, toward home."

"Isn't that what we're doing?" Berta asked. Her view ahead was obscured by her taller friend's back.

"Nope," he replied. "The sun is still coming up in front of us. We're going east."

"But we have to go west to get home," Berta objected.

"Of course we do," he replied. "But if we go that way and Rajani does, she'll just catch us again. So maybe if we go east, in a while we can get back down on the Ivory Road. Maybe we can find a caravan, and somebody will speak Gasparto. Those traders have to know a lot of languages so they can talk to the people they buy and sell with."

Berta squeezed him around the waist, an affectionate hug. "You're right, Gabe!" she crowed. "I don't think anybody living in this part of the world speaks Gasparto or Hindai, but traders would! We'll just tell them that we were kidnaped from the Dominion and taken east, and that our parents will give them a reward if they can get us back home. Traders are always interested in money, and that would be just like another trade."

"Maybe we ought to stay off the road for a while, though," Gabriel went on, trying to think things through. He and his pampered princess were alone, thousands of miles from home, in a land they knew little about. One mistake and they might be in worse trouble than they had been before.

Along this stretch of the Ivory Road, the broad paved roadway ran between half a mile and two miles from the Huang, up a long slope from the river's northern bank. North of that, the land climbed to a long range of rolling hills, mostly wooded. Many little streams ran down gullies to the river, but getting past these was not a problem on horseback. In many places as they followed this narrow trail, they had glimpses of the road.

Toward midday they stopped, letting Bai Shu drink from one of the streamlets that had some water in it. The horse was now fully recovered from this morning's headlong run. They climbed down from the saddle and pulled the pack off the back of it, to see what was inside.

"Is there any food in there?" Berta asked hopefully. It seemed as if it had been a long time since this morning's "meal" of trail bread and water. Gabriel was eagerly pulling all of the contents out, but shook his head, disappointment on his dark, handsome features.

"I guess Rajani had all the food in *her* packs," he said. "We have a couple of skins of water, but other than that there's nothing in here but our spare clothing and bed rolls."

He passed her a water skin so she could drink, and looked around at the woods. The vegetation wasn't all that dense, nor the trees all that tall. It was very different country from the jungles they'd passed beside on the ride up from Delai. His family had taken him camping a few times, and Mama had told him how, when she was around fourteen or fifteen years old, she'd spent most of a year camping out. But even she hadn't been trying to live off the land. How would he know, in this unfamiliar forest, what was edible and what was poison?

A black squirrel with long, furry ear tufts came crawling around the side of a nearby tree trunk and chittered at him. Now squirrels, rabbits, and pigeons were edible, he knew. If only he had a bow! They had set up an archery butt in the back yard at Shadow Manor, and he had his own little bow that he'd practiced with until he could hit the target most of the time. Mama and Papa used it for throwing daggers, too. A wave of homesickness surged over him. He'd been holding up pretty well emotionally since they'd been abducted, but he was beginning to long for Mama and Papa, and little Miri.

Heaving a great sigh, Gabriel walked over and sat on the stream bank with Berta, taking a drink from the water skin. "Don't worry, Berta," he said, patting her on the arm. "We'll find a caravan soon, and they'll have food. And it's past midsummer. Maybe there are blackberries, or something!" The look in her green eyes made him sorry he'd mentioned food.

They did find blackberries, looking very similar to the wild blackberries growing in the countryside around Parat. But no rabbits committed suicide at their feet, no pheasants flew past within grabbing range. The berries were good, but they did little to quiet the children's hunger. At least they were in no danger of dying of thirst, with little streams crossing their path every mile or so.

Every time a view of the road opened up, they would peer down at it eagerly. Once they saw what looked like a local farmer with a cartload of something like onions, moving slowly along the road behind his horse. And two riders who might have been messengers, assuming there was such a thing in this part of the world, came heading west at a hand gallop, bent low over their mounts.

"I thought the Ivory Road was supposed to be a huge artery for commerce in the east," Berta said. Her education had been a little more thorough than Gabriel's so far.

"I dunno," he replied. "I've seen more traffic on the main road between Prusz and Parat in half an hour than we've seen on this road all day. Maybe it gets more traffic in some parts of the east than others, like between Hanshu and Indaya. There's not many people out here, so probably it would be only local farmers taking produce to the river port towns like we saw earlier, or big caravans traveling all the way between Miradil and Hanshu. There can't be all that many of them, even in the summertime."

"You're probably right," she said. But her heart was sinking. Would they have to spend the night in the woods, with the wolves and bears – and no goddess to defend them?"

Finally, as the sun was sinking toward the western horizon, they decided to go back down and travel along the road itself instead of skirting it half a mile to the north. Going was much faster on the pavement, without having to pick their way across streams and ravines, and they had a better chance of seeing any fellow travelers. That the road was the natural place for bandits to ambush travelers was in both their minds, but what could they do? They were tired, and hungry, and getting desperate.

Just before the sun went down they came to a wide and level spot beside the road that had been cleared of vegetation. "I think this is a caravan camping spot," Berta said. She didn't remember seeing it on their trip yesterday, but they had been moving pretty slowly. Could she and Gabriel have already gone past the spot where the ferry had dropped them? During a lot of today's travel along the trail, trees had obscured their view of the river.

There were several stone fire rings scattered around, and they were sure this must be a spot maintained by the government of whatever country this was, or perhaps by an association of traders themselves, to provide a spot where caravans could camp for the night in relative comfort.

There was even some firewood stacked up beside one of the fire circles, and they decided to lay their bedrolls down beside it. The weather was clear, so it was unlikely they'd get rained on during the night. "Do we have any Lucifer matches?" Berta asked Gabriel. It was he who'd rifled the pack at midday.

"No," he said, "but I think I can get a fire going." He reached into a pocket of his trousers and pulled out a little knife like the kind cooks used for peeling potatoes. Its tip was blunt, and the blade didn't look very sharp, but it was a knife! Berta's eyes widened.

"You had a *knife*?" she gasped. "Where did you get that?"

He grinned at her, a look reminiscent of his mother's. "I lifted it from Rajani's kitchen while we were packing up to leave Delai," he said. He was unaware that both his parents had been thieves in their younger years, but it seemed the proclivity ran in the family. "It's not sharp enough to do much with, but it's steel. And it seemed like a good idea to have one. She took my pocket knife, after all."

Gabriel had received a handsome folding pocket knife with a carved antler handle for his seventh birthday, and it had been one of his most treasured possessions even if the blade was only a little over two inches long. It had been in his pants pocket when he was at the Nima gathering with Berta, but not there any longer when he'd woken up hours later.

The stone the fire circles were built from was the same as what they'd seen in outcroppings along the trail during their travels today, some kind of hard granite. But there were other stones scattered around the flattened area of the camping ground, and while gathering up the firewood to arrange in the circle he'd picked one up that he thought was flint.

First, though, the knife needed some sharpening. He ran the edge over the smooth stone of the fire circle, first one way and then the other, and finally stropped the blade on his leather boot. Now it was sharp enough to shave some tinder from a dry branch. He peeled little curls of wood up along the sides of several small sticks, arranging them in a little teepee. Then he took some more curls off and piled them up beneath the teepee.

Forgetting the growling of her stomach and the approaching darkness for the time being, Berta watched him in fascination.

"Where did you learn that, Gabe?" she asked. While continuing his work, he grinned at her.

"Papa taught me," he said proudly. Tevo had picked up some curious skills in his younger years, even as Leila had. Life in Parat was enjoyable, but Gabriel was intrigued by the idea of living off the land – camping out with only one's skills to survive on. Maybe if they had to go a few more days before they found a caravan, he could make a bow or a throwing spear, to catch them some game.

Now came the tricky part. Gabriel, crouched over the little pile of wood shavings, scraped the knife over the small stone he thought was flint. Only a hundred years ago, before Lucifer matches were invented, everyone had had to start fires this way. Sparks flew – the stone *must* be flint! But getting them to catch the wood shavings on fire proved to be a lot trickier than he'd hoped.

Finally, though, blowing gently on a spot where a spark had briefly caught, Gabriel got a little flame to flicker up. Then he gradually fed it more and more small fuel, until they had a merry little blaze going and they could start adding more wood to the fire. There was enough of it nearby that they could probably keep the fire going all night. Now if only they had something to cook over it – like a nicely stuffed hen or maybe a small suckling pig! He winced as his stomach writhed in reaction to the thought, and took a drink of water from the skin they'd refilled at one of the many little streams this afternoon.

The evening was not particularly cold, but the fire was cheerful and they sat as close to it as they could tolerate. The sun had been down for over an hour, and they were huddled together on their stacked bedrolls, staring into the flames and talking quietly about home, when they heard the clip-clop of hooves approaching from the road to the east.

Gabriel was on his feet in an instant, seizing Berta by the hand. "Quick!" he hissed at her, "Into the trees!" Leaving the fire behind, they ran together into the darkness to the north. They'd removed Bai Shu's saddle and bridle, and he was grazing in the grass verge along the edge of the woods.

Peering out of the darkness, they soon saw a single horse approaching. It appeared to be as big as Bai Shu, but much shaggier.

A plow horse! And the rider was a slight figure – a woman? The person dismounted at the fire and looked around, puzzled. Then she or he called out in a language that, from its sing-song cadence, Gabriel guessed was Hando. He had heard it spoken during their journey from Delai, but had not learned any of it as yet.

The children made no response, but the horse smelled Bai Shu and whinnied at him, receiving an answering whinny. There was no use hiding, and maybe this traveler could even help them. "Hello," Gabriel said in his deepest voice, in the Hindai language Danava had taught him. "Do you speak Hindai?"

"A little," the person replied in the same language, heavily accented. From the voice, it was not a woman but a very young man. "Come out," he said, "I won't hurt you. I would just like to share your fire, if I may." Gabriel kept his right hand on the knife in his pocket and took Berta's right hand in his left. "Let me do the talking," he murmured, as they returned to the fire.

The figure standing by the fire was no more than five and a half feet tall, a boy who looked to be around fifteen years old. He had a spotty complexion and the beginnings of a downy blond beard, a big grin splitting his homely face as they came up. "I'm Petyr," he announced cheerfully. From his garb he was a farm boy, and his mount seemed to back up that conclusion.

"I'm Aadi and this is my sister Alisha," Gabriel said. Much of the dye Rajani had applied to Berta's hair and skin had washed or worn away, and she was not looking much like a Dravim girl anymore – especially not with those green eyes and a quarter inch of fiery red roots at the base of her streaked, muddy brown hair. Gabriel said a silent prayer to Betsalel that the cloak of his shadows would provide enough cover that Petyr would not question their claim to be from Indaya.

Petyr was peering into the darkness, expecting more people to come out of hiding. When none emerged he looked questioningly at the children. They scarcely looked old enough to be traveling on their own. "Where your... parents?" he asked, searching for the words. On this stretch of the Huang there were many Hindai speakers to the south, but most people preferred Hando as a trade tongue.

"With the caravan," Aadi improvised. He was beginning to think Petyr posed no threat, but he also did not look like the savior they were trying to find.

"Caravan?" the boy asked. "The one going east, about twelve miles…" He gave up on recalling the word for "back" and just pointed. Aadi's face lit up in a grin.

"That's the one!" he said. Sensing that Petyr might have a hard time following what he was saying, he launched into a long, confusing, and rapidly-spoken explanation for why this seven-year-old Dravim boy and his odd-looking sister were camped out alone instead of safe with their family in the caravan just a few miles up the road. From Petyr's expression, he was only getting around half of it – and blaming himself, not the teller, for his failure to comprehend.

"We're going to catch hell when we get back," Aadi concluded. "Papa probably won't let us go off alone again. Say," he added as if it were an afterthought. "Do you happen to have any food to spare? We didn't expect to be stuck overnight and our lunch was gone a long time ago."

All that was spoken more slowly and carefully, and Petyr's grin returned. He turned to his horse, who'd been standing there placidly the whole while, and pulled a bulging pack down off its back. Then he unsaddled it, took off the bridle, and slapped it on the rump. He said something to it in a tongue Gabriel recognized as the Rusich spoken by the horse tribes, and it ambled off toward where Bai Shu was grazing.

As soon as the horse had gone Petyr dug into the pack. He came up with small, dense loaf of black bread and a half-wheel of hard white cheese, plus a wooden plate on which he set them to begin carving off slices with a sort of hunting knife he carried in a sheath at his belt. "I eat… ate, earlier," he told them. "But help yourselves. Do you want some apples?" Their answering grins spoke louder than words.

Chapter 23

Nimble and Milacek, as well as their riders, had been granted the power of tirelessness by Betsalel and could run for many miles without rest. But that did not mean that they could do without food and water, or sleep – or the need to relieve themselves from time to time.

Leila and Tevo, in the guise of two middle-aged Gholim tribesmen, came to another river port a hundred miles to the east of Ghezh as the sun was sinking, and concluded that they could not simply keep going day and night. If mounted on horses, the fastest available method for traveling east in these parts, the children were still unlikely to be galloping for hours every day. Betsalel confirmed that they had gained noticeably on the kids by day's end. A few days of this, and they would surely catch up with them!

So, still maintaining the illusion of the two tribesmen and speaking in Rusich, they stabled the hungry horses for the night and took a room together at an inn in the town of Dzihbat. It was no more than half the size of Ghezh, and this inn was one of only three. It mattered not. They consumed huge bowls of a stew they suspected had horse meat in it, then fell into the room's two narrow beds to sleep soundly until morning.

When daylight began to lighten the room's small window they rolled out of their beds and stood embracing on the little carpet that stood between them. "Whew!" Leila said, inhaling Tevo's scent. A day of hard riding had left him smelling of horse and perspiration. "Do I smell as bad as that?" He kissed her neck tenderly.

"We both reek, my dear," he acknowledged. "Shall we use the bathhouse?"

Needing to remove illusory clothes to reveal an illusory nude body beneath was a nuisance, and a skill Tevo would not have polished yet. Besides, bathing would take an hour away from the time they could be drawing closer to their beloved son. "I don't mind your stink if you're all right with mine," Leila murmured into Tevo's ear. "We can bathe when Gabe is back in our arms again."

"Probably a little before then," he suggested with a laugh. "We wouldn't want our boy to faint."

They took on a hasty but hot breakfast at the inn before getting on the road again, water skins full and packs laden with trail food. They could not be assured of inns to sleep in each night, after all. Soon the horses were moving at a comfortable gallop, well-rested and well-fed.

And so the days went, as they galloped in pursuit of their son. They traveled fast for ten or twelve hours a day, staying in inns when possible but camping out a couple of times as well. They weren't molested by bandits, as their guise of grim tribesmen and lack of any signs of wealth were equally discouraging. Few could have caught them, in any case, as their horses ran at near top speed for mile after mile.

A few times each day Leila or Tevo would call Betsalel to their personal idols to confirm that Gabriel was still ahead of them. On the second day he reported that the boy seemed to have slowed his progress considerably, and that his parents were now catching up rapidly. By midday on the second day they were close enough that Betsalel could sense Berta, as well. Her Godsight ceremony had given him a slight bond with her, and he had met her more recently in company with his beloved Gabriel; but she lacked the protection he had laid on Leila's son. That was how Danava had been able to control her.

With each day's progress the gap closed, and Betsalel was now able to actually see the children (though not reach out to them). They were traveling with a Hando caravan, he reported, definitely heading east. No wonder they were catching up so fast! Their recent experience had shown that caravans usually moved at little more than a fast walking pace for a man. Each night Leila and Tevo fell into a deep sleep, dirty and reeking but jubilant. Soon they would be reunited with their child, and they could all go home.

Chapter 24

It was well past dark by the time Rajani limped into Khirzai, leading her equally limping mare. It was hard to say which of them was more dispirited. Her riding boots, it turned out, were not all that good for trudging miles along the hard stones of the Ivory Road. She'd met few fellow travelers along the way, and no more bandits – fortunately for them.

She found a room in one of the inns that lined the river front. Here, surely, the children must come if they hoped to return to their home. And here she would await their arrival – unless, possibly, they had beaten her here. As tired and footsore as she was, she thought she had better not rest until she had at least done a superficial check for them or that oversized Shuang horse of theirs.

The sorceress left the mare with the stableman and had a boy carry her packs inside to stow in her room. She didn't tip him, and one look at her face told him not to bother hinting. Rajani changed into fresh clothing, there being quite a bit of blood spattered on what she was wearing, and into some soft leather shoes that were more comfortable on her sore feet. Then she took a late supper in the inn's common room before going out to canvas the riverfront area for signs of the children.

She returned, bone weary, at close to eleven in the evening. The inns and taverns were all closing their doors now, and she had visited all of them. No one had seen a pair of Dravim children on a tall horse, and she was convinced that they had not come here yet.

Shit, I hope there weren't more bandits waiting to snap them up, she thought as she laid her stiff, sore body down in the inn's none-too-soft bed. A pack of horseless bandits as hard-up as the ones who'd attacked them today would probably have slaughtered the girl, dressed in cheap second-hand clothing, as a useless mouth to feed – never guessing they were throwing away tens of thousands in gold to obtain a horse that was worth around eight gold pieces at most. It was not a happy thought on which to fall asleep.

In the morning Rajani felt somewhat rejuvenated. At her age it took longer to recover from injuries, and she spent most of the following day just resting. The inn's stableman claimed he knew a horse healer, a Gholim shaman who worshiped the horse-tribes' god Roschig, and she paid him more of her dwindling supply of coin to obtain the man's services. Soon the mare was her old self again, cheerfully hanging around the paddock behind the inn and gaining back some of the weight she'd lost on the trek from Delai.

Each day thereafter Rajani went out after breakfast. She checked the stables behind each of the small city's ten inns, but no one had seen the big Shuang. In those inn's common rooms, and at other places along the river front where the children might go when they came into town, she asked after them but got no joy.

She had known this would be the result, for each morning before setting out she called Danava to her idol, asking after word of the princess. No, there was no sign of her. The goddess' range was poor here, where only Rajani worshiped her. She needed to spend more time with her worshipers in Indaya and its surrounding nations in the south, where her cult was well-established.

The Destroyer's arch-priestess sensed that her goddess was still feeling resentful about having been asked to perform a healing on the horse, shaken by having the limit of her powers revealed. She tried not to bother her more than necessary, and she had to do something with her time while she waited.

So every day was spent searching – for the horse, for the children, for any word of them from travelers coming west. And every night, she lurked in the inn's common room drinking hot tea or, sometimes, warmed kumis. She had not found much to love about the culture of her mother's people, but she had developed a taste for the mildly alcoholic fermented mare's milk the tribespeople made. It helped to take her mind off her growing worry that the children were dead, lost forever.

Leila and Tevo, still wearing the guise of the grim-looking Gholim tribesmen they'd maintained during their relentless pursuit of the children, pulled off of the road in Khirzai as the sun was going down. So close, now! Betsalel had said that they were no more than two hundred miles ahead of them from here, and at the rate they were catching up they might reach the caravan by dark two days' hence.

But what kind of a fight might they be in for? Another thought had occurred to Leila – suppose their idea of Rajani selling the kids to the khan was wrong, and suppose they'd parted company with her because she had *already sold them* – to someone on this caravan? Betsalel had been unable to resolve any details beyond the fact that they were traveling with a caravan, and that the children were together.

They stabled their horses, which had been leaving a trail of astounded inn stablemen along the Ivory Road. A side effect of the spell Betsalel had placed on them led them to recuperate the extra energy spent by eating as much food as three ordinary horses might – all without ill effect. Leila made sure there was a lot of grain in the feed, too. They'd brought plenty of money with them, and Gaspari florins were good anywhere in the world.

Over the days of their ride they'd become more accustomed to the long hours in the saddle, less anxious to fall into a dreamless sleep as soon as they'd eaten some supper. After eating the meal provided in the common room (another stew, this time with mutton and barley in it) they made inquiries and learned that private baths were available.

Oh, the joy of soaking in hot water, washing off the better part of a week's worth of curdled sweat and road grime! Leila was in ecstasy, and after getting out she put on some clean clothes before dressing herself once more in the illusion of the Gholim mercenary (or caravan guard, or whatever it was they were supposed to be – they'd been going for a forbidding appearance that wouldn't stand out with the locals, and hadn't developed much of a back story since the pair rarely spoke except between themselves).

The two retired to their room after the baths, and embraced. There'd been no lovemaking for days, and they were eager for each other's newly washed bodies. It was only later, after putting on some underwear, that they called Betsalel. What he had to say soon had them getting fully dressed again.

"There is someone in this area who is under the protection of Danava," he announced as soon as he had manifested in his idol and extended his senses. "A woman, I believe, and surely it can be none other than this Rajani. The Destroyer has few adherents in this part of the world."

"Can you guide us to her, master?" Leila asked, as she slipped into her assassin's gear. Though motherhood had softened her curves somewhat, she was still able to fit into the outfit that had been her uniform during her months as a member of the Makucha Nyeusi nine years before. It had lots of secret pockets and places to hold her daggers, little vials of poison, or whatever else you might need when stepping out the door with murder on your mind.

"I will guide you as before," the black god promised. Many times, remaining tiny while manifest in an idol in Leila's pocket, he had silently guided her by turnings to take her where she needed to go. Tevo owned no burglar gear. He'd filled out a lot since his teens, more muscular now. But the clothes he'd brought to ride in were comfortable enough for fighting in as well.

And he was armed. Leila had taught him to throw daggers, a fun way for them to bond in the early days of their relationship; and he'd shown an aptitude for it. In addition, he had a Gaspari saber on his left hip. In his illusion it was replaced by a tulwar, a similar weapon favored by the horse tribes. He would probably have been defeated had he tried to spar with Imbaso's old classmates at the university in Wena, but he was competent enough with it to get by.

Manifested simultaneously in both small idols, a feat he had become practiced at over the past weeks, Betsalel permitted them to speak to each other telepathically, as well as to him. They discussed what they would do as they made their way, turn by turn, to an inn near the eastern side of Khirzai.

Only Tevo entered, appearing to be the same middle-aged Gholim tribesman he'd been for much of the time since they'd left Ghezh. Leila went invisible outside, guarding the door as she waited to learn what he found inside. "There are four women in here who could be Rajani," Tevo reported. He was at the bar, ordering a glass of kumis.

"I am not certain which it is," the Shadow God said. In these close quarters, Danava's protection was interfering with his psychic powers.

"I'll smoke her out," Leila said through the bond. "Tevo, watch the room. Whoever chases me out, follow without her noticing."

149

"Yes, ma'am," her husband replied silently, amusement flooding his tone though he had not spoken aloud. She had been bossing him around since the night they had first met.

Rajani sat in her usual corner with her back to the wall, staring glumly into her fourth mug of kumis. Her anxieties had reached the point where they gave her no rest. The children were dead, or perhaps in the custody of another and had slipped downriver on a boat some night while she was sleeping. She was ruined in the Khanate, and she would have to abandon her comfortable position in Ashbat never to return.

Without the Gaspari emperor's daughter as hostage, Oghul would be unable to hold the tribes together – and within months chaos would reign. Nor did she have any doubts the blame would fall on her, never mind that no one else he might have called on could have done better. Perhaps she should just give it all up and go back to Delai. She could sell the horse, let Danava carry her home, and start all over again. There was a raja or two in Indaya's neighboring kingdoms who might be happy to hire a court sorceress.

At this moment the inn door opened. It had been opening and closing all night, and she paid it no mind – until a small, piping voice called out in Gasparto, "Please! Can someone help me?" Rajani's eyes lifted and saw her there in the doorway – the girl! Somehow she had shed the dye that had been applied weeks ago in Delai, for her hair glinted as red as a Gaspari autumn and her skin was as pale as milk. As the sorceress lurched to her feet, eyes blazing, the girl's green eyes grew wide with shock and fear, and she turned to run back out the door.

Rajani dashed after her, out into the night. There were no streetlamps in Khirzai, indeed very few such amenities anywhere in the Khanate. Where had she gone? There! The sorceress' aging eyes, which were not as sharp at night as they had once been, picked out movement as the tiny figure fled down across the Ivory Road toward the docks.

How could she run so fast? With those short little legs, even an old woman like Rajani should have been able to catch her within a block. But it was all she could do to keep the little figure in sight. No time to wonder how it could be that Berta was here, alone, and with her long red hair and milk-white, freckled skin restored to the appearance it had had when the sorceress first abducted her. Even the clothing was the same, but Rajani's entire mind was focused on the pursuit. She utterly failed to notice the invisible man who loped along behind her, maintaining a distance of six feet so that she remained outside his bubble of silence.

The girl was running toward the docks, but soon there would be nowhere else for her to go – unless she planned to jump into the mighty Huang and drown herself. Rajani ran her to ground at last beneath one of the few lights in the area, a lamp burning beside the entrance to a dockside warehouse. By now Rajani was feeling every day of her sixty-four years, panting and puffing. Yet the child seemed not even winded! She turned at bay, and suddenly the half-Gholim sorceress was looking at a small dark woman she had never seen before. Mid-twenties, and was there perhaps a resemblance to the boy Gabriel?

"Where are the children?" the woman demanded, and Rajani reeled backward.

"That's what *I* want to know!" she snarled, reaching into her pocket to pull out her idol. Danava would soon deliver whatever answers this strange woman could provide. She was calling the goddess even as she pulled the idol free, planning to put it on the ground where the Destroyer could achieve the proper degree of intimidation. If this woman was, as she suspected, Gabriel's mother, she was protected by Betsalel and Danava would be unable to attack her using supernatural means.

The blow from behind took her completely by surprise, all of her attention fixed on the woman standing in the glow of the warehouse lamp. Tevo's saber came down as soon as he realized what she was doing, hacking two fingers from Rajani's hand. They fell to the stones of the jetty along with the idol of Danava, cloven in two.

Rajani shrieked, a thin wail that pierced the ears of Leila and Tevo like an awl. She held up her hand, spurting blood, then looked down in dismay at the shattered idol. Her goddess could not come to her now. Leila quickly freed her own idol from her pocket, and Betsalel vacated Tevo's as he grew beside his arch-priestess.

"Heal her, master!" Leila begged. She didn't want this woman bleeding to death before they had learned everything she had to tell. Rajani watched in astonishment as the Shadow God, whom she had never before met (though she'd seen his idols a few times) caused the bleeding to stop and the stumps of her missing fingers to heal. They did not, however, grow back. Yet still, this supposed God of Death had been able to perform a healing greater than the one Danava had struggled at. Was she overmatched against this foe?

Gasping, the physical pain ceasing though the psychic pain was deep, Rajani realized that the small woman had been joined by a not-particularly-large young man. Both of them were dressed in the kind of clothing one associated with the *hashishin*, dark in color and loose enough to permit free movement, but gathered at the wrists and ankles. The woman held a dagger to her throat.

And then there was the eight-foot black god looming over them all. "I do not *know* where the children are!" Rajani cried. "I am the one who took them, yes, but they escaped me days ago when bandits attacked us as we were traveling west toward Khirzai. My goddess has lost their scent, and they have not come here. I fear them dead!"

Leila and Tevo heaved a sigh of relief. They knew the children were alive and well, only a few hundred miles away. And if Rajani had not sold them to anyone, then the people they were traveling with must wish them well. They had only to catch up, and reclaim their son and his friend before having Betsalel transport them back home!

But there were a few details yet to be dealt with. Had she told the truth? "Master," Leila said, "can you see into this one's soul?"

"Not at all," he replied. "She is under the deepest protection of Danava, an arch-priestess if I am any judge." Rajani looked in alarm at the towering figure who had demonstrated powers beyond those her goddess could command.

"I swear, I tell you true!" she insisted. Betsalel lacked the weaponry Danava normally bore, but it would not be hard for him, at this height, to tear her limb from limb.

"Will you open yourself to me?" he asked her, and revulsion flooded her soul. To be so violated! But it was better than death.

"I grant you permission to look inside and see that I speak truth," Rajani said. "No more! No other permissions will I give you, for I am pledged to my goddess." Betsalel reached out a hand and touched the sorceress gently on the forehead. When he pulled back his hand, his usually serene features were troubled.

"You have endured much, Rajani," the Shadow God said solemnly, "and the blame for what you have become lies elsewhere. But what you do with that is on your own head, I am afraid." The sorceress shivered. Her interactions with Danava had never been like this!

Betsalel went on, "She spoke the truth. The children escaped her while she and her daemon were engaged with a group of bandits. She has been waiting here these past few days, hoping they would come this way. But they have not, as we knew."

"Why did you steal the children?" Leila burst in. She suspected the answer, but needed to hear it from Rajani's lips.

"For gold, of course," the old woman answered. She felt utterly defeated. Her goddess was out of reach (and why had the towering Black One called her a "daemon"?), her strength was gone, and it seemed that these two who had taken her knew more of the children's whereabouts than she did herself.

"Gold from whom?" Tevo asked. He, too, was sure what the answer would be.

"Oghul Khan!" the sorceress replied. "Without hostages against the Gaspari emperor, his rule over the Gholim tribes will soon collapse. He means to use the girl – and her companion – to force the emperor to give the Khanate a trading enclave within Miradil. From there, he will take the city – paralyzing all of the trade between east and west. And Miradil would become his stronghold, from which the Gholim tribes would eventually conquer the helpless Dominion! Can you not see it?"

The monstrousness of the plot against the land that had been his home for his entire life nearly moved Tevo to draw his saber again and relieve the old woman of her head. But pity stayed his hand. Betsalel had said that Rajani's circumstances had led her to her villainy. And she was now helpless, at their mercy, and without protection of the "goddess" that had given her strength. In a day or two, they would reach the caravan that Gabriel and Bertha were traveling with. A few minutes after that, they would be home. Let the old woman slink back into whatever refuge she could find. She was defeated, irrelevant, and there was no need to kill her.

Chapter 25

As soon as dawn came, the three chance companions around the fire circle in the caravan camping site were up and preparing to leave. What amazing luck it was, Gabriel thought, that the person who chanced to join them here was the kindly, good-natured (and none too bright) Petyr. He even shared some more of his food with them before they parted company.

"Are you going to Khirzai?" Berta asked, as they sat around the rejuvenated fire eating a sort of fruitcake Petyr's mother had packed for him.

"Nope," he replied cheerfully. "I'm going to my uncle's farm, to help them out with harvest. It's another twenty miles west, then up a dirt road into the hills another ten. I should be there in time for lunch, if I can get Roki to… go fast."

Gabriel eyed the plow horse with a grin. The animal was standing companionably close to Bai Shu, asleep on his feet, and did not look as though "fast" was one of his available speeds. Perhaps Petyr had meant to say "faster than a walk." He was relieved to know that the farm boy would not be telling anyone in Khirzai about meeting two Dravim children heading east, returning to the caravan they'd been separated from.

Petyr gave them a hand getting the saddle back up onto Bai Shu's back, earning their gratitude again. At more than a foot taller than either of them, not to mention stronger, it was relatively easy for him. With profuse thanks to their benefactor they got on their way east, wishing Petyr and his uncle a good harvest.

Now that they had a definite goal in mind, Gabriel put his heels to Bai Shu's sides and nudged him up into a gentle canter. They went along at this pace for a quarter of an hour, then slowed to a trot for a similar time before moving faster again. Mindful of the morning bandit attack though (was that only yesterday?), he kept his eyes peeled for anyone lurking in the trees a few paces from the road.

The caravan Petyr had seen on his way west must have camped not long after he rode past them, for the children had been on the road for less than two hours when it came into view. It was already underway, but Gabriel would be willing to bet it hadn't been moving for long. He'd never traveled with a caravan in his life, but Mama had told him of her experiences and it seemed they tended to stop early, leave late, and move at a snail's pace during the few hours when they were actually traveling. He supposed it must be hard, getting all those people and animals going in the morning.

Berta squeezed him around the middle and murmured "Gabe, I'm scared. What if these aren't nice people? What if they give us back to Rajani?"

"Danava hasn't found you yet, has she?" he replied with more confidence than he felt. "So Rajani must have taken her goddess west to Khirzai. These people are traders, legitimate business people, not bandits. They're not going to ride back a hundred miles to deliver us to a kidnaper. And they'll be happy to take us in when we promise them that our parents will pay a reward. Don't worry!"

Slowed now to a trot, they came up behind the large, ox-drawn wagon that was bringing up the rear. The load was covered in tarpaulins, and a couple of riding horses were hitched to the back. The driver rode the box beside an adolescent boy, either a helper or perhaps his son. He was dark, probably Dravim, and Gabriel addressed him in Hindai. "Good morning, sir," he said politely. "Can you tell me who is the operator of this caravan?"

The man eyed him and the strange-looking girl behind him on Bai Shu's saddle with curiosity, and answered in the same tongue. "That would be Sri Jiao Jing, a trader of Hanshu. You will find him near the head of the caravan. Look for a man in red garments riding a tall black Shuang gelding."

"Thank you, sir!" Gabriel said, and put his heels into Bai Shu's sides to move ahead.

"I think it would be a good idea if we didn't tell this trader our real names," Berta said quietly to Gabriel as they moved up the line of carts, wagons, and riders. There were even a couple of enormous two-humped camels, laden with boxes and bags. "Why don't you be my brother," she went on, hatching their cover story. "You're bigger than me, so you can be eight and I'll be seven. Your name is, uh, Jurgen, and I'll be Gudrun. Our father is a wealthy Palamban merchant who lives in Miradil, but you take after him more and I take after our mother."

Gabriel grinned as they rode along. Berta's caution was a good idea, he realized, but she was showing an inventiveness to rival Mama's tales. "So, we were abducted from Miradil?" he asked.

"Yes, and if this caravan master or one of the other merchants here can get us back to the Dominion, preferably Miradil, our father will give him a big reward. We were taken by a crazy old Nima woman who wanted to train us to be sorcerers and worship Danava, but we escaped her."

"That should do," Gabriel replied. "But we don't have to go to Miradil. If we could get to any seaport where there's a Temple of the Eight, or any town with a temple of Betsalel, the Shadow God can have us home in Parat in a few seconds."

"I hadn't thought about that," Berta said. Gabriel had been transported by the black god on several occasions and he'd mentioned it was possible, but she had never traveled that way herself.

They were rapidly approaching the head of the caravan. It was led by a conveyance that somewhat resembled a Nima wagon, minus the bright colors and decorative touches. A middle-aged Hando man was driving the team of four horses, moving along at a slow and steady clip. And galloping toward them was a figure that could only be Jiao Jing. The man's red garments were visible a long way off. He must have been scouting ahead, they guessed.

As he drew closer on his fine-looking Shuang horse they realized that he appeared to be in his later forties and bore a strong resemblance to the man driving the lead wagon – the two were probably brothers. His red tunic was silk, with brocaded dragons all over it, but it was worn over more practical leather clothing. He reined up and eyed them questioningly. "Do you speak Gasparto?" Gabriel blurted out. As they were, truly, two kidnaped children from the Dominion they would of course speak that language. And he'd as soon not get into why they both also spoke flawless Hindai.

A look of surprise came over the man's face, and he answered "Yes, I am fluent in that tongue. I travel between Hanshu and the Dominion twice yearly. I am Jiao Jing, master of this caravan, and this man on the wagon is my brother Jiao Shao. Shao, please halt for a few moments while I speak with these visitors."

His Gasparto was accented but clear and flawless. And his brother must be fluent as well, for he immediately pulled back on the reins. Down the length of the caravan, other drivers stopped as well – all of them burning with curiosity to know why.

"You are from the Dominion, boy?" the caravan master asked. His manner was commanding but not unkind.

"Yes sir," Gabriel said. "My father is Vandasi of Miradil, a wealthy Palamban merchant, and my mother is of the Dominion. I am Jurgen and my sister is Gudrun. We were visiting in Miradil a few weeks ago and we were kidnaped by a crazy old Nima woman. She was a sorceress, a follower of the Indayan goddess Danava, and she wanted to raise us as her own and force us to serve the black goddess as well."

Jiao Jing climbed down from his mount, and said "Please, let us rest beside the road for a while so that I may hear your tale." He helped the children down, gaze lingering on Gudrun's dark-streaked skin and brown hair with fire-red roots. His eyes widened. "This sorceress was taking you to Indaya, then?" he asked.

"That's right, sir," Jurgen replied. It wouldn't jibe with their hastily-concocted story for her to have taken them to Indaya in the first place and then immediately headed back west. He wished they'd had more time to think this through!

"We were attacked by bandits around seventy miles west of here," Jurgen explained, "And the Nima woman's horse was killed. Gudrun and I got away, from the bandits and the sorceress both, since the bandits were on foot. But we need to find our way back to Miradil, or to the Dominion at least. My father will pay a very generous reward to anyone who will return us to him. Can you help us?"

"Oh, you poor children!" the trader exclaimed sympathetically. "What an ordeal this must have been for you. I will certainly see about getting you returned to your father, but the caravan must go on. And I fear we might meet your sorceress on the road if we return to the west. Please, let me tie your horse to the wagon and you can come inside. I suppose you must be hungry?"

Petyr's fruit bread had been delicious, but there hadn't been that much of it and that had been hours ago, in any case. "Yes please,

Mister Jiao," Gudrun said. Berta was not accustomed to hanging back while others decided what was to be done. The caravan master tied his own horse beside theirs at the rear of the lead wagon, then helped them up into it. As he climbed in behind them, he motioned to his brother to begin moving again. Caravan travel was slow enough without any unscheduled stops.

The wagon proved more roomy than Rajani's had been, with comfortable beds for four people and kitchen facilities. The paved road was reasonably smooth, and their host soon had a kettle of water going on a small kerosene stove. As they waited for the water to boil, and for a mixture of dried noodles, vegetables, and meat to become soup, they talked.

"I think it best if I take you to my home city of Tzinshai to arrange your safe return home," Jiao Jing said. "It is far to the south and east of here, but we can cross the Huang at Purah and travel by horse on the roads to Tongnan. It is near the eastern border of Hanshu, and from there we can take ship to Tzinshai. I have contacts with the governor there, and he can provide us with a safe escort."

"What about the caravan?" Jurgen asked. He hadn't really expected the first trader he spoke with to be willing to go to so much trouble for them.

"My brother can manage on his own," the trader said off-handedly. "We have run the business together for many years, apprenticing to our father when we were boys. I am the nominal master, as I am the elder brother – but they can do without me for the rest of the trip."

Both children had to bite their lips at the mention of Purah. According to their story, they had not yet been to Indaya. It would hardly do to say they had just come from there a week or so before. But it seemed as if Jiao Jing would be taking them still hundreds or thousands of miles *further* from their home, not back toward it. "Couldn't we get on a river boat and go straight back to Miradil?" Gudrun suggested.

The trader frowned, then turned to the stove. The soup seemed to be ready, and he poured it into a couple of large pottery mugs, handing one to each of them along with a pair of short sticks. They accepted them and then looked at each other blankly before casting questioning glances at their host. He smiled. "You've never seen chopsticks, I suppose?" he asked. The subject seemed to have gotten changed.

While the soup cooled, he showed them how to use the chopsticks and fish the little pieces of meat, vegetables, and noodles from it. It was different from anything they'd had before, but it was warm and hearty and they happily ate it all.

Gudrun had a well-focused mind, though, and after they'd finished their early lunch or whatever it was she resumed her former train of thought. "This Purah place you mentioned," she said, and a momentary shadow crossed the trader's eyes. "Are there riverboats stopping there?"

"Yes," he said. "But I am concerned that this sorceress of yours may catch us. She was afoot when you left her, but how long may it be before she finds another horse? The caravan moves slowly, and I am anxious to part with it. If we take a riverboat, it may be she can use her arcane powers to learn of it and intercept us as we try to travel west. Better to get you far out of her range until she has abandoned the chase."

This didn't seem right to Berta, but Jiao Jing was an elder, respected trader with much experience of the world – and in particular, of this part of it where she and Gabriel were strangers. She didn't bring up the subject of riverboats again. Soon, the children were captivated by the exotic experience of traveling with the caravan, relieved to have left Rajani behind.

Chapter 26

Leila and Tevo were on the road early, anxious to make up the miles. Tireless their horses might be, but neither of them was a race-horse. And at fifteen, Nimble should have been nearing retirement. So they did not run them as hard as they might have. Even a tireless horse could pull up lame, galloping on pavement.

They each had a couple of water skins and food in their packs that could be eaten without any preparation, stopping to relieve themselves and eat something from those packs while the horses had grain from nosebags or drank from nearby streams. The area north of the Ivory Road this far east was well-watered, by comparison with the Khanate lands to the west.

The planned trip back home to report was forgotten. As soon as they had the children, they could *all* go home together, and tell their tale. The khan would never get his trading enclave, and if Rajani was right within a few months the Khanate would be just a pack of squabbling tribes again – punishment enough for him. The old woman had lost two fingers and the payment she had expected to receive, and as long as they got the kids back safe Leila was content to leave it at that. She was not a vindictive woman.

They were in the habit of calling Betsalel each evening, and in an inn room their first night beyond Khirzai the god had disturbing news. "Gabriel and Berta are slipping away from me," he said. "I sense that they move more quickly now, and in a new direction: south. But also, it is as if a part of my power to sense them has been leached away."

His arch-priest and priestess stared at the god in incomprehension. How could this be? "Is it Rajani, master?" Leila asked. Could the woman, whom they had discounted as no longer a threat, have somehow gotten between them and the children once again?"

The Shadow God looked troubled. "No," he said after reaching out with his awareness. "Her I can still sense, and she is receding behind us to the west. This is something else, some darkness that obscures my sight like smoke. It is not impenetrable, but my vision becomes ever less clear. And as we speak they are moving, increasing the distance between us."

"We must leave at once!" Tevo said, panicked. They had been so close, almost home again with their beloved son and his little companion. And now they were slipping out of his grasp? He could not bear it! Leila took his hands, looking into his eyes.

"We must rest," she said calmly. "The horses must rest. We cannot catch whoever has taken the children now if we kill ourselves trying to reach them. But if they are now moving south, they will be traveling through Indaya. We speak the language, and we will find them. If Betsalel's vision is being blocked by some supernatural force, some daemon perhaps, ours is still clear and sharp. We have our wits, and we have our gold. Let us sleep now, and in the morning the chase will resume."

And so it did. The horses ran for hours each day, stopping to eat and drink, as their riders did the same. Inns were spaced along the road at frequent intervals, many of them intended as caravanserai, and the two relentless hunters might pass three of them before finally stopping when darkness claimed the land. As afternoon light turned the stones of the Ivory Road a mellow gold, they spied a caravan in the distance.

In minutes they galloped past the trailing wagons and reached the head, where a middle-aged Hando man clad in finely-made but practical-looking garb was driving a team pulling a wagon that reminded them of the ones the Nima used, save for its lack of decoration.

Jiao Shao looked at the strangers in astonishment as they rode up. Their horses were no steppe ponies, that was for sure. In fact both the mounts and their riders appeared to be Gaspari, though the woman was awfully dark. Nima? She was as small and slight-seeming as any Hando woman, yet there was an air of grim competence about her. She sat astride her tall gelding as if she'd been born to the saddle.

"You are the master of this caravan?" she asked in flawless Hando. Gaspari traveling the Ivory Road were rare. Gaspari, or Nima from either side of the continental divide, who spoke proper Hando as well as any native speaker were unheard-of. Shao pulled up, and called back for the caravan to halt. He was beginning to get an uneasy feeling that this halt and the last one were connected.

Tying off the reins and pulling the hand brake, Jiao Shao climbed down from the wagon and bowed – first to the woman who had addressed him, and then to her companion. The two dismounted and bowed to him in turn, though he sensed a powerful urgency driving them to cut the formalities short.

"I am Jiao Shao," he said smoothly. "In my brother's absence, I am master of this caravan. How may I be of service to you, honored visitors?" For this approach, Leila and Tevo had decided that illusion would serve them no better than the truth. They had dropped their disguises as messengers (Gholim tribesmen no longer blending in, this far east) as soon as the caravan came into view.

"I am Tevo Karmarzin, arch-priest of Lord Betsalel in Parat, capital of the Gaspari Dominion," Tevo said. Though far more substantial than he had been at seventeen, he was never going to be a physically imposing man. But being a priest of the God of Death (among other things) for so long had lent him a gravitas beyond what his youth and physical characteristics could have granted him.

Tevo went on. "This is my wife Leila, Betsalel's arch-priestess. We seek two children who were stolen from Parat by a sorceress, a devotee of Danava who calls herself Rajani. Have you seen them?"

"Parat?" the caravan master asked – one eyebrow raised. "Was it not Miradil whence they were taken?"

The caravan remained halted for nearly half an hour, blocking the road east as the sun sank toward the horizon. Jiao Shao, youngest son of his family and nearly eight years younger than his brother Jiao Jing, told them everything he knew.

The pair were the son and daughter of a Palamban merchant originally from Miradil, who had married a Gaspari woman and moved out of the city. On a visit to Miradil, accompanying their father on a business trip, they had been abducted by what they'd described as a "crazy Nima woman" who had intended to raise them as her own and convert them to the worship of the Indayan goddess Danava. The Destroyer had her adherents elsewhere east of the Pahadai, but for the most part she was worshiped only by the Dravim.

The boy had been dark, as dark as any Dravim but with much curlier hair – more like a Palamban, which made sense since he claimed to have a Palamban father. The girl had been very strange looking, her skin brown but streaky in appearance and becoming lighter with each day (and each washing) as they had accompanied the caravan until it a day or two before the bridge to Purah.

"My brother told me only that he was anxious to take the children to safety," Shao continued. "The boy had promised there would be a large reward from his wealthy merchant father for their safe return, and there was some concern that the Nima sorceress might be able to find them again with her mystical powers. In any case, days ago he took them east on horseback planning to cross the bridge to Purah, then travel south as quickly as possible and take ship at Tongnan for our home city of Tzinshai. There he would be able to muster the resources to have the children safely taken back to Miradil."

Leila and Tevo had passed that bridge, more than twenty-four hours before. Betsalel's vision had now become so clouded that he could not be sure in what direction the children lay. And now they must go back, it seemed. If only I'd believed what my heart was telling me, Leila thought. They had guessed that the bridge to Purah must surely be the only way for the children to have begun traveling south, as he had said was the case that first night. But they had needed to speak with the caravan master to be sure. Now they had, and they had lost another day.

The three of them had been sitting on folding stools set up alongside the road. Now Leila rose to her feet and bowed to Jiao Shao. "Thank you, Honorable Shao, for the information," she said. "I am convinced that those children must be the ones we seek. With luck, we can save your brother the trouble of carrying them all the way to Tzinshai."

Chapter 27

Traveling with the caravan had been fun, for a few days. Two active children were more than fast and energetic enough to run from one end to the other and back again as the train of carts, wagons, and laden pack animals made its slow way eastward on the Ivory Road. If they got tired they could just hitch a ride on a wagon, and most of the adults were happy to see them. Driving a wagon in a caravan, crawling through the landscape, could be so boring that any new thing, any distraction, was welcome.

They were able to converse with any caravan members who spoke Hindai or Gasparto, though there were more of the former than the latter. Jiao Jing and his brother were the owners and operators of the caravan, wealthy traders who made money not only from the goods they bought and sold but from the fees paid to them by others who had chosen to accompany them and share the protection of the guards they'd hired. Some of these others were also traders and spoke some Gasparto, though none seemed to be as fluent in it as the Jiao brothers.

There were a couple of adolescent boys along on the trip, and a few women. But there were no other children, and for the most part Jurgen and Gudrun had to entertain themselves. The vast majority of the people were employees, either of the Jiao brothers or of other people who had paid to join the caravan, and they didn't have time to play games with children while they were on duty.

But Shai Lin, the grandmotherly woman in charge of meals served along the road, took them under her wing to some extent. She was Hando, and might have been anywhere from forty-five to seventy with her smooth round cheeks and crinkled eyes. But her hair was mostly silver, cheeks red from many hours spent out of doors, and she spoke Hindai well enough that they could make themselves understood to one another.

When the siblings tired of dashing up and down the road she would invite them to climb up and ride beside her on the cook wagon. Though many caravans might cook over open fires, this one was better organized than most. In addition to stores of food, the cook wagon boasted an enormous wood stove, over which Shai Lin and her helpers would cook enough stew, or other dishes, to feed all of the caravan's employees and paying customers.

Jurgen and Gudrun volunteered to join the staff of helpers at most meals, and got little nibbles of whatever was cooking before everyone else was served. Shai Lin would make sure there was always a little sweet treat in it for them at the end of the meal, too. "You two remind me of my grandchildren," she would say, grinning toothlessly.

Gabriel doubted this woman had any grandchildren that looked like him, and it was even less likely any looked like Berta. Her dye job had continued to erode until she was almost back to her normal skin tone, but the dye had clung more stubbornly to her hair and it was beginning to look as though it would remain a muddy shade of brown until it had grown completely out again. Already there was nearly half an inch of red showing, yet no one remarked on it. Perhaps Hando people were too polite to comment, he guessed.

They ate a lot of noodles, food the Gaspari children were somewhat familiar with. Centuries ago, when Vinizzi had only recently become a part of the Dominion, the famous explorer Marcano Polisi had traveled all the way to Hanshu when the Ivory Road was no more than a dirt track, and brought back noodles with him to Italia – the region of the Dominion of which Vinizzi was a part. The dish had the great advantage that the noodles could be dried after preparation, and would keep for a long time before being cooked. But no noodles served in the Dominion had ever tasted like these.

In the Dominion, noodles (thin, wide, and everything in between) were served with melted butter or sauces rich in meat or vegetables. The noodles eaten in the Jiao brothers' caravan were most often served floating in chicken broth, with vegetables and sometimes meat-filled dumplings. The broth had a peculiarly savory flavor imparted by a mysterious brown condiment Shai Lin called "mushu." Whatever was in it, it was good; and the youngsters were always hungry enough to eat anything – familiar or not – by day's end.

Berta seemed to have put all her cares aside. She was truly enjoying their adventure now, and seemed no longer worried. They had put their rescue and return into the competent hands of the dashing and forceful Jiao Jing, and she could now just relax and wait to be returned to her home. As long as they were not in the clutches of Rajani and her frightening goddess, that was good enough for her.

But Gabriel had a feeling of uneasiness that he could not completely shake. Their host and rescuer seemed uneasy as well, growing ever more anxious as the caravan moved slowly along. Finally he seemed to decide he could wait no longer. On the morning of their third day of traveling with the caravan, he came to them and handed each of them a leather cord on which a pendant was hung.

Gudrun smiled and put it around her neck, then held it up for closer look at the pendant. "Thank you, Mister Jiao," she said politely. "This is beautiful work! What is it?"

"The carving is made from what they call 'dragon glass,'" he explained with a slight smile. "It is found near volcanoes, of which there are many in Hanshu. In ancient times people believed that volcanoes were really dragons living underground, roaring and spewing out their fire. Now we know, of course, that volcanoes are just the earth's hot heart coming forth to the surface."

Both children had heard of dragons, of course. There were volcanoes in the Dominion, as well, and people had found the bones of enormous creatures buried in the earth as well. In Dominion dragon tales the creatures were as big as a house, covered in hard scales, but had four legs with clawed talons as well as enormous leathery wings on which they could take to the sky. They could speak the tongues of men, and were said to love gold and hoard it in their mountain lairs.

The pendant represented a serpentine creature, and even the tiny scales were detailed. But it had no wings. "Is this a dragon?" Jurgen asked. "What happened to its wings?" Jiao Jing smiled indulgently. He had children of his own, four of them, though they were all grown now. Not that he had spent that much time raising them – that task had fallen to his wives while he was away for most of each year on trading expeditions.

"In Hanshu, dragons do not have wings. This is a representation of Ling Zao, the Black Dragon god worshiped in Hanshu. The pendants are talismans of a sort, blessed by Ling Zao, and are said to grant the wearer protection from supernatural harm. Gabriel darted a dark glance at him.

"They're not... true idols, are they?" he asked. He, unlike most people, knew that true idols could be whatever size the deity cared to make them.

Jiao Jing gave him an odd look. "You know about idols, do you, Jurgen?" he asked. Gabriel looked down, wishing he had not spoken.

"My... our, mother's family are in the clergy," he said. "I have seen all of the Eight and spoken with some of them."

"Ah," the caravan master said with a trace of mockery, "a family favored by the gods. Perhaps that is why your Nima woman planned to train you for her black goddess' priesthood. No, little one. These are not true idols – only fine carvings. The carvers of Hanshu possess skills beyond any others in the world."

Jurgen nodded and let the pendant fall to his chest. Whatever its powers, if any, they didn't seem to be reacting badly with the invisible, internal protection Rajani claimed that Betsalel had placed on him. "I want you two to wear those at all times," Jiao Jing went on. "It is my hope that they will shield you from the view of the Nima sorceress. I fear that she may now be mounted once again and hunting for you, and I doubt that I or all our guards would be able to stop her if she should find you."

The children looked up at him wide-eyed. Berta, at least, had been thinking that the threat of Rajani had gone away. "Come," the caravan master said briskly, "gather your things. We are going to leave the caravan now and ride to Purah, thence to travel by road to the nearest Hanshu seaport. I'll soon have you on your way safely back to the Dominion, but we must ride!"

During the caravan's first stop after the children had joined it they had gotten their dirty clothes laundered – and even been bathed themselves. The women had scrubbed Berta hard trying to remove what they took for dirt on her brown-streaked skin, one of the reasons she was now so much paler. They gathered their pack with spare clothing in it, and Bai Shu was soon saddled and bridled. He'd been idling along tied by a rope behind the lead wagon shared by the Jiao brothers since they'd arrived, and was more than ready to get moving.

Before mounting his own tall Shuang Jiao Jing had a few final words with his brother. He'd already told him of his plans to take the children by ship back to Tzinshai, but added a few additional instructions. No one else in the caravan had really been told much about the children, other than that they'd been stranded alone and taken under Jiao Jing's wing.

They rode from back to front, waving goodbye to everyone. Both children had picked up a few words and phrases in Hando during their visit, and there were many cries of "song bié" as they went along. Then they passed the head wagon and Gudrun, who was riding with Jurgen behind her, put her heels into Bai Shu's flanks. They were on their way!

Chapter 28

Leila and Tevo galloped across the Huang on the bridge at Purah and went into the city. They were anxious to be chasing after this trader Jiao Jing before he reached the seaport his brother had said he was taking the children to. But it seemed he had a couple of days' start on them. And they could not be sure what route he would take.

There was a good road here leading south, a major highway that connected with the teeming city of Delai. But Delai was on the far western side of Indaya, and they gathered that Tongnan, the port in question, was beyond its eastern border. They needed a map, and some idea of the political situation here, before they could begin their pursuit.

So it was as themselves that they road into town, eyes searching on either side of them for businesses that might prove helpful. How fortunate that Betsalel's language instruction had enabled them to read the signs as well as speak the language!

Purah was a major trading hub, its bridge making it the nexus through which trade goods flowed north and south. It was less ancient than Delai, but cleaner and more prosperous as well. Hitching the horses to posts outside a three-story brick building that appeared to be less than a century old, they walked past a pair of uniformed guards armed with spears through a pair of glassed double doors. A handsome plaque mounted on the side of the building, engraved in three languages (Hando, Hindai, and Gasparto; the Gholim peoples rarely traded this far afield) identified it as the Royal Indayan Trade Commission.

There might be some forgotten tribes on earth where women ruled and men deferred to them; but Leila knew that throughout the civilized world, Tevo would be much more likely to get respect from officialdom. Even after all she had done for Palambo – at great risk to her own safety, and eventually including the loss of her beloved husband – those people had still refused to let her remain as ruling queen. It rankled, but she was a practical person. "Why don't you handle this, dear?" she suggested. But her appearance subtly changed so that she was considerably better dressed than she'd been a minute before.

There was a waiting room at the end of a hallway leading from the front doors, with two more guards in it and a very dark-skinned young man behind a desk. Tevo and Leila approached him, she lagging slightly behind. "May I assist you?" the young man said, beginning in Hindai. He was fluent in Hando and conversant in Gasparto as well, but preferred to speak in the tongue of the gods when he could.

Somewhat to his surprise, the short, muscular foreigner answered him in flawless Hindai. "My wife and I are searching for some missing children," Tevo said. "We are newly arrived in Indaya and must travel as quickly as possible to the port of Tongnan." The clerk raised an eyebrow.

"Are you aware, sir, that Tongnan is in Hanshu rather than in Indaya?" Tevo stifled the urge to bite his head off.

"Yes," he said stiffly, "I am aware of that. I have not had access to a map, but we believe our children have been taken through Purah on the way to this port. We hope to catch them on the road, if we can determine which road they were taken by."

"You are Gaspari?" the young man asked, and Tevo nodded. "These missing children are also Gaspari, then?" The two visitors just stared at him as he reached into a drawer of the desk and produced what they recognized as a Hindai copy of Emperor Ostden's proclamation. He held it out to them. "The dark boy and the red-haired girl, these are the ones?"

Tevo exchanged a glance with Leila. Jiao Shao had told them that the girl who called herself Gudrun had arrived at the caravan with pale skin streaked brown, and shoulder-length muddy brown hair that was showing red at the roots. Tevo shook his head. "No, those are not the ones. Our son is dark, yes, but our daughter has brown hair. They were traveling with a caravan in our absence, but were taken from it by a man we believe means to transport them to Hanshu with him. He does not realize that we've returned for our children, but we need to stop him from taking them by ship to Tzinshai."

The clerk looked at them thoughtfully. Except for characterizing Berta as their "brown-haired daughter," they had mostly told him the truth and he was inclined to believe them. "I can give you a map," he said shortly, and rustled in a lower desk draw to produce a roll of paper. "This shows the kingdom of Indaya and some of the lands surrounding it, with major roads, cities, and large towns marked. But if you can pay for their services, it might make more sense for you to hire the Royal Messenger Service to pursue your children. They travel in relays, getting fresh horses every fifty miles or so, and could reach the border with Hanshu in far less time than you could travel it yourselves."

"They do not travel outside the borders of the kingdom?" Leila asked, and the clerk nodded. "The border crossing at Balore is controlled. Assuming this person who is transporting your children is innocent of ill intent, he would of course take them through this checkpoint rather than trying to slip into Hanshu on back roads. Provided with notice to be on the lookout for him, the guards at Balore could give him the message that you are on the way, asking him to wait for you."

"That sounds a good idea," Tevo said, taking the map. "Thank you for the map and for the advice, sahib."

"Where are the Royal Messengers headquartered?" Leila asked.

"They have offices in every major town and city throughout Indaya," the clerk assured her. "The Purah office is on this same street. Go back to the foot of the bridge, then continue for another two blocks and it's on your left."

With more thanks, they went on their way. As they walked their horses toward the office of the messengers, Leila and Tevo threw a bubble of silence around themselves and conferred in Gasparto. "What do you think?" she asked. "Shall we hire the messenger service as he suggested, but hope to catch this Jiao Jing on the road before Balore?"

"It might be wise, as a backup plan," Tevo replied. "We are now on Danava's home turf. There may well be as many temples to her in Indaya as there are temples to Betsalel in Palambo. Suppose Rajani is able to communicate with her even though we destroyed her idol?"

Leila shuddered. She was beginning to regret that they had not done something more permanent to the sorceress. But it was silly to worry. They had left her apparently afoot, hundreds of miles from the nearest idol of Danava. It would be months before she could muster her resources. And probably in no more than a couple of days, they would have found the children and returned home safe and sound.

"Let's get the Royal Messengers on the case first," she said. "Then let's go someplace where we can confer privately with Betsalel. If he has any temples along this road we're to travel, maybe we can speed things up." They arrived at the office and went inside, and after a considerable quantity of gold had changed hands a slightly-built youth on a fast horse was on his way with a message addressed to "The Hando trader Jiao Jing, traveling in company with a dark boy and a girl some seven years in age, making for the port of Tongnan in Hanshu."

The message, along with one accompanying it addressed to the commander of the border guards at Balore, would be delivered as quickly as possible – certainly before the trader and his charges could get there, assuming they would be resting at night. Children the age of Berta and Gabriel lacked the stamina for marathon journeys on horseback. They would need to rest, while the message would be passed from hand to hand until it reached its destination.

After that had been done Leila and Tevo walked their mounts in the direction of the road to Balore, which they'd found on the map the clerk at the trading office had given them. It was a nice map, block printed in multiple colors on vellum and annotated in three languages. Duties on the goods that flowed through Purah had evidently been put to good use.

The afternoon was getting on, but neither they nor their horses were tired and they didn't want to waste time stopping for the night. Tonight, at least, they might try to push on. So they exited the city on the road leading east (which would later connect to a major artery heading south), and did not pull off the road until they came to a wide spot carved in the vegetation beside the road.

A light rain had been falling since they had entered Purah, and it was now beginning to come down with more enthusiasm. They dismounted and walked a little way into the forest, where the trees provided a little bit of shelter from the rain. They were already soaked, but the air was so warm that it hardly mattered.

"Did I mention that the bubble of silence also protects you from small creatures like mosquitoes?" Leila asked with a rueful smile.

"I'm glad to hear it," her husband replied. Other than visits with the family to the royal palace in Iskand, he had never been in any tropical climes. But with this much moisture he guessed flying biters might be quite a problem.

"I'm wondering if we should ask Betsalel to add rain to the list of things it keeps out," she went on. Tevo frowned mock-seriously, his dark eyes sparkling.

"I think that might be just a *little* conspicuous, if we were seen to be riding along in a downpour while remaining as dry as the deserts of Palambo," he pointed out. She sighed.

"You're right. Well, let's see what our master has to say."

The Shadow God could easily have manifested in the idols each of them kept about their person and facilitated a three-way silent conference; but when possible, they preferred to let him assume full size and speak aloud, face to face. In moments Betsalel stood before them. They noticed that the rain did not seem to touch him.

"I still have only a very hazy notion of Gabriel's whereabouts," he said sadly. "He is quite a long way off, to the east and south of here, and I cannot sense Berta at all. I believe there are supernatural powers at word, hindering my vision." Leila was none too happy at that thought. Here they were in Indaya, where dozens of daemons had achieved god status. What if the children had escaped the clutches of Rajani and her Danava, only to be captured by the devotee of some other dubious deity?

"Please tell us there are some temples of yours on the route from here to Balore," Leila begged. The hope of overtaking the children and their (companion? abductor?) on the road would be diminished if they jumped ahead, but after countless days in the saddle she was more than ready for a break. If he could carry them to some point halfway along, and determine that Gabriel was now behind them, they could simply stay there watching the road and waiting for their quarry to arrive.

And if they had not gotten past them, at least they would have closed the gap. There had to be a way to catch them before they took ship! Betsalel bowed his head. "I am sorry, beloved," he said in his

174

deep dark voice. It could be a gentle caress, or the crack of doom. It had certainly scared the shit out of *her* the first time she'd heard it.

"Here in Indaya," he explained, "human civilization is old. Perhaps older than anywhere else on earth. Yet for whatever reasons, the One created me and my siblings in Parat. And as civilization in the area that is now the Dominion flourished, our worship eventually spread to the rest of the globe. But before our worship had become well established here, there was already a horde of gods and goddesses – daemons, of course – which men had created for themselves. There are at least three individual deities here who claim the title God/Goddess of Death, including Danava herself. I am worshiped at the Temple of the Eight in Sumbai, but that is nearly as far from Balore as we are now. There are two additional temples to me, small ones founded by missionaries from the Dominion in centuries past. Neither is any closer."

When Betsalel had first claimed Leila for his own he had mentioned that his worship in the realms of the Hando was not sufficient to support his powers as a god. But even after all this time, she had not truly realized how scanty it was. There had been no temples of Betsalel at all as they traveled along the Ivory Road from Miradil.

Leila sighed, and turned to Tevo. "It looks like we're riding to Balore, then," she said. "Thank you, master. And please be sure to tell us if there are any changes in the situation." Betsalel shrank to tiny size again and vacated his idol, which Leila picked up and slipped back into her pocket. "Well," she went on, "at least we know what disguise to take, as we barrel down the road in the darkness." A minute later two slightly-built young Royal Messengers, mounted on surprisingly large horses, went galloping along the highway in the pouring rain.

Chapter 29

Gabriel and Berta were convinced that they were starting to grow moss. Rajani had warned them that they would not enjoy being in Indaya during the monsoon, and they were finding that to be the case. The rain was warm, the air warmer; but it fell for hours every day.

The road along which they rode, the two of them atop Bai Shu while their companion rode his Mei Luo, had been built with a slight hump in it so that water ran off either side rather than pooling and flooding the surface. It was channeled into deep gutters, which carried the water away to either side of the road. Both of them had thought Parat had a lot of rain, especially in the summer; but by comparison with Indaya, the place was as arid as any desert.

They had traveled mostly east for a while on a road leading out of Purah. Then they had connected with a major road running away south and east toward the border with Hanshu; or so Jiao Jing informed them. He had a commanding presence, but he could be jovial as well, and except for being soaked to the skin for hours every day they had no complaints. They were treated kindly, and lacked for nothing.

They started each day dry, after a night spent in an inn. The caravan master generally took a room with two beds, and the children would share one while he slept in the other. They would have a hearty breakfast, lunch on food packed for them by the inn before leaving, and dine at the inn where they stayed the next night. They were spending many hours on the road though, to the point where the children were so tired when they arrived that they could barely stay awake long enough to eat. Both of them were becoming more used to the spices used in Indayan cuisine though, and coming to find dishes that they liked.

The road led through country that was mostly devoted to agriculture. The Indayans kept cattle, water buffalo, goats, chickens, and horses but there was little land devoted to grazing. Instead, fields for the planting of rice and other grains, and garden plots for vegetables, were carved out of the encroaching jungle. Occasionally they passed enormous farms with many acres under cultivation, presided over by grand houses. These, Jiao Jing told them, were probably the homes of rajas. As near as the children could guess, a raja was sort of the equivalent of a count back home.

Rooms and meals in inns were not the only things their benefactor bought for them. He replaced their Gholim traveling clothes with lightweight cotton ones, which dried quickly once they were out of the rain. Their leather riding boots would never dry, but he found them cloth ones coated in rubber. All three of them got wide-brimmed hats, straw covered in oilcloth, that helped to keep their heads dry even though the rest of their bodies were soaked. Temperatures in Indaya were far too warm to make covering oneself in an oilcloth rain suit or waterproof cloak practical.

Traveling southeast along the road, they frequently met or were passed by small men in uniform, galloping along at speed on horses far smaller than the ones they rode. The Shuang breed was not all that popular here in Indaya, it seemed. "Who are those men, Mister Jiao?" Jurgen asked after the third such they'd seen.

"Royal Messenger Corps," he replied. "We have something similar in Hanshu as well, as I believe is also the case in your Dominion, am I right?" The children had never had occasion personally to use the Imperial messengers, but they knew of them. Without such means of rapid communication, it would have been impossible to rule such a vast country.

"Are they just for the king," Jurgen asked next, "or can anyone hire them?" Jiao Jing smiled from beneath his absurd-looking but effective rain hat.

"They charge a pretty penny for their services," he explained. "And the king can of course use those services without paying for them. But each message sent may require half a dozen horses to be stabled, shod, and fed, as well as a similar number of messengers to ride them. It costs a lot to send information over long distances, in a hurry."

"Why don't they just ask the gods for help?" Jurgen asked. His mama had told him she and her friends in Palambo, including Bapa Vandao, had gotten the gods at the Temple of the Eight in Iskand to carry messages to temples all over the country when they were trying to defeat the evil djinn Kivuli.

Jiao Jing reined in slightly and turned to look at the boy. He had mentioned that his mother's family were involved in the clergy, which in the Dominion undoubtedly meant the clergy of one or more of the Eight. The Gasparis did not openly worship any of the hundreds of lesser gods. "Would not that be insolent, an affront, to ask a god to play messenger boy?"

Now it was Jurgen who looked confused. Had he said too much? "I don't think so," he said unsurely. He wanted to point out that his parents did it all the time with Lord Betsalel, but he thought maybe he shouldn't mention that. "There are temples of the Eight all over the Dominion, and you can pray to a god and beg them to carry a message to anyplace they have a true idol. They don't mind, any more than they mind if you ask them to give you strength, or sweet dreams, or any other boon. It's why they exist, to help their worshipers. They can even carry you from one idol to another, through the plane of spirit."

Jing was shocked. The Eight could carry their worshipers from place to place? He had never heard of such a thing, but then he'd never been a worshiper of the western gods. There was no temple of the Eight in Tzinshai, where he'd been born and raised. Andros, Mulia, Belantos, and Dionos had temples there – as did two dozen of the most popular deities of the Hando, including Ling Zao. He had worshiped the Black Dragon from a young age, had spoken with the god on several occasions, but there had never been any suggestion that he could ask the dragon god to give him a lift to someplace else.

Miradil would have been his chosen destination, but there were no temples to Ling Zao there. He was an official of the Hanshu trading enclave there, however. Perhaps if he could somehow obtain a true idol, he could install one there within the enclave's suite of offices. Think of the thousands in gold that might be saved, if one could travel back and forth between Miradil and Tzinshai in a few seconds!

"I had not known that, Jurgen. Thank you for the information. It's a pity there are no nearby temples of the Eight, or I suppose we might save this rainy trip."

"Yes!" the boy replied enthusiastically. "If we could visit a temple of Betsalel, or any of the Eight, we could have them take us immediately to Miradil so you could claim your reward."

"I fear the nearest one is thousands of miles from here," their companion said regretfully. They rode on.

Thereafter it seemed that they spend even longer on the road each day. The height of summer had passed, but the days were still long and they traveled from barely past sunup until nearly sundown every day with only a few brief stops to have a little food or relieve themselves at the side of the road. Water was usually drunk from their skins without stopping.

They cantered the horses, alternating with a trot, or sometimes walking them if they became overheated. The nearly constant rains helped to cool them off, and the lack of mud on the stone pavement of the road helped them maintain a good pace. Jiao Jing seemed ever more anxious for them to reach their destination, not stopping for longer than necessary even when they came through good-sized towns.

"Couldn't we stop to see what the markets have?" Gudrun asked. The colorful markets were Berta's favorite thing about Indaya, and she was thinking wistfully that it might be fun to visit with her whole family – at some other time of year, when it was not raining constantly.

"You said that your Nima sorceress was a devotee of Danava, did you not?" Jiao Jing replied. They had mentioned that, back when they'd been traveling with the caravan. She nodded. "In this part of Indaya the worship of the Destroyer is widespread," he explained. "If, as your brother says, the goddess could transport the sorceress from one idol to another, she might appear in any of these towns we're passing through. I hope that the talisman pendants may keep you hidden from her, but I cannot take the chance that if we get close enough, she may be able to scry you. We need to keep moving."

That gave both children an uneasy feeling in the pits of their stomachs. They had not told their benefactor that Danava had in fact already transported Rajani and them across thousands of miles, as that would have conflicted with their hastily concocted story. And once they'd escaped the black goddess' immediate range on the

Ivory Road they had thought themselves safe from her for good. They should never have agreed to let Jiao Jing take them through Indaya, the heart of her power! They did not know, of course, that Rajani had lost her idol back in Khirzai.

Now all three of them were anxious to reach their destination, and it was with great relief that they came at last to the border city of Balore. The place was massive and ancient, ringed by stone walls that rivaled those of Miradil – one of no more than a handful of cities in the Dominion that was still fortified against invaders.

The road that they had been traveling on led here, to a pair of massive gates on the city's west side. Armed guards in splendid peacock uniforms of red and blue manned the gate, and as they arrived near midday traffic was already backed up for a quarter of a mile as each party entering must show papers. The guard post at the Hanshu border, a short distance away on the road that exited via Balore's east gate, would require documentation again for any wishing to enter the Blessed Kingdom.

As a trader who spent more time in foreign lands than he did at home, Jiao Jing always carried passes, certificates, and identification with him. He had signed and sealed permits allowing him to trade in Indaya, the Gholim lands, the Dominion, and Palambo – though he seldom traveled to that hot southern land.

One of the guards at the gate presented Jing's documentation to another guard, acting as a clerk, who sat at a broad desk set up beside the gate entrance. He read it over, then glanced up at the Hando man standing there with the two small children mounted on a tall horse behind him. Then he rummaged in a folder and came up with a sealed message.

"Jiao Jing?" he asked, and the caravan master nodded. "These children are accompanying you?" Another nod.

"I found them lost on the Ivory Road and am making arrangements to return them to their home," he said. There was no hope of passing two such as these off as his own grandchildren. The clerk smiled, and handed over the message.

"The Royal Messenger Service delivered this to us, to be given to you, two days ago. You may proceed into the city."

Still leading both his horse and the children's, Jing nodded his thanks and passed through the gate – getting out of the way for the next person to enter. The city had six gates, all of them similarly controlled during the day and locked up tight at night. But this one, and its opposite number facing the Hanshu border, got the most traffic.

Gabriel and Berta, their eyes alight with curiosity, sat astride Bai Shu waiting for their benefactor to read his message. What might it be, that was so important the sender would pay "a pretty penny" to have it delivered? And it could only be from someone who knew he would be coming to Balore!

Jiao Jing studied the message, and his face clouded. Then he wadded it up and stuck it in a pocket of his tunic. Miraculously, the rain had been in abeyance since they left the inn this morning. He looked up at the children, eagerly waiting to hear the news. "That was from my brother," he said, looking grim. "The news is bad. Your Nima sorceress found the caravan, and was looking for you two. He told them nothing, but he fears she knows you were there and will soon learn where you were taken. I had hoped to stop a day here, but we must be on our way immediately." The children's eyes were wide with fear.

Chapter 30

The rain slowed them more than they'd expected. It blinded them, it soaked them, and it seemed to defeat even the spells of tirelessness that had been laid on their horses. Their disguises as members of the Royal Messengers worked well enough when they were galloping along the road, though it was difficult to create the illusion of messengers being steadily soaked by the rain. But real messengers would not keep galloping past a Post Station as dusk was closing in.

After only a day, they abandoned the notion as raising more questions than it eased, and instead became a pair of sober, well-dressed Dravim businessmen who were in a hurry to get to Balore and meet a shipment of goods from Hanshu that was due to arrive there. The cover story worked well enough, and explained why they stopped late, left early, and immediately urged their horses into a run.

But at night, as they rested for a few hours in an inn, Leila's spirits sank. "Poor Gabe, poor Berta!" she moaned, lying on the narrow bed fully clothed as Tevo tried to comfort her. If the rigors of travel by horseback through an hours-long downpour had left her feeling emotionally exhausted, how bad must it be for two small children? She desperately wanted to hold her son in her arms, to comfort him – and equally, she missed her dry, comfortable home and her adorable little daughter. Yet she no longer wanted Betsalel to take them home for a visit. She was too anxious, too worn by their ordeal to inflict herself on those she loved.

They continued to call the Shadow God nightly. He reported that their quarry was still dimly sensed, moving in the same direction they were – but no closer, it seemed, than had been the case as they were leaving Purah. Somehow this Jiao Jing (about whom they knew nothing save what they'd been told by his brother and business partner), even burdened with the children, had managed to maintain his lead.

Betsalel was physically linked with Leila, as a part of his idol from the Blackwald still resided within her body; and he immediately sensed her distress. Touching her shoulder, he sent a flood of calm, of healing flowing through her and she straightened up. "Thank you master," she said softly.

"We will find the children and bring them back safe," he promised her. "Sooner or later. For now, rest and sleep. Your dreams will be pleasant." As if in a trance, she lay down on the narrow inn bed and immediately fell into sleep.

Whenever they came among people, meeting them coming the other way on the road, they asked about the Hando man traveling with two children. Most looked blankly at them, either having not passed them on the road or being simply too caught up in their own concerns to have noticed. Yet one or two admitted to having seen such a party – moving fast along the road to Balore, some two days previously.

"It's all right," Tevo assured Leila when she fretted about it. "We sent the messenger. This Jiao Jing is a trader, a man for whom money sings the song he loves best. He can save himself weeks of trouble, and much gold in travel expenses, by simply waiting for us in Balore. And when he gets our message, he will realize it is the most sensible way for him to obtain the reward he seeks."

She kissed him. "You're right," she said – trying to convince herself it was so. Yet it still bothered her. Why would this unknown man be dragging her son and his friend all the way to some port on the southeastern coast of Hanshu, when they had told him they needed to be returned to Miradil? Surely the Temple of the Eight in Sumbai would have taken little more time to reach from Purah, going straight south instead of south and east. And there, as Gabriel could surely have told him, they could all have been taken to Miradil in a matter of seconds. She stifled her fears, and they moved on.

At last, after days on the road under blinding rains, they came to the border city of Balore. Not much had impressed the two sophisticated Dominion citizens since they'd come east. Towns and cities in Indaya were often dirty, run down, and lacking in amenities they'd come to expect. But the mighty outer walls of Balore rose a hundred feet high, and a third as thick. The gates were broad, made of iron clad in bronze, and there were iron portcullises and murder holes above as they rode through to the checkpoint where guards waited to check everyone who entered the city. Clearly there was a reason Belantos held such power in this part of the world.

After discussing Balore with fellow inn patrons at the past couple of stops, Leila and Tevo had decided to arrive there as themselves. While she had in the past successfully cashed bank notes that were nothing but blank paper, they had no way of knowing how far from them their identification documents might be taken when they presented them. Better to be the two people mentioned in the only genuine documents they'd brought along.

The guards had no problem admitting the pair of Gaspari citizens, who had signed and sealed documents authorizing them to search for the two missing children and return them to the Dominion immediately should they be found. The clerk at his desk looked up in surprise at that. The woman certainly didn't look like any Gaspari he'd ever seen, but he recalled that the Nima were sometimes that dark. The two spoke flawless Hindai, a surprise, but he didn't doubt they were really Gaspari.

"You are searching for missing children?" he asked them. "They are no longer missing," Tevo explained. "They were taken in by a Hando trader named Jiao Jing, who found them on the Ivory Road and has taken them south for some reason we're not sure of. We sent a message to the commander of the Balore Guard, with another message to Jiao Jing asking him to wait here for us so we could collect the children and pay him the reward for their return. Do you know if that message was delivered?"

The memory sprang back for the clerk, but he wanted to make sure and pulled out his book. Yes, it had been checked off. "I handed the message to that Hando gentleman myself, only day before yesterday," he said. "He had two small children with him, a dark boy and a girl who looked as pale as any Gaspari but had strangely colored hair. I noticed him reading the message a minute or two after they'd passed through the gates. But I didn't see them after that."

Leila sagged in relief. The message had been delivered! Surely, Jiao Jing's greed would have led him to stay in Balore, awaiting the big cash payout that had been promised. But now, how were they to find him? Remaining without illusions, the two of them began accosting citizens at random and asking them, "Did you see a middle-aged Hando man with two small children, mounted on two Shuang horses?" The horses themselves were more common here this close to the border than they were elsewhere in Indaya, but a lone man with two children clearly not related to him was more likely to stand out.

Eventually they found someone who had seen them, but the man had little to tell his inquisitors. "He was reading something, then wadded it up and stuck it in a pocket. After that they left the area, heading along the main artery to the east. I haven't seen them since." Her sense of dread growing, Leila tipped the man generously and they moved up the city boulevard that was the continuation of the main road that had brought them here. It was narrower and far more crowded within the city, but would eventually lead to Balore's east gate and the short trip to the Hanshu border.

"I have a bad feeling," Leila said to Tevo as they rode along; and for once he didn't try to comfort her. The same bad feeling had been creeping over him since they'd spoken with that man whose food cart was parked near the west gate. Why, if Jiao Jing was entranced with the prospect of riches to come, would he wad up the message instead of carefully folding it?

Balore was smaller than Parat, but not by a whole lot. The population density of the cities east of the Killtops was far greater than in most of the Dominion. They might stay here for a month, searching every day, and never find the children and the man who was supposedly escorting them to safety. The only sensible approach for Jiao Jing, after reading their message, was to leave a message of his own with the gate guards telling the people coming to collect the children where they could be found. And he had not done so.

As they continued along the road, picking their way around slow traffic, their hearts sank lower and lower. Only a few days ago, they had been sure that they would soon be reunited with their son, he and they and Berta all soon safe at home. Yesterday, after their miserable trip through monsoon rains from Purah, their hopes had been high again. The greedy merchant, who had been willing to take such pains to assure the kids didn't fall back into the clutches of the woman who abducted them, would surely be waiting for them – and his princely reward – when they arrived in Balore.

And now, their inability to gallop through the center of this teeming border city was gnawing at their composure. It took nearly two hours to clear the east gate, then Leila called Betsalel to the idol in her pocket. He spoke mind-to-mind with both of them, saying "I can sense Gabriel dimly. He is still to the east of us, and south." Damn!

For the border crossing into Hanshu, the pair took the guise of Hando merchants – clad in silk tunics above practical traveling clothes. Their appearance, and their flawless command of the language, let them pass without submitting documents. Soon they were thundering down the road that bent south to the Hanshu port city of Tongnan, climbing the range of low hills that formed the southern end of the Shan Ling mountains. Much further north that range gave birth to the mighty Huang, though it was as nothing compared with the Pahadai.

"They're only two days ahead of us," Leila said as they urged their mounts along. The tall Gaspari horses were close enough in appearance to the Shuang breed that they'd gone unremarked at the border crossing. "There surely would not be ships leaving for Tzinshai on a daily basis. If the Eight will it, we may find them stuck in port waiting for a ship to sail."

Tevo smiled grimly at her and held up his left hand, thumb up. It was a gesture that mean many things in the Dominion, including "may it be so." They had not eaten lunch today, and though both of them felt as if they wanted to gallop all the way to Tongnan without stopping, their stomachs and their bladders had other ideas.

Already the terrain and climate were changing, it seemed. They traveled under gray skies, but the torrential rains that had plagued them along the road from Purah did not fall here. People were everywhere: soldiers moving along the road on foot or mounted on tall Shuang horses, peasants laboring in the fields on either side, farm carts rattling along pulled by donkeys or even large dogs.

They guided Nimble and Milacek off the highway into a wide flat area that had apparently been carved out of farm fields to provide travelers with a place to rest. There was a small building at one side, which proved to be a tavern of sorts. It served food, beer and ale, rice wine, and tea. After using the privy Leila and Tevo took their food and drink to a table outside, and sat conferring as they refreshed themselves.

"I don't think two Hando merchants would be asking around about missing Gaspari children," Tevo pointed out. "but perhaps we might be business associates of Jiao Jing's, seeking him out to make a trading proposition?" Leila agreed. If they could find the caravan master, they would find the children. But asking about them might just cause suspicion. And if people thought you were looking for someone to give them money, they were much more likely to be helpful.

Chapter 31

The weather had turned, if not exactly dry, at least more like the damp weather you often got in the Dominion in spring and fall. Hanshu was a very different place from Indaya, it seemed, though they had only had to climb a range of low hills to make the transition. It was currents in the ocean to their south, as well as the land terrain, which produced the different weather. But the children knew nothing of this. They were only thankful to be riding through a light mist instead of a downpour.

As they left the hills behind, the clouds overhead began to break up; and sunshine came streaming in over their right shoulders as they cantered south toward the sea. Jiao Jing's report that Rajani was on their trail had filled Gabriel and Berta with fear, and they were all anxious to reach the seaport ahead. That woman, with her black goddess at her command, might do anything at all to them. And if she caught up with them she might snatch them away in an instant – back to Delai, or perhaps even to the palace of this Gholim "king" she'd talked about.

When they'd had a few moments to speak in private, Berta had confided to Gabe that she suspected Rajani had been hired to catch them so that the Gholim khan – which she said was what they called a king, except they didn't really have kings the way other countries did – could use her to force her father to do things he didn't want to do.

The Dominion had the Killtops as an impenetrable border on the east side, and was surrounded by water on the other sides. There was a small border with Palambo, which country was now friendly with them of course, but only the Gholim tribes were really their neighbors – and then only in the narrow strip of land where the Ivory Road ran beside the Huang at Miradil. Therefore, Berta's logic ran, the khan must want something from the Dominion and had chosen the despicable ploy of kidnaping the emperor's daughter to achieve it. Gabriel was impressed. He knew far more of religion than she did, but her grasp of politics and history was well beyond his.

"What happens when we get to Tongnan?" Jurgen asked. "Will we have to wait long for a ship to Tzinshai? Will we take our horses?" The expression on Jiao Jing's face was worried.

"I very much hope we will not have to wait long for a ship to Tzinshai. The sea route between Tongnan and the ports east of there is very well-traveled. We should be able to find passage for ourselves and our horses within a couple of days after we arrive, though we may have a few stops on the way. But once we are on the water, I feel confident that your Nima sorceress will be unable to track us."

"The goddess Danava seemed very powerful," Gudrun said worriedly. "She threatened to kill me with a thought if I did anything wrong."

"Ah," Jiao Jing said more confidently, "but Danava is primarily a deity of Indaya. There are few who worship her elsewhere, and her power in Hanshu, especially along the coast, will be reduced. Is it not true that in the lands of the Gholim tribes you were able to get out of her range in just a few minutes on horseback?" Berta subsided. He had a point, and she shook off her worries. But she still wished they could have gone to a temple of the Eight. It would have made getting home so much easier!

They rode hard through the afternoon and came into the outskirts of Tongnan after dark. The children were so tired they were in danger of falling from the saddle, and Jiao Jing assessed them anxiously. They were his ticket, his once-in-a-lifetime chance, to everything he'd dreamed of; and he was as protective of them as if they'd been his own.

It was too late tonight to do anything about seeking passage on a ship heading east, and they were soon ensconced in an inn room near the waterfront. Tongnan was a bustling port, home to offices of many trading companies, shipping companies, and the residences of those who worked in the shipping business. From here, one might reach any port in Hanshu, as well as all of Indaya's coast and all of Palambo's beyond the Talj Jabal. One could even sail all the way around Palambo to reach the western ports of the Dominion. Jiao had noticed sailors drinking in the common room when they came in, and after the exhausted children had been tucked into bed he returned downstairs to hear what they might be saying.

Most of those here were Hando like him, though there were a few Dravim among them. The Gholim possessed their own shore, far to the north; but it was locked in ice for much of each year and none of them ever became sailors. Ordering a beer from the bar, he took a seat beside the cold hearth and leaned up against the wall, sipping slowly. It was said that the making of beer had been invented in a region that was now part of the kingdom of Palambo, thousands of years ago. But in Jiao's opinion only his countrymen knew how to make a beer that was worth drinking.

The talk swirled around him as he strained his ears, listening for news. He had been long out of Hanshu, months this time. What had been going on in his absence? There was talk of the storms along the southwest coast of Indaya, of whores and brothels. The news Jiao really wanted to hear would not likely come from the lips of common seamen, he realized. But then he heard one tell another, "I'd like to go with you, but we sail for Szeding on the morning tide. If I'm not back at the ship by midnight, the mate will have my hide."

Szeding was the next port east from Tongnan, Jiao Jing knew. He approached the sailor who'd been speaking. "Excuse me," he asked politely, and the man looked him up and down. His clothing bespoke wealth, yet if he were drinking in a waterfront inn he could not be of the aristocracy. "I couldn't help but overhear that you're sailing toward Szeding tomorrow morning," he went on. The sailor nodded, waiting for him to get to the point.

"May I ask what vessel?" Jiao said, extending far more courtesy to this lowly sailor than was customary.

"The Piao Qin, out of Dongyi," he replied. The merchant smiled. He did not know this particular ship – most of his trading activities took place along the Huang and the Ivory Road beside it. But the mention of Dongyi boded well.

"You will sail to Dongyi eventually?" he asked, and got a nod in return.

"We're stopping at Szeding and Tzinshai on our way around the coast, then will be docked in Dongyi for a couple of weeks for maintenance before returning south," the sailor explained.

"Might you have room for myself and my two young wards, and two horses?" Jiao asked eagerly. The seaman looked unsure. It was his job to trim sail and scrub decks, not keep track of passenger berths or space in the cargo hold. But he knew they were not overladen. The ship had come from the southernmost tip of Indaya, with rice, ivory, tiger skins, and spices on board for sale along the Hanshu coast.

"It's likely we can squeeze you in," he admitted. "But you'll need to speak with Fong Zi, our purser, in the morning. *Early* in the morning. We're taking on some supplies before we leave, but sailing only a couple of hours past dawn."

"Perfect!" the merchant replied. "We will be there first thing. Where is the Piao Qin docked?" The sailor gestured.

"Go out this door, walk to the waterfront. Turn left and go down to the third pier, then down it to the end. You can't miss it." Jiao Jing thanked the man and hastily downed the last of his beer, then left the common room and went straight to bed.

Gabriel's eyes fluttered open and he found Jiao Jing moving about the room. He was already dressed and was gathering the contents of his pack, but no light yet showed through the room's narrow window. A candle was lit on the nightstand between the beds. "Is it time to get up?" he asked sleepily, and Berta stirred beside him.

Their benefactor smiled. "I had a piece of good luck last night in the common room," he told the children. "A ship is leaving this morning for Tzinshai, and it seems likely we may be able to take passage on it. Soon we'll have you well out of the clutches of your Nima sorceress!"

At the mention of Rajani Gabriel put his feet on the floor and began looking around for his clothing, and Berta was quick to do the same. Before long they were downstairs, and were able to get some hot tea and cold buns filled with a sweet bean paste for breakfast. Then Jiao paid the bill and they collected the horses before hurrying off in search of the Piao Qin.

Honorable Fong Zi, purser of the Hando merchantman, was on deck soon after sunrise. Supplies were being loaded, and it was he who would accept bills from the grocer, the butcher, and the chandler and assure that they received their payment. The late-arriving party of travelers seeking passage was assured that they and their mounts could be accommodated, provided they did not mind sleeping in hammocks in with the common seamen, and taking their meals with the crew.

The horses would be stabled below decks, but extra payment would be required for their food and for the labor of mucking out their stalls. Jiao Jing agreed to all of this readily enough, and handed over the amount requested without haggling. He was extremely anxious to leave Tongnan, and was convinced that Ling Zao was smiling on him from the celestial realm, for him to have found a ship so quickly. They had not been in the port city for as long as ten hours when the Piao Qin slipped her moorings and was towed out into the bay by her boats before hoisting sail and beginning the journey east and north along the coast of Hanshu.

The children were fascinated. The weather this morning was clear and warmish, with a stiff cool breeze and clouds on the horizon behind them. Neither had ever been on a ship of this size, though they'd both ridden on river craft and had sailed on small boats a little way off the coast of the Northern Ocean. The seawater here was far warmer, and colorful little fish swam just beneath the surface.

Jiao Jing wondered what sort of sailors they would prove to be. Few citizens of the Dominion were mariners, the waters of the Center Sea being vast but not to be compared with those of the untamed world ocean. He himself had not spent all that much time at sea, and he knew that should the weather turn rough he'd be groaning in misery soon enough. But for now the voyage was pleasant, and the children so excited by the novel experience of sailing on the sea (though within sight of land the entire way) that their anxieties and concerns had been forgotten. And Jiao's anxieties had faded as soon as Tongnan fell behind them. Those who pursued would never catch them now – and soon, he would be in his home territory with all of his resources at his command.

Chapter 32

Leila and Tevo arrived in Tongnan as late as Jiao Jing and the children had, two days earlier. They and their mounts were not nearly as tired, though. They put up in a decent inn a few blocks inland from the docks, now appearing as a pair of Imperial guards. Chasing down the children and the man they now knew must be their new abductor would have to wait for the morrow. They ate a late, but still warm, supper, and then went to bed.

The morning saw them up early. In their mad dash for the coast, they had not had much chance to develop their cover story. But here, they hoped, they might have a chance to find their quarry. "We'll be acquaintances of Jiao Jing's, I think," Tevo said thoughtfully. It wouldn't be unreasonable for two of his colleagues in the trading business to be asking after him… and of course they might mention he was traveling with two small children. "A few months ago Jiao sold us certain goods he was importing from the Dominion, and we have been trying to find him to tell him we'd like to buy another shipment. We'd hoped to catch him on the Ivory Road, but learned from his brother that he'd gone south to take ship."

If you thought hard about it the story was a little thin. Why would traders, for whom coin was such a consideration, chase their fellow merchant halfway across Indaya and Hanshu when they might simply wait for him to return to Tzinshai and put in an order for the goods they wanted there? But Leila felt confident that most people wouldn't question it – and if any did, she was very good at ad-libbing excuses. She'd gotten a lot of practice at it, in her younger life.

So, leaving their horses happily gobbling up twice the expected quantity of grain in the inn's stable, the two middle-aged merchants set out for the docks to learn what they could of their old trading partner. Leila eyed the port facilities with appreciation. She had grown up in one of the Dominion's foremost seaports, but it was no bigger than the one here. A deep, broad bay indented the coastline here, where the mouth of a small river came out, and stone or concrete breakwaters extended the sheltering headlands on either side still more. This part of the world got storms far fiercer than ever were seen on the Center Sea.

Along the bay shore a broad paved street ran, lined on the landward side with warehouses, inns, taverns, and brothels. To seaward, long stone jetties jutted out into the water. Many ships rode at anchor in the bay itself, those that didn't need to offload or take on heavy cargo. Between these and the many craft (everything from small fishing boats and the square-sailed boats the Hando called "junks," to multi-masted merchantmen) moored to the docks, there were more than a hundred ships here. Who could keep track of them all?

Ah, in fact that would be the Royal Office of Sea Commerce, as the official sign announced it. It stood across the shore road from the largest of the piers, located at the halfway point between one breakwater and the other. And it made the similar facility Leila had visited in Jena, before taking ship as Suleiman Abasa for the shores of Palambo nine years ago, seem tiny by comparison. Hanshu was an ancient land, with a civilization far older than that of the Dominion. Was it any wonder they had such things as the organization of commerce well in hand?

After a short wait, one of a dozen clerks (all men, Leila noticed; were the skills of women even less valued here than was the case in the Dominion?) saw the two traders. From the look of them, he guessed them to be brothers. Tevo had continued, subconsciously, to pattern his illusions after those Leila produced. "We seek passage to Tzinshai," Leila (the elder "brother") told the clerk. "Preferably without any stops along the way."

The clerk made reference to a large chart set up on the wall behind his counter, then got out a ledger. "Do you have cargo to ship?" he asked them.

"Not this time," the trader replied. "We have our horses to bring along with us, and a small amount of personal baggage, but that is all."

The clerk nodded sagely, and pulled out a different ledger. "You would prefer a comfortable cabin?" he asked, having seen that their clothing was richer than that of most travelers.

"It does not matter," said the other trader with a hint of impatience. "We care not about the accommodations, only about reaching Tzinshai in a hurry."

"The ship leaving soonest will sail with the morning tide tomorrow," they were informed.

"Have there been any ships sailing that way in the past couple of days?" the elder trader asked, which puzzled the clerk. Of what use to learn of ships one could not travel on, since they had already left? But it required only flipping backward a page or two to produce the answer.

"The Piao Qin sailed two days ago," he replied. "And the Feng Shi left on the evening tide three days before that."

With sinking hearts, they obtained the location of the Cai Yuan, which would sail tomorrow, then thanked the clerk and left the building. Within a bubble of silence, Tevo cursed. "Jiao Jing and the kids have to have gotten here in time to take the Piao Qin," he said. They had been frustrated at every turn since beginning this trek, it seemed. "But there's probably no way to find out if that's really the case."

"We've got the whole day," Leila told him calmly. "We can visit every inn close enough to the waterfront to have been where they stayed, and ask after our old friend Jiao Jing. And we should go ahead and book passage on the Cai Yuan. If by some fluke he missed the earlier ship, we'll be shipmates. And what a reunion we can have!" Her maternal ire had been aroused by the betrayal of the Hando merchant. What more could he want with her son – and more to the point, the Gaspari princess – beyond a big cash reward? She didn't like contemplating the answer.

The two Hando traders found the Cai Yuan, a quarter of a mile east of the Office of Sea Commerce, and arranged with the purser to be aboard, with their mounts, early the following morning. That left them with part of the morning, and all of the afternoon and evening as well, to go bar-hopping.

Yet both of them were filled up with anxiety, and working hard to hold off despair, as they started at the western end of the street and worked their way along the waterfront – visiting every inn that offered lodging. They had thought themselves competent, and with Betsalel's backing nearly invincible. How could it be that, weeks after they'd begun the search, they were no closer to finding their son than they'd been when they started out?

195

They ordered hot tea in the first few inns they came to, something you would not find in many inns in the Dominion. Toward noon they ordered lunch, as well. In each place they would appear to be about their business, two colleagues or perhaps brothers relaxing as they waited to board a ship. But then the casual questions would begin. "Say, barkeep, I'm wondering if you might have seen our business associate Jiao Jing? He was supposed to have met us here yesterday but has not gotten in touch with us. He's traveling with two small Western children, a dark boy and a lighter girl..."

Neither of them had yet set eyes on the man who had stolen the children away, so they weren't able to describe him except in general terms. They assumed he would be an older version of his brother. Gabriel they could describe in minute detail, but though Jiao Shao had said that Berta's skin and hair had been darkened they had no way of knowing what she might look like now. How fast would the dye wear off, and would Jiao Jing attempt to disguise her appearance by dying her hair again? So the descriptions were vague. But it was unusual enough, they hoped, for a Hando man to be traveling with two children who were clearly not his relations, that it might have been remarked on.

But they met with no success. In inn after inn, the innkeeper or his employees confirmed that they'd seen no such people. Then finally, two hours after lunch (the merchants had switched to rice wine, but their consumption of what they ordered had become part of the illusion) the fiftyish woman tending bar at an inn well down toward the eastern end of the waterfront replied, "I know no Jiao Jing, but there was a man like you describe staying here with two small round-eyed children two nights ago. They came in late, and the children went right to bed as soon as they had been shown to their room. Then they were up almost before dawn the next day. They ate breakfast, then left with all their belongings. I assumed they were leaving by road, since they were mounted, but perhaps they caught a ship."

Leila couldn't stop herself, no mind how out of character it was for this middle-aged trader to ask, "How did the children look? Were they well?" The woman looked at him oddly.

"They were very tired when they came in, almost dead on their feet," she said. "I'm short of help now so I've been working morning and night. I served them breakfast the next morning and it appeared they could have used another couple of hours' sleep. But they were cheerful enough, and not unwell. They ate heartily."

The innkeeper wiped the bar with a cloth, then added "I must say that girl was the strangest-looking child I have ever seen. Her skin was pale and freckled, but streaked with something that looked like dirt but would not wash off. And her hair was streaked brown and black, but with nearly an inch of bright red at the roots. Why would someone do that to a child?"

Leila didn't reply. She and Tevo left the inn shortly and walked outside. The clear weather had given way to clouds, and the wind was rising. It would probably start raining before long, and they began walking back to the inn where they were staying. "At least he's not terrorizing the kids," Tevo said thoughtfully as they walked along.

"Not yet at least," his wife replied. What had he told them to convince them to go along with him willingly – that he was taking them to safety? She thought her son was quite bright, but he was only seven, after all. And he had led a sheltered life compared with the one his mother had endured. Might he be naïve enough to accept Jiao Jing's lies unquestioningly?

"Do you think it's possible," she asked, "that they did go by road instead of getting on a ship?" Leila was beginning to doubt her abilities, after failing so many times since this trip had begun. It was time to consider their moves more carefully, and plan for contingencies. Tevo considered for a long moment, then replied "I don't think so. If Jiao Jing meant to take the children by road to Tzinshai, he could have gone by a much more direct route from the Ivory Road – one he's probably taken many times in his life, if what his brother told us was true. There could have been no reason to come to Tongnan except to take ship."

The two Hando merchants spent the rest of the afternoon and evening drinking in the common room at the inn where they were staying, as a cool, gentle rain fell steadily outside. This weather, if it persisted, would likely not interfere with the sailing of the Cai Yuan come morning.

This time they truly drank – beer and rice wine, hot tea with supper, then some more rice wine afterward. They hoped to hide from their fears and discouragement in a bottle, but it did little good. Fairly early in the evening the two went upstairs to their room, and Leila and Tevo made love passionately, almost desperately, in one of the room's narrow beds before falling asleep locked in each other's arms. In the morning they would be off to Tzinshai.

Chapter 33

The White Bird, she was called. But the Piao Qin bore little resemblance to her namesake. Over two hundred feet long, broad of beam and with a high prow and stern, she was a junk grown large with four masts. Her sails were square, woven of sturdy hempen canvas, and were as close to white as anything about her. Her hull was painted dark green, but the paint had faded through many voyages along the coasts of Hanshu and Indaya.

The accommodations Jiao Jing had so hastily bought for them were miserable. A little light filtered in from unglazed windows set high around the crew's quarters. The captain and some of his officers had cabins of their own with bunks, but the crew – and its paying passengers – slept in hammocks slung one above the other, packed close together, in one large space beneath the forward deck.

At first Gabriel and Berta, still maintaining their pose as Jurgen and Gerdur though they no longer looked remotely like brother and sister, were intrigued by the idea of sleeping in hammocks. But the reality of sleeping in a room full of unwashed, snoring sailors soon made them wish they could throw their bedrolls onto the deck and sleep there instead. Jiao Jing would not hear of it, though.

He was no happier with the Piao Qin's facilities than they were, but now that he nearly had his little prizes where he wanted them he was not about to risk them in any way. Suppose one of them fell overboard, or caught a chill from sleeping out in the damp sea air?

So they endured, and in time the children became accustomed to it and were able to sleep. During the day they were permitted to roam the ship, provided they stayed well out of the way of the crew as they went about their work. Jiao mostly kept to himself, one eye always on the children as they explored the decks. Despite the physical discomforts of the voyage they seemed to be lighter of spirit than they'd been during the hard ride across Indaya to Tongnan.

Seemingly his invocation of the Nima sorceress had done the trick, convincing them he was their rescuer and that they were now safe. He wondered idly whether the old woman might truly be on their trail. From what they had said of her, she must have run into some difficulties or she would surely have caught them – probably before they had reached the caravan, or soon after.

Jiao knew little of Danava. He had been a devotee of Ling Zao from early adulthood, fascinated by the black dragon's purported ability to grant his worshipers the power of amassing wealth. And while the god had never specifically granted him a coin-related boon, he certainly had prospered. But he had all the wealth he needed, now. He wanted something else, something more.

The Destroyer of Illusions was worshiped in Hanshu, it was true. But her powers were mysterious and unknown to him. Likewise, while Jiao had been a faithful worshiper he had never delved into the deeper mysteries. Had he learned that it was possible for Danava's arch-priestess to carry a small true idol with her and have her goddess manifest wherever she might be, he would have been less sanguine about having snatched her prize from under her nose.

There were many ports along Hanshu's southern coast, but the Piao Qin stopped only at Zedong – the largest of them. Jiao Jing and the children stayed aboard. The kinds of goods they'd taken on along the coast of Indaya were best sold in the largest ports the kingdom had to offer: Tongnan, Tzinshai, and the ship's home port of Dongyi. Now it would be a mere four-day sail to Tzinshai, a day in port there, then another four days north to Dongyi. Or so should be the case with fair weather and good winds.

But on the third day the sun came up before them in a blaze of blood, and the captain warned the crew, "A blow is coming. Make sure everything's tied down, and better tell Honorable Jiao Jing to keep those Gaspari brats below." By midday the Piao Qin was anchored two miles offshore, head into a gale and all canvas down as she pitched on the waves and sheets of rain lashed her decks.

Below, in the crew's quarters, Jiao Jing and the two children retched miserably until nothing but bile came up, moaning while spray blew in through the high windows and turned everything cold and damp. By the following morning the storm had eased and the wind was now blowing from the west, so the crew upped sail again. But the seas remained rough, rain falling as often as not, until they had rounded the southeastern corner of Hanshu and had nearly reached their next port of call.

Jiao was the first to regain his strength. He might be well into middle age by the standards of the Gaspari Dominion, but the Hando lived longer than westerners did and he was still vigorous and active. Gabriel and Berta had been unable to hold down any food since the storms began, but he made sure that they drank water and did not become dehydrated. When they reached port in Tzinshai, the children remained limp in their hammocks – resting peacefully now – while he went ashore and began marshaling his resources. Soon, very soon, his plans would come to fruition.

Chapter 34

The accommodations on the Cai Yuan proved to more comfortable than Leila and Tevo had expected. She had traveled from north to south across the Center Sea, and had had to call on Betsalel to save the ship from being wrecked on a lee shore during a storm on that voyage; but she had no experience of ocean travel. Tevo had gone along the Dominion's Center Sea coast on small vessels many times during the first couple of years after Betsalel had been restored to the Dominion's pantheon, but had never been far from shore or in rough waters.

So both of them were surprised by the neat little cabin with its glassed porthole, two narrow bunks, and furnishings secured to the deck. It even included a privy stool, similar to the arrangement on the ship Leila had ridden to Palambo all those years ago.

They had not been under sail for long before a rain squall sent them retreating below, and they decided to call the Shadow God since they were apparently confined to quarters for the time being. He grew only to a height of five feet, in consideration of the cabin's low ceiling. "A ship?" he remarked, with an air of discouragement.

"We're pretty sure that Jiao took the kids by ship to Tzinshai three days ago," Leila explained. "It doesn't make sense that he would have taken them to Tongnan unless they meant to sail, and a ship left heading in that direction not long after they would have arrived. Can you sense them?"

Betsalel closed his two "normal" eyes and reached out with his senses. Out at sea, thousands of miles from his greatest concentrations of worshipers and with only Leila and Tevo near at hand, his strength was greatly reduced. After searching in vain for a full minute, he opened his eyes again and said apologetically, "I cannot sense Gabriel at all. The extra day must have put him beyond my reach, here."

Leila put her head in her hands. She was not often susceptible to despair, and refused to believe that they would not *eventually* get the children back safe and sound. And there would be retribution for this Jiao Jing, whatever his motivations for stealing them away – when they might have been home weeks ago, if he had simply let them continue traveling with the caravan. But it was so damned discouraging! Time after time they had thought their son nearly within their grasp – yet they were no closer now than they'd been when they started out, it seemed.

"Have you been keeping Ostden and Lisabet informed of developments?" she asked her god. He nodded sadly.

"The empress is a strong woman," he replied. "She has refused to give up hope, though I've had no good news for her. Just the knowledge that her daughter is alive has been enough for her to maintain her composure. And there have been no demands or ultimatums from the khan, so Ostden knows that he does not have the children in his grasp. He is very anxious *not* to have to make a choice between Berta's safety and that of the realm."

The ship's tossing had increased, and it was only Betsalel's divine powers that enabled him to remain standing on the floor as his arch-priest and priestess sat on the bunk talking with him. "Master, I want you to take me home for a few hours," Leila said looking up, her deep green gaze steady.

"Tevo must remain behind so I can return with you here, as I fear I might be unable to return to this idol if no people are near," he replied. "But other than that, there should be no problem. Approach me, and I'll carry you to Shadow Manor."

To Tevo, Betsalel added, "I'll return here for a while after dropping Leila off, in case there's anything else you need." His arch-priest smiled wanly in response. He missed his little girl deeply, and ached to hold her in his arms. But how could he deny his beloved wife the chance to do so? Perhaps he could get a turn soon enough. Presumably there'd be nothing much for them to do during the five days or so that it was supposed to take to sail to Tzinshai. As Leila seemed to vanish from Betsalel's arms and the idol took on its customary resting posture, the decks lurched and the idol threatened to topple over. Tevo jumped up to steady it, his stomach lurching in sympathy. He'd never been all that great a sailor.

A sensation of absurd happiness seized Leila as the familiar environs of the ballroom at Shadow Manor came into focus around her. Home! Oh, if only it had been *all* of them coming home! The past weeks' adventures had not been without interest, seeing places she had only read about before; and someday, it would be nice to go back and visit the "realms of the Hando" under more pleasant circumstances. But not for a long time!

As Betsalel tenderly, lovingly set her down on the carpet, she turned to thank him. She had known a mother's love, and now a father's as well – the father she had once vowed to kill – but the love her god bore for her was beyond any human love. He was literally a part of her, and knew her joys and her pain. "I'll call you when I'm ready to go back," she promised. In her heart she knew that only Tevo and the need to find their son would tear her away.

It had been early afternoon in the Southern Ocean along the coast of Hanshu. Here, so many miles to the west, it was early morning. *Very* early morning. Was anyone even awake yet? Leila walked through the door to the living room, then headed for the kitchen. She heard the sounds of Elyzia stirring, probably baking pastries. The woman arose hours before anyone else in the house, all to make sure that there would be hot and delicious treats for breakfast.

The older woman was bent over putting a pan of strudel into the wood-fired oven as Leila entered the kitchen, and she nearly jumped out of her skin when she closed the door and turned to see she was not alone. "Mistress!" she squeaked, "When did you get here? You like to have scared the life out of me, creeping up like that!"

Leila's mouth widened in a happy grin. "I'm sorry Elyzia, I didn't mean to startle you," she said – stepping forward and enfolding the housekeeper/cook/nanny in a warm hug. The woman's face lit.

"You're back, does that mean you've found our Gabriel? And the little princess?" The grin vanished.

"We're on their trail, but we have not caught up with them yet," the lady of the house admitted.

Elyzia looked disappointed, but said nothing. Leila added, "Tevo and I are taking passage on a ship from Tongnan to Tzinshai, in the kingdom of Hanshu. That's the biggest of the Hando realms, actually the only one ruled by the Hando people. Anyhow, I just felt I needed to see home again, hold Miri in my arms, before continuing the journey. Is everyone well?"

"They're all fine," Elyzia said with a smile. "Those baby sisters and brother of yours are becoming proper little Gasparis. Miri misses Gabe and her mama and papa, but having her aunts and uncle here, and her grandma, is helping her to think about happier things. They've been visiting up at the palace a few times, too – and Lord Betsalel has been keeping us posted about your trip."

Leila breathed a sigh of relief. It was such a blessing, having the services of a god. Had they mailed a letter from the Ivory Road, it would probably not be arriving here for another month at least. "I think I'll take a hot bath," she announced. Bathing facilities had been few and far between since they'd turned south, and it was unlikely any baths would be possible aboard the Cai Yuan. Likewise, there had been no opportunity to do any laundry in weeks. She and Tevo could use clean underwear, and maybe some new traveling clothes.

By the time Leila had soaked herself clean and washed her hair, then donned clean clothing, the rest of the family was up and seated around the breakfast table as Elyzia brought out the warm pastries, slices of ham, and scrambled eggs. Even in summer, Gaspari fare tended to be heavy.

The housekeeper had not revealed Leila's presence, and when she walked into the room everyone but Vandasi – who was strapped into a high chair – jumped from their seats and mobbed her. "Mama, mama!" Miri squealed, jumping up into her arms. Oof! It felt as if her daughter had grown in just the few weeks she'd been gone. Leila's own small stature was due more to a lack of nutrition in her childhood than to heredity, and it seemed likely that someday both her children – especially Gabe, whose father had stood six-foot-two – would tower over her.

Leila took a seat with her little girl clinging to her like a limpet, hugging her as if she never meant to let go. A surge of love washed over her, so strong it brought tears to her eyes. The tears flowed stronger as the longing to hold her beautiful boy came over her. Miri looked up into her face. "Mama, why are you crying?" Leila smiled through her tears.

"I'm just so happy to see you," she said, and buried her face in her daughter's soft curls.

Night had fallen aboard the Cai Yuan by the time Leila reappeared inside the darkened cabin shared by the two Hando merchants. A ship's lantern glowed on the wall, and the decks were still heaving in the storm. Yet Tevo, his illusion gone, lay sleeping comfortably on the narrow bunk.

The motion was already making Leila wish she had not had that hearty lunch. It had been a lovely day in Parat, and her visit had been joyful. "How is it Tevo sleeps so soundly, master?" she asked the god in hushed tones. "Did you lay your blessing of sleep on him?" The granting of sound sleep and pleasant dreams, along with the surcease of death, were among the powers traditionally associated with the Shadow God. The cheating of death that had come too soon was a more recent aspect of Betsalel's, but it was now a widely accepted part of his church's tenets in the Dominion and Palambo.

The Shadow God (a little shorter than Leila, here in this cramped cabin) smiled. "I gave him something more permanent," he said. She looked at him questioningly. In the dim lantern light, only his eyes were visible. They seemed to twinkle. "I'll give it to you as well, the gift of immunity to motion sickness. You must be at your best when this voyage ends, ready to chase down this Jiao Jing."

He touched her shoulder, and immediately Leila felt the sensation of dizziness and nausea vanish. She still must use her superior agility and balance to remain standing as the floor rose and fell beneath her feet; but she now felt no more distress from the motion than she would have standing on dry land. "Thank you, master!" she cried, embracing her god. It always amazed her, the wonders he could work. Especially considering that he was unable to reach out and find the missing children. But he always had been a god for whom physical closeness was important.

Betsalel dwindled to pocket size and Leila snatched up the idol as he vacated it, before it should roll away and get lost in some dark corner of the tiny room. She felt so uplifted by her trip home, surrounded by loved ones and physically pampered with hot water and familiar foods, that she needed to share her joy with the man who was half the reason she had returned so soon. She touched Tevo on the shoulder.

He had raised the rail on the inner side, to keep him from rolling out of bed as he slept. As he roused at her touch, Tevo grasped the rail and hauled himself into a sitting position. His dark eyes lit with love as he beheld her there standing over him, a happy smile on her face. With an answering grin he said, "You look pretty good – he did you, too?"

Leila nodded, then stepped over the rail and squeezed in beside her husband – snuggling up against him for a hug and a kiss. "Mm, you *smell* pretty good, too!"

"I got a bath while I was home and some clean underwear for both of us," she said. She sniffed him. "You should probably go home for a while too, maybe tomorrow. Everybody's fine, but Miri really misses her papa."

He squeezed her back. "Did you eat dinner?" she asked him, and he nodded. "Betsalel gave me his blessing right after he got back from dropping you in Parat," he said. "By then I'd already lost my lunch, I'm afraid. And because of the storm there wasn't the usual full dinner service. But I managed to stagger over to the dining room and they gave me some fruit and biscuits. They were really surprised to see me up and about, though I tweaked the illusion so that Honorable Ming Shao looked a little the worse for wear. I told them my brother was too seasick to leave his bunk, but I took a little extra back with me. You want some?"

"Maybe later," she said. The ship's biscuit kept for emergency rations would ward off starvation, but that was about the best you could say for it. "How about some goodies from home, instead?" She pulled a bundle out of her pack and opened it on the bed. There were a couple of Elyzia's pastries, now cold, some wrapped sandwiches with ham and rich buttery cheese on dark rye bread, apples, and oranges. And a couple of bottles of ale from Parat's famous brewery. In short, a feast!

The two travelers such a long way from home sat happily devouring their impromptu picnic, unmindful of the way their "table" rolled from side to side. Thank you, Lord Betsalel! They cleaned up the mess afterward, brushing away the crumbs. Then, after talking quietly for around an hour, they slept.

Chapter 35

Berta's eyes fluttered open. She was lying in her hammock below decks on the Piao Qin, and it was not moving! Ugh, she felt weak. Achy, smelly, tired … and hungry? She struggled into a sitting position and looked around her. Daylight was streaming in through the windows far above her head, and it seemed no one was here except Gabriel, in the next hammock over.

"Gabe!" she cried out. The last few days were a blur in her mind – heaving decks and swaying hammocks, the creaking of the ship's hull, feeling so sick she had wished she could die. She dimly remembered Jiao Jing, who was sick too, making sure she drank enough water. But she couldn't remember the last time she'd eaten anything that had stayed down.

The ship still moved, slightly. But it was a gentle movement like the slow breathing of someone asleep. Gabriel poked his head up and looked at her. "Berta, where is everybody?" he asked.

"I think…" she said, looking around and listening, "I think we must have reached port. Maybe all the crew have gone ashore?"

Gabriel couldn't imagine Jiao Jing leaving them all alone, unless maybe he thought they would keep sleeping. He heaved himself over the edge of the hammock and put his feet on the wooden deck, then helped Berta climb down. "Let's go see if anyone is around," he said, and the made their way down the corridor and up a gangway to the deck above.

A crewman on watch, one of the few who hadn't been given liberty during this short stop, looked surprised to see them. During their time spent with the caravan, and again during their travels with Honorable Jiao Jing, they had begun to pick up a little of the Hando tongue. They couldn't understand much of what the man said to them, but caught the words, "You stay here. Wait for Honorable Jiao."

As if they were going to trot down the gangplank and go wandering in a strange foreign city where they didn't speak the language, Gabriel thought. He wished he knew if there were a Temple of the Eight, or of Betsalel, here. Surely Jiao Jing would have mentioned it, though, when he'd told him about the gods' ability to transport worshipers between idols?

He gestured at his mouth, looking the crewman in the eyes, and said "Eat?" in his halting Hando. The man understood immediately, and smilingly led the children to the galley. Before the weather had gotten rough, they'd taken meals here with the crew on several occasions. The fare usually consisted of ship's biscuit and some kind of stew, frequently with fish in it.

Today, though, it seemed fresh supplies had been brought on board. The smiling cook gave them big steaming bowls of noodles in chicken broth, with fresh green vegetables and little meat dumplings floating in it. Neither of them had tasted anything so wonderful since they'd left home. They were working on second helpings when Jiao Jing appeared. He had changed clothes since they had last seen him, and appeared to have had a bath as well. But his expression was one of anxiety.

"Are you well?" he asked, examining them in the light of day. For much of their storm-tossed passage, they had scarcely been able to see once the shutters had been closed on the crew cabin's little windows. The girl looked wan, almost all of the skin dye worn from her pale, freckled skin. Yet there were spots of color in her cheeks, thanks to the hot and hearty soup.

"We're all right, Honorable Jiao," Gabriel assured him. "Just a few more meals and we'll be fine. Is this Tzinshai? When can we go home?" Clearly, the boy was feeling better. While he'd struggled to get water down them, neither of the children had had much to say beyond feeble groans.

"This is Tzinshai," the merchant admitted. "I have been ashore, consulting with my employees and visiting with my wives." He gestured at his clean raiment. They looked at him eagerly. It had been such a long, hard trip, but finally they were here! Soon surely, they would be safe back at home.

"But the news is not good," he went on grimly. "I have learned that a woman such as the sorceress you described has been seen in the city, asking after two young Gaspari children. You must not leave this ship!" Their faces fell. "Don't worry," Jiao assured them, "the Piao Qin leaves for Dongyi tomorrow morning, and we will all be on it. From there we can go to the Celestial City, Tiangong, and seek protection from the king. He has sorcerers of his own at the palace, who can ward you from this Rajani and her arts. And from there it will finally be safe to take you home."

Now that the ship had taken on fresh water, the cook provided the children with enough hot water for them to bathe – in washtubs set on the floor of the galley. Jiao had brought them fresh clothing as well, traveling clothes of the sort Hando children might wear, and for each of them a red tunic of silk brocade with dragons on it. "Red is considered a lucky color among the Hando," he explained. May it, and your dragon talismans, shield you from the arts of Rajani."

Gabriel and Berta felt so much better after the hot lunch, not to mention being clean and dressed in fresh clothing, that they were almost willing to overlook their disappointment. For weeks they'd been told that once they were in Tzinshai they would be safe, and would soon be returned home. Yet now it was to be more days, perhaps as much as two more weeks, before they would reach Tiangong. From what Jiao said of the place, the Celestial City was one of the wonders of the eastern world. So perhaps, it would not be so bad to go there. Just so there were no more storms!

There were not. Weather conditions in the Eastern Ocean along Hanshu's east coast were far different from those to the south and west; and the further north they sailed, now in late summer, the more clement the weather became. Days were bright and breezy, nights calm, and the horrors of the journey from Tongnan were forgotten as Jurgen and Gerdur ran around the decks, threw lines over the side in hopes of hooking fresh fish for supper, even volunteered to help the cook in the galley as he chopped vegetables and rolled dumplings for soups and stews.

By the time they pulled into port at Dongyi, five days after leaving Tzinshai, both children had a much better command of Hando than they had owned a couple of weeks previously. They lacked some key words and phrases, ones that would have let them be understood had they wished to flee from Jiao Jing and tell the authorities, "We have been kidnaped and wish to be taken to the temple of Betsalel." But if they should really need to get away, they would at least not be as lost and helpless as before.

Yet they were only seven years old, used to accepting the authority of adults. Honorable Jiao had been nothing but kind to them, offering no threats such as they had received from Rajani and her goddess. He had spent a lot of money seeing to their needs, as well, and was a respected merchant. They were sure that he was taking them in good faith to where he could return them safely home and collect the reward they had promised him.

So there were no thoughts of escape. They stayed the night in a comfortable inn near the broad highway that led from Dongyi to Tiangong; and in the morning the three of them, mounted on their tall Shuang horses, were riding along it headed east. The Celestial City awaited!

Chapter 36

Only three days behind, the Cai Yuan caught much of the same weather the Piao Qin had endured. Summer was a time of storms all along the continent's southern coast east of Palambo. But Leila and Tevo endured the voyage in much greater comfort than the children and their "rescuer" had.

They had a cozy private cabin to relax in, for one thing – safe and dry while rain lashed the decks above. Their god's gift of immunity to motion sickness meant that their appetites remained hearty. If the weather wasn't too bad Honorable Ming Shao and his elder brother Honorable Ming Tai would make their way to the dining room for whatever the cook had prepared for them. Leila and Tevo were coming to find they liked the flavors of Hando cooking.

The storms were a great excuse for them to remain in their cabin, as well. There, one or the other of them could have Betsalel take them home for a hot bath, clean underclothes, and a visit with the family for a few hours. It was a pity they couldn't both go together, but Betsalel was uncertain that he would be unable to return them to an idol that had been left completely alone.

They spent a lot of time in that cabin reading books they'd brought from home, nibbling on goodies Elyzia had insisted they take back with them, and making love. After a bath, a shave, and a change to clean clothes Tevo looked so much better Leila just wanted to devour him.

Not even giving birth to two children and living a life of ease had managed to put much weight on Leila's frame. She got that natural tendency toward lean muscle from her father, she thought – along with her dark skin and black hair. But after days of lying about and snacking, she felt as if her traveling clothes were beginning to get a little snug. Horrors!

She took to sneaking out of their cabin at night, under the cloak of her shadow power, and doing gymnastics up in the rigging – if the wind wasn't blowing too much. Though stormy it was warm, and if her underwear got soaked it wasn't a problem – she could wring it out before coming back inside and it would dry, hanging in their cabin, by morning. Soon she felt she was back in fighting trim.

The weather had eased by the time they reached Tzinshai, with overcast skies and a light breeze blowing. The two Hando merchants descended the gangplank with their minimal luggage at two in the afternoon, among a small flood of other passengers. Cai Yuan was a merchantman, but her owners made good money ferrying passengers as well as cargo. She would offload the last of it here, then take on a new cargo of Hando goods and begin the journey south again.

Feeling remarkably well and rested, Leila and Tevo were in high spirits. Tzinshai at last! Soon they would be able to collar this Jiao Jing and find out exactly what he thought he was doing. He knew they were coming after the children, had received a detailed note telling him to wait for them in Balore and receive a generous reward. Instead, he had taken the kids and fled as quickly as he could into Hanshu.

But how to find him? Tzinshai was a major seaport, second only to Dongyi along Hanshu's eastern coast. Betsalel reported that he had no clear sense of Gabriel here, so whatever masking effect had been applied was still working strongly – or else, something they were not willing to think about yet, the children were not here.

The Royal Office of Sea Commerce was clearly visible, a three-story brick building in a central location along the waterfront. Unlike many of the world's major harbor cities Tzinshai had no navigable river flowing through it. The bay that formed its harbor was entirely man-made, excavated in ancient times. It was roughly rectangular, lined in stone and concrete, and the entrance to it was flanked by fortifications. A wall surrounded the city itself, but there was evidence that it was falling into disrepair. Hanshu had been a united nation for centuries, and it had no serious enemies.

The horses were in a state of bliss to be free of the miserable confines of the below-decks stalls they'd lived in for the past several days. The traders left their mounts tied to a post outside and went in, whereupon Honorable Ming Tai approached a window in the office and spoke with the clerk. "Greetings, honorable sir," he said, with a slight bow. The clerk gave him a deeper bow, as a token of respect to an elder. Hando culture, Leila had noticed, reverenced older people much more than was the case in either the Dominion or Palambo.

"I am Ming Tai, a trader of Tongnan," the older man told the clerk. "My brother and I have just arrived and are seeking a fellow trader whom we met in Tongnan a little over a week ago, Honorable Jiao Jing. He mentioned that he was traveling here, where his trading office is located, and we are hoping to set up some business arrangements with him. Might you direct us to his company's offices?"

Jiao and his brother were primarily land traders, carrying the goods of Hanshu and Indaya along the Ivory Road and trading for the goods of the Dominion and Palambo in Miradil. But the clerk, a man in his early thirties, had worked here in the Tzinshai office for more than a decade and he knew of the Jiao trading firm. "The Jiao brothers' firm is called Black Dragon Imports," he told the older man. "You will find their warehouse on the Street of Pearls. Go down Sunset Street, which is next to our office on your left as you came in. Then go five blocks up and you will see a sign for Street of Pearls on the building at the northwest corner of the intersection. Go down that street to your right another three blocks, and you will see Ling Zao on their sign. Their trading office is on the ground floor of the building."

The Ming brothers thanked the clerk for the information and were soon riding down Sunset Street (which led west away from the harbor), looking around them and conversing (in Gasparto) within a bubble of silence. The illusory men's mouths did not move.

"Ahh, it feels good to be moving on land again," Leila said.

"I agree," Tevo replied. Boat travel had never been his favorite means of transport. Though he had not really learned to ride until he was an adult, he greatly preferred being in the saddle – especially with a mount as sweet as Milacek.

Thank Betsalel they were able to read all the signs! The literacy rate must be high in Hanshu, for their curious-looking ideograms were everywhere – on signs, or painted on the sides of buildings. Most buildings in this part of town, near the waterfront, appeared to be of brick or stone and between two and four storeys in height.

They soon came to the Street of Pearls, slightly narrower than Sunset Street but still a broad thoroughfare. All the streets surrounding the harbor were bustling with commerce, and they needed to be broad to accommodate large wains full of trade goods moving to and from the ships.

The headquarters of Black Dragon Imports were impressive. The building was of unpainted dark gray stone, three storeys high, and had a small window overlooking the street beside a door painted red. To the right of that were broad double doors of heavy red-painted wood banded in iron, for the loading and unloading of freight. And above those a long wooden sign announced the company name above the sinuous figure of a black dragon.

Leila got a strange feeling in her gut as she beheld the sign. It was not exactly terror, such as Cyryl Kubasz had told her the signs of Betsalel had produced when he and his posse of thief takers had tried to break into the original Shadow Manor. It was more like a hint of unease, a vague foreboding.

She called the god to his idol in her pocket. "Master, is that sign something beyond a commercial nameplate?" The thing was twenty feet across and six feet high, whereas most businesses in the Dominion preferred less ostentatious signage. The Shadow God spoke in both their minds.

"Ahh," he said. "Now I understand. That is Ling Zao, the god of earthquakes. He is an ancient daemon, though not worshiped much outside of Hanshu. I have never met him, but I can sense his essence. He is also, curiously, considered to be the god of financial prosperity. This sign is imbued with his protection, and if you came here with ill intent you might find yourself very reluctant to go inside."

"I'll be sure to hold good thoughts then," Leila replied as silently. Linked thus with the god, she and Tevo could communicate mind to mind. In truth, both of them were angry with Jiao Jing for the chase he had led them on. But they didn't intend to rob or kill him, so they hoped the daemon's protection would let them through. It did.

They opened the door and went into the trading office, a room no more than ten feet wide but more than thirty feet deep. A counter ran across the width of the room six feet inside the door, restricting visitors to a small lobby area. Behind the counter three desks were set up in a row down the left wall while the right one held shelves for files and office supplies. At the back a door led, one might assume, to the warehouse.

A young man working with papers at the desk nearest the front door stood up as they came in and walked to the counter. The men who had come in appeared to be fellow traders from their garb, men in their mid to late forties. He bowed politely and said "Welcome to Black Dragon Imports. How may I help you?"

The two bowed to him in turn, and the elder man said, "I am Ming Tai and this is my brother Ming Shao, traders from Tongnan. We would like to speak with Honorable Jiao Jing, if we might." The young man eyed them curiously.

"I'm sorry," he said, "but my father is not here at this time. He and my uncle are conducting a caravan from the west, and will not return to Tzinshai for another few weeks."

The brothers exchanged glances. Was it possible Jiao would not even communicate with his own son? It seemed awfully unlikely. "But we met with Jiao Jing in Tongnan not two weeks ago," Ming Tai said. "He was traveling with two young western children, and said he was on his way here by ship to arrange for their return home. Did he not arrive safely?"

Jiao Sing had a moment of doubt. Father had warned him to be on the lookout for Gaspari agents pursuing him and the children he had said he was taking to the king. But these were just a pair of Hando merchants. If they had truly seen him in Tongnan they would know he was lying about Father still being out with the caravan, and that could be awkward. Plus, it might spoil a business opportunity.

While the son of the man they sought was conducting his internal debate Leila reached for her god again. "This man before us," she asked, "is he under the protection of Ling Zao?"

"Yes," the answer came at once. "He and the other two in this office all bear that daemon's protection." In the case of daemons who had been worshiped as gods for millennia, the distinction between god and daemon was one of origin, only. They could have powers every bit as great as any of the Eight, especially in places where they had more worshipers.

That ruled out the possibility of Betsalel looking into the man's mind and learning the truth. But perhaps Ming Tai might cozen him into revealing it? "It's all right," he said in confidential tones, "you can tell us. Your father was concerned that people wanting to take the western children from him were in pursuit. A couple of days after he sailed from Tongnan, we met these pursuers. A pair of Gaspari agents, a man and a woman. We told them we had not seen Honorable Jiao or the children, but they seemed to have some secret source of knowledge that he had passed through Tongnan. As my brother and I were traveling here in any case for some business dealings, we thought we would stop by and warn your father that they have hired the Royal Messenger Service to bring word here. They wish to enlist the aid of the Wan Hui Tong to capture the children and do away with your father, thus avoiding having to pay the reward that was promised for the children's return."

Jiao Sing's eyes widened. The Wan Hui Tong! That almost legendary criminal gang had operated in Hanshu for nearly two centuries, and was rumored to have branches in every major city. And the Royal Messenger Service might well have brought word even before Father had left again. But the Tong would be looking for him in Tzinshai, and he was already gone. By now he should be almost to Dongyi.

"I thank you, Honorable Ming Tai," he said formally. "But you need not fear for my father's safety or that of the children with him. They left again on the same ship that brought them here, two days ago. They will now be safely out of the reach of both the Tong and these Gaspari agents you saw. But I appreciate your concern, and will tell Father of your kindness when next I see him."

The impassive Hando traders walked their horses back the way they had come, avoiding traffic. "Wan Hui Tong?" Tevo asked.

"It's a real thing," his wife replied. "I read about it in that book we had on the voyage from Tongnan. Supposedly it was founded centuries ago and now controls a lot of the criminal operations in Hanshu. I have no idea how you'd go about hiring them, though."

"Too bad," he replied. "They might have better luck than we have, so far." After a moment he added, "Could Jiao and the children have gone back to Tongnan?" He was pleased to have Jiao's son admit that his father had been here, and with the children. But try as he might to shield himself against disappointment, the knowledge that they had once again eluded him and Leila was like a knife in the guts.

"I don't believe it for a minute," Leila replied.

"What, you think the kid lied?" Tevo asked. "Do we need to find out where the Jiao family lives and check there?"

"I'm tempted to stick around town and find out where his grandchildren are so we can snatch them. See how *he* likes it," she said grimly. Tevo got a little shiver. He had rarely witnessed his wife at her most lethal, but he knew she was a force to be reckoned with.

"But no," she went on. "We need to check at the Commerce Office and see where the ship went. I don't think it's going to have been Tongnan." Ming Tai spoke once more with the clerk he'd talked with not half an hour before. "The Piao Qin? Out of Dongyi?" The trader nodded.

"She sailed for her home port two mornings ago," he said. "According to the record, she will be there for a further two weeks undergoing annual maintenance before returning to Tzinshai. Are you interested in arranging for her to carry your freight?"

"Uh, no... We will not have freight to carry until after we have met with Honorable Jiao Jing, I'm afraid," the trader replied. "We are interested in joining him in Dongyi. Are there any ships departing soon?" The clerk checked the chart on the back wall, then consulted a ledger.

"The next ship sailing for Dongyi will be day after tomorrow. I have no others, but probably there will soon be some arriving. They don't get into our ledgers until they have made port and registered with us, I'm afraid."

Jiao Jing and the kids were already two days ahead of them. Could they let them expand that lead to the better part of a week? "We haven't been in this area in some years," the younger of the traders said. "How is the highway between Tzinshai and Dongyi, these days?"

The clerk smiled. "Our great king Wang Qian, may he rule forever, has done much to ensure the smooth flow of commerce within the realm. Only five years ago a project to widen and level the coast road was completed, and it is now one of the finest highways in Hanshu. There are inns at frequent intervals, and the road is patrolled by the Royal Guard lest bandits molest travelers. You should be able to reach Dongyi by horse only two or three days later than you might sailing on the ship that leaves two days from now. Do you need to acquire horses?"

Aha, Leila thought. That sounded a lot like a sales pitch, and now I see why. "Thank you," Ming Tai said somewhat stiffly. "We are already mounted. Good day to you." The clerk's smooth face masked his disappointment as the two wealthy-looking merchants took their leave.

They had emerged from the Cai Yuan remarkably well-rested, and the horses were eager to move. But they needed to acquire a few supplies before they could begin the journey north. The Commerce Office clerk had expected it to take four more days on the road than would be required to sail there. But he didn't know that these merchants' horses, and the merchants as well, were tireless. If they rode hard, they might even shorten Jiao Jing's lead. Within an hour, well-laden with food and water, Nimble and Milacek were galloping north on the highway to Dongyi.

Chapter 37

The road between Dongyi and the Celestial City ran beside a river, the Sheng Jiang, that was slow and broad as it spilled into the Eastern Ocean. But as that road continued east and north, the river lay below it and a mile or so to the east, rushing clear and cold through a deep canyon.

Compared with their trip south and east through Indaya during the monsoon, this was a pleasant ride. The days were warm enough to be comfortable, and though there was often rain in the afternoons it was not the drenching downpour they'd experienced before. Jiao had provided them all with hooded cloaks that repelled a great deal of the rain, as well.

Nights were spent in comfortable inns, where they ate hot suppers in the evening and usually breakfasted on tea and cakes before getting underway again. Each morning they had the cook pack them a lunch that could be eaten on the road. There was much traffic on the road in both directions, but far fewer wains and wagons than they had seen on other highways.

"Why are there so many people on foot here, Honorable Jiao?" Gabriel asked.

"Tiangong is not by any means the largest city in Hanshu," the trader explained as they rode along. "But it is our capital, and the most beautiful and holy place in the kingdom. Most of the people you will see coming and going along this rode are not merchants or jobbers, but pilgrims."

"Pilgrims?" Berta asked. The city she'd been raised in was considered the holiest in the Dominion, and many pilgrims came there to worship at its Temple of the Eight. Jiao realized that he had blundered by mentioning it, and considered carefully before answering.

"Many gods who are worshiped in Hanshu have their chief temples in Tiangong. The priests will tell you that you are more likely to have your prayers answered if you worship there, rather than at any of their other temples or shrines."

I wonder if there is a temple of Betsalel there, Gabriel thought. But he didn't say it out loud. He was beginning to get the sense that

Jiao Jing was not in any hurry to see them returned to their parents. Ever since he'd mentioned that the Shadow God could carry them home, their rescuer had abruptly become very concerned about Rajani catching up with them. Instead, he asked "Tiangong is where the seat of Hanshu's government is located?"

"The royal palace is there," Jiao replied, "and the head offices of the royal government are located there as well though not within the palace itself. Most of the daily operations of government are run through the provincial capitals around the country."

"We have something like that in the Dominion," Berta put in. She had largely abandoned trying to pretend she was Gudrun, younger child of a Palamban merchant.

"Except in the Dominion," she went on, "The counties rule themselves without much interference by the Imperial government. They must obey the constitution, and Imperial guards are garrisoned in most cities to help keep the peace, but people in a local region mostly do things however they prefer. It's kept us from having any major wars for more than a thousand years."

Jiao eyed her. Except for her hair, which was still mostly dark brown with nearly an inch of red roots, the girl was unmistakably the Gaspari empress's daughter. He had never beheld any of the Imperial family before having this girl and her dark little friend fall into his hands, but he had seen portraits of them.

There was an excellent recent one, in oils, hanging in a place of prominence within the headquarters of the Imperial Trade Office, where he'd had occasion to go several times a year since long before Ostden had succeeded to the Gaspari throne. In the picture little Berta Piastin had been no more than four, the Imperial heir a baby sitting on his mother's knee.

He wondered who the dark boy really was. His claim to be the son of a Palamban was certainly believable, from his appearance. But whatever his origins, the girl clearly relied on him to be her anchor in their distressed circumstances. Jiao was content to let him come along for the ride. If the child was best friends with the daughter of the emperor, his family must surely be wealthy and well-connected.

Returning his attention to the discussion at hand, Jiao said "Our king is considered to rule by divine will. Therefore his decrees have the power of law. But most of Hanshu's rulers have seen fit to let things go on as they have been, without making changes. The government runs smoothly enough, and the peasants are well under control. We, too, have long been at peace."

Their journey continued at a comfortable pace, with several brief stops per day so that the middle-aged man and his young charges could relieve themselves, have some food and water, or just stretch their legs. Jiao did not fear that the children would try to escape, though it was clear they were both expert riders. They were thousands of miles from home after all, in a strange land where no one spoke their language; and he was their only friend.

The road climbed ever higher, still following the course of the Sheng Jiang. If you stopped beside the road and listened, you could almost hear the waters rushing along a mile away and a thousand feet down. The journey to Tiangong should take six days, Jiao had told them, and on the third night they stopped at an inn beside the road in the small town of Xia Gu, which spread north from the road almost to the river canyon.

At this point they were only in the foothills of the Shan Lings, and there was much agriculture in the region. Fruit trees marched across the hills on either side of the road, and Gabriel and Berta nearly made themselves sick gobbling down fresh plums and peaches. There had been little fresh fruit available on their long, hard journey and this was a treat beyond compare.

The children turned in early, and Jiao Jing made for the common room after making sure they were tucked in and sleeping. He knew this inn of old, having often traveled the road from Dongyi to Tiangong acting as an agent for his father before he and Shao had taken over the business. It was still run by the same man, Lee Ho Sing, who had been operating the place a quarter of a century before.

He was aged now, once glossy black hair gone silver; but his face was unlined and he seemed as spry as ever. He immediately recognized Jiao Jing as well, though they had not met in nearly a decade. "Jiao Jing, my old friend," the innkeeper said with a deep bow, "what brings you to Xia Gu? I have not seen you in many a year."

Jiao gave him a friendly smile and a bow nearly, but not quite, as deep. In the subtle and complex social hierarchy of Hanshu, a wealthy, well-traveled merchant had an edge over the owner of a single small town inn. "Well met, Lee Ho," he replied. "I suppose you might say that I am just another pilgrim. My business activities no longer bring me this way, I'm afraid."

The innkeeper poured two cups of plum wine and passed one over the bar. Then he looked right and left and said in a low voice, "What's with the two western children? Do you have a wife I don't know about?" Jiao grinned in amusement at the idea of Berta and her dark little friend being offspring of his. Surely, it would have required at least two extra wives to produce two such different children.

"They were found wandering on the Ivory Road," he explained. "They were kidnaped out of Miradil by some Nima witch, or so they told me, and I'm taking them to Tiangong to make arrangements for them to be returned home." Lee Ho eyed him thoughtfully.

"So, you were eastward bound when you found them?" Had the caravan been heading west, they might merely have taken the children along with them until they got to Miradil.

Jiao nodded. "Heading east, and already nearly halfway to Changtze," he said. "They claimed that this witch had arcane powers, and was a devotee of Danava. I thought it best to take them as far as possible from the seats of the Destroyer's power." They both downed their cups of the light, sweet wine and Lee Ho poured more.

"You're going far out of your way to help these children," he remarked casually. "Out of the kindness of your heart?" He knew Jiao Jing too well. The trader's smile didn't reach his eyes.

"What do you think, Lee Ho? Of course they have promised that their parents will pay a large reward for their safe return. They are, so they said, the children of a wealthy Palamban merchant and a Gaspari woman."

Lee Ho had gotten a good look at them when they came into the inn, and he had never seen an odder-looking pair. The boy might pass for Dravim, he supposed, but if the girl was truly his sister they must have had different fathers. "And you believe them?" he asked, careful not to pry too hard though his curiosity was burning within him. Jiao took another sip of his wine.

"That they are brother and sister?" he said. "I doubt it. That they are the children of a wealthy Palamban merchant, I am not sure. That there will be a magnificent reward, I have no doubt."

"And what of this Nima sorceress?" Lee Ho asked. If the children were a valuable target pursued by someone with supernatural powers, having them under his roof might be a risk. "Days behind us, if she has not lost the trail altogether," Jiao Jing assured him. He had no worries about Rajani. She would have caught them while they were traveling through Indaya, had she been after them at all.

But the Gaspari agents who had sent the message to him in Balore were another story. From the tone of their letter, they would not give up so easily. And likely they had the resources to track him all the way to Tiangong, though he had a good head start. But he could not just stroll into the royal palace and demand an audience with the king. How long would it take for him to be seen, and how long might negotiations go on before he had gotten what he wanted? It would be better if the agents could be stopped, somehow.

"Lee Ho," he asked casually, "do you still have contact with some of the local bully boys?" Things had quieted down in Xia Gu over the past decades, but there had once been bandits and outlaws along the road and years ago the inn had hired young men, little better than the bandits themselves, as bouncers and guards to protect the inn and its patrons.

"Just Zhin Gao over there," the innkeeper said, gesturing with his head. A hulking young man in his early twenties stood leaning up against the wall near the front door, looking out into the room and cleaning his fingernails with a small dagger. Jiao grinned.

"A lovely specimen," he remarked. Lee Ho shrugged.

"We don't have the need for security here we did twenty years ago. Why, did you want to hire him as a guard on your journey to Tiangong?"

Jiao shook his head. "The road is safe enough," he said, "but I'm concerned about that sorceress. Should she be on our trail herself, or if perhaps she has hired others to chase us down, they will likely be traveling up the Sheng Jiang road just as we are. I would like to have someone watching our back trail for pursuers, someone who could… detain any who come. Once I have gotten the children to Tiangong, I hope to return them home and claim my reward within a couple of weeks. But I can't have the sorceress showing up there before then. There is a temple to Danava in Tiangong, and her powers will be enhanced."

There was a temple to every god, goddess, or minor deity known to be worshiped by man in Tiangong, Lee Ho knew well. A large part of his business was from the pilgrims traveling there. He called to the thug at the door, "Zhin Gao! Come here!" The man tucked his dagger away and came at once. He knew who paid his wages.

When the young man had arrived at the bar Lee Ho introduced him to his old friend. "Zhin Gao, this is Honorable Jiao Jing, a wealthy and important merchant of Tzinshai. He has a business proposition for you."

"Thank you, Lee Ho," the trader said, then addressed the "security man." He had to look up to do so, as Honorable Zhin overtopped him by several inches.

"I am taking two western children to Tiangong to see that they are returned to their parents," he said. "There is a possibility that I am being followed, by the Nima sorceress who kidnaped them in Miradil or by agents she has hired. I need some people to watch the road, and if any come asking after these children to stop them from coming after us. Do you have some friends who could help you in this? I will pay well."

Zhin looked him up and down. He certainly dressed the part of a wealthy merchant, and his boss had vouched for the man so he was probably good for the coin. Standing around the common room every evening ready to expel rowdy drunks and take down cutpurses was boring work, and paid little beyond an evening meal and free drinks. The merchant's proposal sounded far more interesting, and likely a great deal more rewarding.

"Sure," he said, "I can round up a few friends. You want this person or her hirelings tossed into the canyon?" Jiao Jing paled. He was not a murderer!

"No, nothing permanent please. I just need anyone who is asking after me or the children to be delayed. Drug them, perhaps, rob them of their gold, hold them captive for a couple of weeks and then let them go. Without money, they will be unable to continue their pursuit with any speed. By the time they can follow me to Tiangong, the children and I will be long gone."

Chapter 38

The clerk at the Royal Office of Sea Commerce had not been exaggerating. The coast road between Tzinshai and Dongyi was the equal of any highway the Gaspari Dominion could boast –broad, well-paved, and with up-and-downhill stretches kept to a minimum. Clearly Hando engineering had been developed to a high art, for much of the coast was rugged and hilly, with small streams spilling out into the Eastern Ocean along its length. As the Ming brothers galloped along the road, they must have crossed more than a hundred finely-made stone bridges.

There was little conversation during the day. They let the horses run at a comfortable pace from morning until night, stopping only when their shaken bladders could stand it no longer. They ate trail rations, and drank from their water skins, in the saddle. The time spent on the Cai Yuan, trapped below decks during days of storm, now glimmered in the travelers' minds as a vision of better times – times when they'd been clean, well fed, and had leisure to enjoy each other's company.

They usually kept going until dark, or even beyond it if a moon was in the sky. It all depended on the availability of an inn with stabling for the horses. Nimble and Milacek needed a lot of grain to fuel their marathon runs each day, or they would have taken the energy they needed from the substance of their bodies and melted away into nothing. While the stable hands marveled at the appetites of the traders' horses, the brothers themselves would be hastily downing as much of whatever hot food the inn had to offer as they could. Then they would fall into bed.

Thus, it was only midday of the fifth day after they left Tzinshai that Leila and Tevo came at last to the outskirts of Dongyi: Hanshu's second-largest port city, serving most of the northern part of the country. It reminded Leila of her first sight of Iskand in Palambo – thousands of miles to the south and east of here, but as busy and as sprawling. She and her companions had come in by riverboat from the south and had ridden their horses past miles of river docks before reaching the city proper.

Here, though, there was little river commerce. The Sheng Jiang, the "Holy River" that spilled its waters into the Eastern Ocean north of Dongyi's center, was navigable for only around two hundred miles upstream. Then it became a raging mountain torrent, spilling out of the Shan Ling mountains' eastern slopes. Most of the goods that came into Dongyi by ship left by wagon, along the kingdom's excellent roads.

Leila and Tevo felt pleased with themselves. They had gotten here in no more time than it would have taken a fast sailing ship such as the Cai Yuan to make the journey. Of course, it had required them to pay for food and lodging in a succession of inns, and ride hard all day until their backsides were as stiff as their saddles; but here they were. And now, the question was: where were Jiao Jing and the children?

The coast road had spilled out onto a still broader, curving, stone-paved road that ran along the waterfront for miles, and as they approached the center of Dongyi's natural bay they spotted the place they were looking for: The Royal Office of Sea Commerce.

This time, though, the clerk was less helpful. There were no ships traveling between Dongyi and the Dominion. People in Hanshu wishing to export goods to the Dominion usually had them taken by road around the southern end of the Shan Lings, before loading their cargo onto river boats. And in any case, if Jiao Jing had intended to return the children to the Dominion by ship, and had not wanted to use river transport, he would have taken ship from Tongnan south to the ports in southern Palambo. From there, one could go by ocean all the way north to the Straits of Andala and thence into the Center Sea.

Likewise, the clerk at the Sea Commerce office did not know of any Black Dragon Imports office in Dongyi. The two middle-aged traders left there with directions to the Dongyi government offices in the center of town, where they might learn whether such a trading company was registered. All who did business here were required to have a government-issued license. Except in places like the lands of the Gholim it seemed, bureaucracy was the way of the modern world.

Two hours later, beginning to get discouraged, Ming Tai and his brother left the small offices of Black Dragon Imports' Dongyi branch. They had no warehouse in this city, it had turned out, just a little hole-in-the-wall office where a pair of functionaries handled transactions. Many of Hanshu's finest goods came through this port, and some of them would eventually find their way to Miradil.

But the clerk had not seen his boss in ages, did not even know Jiao Jing by sight. He had been hired by one of the Jiao family years ago, and did all of his correspondence with the Tzinshai office by mail. Leila was inclined to believe him.

On the street outside, the traders mounted their horses and turned the animals' heads back toward the harbor. "Back to the Sea Commerce office?" Tevo asked, trying to stifle his frustration. After their headlong rush to get here, they had been brought to a standstill.

"The guy at the Tzinshai Commerce office said the Piao Qin would be undergoing maintenance here for another couple of weeks," Leila replied. "It should still be here. Let's find out where it is, and see if we can talk to any of her crew. Someone might know where their passengers were heading from here."

They found the Piao Qin, a smaller and older-looking ship than the Cai Yuan, winched up on runners in a huge dry-dock facility. A dozen men were swarming over her, scraping her bottom, caulking her seams, and checking the integrity of her fittings, lines, and sails. Such maintenance was the cost of doing business along the coast of the Southern Ocean, where storms could put you on the bottom if your craft was less than seaworthy.

While the dozen men worked away at putting the old cargo junk back into service, two others – more finely dressed – stood watching the labor and taking notes. The visitors approached them. Giving a bow carefully calculated to indicate a greeting to an equal, Ming Tai introduced himself. "Greetings, honorable sirs," he said with exquisite politeness. Civility was of crucial importance in Hando society, Leila and Tevo had learned.

"My brother and I are business associates of Honorable Jiao Jing, proprietor of Black Dragon Imports. We have come from Tzinshai with important news for him, having learned from his son that he had traveled to Dongyi on this vessel." The older of the two men nodded and returned the trader's bow.

"I am Sing Tze, owner and captain of the Piao Qin" he said. "Honorable Jiao Jing did indeed sail with us from Tongnan, staying only one night in Tzinshai before continuing north with us. He and his two young wards were very anxious to be on their way. They and their horses debarked as soon as we had come into port four days ago, and immediately rode off."

"Do you know where they were bound?" Ming Shao asked, and Sing Tze shook his head.

"We do not ordinarily carry passengers," he explained. "Honorable Jiao and his charges slept in hammocks in the crew's quarters and dined with them in the mess. I rarely had the chance to speak with them, being busy running the ship; but one of my crewmen may know more."

He called to one of the men nearby, who was standing near the ship's keel removing barnacles with a steel scraper. "Yuan! Come here a moment." The man turned and looked at him, puzzled, then set down his tools and came to stand with the group. He saluted the captain, and looked at him questioningly.

"You spoke with our recent passengers during our voyage up from Tzinshai, did you not?" Once the weather had eased the children had been all over the place, and though they'd been supposed to stay out of the sailors' way there had been some interaction. The captain didn't mind, so long as the work got done. The little ones had been strange-looking, but cute.

The young seaman smiled. He was around Leila's age, and not a great deal bigger than she was in truth. Ming Tai, of course, towered above him. "Honorable Jiao did not have much to say," he replied, "and the children mostly spoke some barbarian tongue – Gasparto, maybe, or whatever it is they speak in Palambo." He'd never been to either of those far-off lands, though he'd traveled widely in his young life.

"But the little ones seemed eager to learn," he went on. "While I was scrubbing decks they would come and talk with me, asking for words and trying to carry on a conversation in Hando." Leila's heart clenched. In the weeks she'd been searching for her son, this was the first time she had spoken with anyone who had seen him and interacted with him as a person since they had left Jiao Shao and his caravan on the Ivory Road. She looked expectantly at Yuan, hoping he would have more to say.

"They asked me about Tiangong a lot," Yuan concluded. "I think Honorable Jiao may have told them that he was taking them to the Celestial City." Ming Tai slipped a handful of silver to Yuan and thanked him, then thanked the captain as well before he and his brother took their leave.

The port's dry-dock facilities were far to the northern end of the harbor, and the road that ran along the waterfront soon intersected with the Sheng Jiang road – the river road that ran all the way north-by-northwest to Tiangong, on the lower slopes of the Shan Lings. As they urged their horses to a canter, Leila called their god.

"We think they may have gone to the Celestial City," Leila told him. In the book she'd read during their sea voyage, it had said that Tiangong was the seat of the royal government and also called "The City of a Thousand Gods. "There is a temple of the Eight in Tiangong," Betsalel replied. "Shall I carry you there?"

Leila and Tevo considered. Were they to go to Tiangong at once, there might be some issues with bystanders when the idol of Betsalel suddenly sprouted two horses and their riders. But of deeper concern was their uncertainty – they had only the sailor Yuan's "may have" to convince them that Jiao was even taking the children there. The trader had been doing business within Hanshu for all his adult life and probably had contacts all over the country. The river road had dozens of offshoots, some of them major roads leading to cities in the interior. If they hurtled headlong to Tiangong, would they be back to waiting as they had begun in Ghezh, hoping that the children's abductor would appear?

Leila dismounted and pulled out her tiny idol, holding it in the palm of her hand. The miniscule god stepped carefully, rotating through a full circle until he was once again facing up the river road in the direction of Tiangong. "What little I can sense of Gabriel tells me he is in that direction," the Shadow God said.

"Let's pursue them on horseback for now, and check again at each crossroads to make sure they are still moving in that direction," she replied.

Tevo nodded agreement, and the god said "Very well. We can always go directly to Tiangong as soon as you have decided that's where they are truly going."

Lunchtime had been hours ago, and both of them were starving. But neither of them were willing to stop for the night in midafternoon, even if that might be more convenient. They stopped at an inn and got the horses nosebags full of grain to munch while the two Ming brothers devoured mounds of wheat noodles drenched in a savory sauce and laden with vegetables and prawns. They were not on the road again until around five, but this far north (a hundred miles or so south of Parat) the sun still went down late in Canis. There were another four hours at least before it would become too dark to see.

Chapter 39

They had left all crossroads behind, and the road had become both steeper and more winding. The Sheng Jiang, now a shallow, rushing mountain stream no more than fifty yards from bank to bank, ran a quarter of a mile away to their right. And ahead on the mountainside above, the Celestial City glowed in the midday sun like a beacon.

"It's so beautiful!" Berta gasped, looking up. Today she was the one guiding Bai Shu, as Gabriel sat behind her with his arms wrapped around her waist. Ever since they had left Tzinshai, he had been feeling increasingly uneasy about Honorable Jiao. As he thought back on it, ever since they had first met the man there had been something… not quite true about him. He was usually friendly, even grandfatherly. But things he told them did not happen, and his story kept changing. He and Berta would have been back in Parat weeks ago, except for Jiao's insistence that they must keep moving to avoid Rajani's clutches. But once they had left Indaya behind, wouldn't her powers have been weakened? He wasn't sure what their rescuer's motives were, but increasingly he distrusted the man.

All this was driven out of his mind, though, by the sight of the Celestial City above them on the road ahead. They had been riding toward this goal for days, yet the reality was more dazzling than anything he'd been told. It stood like a jewel set into the mountainside, polished stone in a dozen different colors gleaming from its walls. Above the walls, the citadel of the royal palace shone stark white, but glittering in the sun in a way that suggested it had been built from some crystalline mineral.

Tiangong's setting itself was lovely enough. The eastern slopes of the Shan Lings were cut deeply by heavy rains in some areas, soft sandstone carved into fantastic shapes. In other spots, including the area immediately around Tiangong, the mountains were of pale gray stone and heavily wooded with conifers of types the Gaspari children had never seen before.

Sensing his riders' eagerness, and eager enough himself for a comfortable stall and a bag of grain, Bai Shu picked up the pace a little. Jiao glanced sideways at them, and nudged his own mount to a little more speed. They were so happy to be walking into the dragon's mouth! This journey had not been without effort or expense, and that first leg of the voyage from Tongnan had been bloody awful – but overall, it had been a walk in the park. And the reward would fulfill ambitions he had held for his entire adult life.

Tiangong was one of many walled cities in this land. Both children had visited Miradil, the only city of any size in the Dominion to have maintained its wall. But in Indaya, and here in Hanshu, they had seen a lot of them. Peace had settled over the land to the point where fortified places were beginning to become obsolete, however. In the modern era's atmosphere of negotiation as an alternative to armed conflict, such places might soon vanish altogether. It would have been a crime to set petards beneath the walls of Hanshu's Celestial City, in any case.

Berta thought the walls must surely be built of the same light gray stone as the mountains that surrounded it. They were twenty feet thick, at least, and though she supposed that the interior of them might be filled with rubble, it still made sense that they were constructed of the material that was in greatest local supply. Her education had included a lot of the martial history of the Dominion, though her sex meant she would never fight to defend that land – or rule it.

But over that gray stone had been laid slabs of green, red, yellow, black, deep blue, sparkling metallic gold and more – set in designs which, Berta gradually realized as they drew closer to the gates, represented the gods. Or at least, the symbols of the Eight she was familiar with were there. But what were all those others?

Gabriel, who sat a few inches taller than Berta in the double saddle behind her, leaned close and whispered in her right ear – on the side away from where Jiao rode. "See that red oval on black?" he murmured.

"Yes," she breathed.

"That's one of the symbols of Betsalel! Maybe there's a temple of Betsalel here, or a temple of the Eight, and we can go right home!" She took a hand off the reins and reached back for his, to give it a squeeze. As they lay snuggled in inn beds at night, they'd begun to discuss their situation. Berta trusted Jiao no more than he did, now.

As had been the case at every city gate they'd come to on their journey, the travelers were required to provide identification to the city guards and explain the purpose of their visit. It seemed silly to Gabriel, and he imagined enormous rooms, whole buildings, full from floor to ceiling with the books in which the guards recorded this information. Would any of it be looked at again? And so little effort was made to ensure that people entering the city were telling the truth. Why not just throw the gates open and let people go in and out as they pleased – at least until an army showed up?

Once inside the Celestial City, the children's eyes were wide as they took in the sights all around them. Tiangong seemed to have been built on a medium-sized, not-particularly-steep mountaintop, or at least the southeastern slope of it. Everything in the city led up from the gates, and all of it was overshadowed by the Royal Citadel, gleaming white at the summit.

Jiao seemed to know the place, and he led them without hesitation along winding streets that looped back and forth as they climbed higher toward the palace. Would he be taking them right to the king? Berta and Gabriel both fantasized about such a meeting.

For Princess Berta, elder child of a man who ruled nearly a third of the known world, the vision was of royal pomp and every courtesy shown, as she greeted the Hando king and was shortly returned to her family – with her beloved friend Gabe along for the ride. For Gabriel, there were troubling questions. He loved Berta, and her parents were quite all right too. So was his Bapa Vandao, who was a king as well. But this Hando king, whose name they didn't even know – would he take them under his wing and make sure they got home safely, or prove to be no more honorable than the "king" for whom Rajani had stolen them in the first place?

There were to be no kings in the immediate future, as it turned out. Before the party had climbed more than halfway up the hill, they came to a stop at a fine-looking residence of wood and stone, and Jiao commanded them to dismount. "Where are we?" Berta asked sharply. As the weeks had gone by, a lot of her princess-ness seemed to have reasserted itself. Jiao had given them no reason to fear for their lives, and she was slowly returning to her bossy (if adorable) self.

Jiao looked a little annoyed. He had been happy enough when the children were cowed, willing to accept everything he told them. The growing attitude of entitlement and authority he detected from the little princess did not please him. "We have arrived at the home of my friend Bian Tu, where we will stay until I have made arrangements with King Wang Qian for you to be returned to your family," he told them. "You will be made comfortable here, but you will show Honorable Bian every courtesy. Am I understood?"

The children exchanged glances. This was as close to domineering as their rescuer had been since they had met him. Was he now showing his true colors? "Of course, Honorable Jiao Jing," Berta said meekly. She needed to have a consultation with Gabe, as soon as they could be alone together. But at least, it looked as though the accommodations here might be far more comfortable than those they had endured over the past couple of weeks.

Chapter 40

The journey along the river road was proving to take far longer than had the trip from Tzinshai. This northern section of Hanshu was packed with humanity, it seemed, and every population center in it was connected to the river road that led to the city of cities, Tiangong. And at every intersection, either Leila or Tevo must dismount and have Betsalel check to make sure their quarry was still ahead of them.

In between stops they urged the horses forward at increased speed, hoping to make up for lost time. But it was still late on their third day of travel when they arrived at the small city of Xia Gu. In addition to using Betsalel as a guide, they had taken to making inquiries at the inns of whatever town they stopped in for the night. From the number of hostelries along this road, many travelers came this way. But they had been fortunate enough, last night, to visit the inn where Jiao and the children had stopped.

"Oh yes," the elderly female innkeeper had told them. "A nice-looking man of middle years, respectably dressed, with two small children. I fed them breakfast just three, or was it four, mornings ago. Very strange looking, the girl was." Now another day had ended. Had they gained any on their quarries, or were they still lagging more than three days behind?

Xia Gu was not one of the larger towns along the river road. Three inns faced the road, along with a grocer and some other shops that were now closed for the evening. There were quite a few people still out on the streets, though, some hurrying home for supper probably while others loitered waiting for whatever the town offered in the way of night life to begin.

The first inn on the right looked a little more substantial than the others, and the Ming brothers stopped there first. "Might as well put up here for the night," Ming Tai said. They rode their horses around to the back and left them in the care of a stable boy, then hefted their packs and went in through the inn's front door. The evening was young. A little refreshment, then they could probably canvas every inn within three blocks of the river road before going to bed.

As they entered the inn, the brothers passed by a tall, muscular young man leaning up against the side of the building. He scarcely gave them a glance as they went inside, and they paid him no mind. The innkeeper, a fellow who looked to be in his late fifties or early sixties, took their coin and showed them to a comfortable room on the second floor. After dropping their packs, the pair returned to the common room.

"May I offer you some plum wine?" their host suggested as the merchants seated themselves at the bar.

"That would be fine, the younger replied."

After they'd been served the older said, "I'm wondering if you might have seen our business associate, Jiao Jing, recently?"

The innkeeper's dark eyes glittered, but he answered in the negative. "Jiao Jing? Don't know the man. A fellow trader?"

"That's right," said Ming Tai. "He's around our age, maybe a little older. Traveling with a pair of young children from west of the Pahadai. We're hoping to catch up with him to bring him news from his son in Tzinshai."

The man behind the bar shrugged. "Sorry, haven't seen him. Would you care for some of tonight's special? The cook's just taking it off the stove." In fact delicious smells were wafting out from the kitchen.

"Sounds great," Ming Shao said. "We'll take that table over near the fire, and bring a bottle of that plum wine if you would. It's delicious!"

"We make it right her in Xia Gu," the innkeeper replied with a smile.

Ming Tai and Ming Shao seated themselves by the fire. Though it was still summer, as the river road had climbed they were finding that night brought a nip to the air. It was far cooler here than it had been in Indaya only a couple of weeks before. The special proved to be a bowls of snowy white rice topped by a dish of beef strips and vegetables in a dark, savory sauce. As they'd ridden north and east, the flavors of the local cuisine had begun to take on more and more piquancy. Odd, Leila thought, as she sank her teeth into another delicious mouthful. In her experience it was usually the warmer southern regions where the cuisine was most fiery – probably an effort to cover up the taste of meat that was beginning to turn.

It had been a long day on the road. The food was hearty and filling, the plum wine light and delicious. Ahh! Leila drained one glassful, then poured another from the carafe the innkeeper had brought to the table. The sun was not down yet, but somehow she felt so drowsy…

Lee Ho Sing watched the sleep potion beginning to take effect, and motioned to Zhin where he stood beside the door. The drug was a harmless one, but the quantity those two merchants had ingested would have them dead to the world for the next several hours. He had employed it before, with customers who were getting out of hand.

Two of the cohorts Zhin had rounded up for Jiao's assignment were also in the inn's common room, with another outside and the fourth member of the group wandering from inn to inn on the watch for anyone who might be asking after the merchant and his juvenile companions.

The travelers had set their chopsticks down, their heads sinking toward the surface of the table. But as the three hired thugs moved in on them, an amazing transformation took place. The two middle-aged Hando men shrank, their fine clothing becoming riding leathers of an unfamiliar cut. And one of them had become a small, dark woman while the other was a somewhat larger, but also fairly dark, Gaspari man! What sorcery was this?

"Get them out of here," Lee Ho hissed to Zhin. The bouncer motioned to Sheng and Zhuang, and the two of them approached the table while he stepped out the door.

Run was leaning up against the outside wall, and he told him "We got somebody. Come help us carry them outside." The woman was small, the man not a lot bigger. Run heaved her over his shoulder and hauled her out through the back to the stable yard while Sheng and Zhuang took the man between them and Zhin scanned the room to make sure that the rest of the inn's patrons had not become unduly interested. Nobody, it seemed, had registered the fact that a pair of Hando merchants had somehow transformed into these foreigners.

The four thugs and the innkeeper met in the stable yard. Night had fallen, and they stood around the sleeping bodies in a pool of flickering yellow light from a lantern beside the inn's back door. "These have to be hirelings of the sorceress Honorable Jiao spoke of," Lee Ho declared. "We must get word to him – they are only three days behind him."

"How are we supposed to do that?" Zhin asked. If the innkeeper was the boss of their operation, he was the foreman.

"Go ask if these two came on horseback," Lee Ho commanded. The stable boy who had welcomed the visitors in not an hour before was still on duty, and Zhin soon returned to report, "They came in with a pair of large horses, maybe Shuangs, that have been eating their heads off since they got here."

"I think two of you should take those horses and ride to Tiangong," Lee Ho said in a voice that didn't invite argument. "At the least, Honorable Jiao should be notified as quickly as possible that this sorceress' minions are on his trail – and that we have stopped them. I expect that he will give you considerably more gold than that he already paid, for this news. And with their horses and all their money gone, we should not need to keep these two locked up and fed for a full two weeks. I would think a week should be sufficient."

Before long Sheng, the lightest of Zhin's recruits, was dispatched atop Milacek while Zhuang, the least useful of them, rode Nimble as the two pounded along the river road toward Tiangong. The Gasparis' packs were retrieved from their room, and Lee Ho discovered that they contained a considerable amount of gold as well as several copies of a proclamation from the Gaspari emperor offering a reward for two unspecified children. Two were in Hando, the others in scripts he could not read. He wondered whether their captives were really sent by the sorceress, or perhaps just magician/adventurers trying to wrest Jiao's prize away from him so *they* could claim the handsome reward.

Well, the children were probably already nearly to Tiangong, and out of Lee Ho's reach. He might as well fulfill the task the merchant had given him. The innkeeper had a house on the north side of town, where he his family had lived when he was a young man. But his children had long since grown up and moved away, and his wife was dead. He spent most of his time at the inn, now. The house would do well as a prison for the two minions of the Nima sorceress – or whatever they were.

The inn kept a farm cart and a donkey to pull it, and they soon had the two sleeping Gasparis dumped into the back and covered with a canvas tarpaulin. Lee Ho had an inn to run and had returned inside, leaving dealing with the captives to Zhin and his two remaining cohorts.

"Do we need to tie them up first?" Zhin asked before he left. He knew the way to Lee Ho's small house, having been there on occasion, but had no idea what drug his boss had used on the magicians.

"They should be out cold for another several hours, and it won't take you half an hour to get the house," Lee replied. "Strip them and search them when you get there, see if they have any more documents on them. And I expect my share of whatever additional gold you find. After that you can tie them up – and better make sure you do it right! You saw what they can do, who knows what other tricks they have up their sleeves? Send Ji back here to report after you've searched them. You and Run should be able to handle the two of them by yourselves for a while – they don't look all that formidable."

Hulking Run and scrawny Ji trotted behind the cart as Zhin drove it along one of Xia Gu's north-south arteries toward the river. Sure, they don't look formidable *now*, he was thinking. But the pair in the cart behind him had appeared to be men as tall as he was before they had drunk Lee Ho's drugged wine. What if they could transform into demons once the drug wore off, ripping through their bonds before dismembering their captors? He had rarely seen any examples of real magic, and it made him very uneasy.

But maybe the sleeping pair's transformation was only an illusion? If that were the case, they might appear to be demons but would lack a demon's strength. If they really were only dealing with an undersized couple of Gasparis – or perhaps they were Nima, the woman certainly looked dark enough – this job would be smooth sailing.

Lee Ho's house was a small timber structure on a flat lot big enough for a decent kitchen garden. It had but four rooms: a small kitchen and a living area, and a couple of bedrooms. In the back yard was an outhouse and three plum trees, not a bad place. Better than the apartment Zhin Gao shared with his friend Run, in the strip near the river road. Maybe if he did a good job on this assignment and there was a decent amount of gold in it for Lee Ho, his boss would let him live in this house as part of his payment for helping him around the inn. It wasn't like *he* was using it.

Zhin and Run each threw one of their prisoners over a shoulder and took them into the bedroom that had been shared by Lee's two sons before they had grown up and left home. There were still two sleeping pallets in there, sitting on low wooden platforms. Ji stood watching as they stretched the sleeping captives out on the pallets and began removing their clothing. They didn't stir at all while this was going on, clearly dead to the world.

Ji was watching with a great deal of interest as Zhin stripped the female captive. She was slight, and dark, but not much older than he was and not that bad-looking. A little thin for his taste. His eyes widened after Zhin got her garments off of her and began going through the pockets.

For one thing, there were a lot more pockets than you would expect such a garment to contain. And for another, they seemed to be full of weapons and mysterious small bottles that he suspected were poisons – or perhaps drugs like the one the woman had unwittingly taken with her wine. She had several small leather harnesses attached to her body over the underwear, and a total of four razor-sharp daggers sheathed in them.

Was this woman some kind of Nima or Gaspari version of a tong member? Some of the tongs specialized in running gambling, prostitution, and drug dens, or robbing goods from freight wagons. But some, for instance the Wan Hui Tong, were rumored to have members who specialized in bringing swift and silent death to the enemies of those willing to pay the price.

A little shiver ran down Ji's spine at the thought. He'd been thinking about searching under the woman's underwear himself, but the idea was beginning to lose its appeal. As Zhin searched the woman Run was doing the same for the man, and abruptly he pulled a small dark object out of a pocket and hissed. "The Black One!" he said, and hurled the little statue across the room.

The Black One was not well known in Hanshu. With so much competition, including other gods who claimed the role of God of Death, Betsalel had relatively few adherents. But for those who knew him only slightly, he was a chilling figure of mystery and dread. "She's got one, too!" Zhin exclaimed, holding up the little idol with its tiny red eye.

Had they known these were true idols, through which the Shadow God himself might manifest at any moment, the three might have run screaming from the house. But they took them for talismans, items like the carved pendants Jiao Jing had given the children. Yet who knew what powers such talismans might confer?

"I thought you said the sorceress was an initiate of Danava?" Run asked, giving his friend a questioning look.

"That's what Honorable Jiao said," Zhin replied. "But maybe the sorceress and the cult of Betsalel have some kind of a deal going. Danava's associated with death, too. Ji, take these and go toss them into the canyon, right now!"

Ji paled and recoiled as Zhin handed him the idol. But a glare from the taller man soon had him scampering to collect the other one from where Run had thrown it, then dash out the back door and head for the river canyon. It was no more than a quarter of a mile away. As he ran, he was praying silently to Andros for protection. He'd folded the little idols up in a kerchief to avoid touching them with his hands, but would that be enough?

The Shadow God did not reach out from the Plane of the Immortals to cause the cliff to crumble beneath Ji's feet, nor did his heart stop as he ran. In a few minutes the two small idols were bouncing downstream along the river bed a thousand feet below, where they would eventually become buried in stones or perhaps wash down to where the river ran more slowly and turn up inside the belly of some fisherman's catch. Whatever their eventual fate, they were now out of reach of any of Betsalel's believers.

Chapter 41

Leila awoke to a dull aching in her head and a considerably more pronounced aching in her arms, legs, and shoulders. What in all the hells? She and Tevo had just been enjoying a delicious meal... where? That inn along the river road, that was it. They were in Zi Goo or someplace like that, and the innkeeper hadn't seen Jiao or the kids. They'd scarcely expected to strike gold in the first place they'd stopped, but this inn was a convenient place to stay. After supper they were going to go out and canvas the other inns in the area nearest the road.

Her eyes were open, but she could barely see anything. There was a faint grayness coming through a window over there on the other side of the bed, as if dawn were coming... Bed? She was lying on a bed, the kind favored in Hanshu: a hard wooden platform with a stuffed cloth pallet laid on it. Her arms, she could feel, were tied behind her, bound at the wrists. Her legs were drawn up to her chest and tied at the knees and ankles. What?

Oh, if only they'd checked with Betsalel before choosing that inn! It struck her as odd, though, that an old and seemingly respectable inn situated within a stone's throw of the road on which thousands of religious pilgrims traveled should have taken to robbing its customers. She and Tevo had been carrying large amounts of gold, and their appearance as well-heeled merchants must have been enough to trigger the innkeeper's greed.

But if that was what had happened, why had they not just been dumped into the river canyon? Leaving them alive was a big risk for the thieves, as the penalty for robbery in Hanshu was usually death or mutilation. Did they hope to get something more out of them... locations of more gold, or what? It just didn't make sense.

Leila heard a faint groan behind her and realized that Tevo must be waking up, too. With a lunge and a twist she brought her hands around under her legs and in front of her, then straightened her legs and rolled over so she was facing the other bed. Yes, it was definitely getting lighter in here. She threw a bubble of silence over them.

"Tevo, are you awake?" she asked. No need to keep her voice down, or speak in Hando. He grunted, testing his bonds.

"What the fuck happened?" he moaned. Despite their situation, she smiled in the dim light.

"Looks like the famous Makucha Nyeusi assassin and her cute boyfriend fell prey to bandits, I'm afraid."

Tevo's dark eyes popped open, and with an effort focused on her. He scooched a little closer to the edge of the pallet nearest hers, anxious about the relatively small radius of the silence bubble. "Shit!" he said ruefully. Then added, "Why are we still alive?"

"I haven't worked that out yet," she replied. Then a thought occurred to her. "Do you think maybe Jiao set that innkeeper to watch his back trail? He must know we're coming, since he ran as soon as he got our message telling him to wait."

Tevo considered for a few moments. "That sounds more like it. Though I don't suppose he'd mind robbing us of everything we own while he's at it. What do you suppose they're going to do with us?" It was assumed that the innkeeper who'd drugged them must have henchmen at his command.

Now it was Leila's turn to mull the situation. "They might just be going to imprison us here until it's too late for us to stop Jiao from doing whatever it is he's planning to do with the kids. Or maybe they've sent word to him and will kill us if that's what he orders. He won't know exactly who or how many people are coming after him."

Daylight was beginning to come in through the window, and Leila sensed a faint vibration through the pallet. "Tevo!" Leila said suddenly, "Go invisible!" He did, but the pallet vanished as well. He hadn't had the training she had. "Think about just you yourself, your clothes, and your bonds becoming invisible. That's it," she added as he achieved the desired effect. She dropped her silence bubble as her own body and bonds disappeared from sight, and immediately heard heavy footfalls coming their way.

There was the sound of a latch being unlocked, then the room's door opened and a tall, ill-favored young man a little younger than they were stood in the doorway. He had a tray with a pot of tea on it, and some hard biscuits. His almond eyes went round at the sight of the two empty pallets, indented where the bodies that had lain in them had been.

"Zhin!" he cried out in alarm, dashing back out through the door and hastily setting the tray down on a piece of furniture in a room at the end of the short hallway. "They're gone!"

"What?! They can't be!" came a voice from the area Leila took to be the kitchen, and a slightly shorter young man came hurrying down the hall. Now that she thought about it, she had seen the first guy standing outside the inn when they came in last night. And this second one had been leaning up against the wall inside, near the door. She'd taken him for a bouncer, not a bandit thug.

The two bed platforms and a small nightstand between them were the room's only furnishings, and it was clear in the growing light that the two captives were not there. "How the hell could they have gotten away?" Zhin demanded angrily. They'd sent Ji back to the inn with a report for Lee Ho, and the small amount of additional gold they'd found about the prisoners' persons. He had not returned.

It seemed obvious to both of them that the prisoners must have somehow slipped their bonds. They had not stripped them naked, only patting them down thoroughly once the two were down to their underwear. Could they have had, say, more small knives or other hidden weaponry that would let them cut through the stout ropes with which they'd been tied? However they had gotten loose, it had clearly been easy enough for them afterward to slip out the window to the ground.

"Check their belongings!" Zhin cried, and he and Run both hurried to the living room where the prisoners' clothing and weapons had been stashed. Their packs, and the vast majority of their gold, had been left back at the inn with Lee Ho. The moment the two left the room, Leila threw up another bubble of silence and began picking at the knots securing her knees and ankles with her hands. Another few moments and her legs were free, the ropes falling to the floor and becoming visible. She tossed them onto her husband so he could hide them for her.

Tevo, still trussed up, observed the momentary appearance of the ropes with pleasure. His beloved certainly had some useful abilities. Shredding the knots tying her wrists with her teeth, Leila was soon free. She knelt by the other pallet and felt for Tevo's head, giving him a firm kiss on the lips. "I'll be back soon and get you out of those bonds, sweetie," she promised. Then she was gone.

Not wanting to risk meeting one of their hulking captors in the hall, Leila climbed out of the window and went around to the front of the house. The door was unlocked, and she slipped silently inside it. Zhin, the young man who seemed to be giving the orders to his big, ugly friend, was standing with his back to the door – rifling through her and Tevo's clothing, boots, and the assorted daggers and knives that they'd been carrying about their persons. Tevo's saber must have been removed as soon as it appeared, and was probably back at the inn with the rest of their belongings.

The taller man stood back, watching his friend work. Neither had noticed the door opening and closing again. "Everything's still here," Zhin said. "That means they're running around out there in their underwear, barefoot and unarmed. I'm going to go out and take a walk around the perimeter, see if I can spot any tracks. You stay here and guard this stuff. They must not have been gone very long, or they would have sneaked in here and taken it while we were sleeping."

Hmm, not only the boss but the brains of the operation, it would seem… Leila waited until Zhin had gone out the front door. The big guy stood glaring at the pile of clothing and weapons for a few moments as if he were expecting them to move of their own accord, legs slightly apart and muscular arms crossed. Then he heaved a deep sigh, and sat down on a chair beside the room's window. From there he had a view of the door as well as the table where the recent captives' belongings had been set.

Zhin went by outside the window, studying the ground, and his henchman turned to call out, "See anything?" As he did, Leila glided silently past him and began rifling through the collection of items on the table. Their idols were not here! Damn, if she'd been able to call Betsalel the entire gang could have been rounded up without the need to kill anyone. Now, she'd have to do things the hard way.

Leila didn't want to take the time to put on any of her body sheaths, so she took only a single one of the daggers plus an injector ring. She had used a similar ring to quietly dispatch several minions of Kivuli during her mission in Palambo nine years earlier. But this one was loaded, not with deadly oualit, but with a substance closer in effect to whatever it was they'd been dosed with last night.

The thug was trying to relax, but she could see that his senses were on the alert. Once she got close enough to him to use the ring, he would be sure to sense her presence – and he was twice her size. A pity she had not thought to bring a blow-gun on this trip! She considered her options. This guy might only be a hireling, but she didn't doubt for a moment that he would have cheerfully killed her and Tevo if those had been his orders.

Ah, hell. Poor Tevo was still trussed up like a chicken for the spit in the guest bedroom, and likely Zhin would finish his perimeter check and be back here in another minute. Then she'd have *two* big men to face. Sorry, whatever your name is, she said to herself.

Run glanced over at the pile of stuff on the table. Hadn't there been *four* daggers there a minute ago? While he was pondering that question, the missing dagger suddenly sprouted from his throat and he fell forward out of the chair – gurgling hideously as his life's blood pumped out, soaking the room's thin carpet. Yuch, Leila thought. She stepped gingerly, anxious not to be leaving bloody footprints, and had just retrieved the dagger from the dead man's throat when Zhin came back in through the front door wearing a worried expression.

"I couldn't see any sign of them," he began. Then he paled and rushed to where his friend lay sprawled in a pool of blood on the floor. "Run, Run!" he shouted, trying to lift the larger man and turn him over. He was bending over directly in front of the invisible Leila, and she carefully calculated her stroke before sinking her still-bloody dagger into his back just between the shoulder blade and the spine. The blow should incapacitate him for a few minutes, long enough for the free Tevo, but it wouldn't kill him unless maybe the wound festered.

She'd read of warriors who received such a wound and shrugged it off, going on to charge the enemy lines and killing many foes. But if she was any judge of men, Zhin was no such warrior. To prove her point, he fell face down atop his stricken friend and howled in pain.

Leila darted over to the table and scooped up the rest of her daggers and Tevo's as well. It looked like Zhin was out of commission, but should he rise again she didn't want him armed. Seconds later she went visible as she stepped into the bedroom, hoping Zhin would believe whoever had attacked him was still back in the living room standing over him with a knife.

Tevo spotted her and went visible himself, and in moments she had cut his bonds free. "I had to kill the bigger thug," Leila said ruefully. "But I've got the other one, Zhin, down and I don't think he's too seriously hurt. We need to get some answers out of him."

Tevo was standing a little unsteadily beside the bed, trying to work the kinks out of his arms and legs. "Should we appear as demons, or something?" he suggested. Leila considered. He already knew what they really looked like. "Let's just get back into our clothes before we interrogate him," she countered. It was hard to command respect standing in your underwear, even if you were the one holding a knife.

Zhin had gotten up onto his knees, and was trying to reach the bleeding wound in his back. Tears were running down his face. "Augh, you've killed me!" he cried, no doubt believing his assailant was still in the room. Leila went visible while Tevo, clad in shadows, hurried over to retrieve his belongings and get dressed.

Kneeling on the floor over his dead cohort, Zhin stared in disbelief at the little dark woman. "You?" he asked. "You're the one that killed Run?"

"Sorry," Leila replied sincerely. Deadly assassin she might be, but that didn't mean she liked killing people. Not even lowlife scum who deserved it.

Seeing he was only facing one small woman and beginning to realize that he was not mortally wounded, Zhin made as if to rise. In a split second, Leila had two of her daggers in her hands, poised for throwing. "Stay where you are!" She commanded. "I took out Run with one throw, and I doubt I'll need both of these for you. That hole in your back will heal up all right, but you'll be joining your friend if I hit you in the throat – or the heart."

Fear apparent on his face, Zhin sank back down onto his haunches. His pants legs were soaked in blood. Tevo finished putting on his clothes and went visible, making the thug gasp in shock. So that was how they had done it? His earlier fear of the pair's sorcerous powers came back full force, and he didn't move a muscle as Tevo stood there holding a pair of his own daggers. His skill with them was not quite as amazing as Leila's, but it was certainly good enough.

Soon Leila joined them again, feeling stronger and more confident now that she was dressed. She'd replaced the knives in their various hiding places. Darting back to the bedroom, she retrieved the ropes she'd been bound with. "Tevo, let's get him up onto that chair," she suggested. The room boasted two chairs, sturdy ones made from a heavy dark hardwood.

Holding a knife in one hand, Tevo helped Zhin to rise and stagger over to sit in the chair while Leila threw the latch on the front door and did the same for the back. Until they questioned their erstwhile captor, they had no idea how many more members of the gang there were or whether they were likely to show up at any moment.

Leila secured Zhin to the chair, tying each of his feet to its front legs at the ankles and his arms behind the chair back. The wound was still bleeding, and she found a dish towel in the kitchen and wadded it up to press between the chair and their prisoner's back. The tables had been turned.

Zhin was not feeling well. Run had not been exactly a friend, but a person he'd associated with since adolescence; and it had been a shock to find him dead. He and the team he'd assembled were petty criminals, not murderers, and his suggestion to Honorable Jiao that they drop any pursuers into the canyon had been nothing but bravado. True, he'd cracked the occasional skull in the course of relieving a drunk of his purse; but now he was in the hands of trained assassins. It was an effort to control his bladder, as he sat there miserably tied hand and foot – gazing up into the stony faces of the pair they'd kidnaped last night.

"Who do you work for?" the woman demanded. Hando was used as a trade language all over the world east of the Pahadai, but she spoke it without accent – as if she were a native of one of Hanshu's largest cities.

"Honorable Lee Ho Sing," Zhin croaked in reply.

"The innkeeper?" Leila asked, and the wretched captive nodded.

"How many in your gang?" Tevo wanted to know.

"Besides me, there's Sheng and Zhuang, and Ji. And Run, but you killed him."

"Where are the others, then?" "We sent Sheng and Zhuang on your horses, riding to Tiangong to tell Honorable Jiao Jing that we had caught you," Zhin said. He didn't see what difference it made, to tell them whatever they wanted to know. He and the rest of his companions were all probably dead meat anyhow.

These must be underworld nicknames, Leila realized. Weasel, Stupid, Ox, and Chicken. During her years with the Night Guild in Marsine, many of her fellow thieves had taken such street names. She herself had been Penumbra, the shadow. "What about Ji?" she asked. Zhin looked uncertain.

"Honorable Lee Ho wanted us to report what we found after we got you here and stripped you," he explained. "We sent Ji back to him with the gold we found in your pockets. But he didn't come back."

Hmm, perhaps "Chicken" flew the coop? They had not been carrying all that much gold on them, most of it stowed beneath clothing and gear in their packs, but it might have been enough to tempt a small-town, small-time thief to flee his home. "What happened to the rest of our belongings?" she demanded. "Where are the idols we had in our pockets?" If they could recover even one of those, none of this would be a problem.

Zhin's eyes widened, and his face paled. "Those were idols?" he asked in surprise. "Real ones?" Leila tweaked her appearance slightly so that she looked like a slightly more formidable, definitely more scary version of herself.

"I am the arch-priestess of Betsalel," she said darkly. "What did you do with our idols?"

The thug's bladder control abandoned him, and a stain spread on his crotch. There were tears in his eyes again. "I... We... We thought they were just talismans!" he finally got out. "We were afraid they might have been given to you by the Nima sorceress Honorable Jiao warned us about. I had Ji throw them in the canyon." In his mind, he was picturing the Shadow God manifesting in one of those discarded idols and growing until he was tall enough to step over the lip of the canyon, stomping toward the house to rend Shin limb from limb for his blasphemy. Few people who were not members of the clergy truly understood how idols worked.

Leila heaved a sigh. When she hadn't found the idols with their clothing, she'd been afraid something like that had been done with them. She moved on. "Jiao Jing told you we were hired by a Nima sorceress?" she asked, and their captive blinked.

"That's what he said," he admitted.

Leila's regret at having killed Run deepened. Seemingly these young thugs were only misguided young men, petty thieves who'd been sold a fairy tale by the trader Jiao. Even Lee Ho Sing might possibly be excused for his crimes, if he had thought he was stopping agents of a sorcerous kidnaper. "So," she went on, after thinking the situation over, "Jiao Jing told you to stop anyone who came asking after him, and delay them so he could continue on his way to Tiangong with the children unmolested?"

"Exactly," Zhin replied miserably. What had he gotten himself into? Leila stepped back from the captive and motioned Tevo over to stand beside her. Then she threw up a bubble of silence so they could confer in private.

"I'm inclined to believe him," she told her husband, and he nodded agreement.

"We need to get back to the inn and explain the situation to Lee Ho, then get some more horses and hit the road. Shit, regular horses aren't going to be able to make anywhere near the speed we were getting from Milacek and Nimble."

"I doubt there are any temples of Betsalel closer to here than Tiangong," Leila mused. "And it's really only about three or four days' journey normally. As soon as we get there we can consult with Betsalel, and get him to give us some new idols. Then we should be able to comb the city and narrow down where Jiao has taken the children. Oh, and find Nimble and Milacek. I've had that horse for half my life, and I'm not letting him get stolen from me."

Leila dropped her bubble, and spoke to Zhin again. He was staring at her, wondering how it was that they had seemed to speak but he'd heard nothing though he was less than eight feet away.

"How did we get out here?" she asked. "Did you and Run carry us?" The captive shook his head.

"We took Lee Ho's farm cart and his donkey to pull it, and just put a tarpaulin over you guys so nobody would see you. It was still pretty early in the evening."

While Leila watched over the captive, Tevo went out and found the cart. Zhin and his cohorts had unhitched the donkey last night, and it was munching some hay in a little open-faced shed out back. He soon had the beast in the traces again, and led him around to the front door.

Leila and Tevo together heaved the body of Run up off the floor and carried him out to dump in the back of the cart. Then they went back for Zhin, keeping his hands tied behind his back but freeing him from the chair. Though he was bigger than either of them, he was in no shape for any escape attempts and went along meekly. "What's likely to happen when we go back to the inn with the body of your friend here in the back of the cart?" Leila asked.

"Lee Ho might call the City Watch," Zhin offered. "He's been a businessman in Xia Gu for thirty years at least, and his father before him."

"Better if that doesn't happen," she said. "How far is it to the canyon rim?"

"It's about a quarter mile north of here," the bound man replied, gesturing with his head. They sat him on the driver's seat and Tevo led the donkey while Leila walked behind the cart – both of them invisible. It was still pretty early in the morning, but anyone who happened to notice would see only Zhin with the cart.

At approximately the same spot where Ji had tossed the idols the previous night, the invisible man and woman heaved the now-invisible body out of the cart and got it thrown over the edge with considerable effort. It reappeared in midair as it left their hands, sailing on an updraft down to the water below. There was no one to observe.

Run had left behind some bloodstains on the cart's wooden floor, but a sprinkling of dust from along the cliff edge blotted it up and helped to hide the evidence. Still invisible, Leila and Tevo led the cart with Zhin riding it back the way they had come and continued south to the river road, taking it inside the stableyard of the inn.

The former captives became visible again, and helped their forlorn and bleeding prisoner climb down. The stable boy was staring at them in disbelief, motionless until Tevo admonished him, "Unhitch the donkey and put him back in the stable. Do you have any extra horses?" The kid gaped at him, then replied "Yes sir, I mean no sir... I'll put the donkey and the cart away, but all of the horses here belong to the people staying in the inn."

Another complication. Well, one thing at a time. Leila and Tevo flanked Zhin and, holding him by the elbows, chivvied him in through the inn's rear door to the hallway that led into the common room. Lee Ho was on the bar, serving tea and small pastries to inn customers. He dropped the pot almost hard enough to shatter it, sloshing tea across the bar, when he beheld his bouncer in the custody of the two Gaspari agents they'd taken down last night.

"Zhin, what?..." he demanded, looking first to his employee and then to the grim-looking foreigners. "I, uh..." It had suddenly occurred to him that these two had demonstrated magical powers. Why had he imagined a gang the likes of Zhin and his street thugs would be able to keep such in custody? He was probably about to get turned into a toad, or have his inn burned down around his head, for his part in kidnaping them...

But Leila and Tevo had decided to try another approach. They didn't want to end up beheaded for murder thousands of miles from home, but they couldn't afford to leave a nest of hostile enemies behind them, either. Could they trust Lee Ho to take the side of right once he knew what it was? They'd have to chance it. "Sit down, Zhin," Tevo commanded, and the bleeding man took a stool at the bar. "He's going to need some medical attention," the arch-priest went on. "You are Lee Ho Sing?" he asked, and the apprehensive innkeeper nodded.

Tevo nodded, not quite a bow, and thrust out his right hand in the Gaspari manner when meeting someone. "I am Tevodar Karmarzin, arch-priest of Betsalel in Parat, capital of the Gaspari Dominion. This is my wife Leila, Betsalel's arch-priestess. We are hunting one Jiao Jing, a trader of Tzinshai, who rescued our son and his friend from the woman who had kidnaped them. We sent him a message telling him to wait for us in Balore, Indaya, several weeks ago and he ignored it. We believe he is seeking to hold the children for ransom himself, perhaps with the backing of your king. Can you cast any light on this?"

Lee Ho sagged, wishing he had a stool to sit on. Taking off his apron, he came around the bar and beckoned the visitors to sit at a nearby table with them. "I fear that I have been greatly misled," he said, wringing his hands. "I must apologize for what you have been through, but as it appears you are unharmed I hope that there will be no hard feelings. Can I offer you some tea?"

"Only if I watch you drink some first," Tevo said snarkily. You have our packs and other belongings safe?" Lee Ho nodded.

"I have them locked in a cabinet in the kitchen," he said. "And little Ji came here last night with some gold he'd taken from your persons. I put him on the door after that, since Zhin was not here. I, uh…"

"Good enough," Tevo said dismissively. "You also owe us a pair of the finest, fastest horses this fleabite town can provide. Now, tell us everything you know about Honorable Jiao Jing."

Chapter 42

Sheng leaned over the mare's neck, Zhuang beside him on the big gelding. The two were not expert riders, but somehow these horses knew how to glide down the road at a gallop without making them fall off. There'd been a few problems back at the inn when they'd first mounted, the gelding especially not wanting to allow an unfamiliar rider on his back. But once they were in the saddle, with help from Zhin and Run and Honorable Lee Ho, the horses had not bucked or reared – nor attempted to reach around and bite them. They had bolted up the river road at speed, heading in the direction of Tiangong, as if all the demons of hell were after them.

It was then that Sheng had discovered that the bridles those strange Gaspari agents were using had no bits – they were just leather halters with reins clipped to them. Pulling back on the reins as hard as he could and yelling "Stop, slow down!" in Hando had had no effect. He had no idea what the Gasparto for "Whoa" was, so he just hung on and rode.

Zhuang, bigger and stronger than he was, was having no better luck. "Sheng, what do I do?" he called, "I can't make him slow down!"

"Just stay in the saddle and ride it out," he called back. "They can't keep up this pace for very long before they'll get tired. Then they'll slow down. Don't worry!"

Now it was six hours later and Sheng was getting worried. The horses had not slacked their pace in the least, were still running all out, and showed no signs of exhaustion. Their flanks were wet with sweat, their breathing steady and deep, and they still refused to respond to their riders' commands. At least they were staying on the road. He had an awful vision of the horses continuing straight at the next bend and running right off a cliff into the river canyon, which was not as deep here as it was back in Xia Gu but still plenty deep enough to do the job.

Both men were quivering on the edge of exhaustion. Their buttocks and spines had been pounded into a pulp, and their bladders were bursting. The jolting from galloping along the stone-paved road had their kidneys aching. Yet still the horses ran on. Would Sheng have to risk broken bones jumping from the tall horse's back to the stone pavement? He was a small man and fairly agile, but at this point he was so stiff and sore he wasn't sure he could manage it without injury. And there was no way Zhuang could pull it off.

The moon was only about a quarter full, shedding enough light on the road's light-colored paving stones for the horses, but the men could barely see anything. It had been around eight in the evening when they had set off on what Sheng was coming to see as a fool's errand, so must now be in the small hours of the morning. Even if they came to an inn and could get the horses to stop, wouldn't it be locked up for the night?

He stood up in the stirrups of the odd western saddle, trying to take some of the weight off his aching backside, and looked ahead. Was that a glimmer of light he saw, beside the road on the north? At the speed they were traveling it quickly grew closer, resolving itself as a lantern mounted on the outside of a two-story structure of timber and stone. A wayside inn!

And even as they approached it, the horses began to slow. Yes, thank the thousand divines! On the near side of the building was an unfenced side yard with hitching posts and a drinking trough for horses, and a pump where travelers could draw water for themselves to drink.

Nimble and Milacek were parched. Running for six hours hadn't made them tired at all, but they were thirsty – and very hungry, as well. As his mare stopped at the trough and lowered her head to drink, Sheng draped the reins (which were tied together) over the cantle of the saddle and climbed down off her back. He was only nineteen, but he felt like an old man as he stiffly slid down. He nearly collapsed after hitting the ground.

Sheng's groan of pain and relief was accompanied by a "thump" as his larger companion also climbed down from the saddle and collapsed in a heap between the two horses. He was fortunate not to have struck his head on the trough. "Sheng, I can't go any farther," Zhuang moaned. "Can we stay at the inn?"

Lee Ho had given them a purse, some of the money Jiao Jing had paid up front for their services, to cover their expenses on the trip to Tiangong. It was expected that Jiao would pay them still more, once they relayed the urgent news to him. The two men, limping badly and feeling as if their lower limbs were carved out of wood, staggered the few short yards to the inn's door and tried it. It was locked up tight.

"Maybe we can get into the stable yard and sleep in the barn," Sheng suggested. As they turned back they heard a clatter of hooves. The horses had finished their drink and, looking around, had seen no food. They knew where to find some, though – food they'd been devouring when their evening's rest had been so rudely interrupted several hours ago. As one they turned and began galloping down the road at a somewhat more sedate pace – back toward Xia Gu.

Chapter 43

The house of Honorable Bian Tu proved to be spacious and comfortable. It was far less opulent than the Imperial Palace in Parat, of course, and lacked even some of the creature comforts Gabriel was used to at home. Certain details of Shadow Manor's plumbing systems were unique in the world, having been magically provided by the Shadow God. Still, it was a far more pleasant place to stay than any they'd occupied during the weeks since they had been kidnaped.

Their host was a boyhood friend of Jiao Jing's, they'd learned, with whom he had gone to what passed for university in Hanshu. His family were wealthy merchants, as were the Jiao clan, but while Black Dragon Imports sought goods far and wide Bian Mercantile had prospered by staying put in the Celestial City – selling goods of the finest quality to the many temples, the wealthier citizens, and even to the royal palace itself.

The house was similar in size to Shadow Manor, but it was only Bian Tu and a small staff of servants living here now. As had been the case with Lee Ho, his children were grown and his wife long dead. His two daughters and one of his sons had remained in Tiangong, living elsewhere with their own families and helping in the family business. When Jiao had begun formulating his plans, he'd thought from the first of Bian. He was perfectly situated, and his house would make the ideal place in which to hide the children until he'd concluded his negotiations with King Wang Qian.

But first he must obtain an audience with the king, and that he knew would not be easy. One of the reasons the government of Hanshu had so many layers of bureaucracy was that its rulers had little desire to spend their days being badgered by their subjects for favors and concessions.

After the children, still going by "Jurgen" and "Gerdur," had been handed over to Bian's aging housekeeper Zu Lao (the woman had been with him for decades, and had once been amah to his children), Bian welcomed his old friend into his study and poured him some wine.

"It is good to see you, Jing," he said with a smile. The two of them as a team had broken nearly every rule the schoolmasters had set, before settling down to become solid citizens. Both of them had benefited from families that were long established in successful businesses, and both of them had prospered – though Jiao's trading empire dwarfed Bian Mercantile's operation.

"And you, Tu," Jiao said. It had been many years since he had been here, though the two of them had stayed in touch by letter. "This in an excellent vintage!" he remarked. "May I ask where you got it?" Bian smiled.

"Are you sure you're not the one who imported it in the first place?" he asked. "It's Gaspari, from the region around Parat, I understand." The Hando made wine from any fruit available, but grapes were not cultivated within Hanshu to nearly the extent they were in the Dominion.

"Hmm, I suppose it's possible," Jiao replied. "Shao handles a lot of the purchases of wine when we are in Miradil." Now that the courtesies had been met, Bian moved on to the question he was burning to ask.

"Your letter only mentioned that you had a business proposition for the king, and that you would like to put up with me in Tiangong for a while. Who are the children?"

Jiao's eyes glittered, and a slight smile curved his lips. "My dear Tu, I must ask that you swear what I tell you will not leave this room. There are those who seek to hinder me, and no one must know that the children are here, staying in this house. Can I trust you on this?"

Bian's eyes widened slightly. This seemed more like the Jiao Jing of thirty years ago than the respected and widely-traveled trader that man had become. Some might think that traveling back and forth along the Ivory Road with caravans of exotic goods was an adventurous lifestyle. Perhaps it was, compared with running a highly-respected supply house in the kingdom's capital and never leaving one's home town from one year to the next. But this secrecy, the air of danger, was something he would never have expected from his old friend at this time of their lives.

Bian put his hand over his heart. "I swear it, by Ling Zao. None shall learn of this from me. Now, who are they?"

"The girl," Jiao Jing said with a satisfied smile, is none other than Berta Piastin, the elder child of the Gaspari emperor."

"What?!" his friend gasped, "that is who was kidnaped, the 'red-haired girl' in the proclamation?" Jiao nodded.

"What about the boy?" Bian asked. "He looks more Dravim or maybe Palamban than Gaspari. How does he come into it?" Now his old friend shook his head.

"I'm not sure," he admitted. "The proclamation did not name either child, though it was obvious that the girl could only be Ostden's own daughter. Why else would the emperor of the entire Dominion be issuing such proclamations? Besides, when the children came riding into our caravan on the Ivory Road a few weeks ago I recognized her. The woman who had kidnaped them from the Dominion had tried to disguise her by dying her hair and skin, but the dye was wearing off and her roots were growing out. I had seen an excellent portrait of her done just a few years ago. She is taller and slimmer now, but it is the same child."

"They escaped their captor?" Bian asked.

"That's right," his friend replied. "She was a Nima sorceress, they said, a devotee of Danava. Never heard of the Nima having anything to do with the Destroyer, so maybe she was only posing as Nima. Or maybe they lied about that, too. They told me they were brother and sister, name of Jurgen and Gerdur, and that their father was a wealthy Palamban merchant based in Miradil and would pay a handsome reward for their return."

Jiao's old friend was goggling at him. "But you'd seen the proclamation by then?" he asked.

"Of course I had," he replied. "Messengers were carrying it all along the road. I'm surprised someone else hadn't already seen them and taken them away from this sorceress person. Unless perhaps she really *was* a sorceress... Anyhow, I knew that the proclamation did not say that the girl was the emperor's daughter because if it did a thousand people would be searching for her – each planning to demand far more gold than the reward that was offered, or some other concession from the Gaspari emperor. It is true the girl is not the heir to the throne, but she is surely much loved by her parents. The Gaspari empress is a beautiful woman, and likely Ostden will do anything he must in order to save their daughter."

The wheels were turning in Bian's mind. "So... you became the thousandth man, and rather than getting on a riverboat and returning to Miradil with them you brought them here – to offer this opportunity to our king."

"Exactly!" Jiao replied, pleased that his friend had figured it out so easily. "I have enjoyed much financial success," he went on, "but I want more. I want political power. I will ask only that King Wang Qian grant me the governorship of Tzinshai, and I will give the children to him to do with as he pleases. He may simply return them to their parents, claiming their eternal gratitude and improved relations between Hanshu and the Dominion, or hold them for whatever ransom he desires. Enclaves in other Gaspari trading centers beside Miradil, perhaps? A marriage between young Aleksei and one of his granddaughters? The possibilities are endless!"

Bian took another sip of the fine, dry white wine. He felt slightly stunned. Those odd-looking little children he'd casually sent off with Zu Lao were undoubtedly the subject of an international manhunt. He hoped he would not have to have them in his house very long. "So you have not revealed to them that you know who they are?" he asked, after mulling the situation over for a few moments.

"We've continued with the fiction that I believe they are Jurgen and Gerdur, brother and sister. They are only little children, after all, and gullible. The boy mentioned that his mother's family are affiliated with the priesthood of Betsalel, and told me that if they could get to a temple where the Shadow God is honored the god could transport them home. There are temples of the Eight all over the Dominion of course, but fortunately few of them east of the Pahadai."

"So how did you avoid taking them to a temple of Betsalel?" Bian asked. Jiao smiled again, an oddly foxy expression on his round, blunt-featured face.

"I invoked the threat of the Nima sorceress, of course! I doubt the woman is really a sorceress, but the children are clearly afraid of falling back into her clutches. Evidently she threatened them with death. They managed to get away from her when bandits attacked their party as they were riding along the Ivory Road. That part of the story is a little unclear. But I convinced them that this Rajani person was on our trail, magically divining our location as we made our way through Indaya to Tongnan. Initially I told them I was taking them to Tzinshai, as it is my home base, to use my contacts there to arrange safe passage for them back home. But of course when we arrived there, I learned that Rajani had been asking after us and we must flee north. And so forth. They have been obedient and cooperative, so I doubt they think anything is amiss."

Bian poured a little more wine for each of them, then sat back in his chair. "Well, I hope you are able to get in to see the king soon. It seems likely that these others you mentioned who 'seek to hinder you' may soon arrive in Tiangong. Best if all of you were gone by then."

"Can you arrange an audience for me?" Jiao asked. He'd sort of assumed that as Bian Mercantile were purveyors to the palace, Tu would be able to get him in for an interview. This offer could only be made directly to the king, of course. Wang Qian was a few years older than Jing and Tu were, and from all accounts a shrewd and sober monarch. His dynasty had ruled Hanshu for centuries – centuries during which opposition had been quashed and peace had brought prosperity to the land.

Bian looked unhappy at the suggestion. "My dear Jing," he said, "you must realize that as far as the king is concerned I am little more than an up-jumped grocer. I command a great deal of respect from Honorable Sum Zhi, the castellan. And those under him look on me with favor too. I have met his majesty briefly on a couple of occasions, but I doubt that my name will buy your way into the palace without going through the usual channels."

Jiao looked disappointed. "And the 'usual channels'?" he asked.

"There I can help you. You will need to go to the office of the seneschal, Shian Tze Din. It is he who arranges his majesty's schedule and makes his appointments."

"You can provide me with a letter of introduction?" Jing suggested. "Even if as you say the king does not regard you as a person of import, might not this seneschal?"

Bian sighed. "Think, Jing," he said. "You say there are those who seek to thwart you. Suppose they go to the palace and tell Shian, 'we are looking for some missing children who we believe were taken by Jiao Jing.' And you had arrived earlier with a letter of introduction from Bian Tu, well known as the supplier of goods to the palace. Where do you suppose they will go looking for Honorable Jiao and these missing children? You cannot let anyone at the palace, anyone in Tiangong at all, know that you are staying here, or all may be lost."

Jiao frowned. Of course, how could he have been so foolish? It would hardly do to repay his old friend's hospitality by bringing down those Gaspari agents on his head. He hoped that the agents would have been picked up by those he'd left watching the road in Xia Gu, and would be delayed until after the children were in the hands of the king and he himself was back in Tzinshai. Yet suppose they slipped past in the darkness, or came by some other road? Better to do as Bian said.

"You're right, Tu," he said apologetically. "We are all tired from our long journey, and I hope that tonight we might bathe and rest. Tomorrow, I will leave the children here with you and your servants while I go to see this Shian Tze Din."

"Good," Bian replied. "But how will we entertain these children while you are gone? If they are not to suspect your intentions, they will find it odd if they are not allowed to go out and see some of the Celestial City. It is one of the marvels of the eastern world, after all."

Jiao considered. "I do not believe that my adversaries can reach Tiangong for another few days at least. Probably not until after I am long gone. It should be all right if you want to take them out into the city to see the sights. Just make sure that the girl has her head covered. That hair is too distinctive."

"All right, Bian replied, "I'll do that." He liked children, had raised four of his own and enjoyed visiting with his grandchildren often.

"They only have a few words of Hando," Jiao reminded him, "So communication may be a little difficult. Just be sure not to let them anywhere near the Temple of the Eight."

Chapter 44

Leila and Tevo cantered, then walked, then cantered again along the river road going east-by-north to Tiangong. They'd left behind them one extremely chastened innkeeper and a sorry group of hometown thugs. The absence of the largest of their number had not been discussed, and Leila wondered what Lee Ho Sing would think about the large pool of dried blood in the middle of the living room carpet, next time he visited his house on Xia Gu's northern edge.

These horses had been the best available in a hurry, and they were not all that good. The larger Shuang breed, similar in size to the horses of the Dominion, cost more to keep and were usually owned only by the wealthy. Instead, they were mounted on a pair of scrubby, tough little horses more like the breed favored by the Gholim. They could go a long way on relatively little food and water, but with their short strides they had little speed.

Anxious to see the last of them, Lee Ho had not only purchased the horses and their tack but loaded them down with supplies for the road: cakes, dried meat, fruit, water, wine, and grain for the horses. He hoped never to see them, their children, or his old "friend" Jiao Jing again.

Their current mounts' backs were narrow and bony beneath the minimal eastern saddles, and their trot was backbreaking. Fortunately at a canter the ride was bearable, but they could do that for only a mile or so before they would need to return to a walk, keeping the animals from getting exhausted. It was going to be a long three days to Tiangong.

They'd been at this for several hours, eating from their packs while staying in the saddle, but both of them needed to relieve themselves and they pulled off to the south side of the road where some grass was growing. The horses eagerly cropped at the tender shoots while Tevo stood on the road bed and pissed off into the nearby low shrubbery. There'd been a fair amount of traffic on the road through much of their journey so far, but there was no one in sight just at the moment.

Leila picked her way a little further south to where there were some larger bushes and crouched among them, britches down around her ankles. Suddenly she heard a shout. "Leila, somebody's coming fast!" Most traffic on the river road moved at a sedate pace, as a great many of the religious pilgrims were elderly, infirm, or afoot.

Finishing her business, Leila quickly hiked her pants back up and emerged from the bushes, daggers in hand. She and Tevo had assumed the aspect of a pair of Hando youths who would not have been out of place in Zhin's little gang. They found that appearing to be a part of the local scene while still unapproachable worked best for speeding their travels.

A pity, Leila thought, as she peered up the road in the direction of the approaching hoofbeats, that she hadn't figured out how to create the illusion of pissing standing up. In Palambo and Hanshu as well as in her homeland Leila had observed the way in which women were treated as subordinate to men. Despite that, she didn't envy them many things. But being able to relieve oneself without getting into a vulnerable crouching position was one of them.

"There are no riders!" Tevo exclaimed, as the hoofbeats drew nearer.

"It's Nimble!" Leila crowed.

"And Milacek!" he added.

"Nimble!" she called, and the horse slowed as he approached them. His companion did the same. The two newly acquired horses looked up and greeted their larger brethren before returning their attention to the grass.

Leila threw her arms around the neck of the big chestnut gelding. Her old friend, with whom she had had so many adventures! Tevo, who was similarly making much of Milacek, said "Looks like our Sheng and Zhuang must have gotten thrown off, but not right away." His wife laughed out loud. She'd been surprised, really, that their horses had even permitted the young thugs to mount them.

"Nimble's too well-mannered to buck anybody off, I think," she said. "They probably dismounted for some reason and the horses just took off. Look, the reins are knotted over the cantles. I don't know what might have happened if they'd been left hanging down."

The joyful reunion concluded, the gelding and mare approached the roadside grass with a great deal of interest. "Oh!" Leila realized. "They must not have finished eating their supper last night when they got stolen. They're probably starving!" The horses' nosebags were among the contents of their packs, and they got them out and filled them with grain they'd packed along. Soon Nimble and Milacek were happily recouping some of the energy they'd expended on their long run.

The horses would be unable to continue the journey until they'd finished their meal, so the humans sat down and broke out some food of their own. As they ate, they talked. "These horses Lee Ho bought for us are going to slow us down," Tevo pointed out.

"But we can't just leave them out here at the side of the road!" Leila said. "There could be wolves, or wildcats – or bandits who might abuse the poor animals."

"Let's put them on leads and move at a pace they can stand until we come to the next inn," Tevo suggested. "We can feed Nimble and Milacek some more grain and water them there while we sell these two. Then we can move on. We should be able to cover quite a few more miles today before we need to stop for the night."

And so they did. The gold the two small horses brought helped to compensate somewhat for all they'd been through. Having been sent to sleep at dusk and gotten back on the road again before noon the following day, they had really lost only a few hours on their journey to Tiangong.

The next morning, as Nimble and Milacek slowed their pace to weave their way through a knot of carts, litters, and pedestrians crowding the road, two of those pedestrians looked up in shock. "It's *them*!" Sheng gasped to his companion. "They're back again!" Zhuang gaped as the horses went past.

"Somebody else must've stolen them after they got away from us. Those ain't the ones that had 'em before."

"You idiot," his companion replied, "it's them in disguise! You saw how they looked just like a couple of rich merchants and then turned into those foreigners. They've just turned themselves into somebody else again." They continued walking, east by south on the long journey home.

After a moment Zhuang added, "If they want those horses, they can have 'em. I'm just glad it's not *me* on that demon's back."

Chapter 45

The day dawned bright in Tiangong, sunlight sparkling in the clear mountain air. Cumulonimbus clouds wreathed the peaks, turned pink by the rising sun, and by afternoon they might have rain; but for now, it was a perfect morning to go exploring.

Gabriel and Berta had spent the night sleeping on very comfortable goose down pallets in a bedroom that had once belonged to Honorable Bian's daughters, and awoke eager to explore this fantastic city. Jiao Jing had told them last night that he was going to the palace to make arrangements for them to be returned safely home, and that Bian Tu would be happy to show them around while he was gone.

They ate breakfast, sweet buns and fresh fruit washed down with sweetened tea, and chattered happily together. Zu Lao didn't much like them saying things she couldn't understand, and was trying to insist that they speak in Hando instead. Their vocabulary had increased just in the few hours since she'd taken them in hand.

"Thank you for the delicious breakfast, grandmother," Gabriel said in what he hoped were acceptable accents. Hando was a complex tongue compared with Gasparto, requiring that you pay close attention to the pitch and tone of your words. The same word could have several different meanings, depending on how high or low you said it.

"That was not bad," the old former amah said acerbically, "but you used the wrong term for grandmother. That is what you call your mother's mother. When you use it as an honorific, you must say 'grandmother.'"

"Sorry, grandmother," Gabe corrected himself while Berta looked on in amusement. Honorable Bian, clad in the garb of a respectable businessman, appeared at the table and poured himself a cup of tea.

"Are you two ready to see something of the Celestial City?" he asked, and they got enough of the gist of what he'd said to reply "Yes please, Honorable Bian!" He surveyed their garb critically. To Zu Lao he said, "Lao-lao, do we still have some of Zia and Sing's clothing in the house?"

"Certainly," she replied. Some of the Bian children's finer outfits had been passed down to their own children, but some others still remained – tucked away in cedar chests in one of the unused bedrooms.

To the children he said, "If you are finished eating, let us get you some new clothing." They looked a little blank at that, and he took a fold of Berta's tunic and rubbed it between his fingers, then gestured to his own clothing and motioned for them to follow him.

It was like opening a treasure chest! Every little girl loves to play dress-up – even ones who really *are* princesses. Each of the four Bian children's outgrown clothing occupied its own trunk – two full of girls' clothing and the other two full of boys'. And what clothing it was! The Bian family – if not as rich as Berta's own – was quite prosperous, and only the most exquisite outfits had been stored away to be passed down to future generations. Most of it was silk, woven into jewel-like brocades and shimmering satins.

Such finery was worn by both sexes in Hanshu, though men usually wore sober black pants beneath their splendid tunics. And of course it ranged in size from clothing suitable for a toddler to garments the Bian children had worn in their adolescence. It was the better part of an hour before the visitors had selected the garb they would wear, as Bian Tu stood by amused. He made sure that each of them had a headdress, as well.

This local garb would not hide the fact that the two were not Hando, but it should help to make them less noticeable in the crowds. People in Tiangong often went about dressed in their best, as it was considered disrespectful to the gods to do otherwise.

Gabriel and Berta took the clothing they'd selected back to their room to put it on. After they'd had their baths last night they'd put on clean underwear, and had not put the black dragon talisman necklaces back on – leaving them on the nightstand instead. After Berta had slipped into blue silk trousers and a deep green brocaded tunic that set off her eyes, she reached for the necklace to hang it around her neck.

Gabriel put a hand on her arm, and murmured, "Berta, let's not wear them." She looked at him blankly.

"But Honorable Jiao said they would help to hide us from Rajani," she pointed out. The boy had gotten into a pair of black trousers and was slipping a golden silk tunic that looked a little like a bathrobe over his shoulders. It had no buttons, but crossed over in front – held closed with a silken tie belt.

"Can we really believe anything Honorable Jiao has told us?" he asked rhetorically. "If these necklaces hid us so well from Rajani, why did she supposedly find us in Balore, and again in Tzinshai? To hear him tell it, we have only just barely escaped her clutches every step of the way, even when we were on the ocean for days at a time. I'm beginning to think that she's not even really after us, doesn't have any idea where we are."

Berta was innocent, but she was no dummy. "Then the necklaces must be for some other reason," she said. He nodded.

"I think they're preventing Betsalel from finding us. You know Rajani said I bore his protection, so his connection with me is strong. And you were introduced to him at your Godsight ceremony, so he knows you too. Think about it, Berta! My mama and papa are his highest clergy in the whole Dominion! You know they have to have asked Betsalel to help as soon as we went missing. So why haven't they found us?"

"But…" Berta was marshaling her thoughts. "Danava must have been shielding us from divine vision when we were traveling in the caravan, and then when she took us to Delai we were probably too far away – no temples of Betsalel nearby." Gabriel nodded.

"That's true," he admitted. "But Betsalel could have taken people to Miradil and had them go out looking for us. Once we escaped from Danava's range, he might have been able to find us, if whoever was sent to look for us had idols with them. But he didn't, and I think it's because of those talismans."

Berta sighed. Danava's death threats, and Rajani's, had struck deep. But it had been weeks since there'd been any sign of the old sorceress. Probably Gabe was right. She scooped up both of the talismans and stuck them into the bottom drawer of the nightstand. "I don't know whether Honorable Jiao mentioned to his friend that we're supposed to be wearing them, but if they're not out in plain sight maybe he'll assume they're under our clothes," she said.

Her friend gave her a grin, dazzling white in his dark face, and a little hug. Then they finished getting dressed, donning their headdresses, and admired themselves in the room's full-length mirror before going back out into the corridor and down the stairs to the sitting room where Honorable Bian awaited them.

He gave them a grandfatherly smile, beaming happily, and said "Excellent! You two look splendid! Shall we be off?" To Zu Lao he said, as they were leaving, "We'll be back in time for supper, as I assume Honorable Jiao will be. Set places for four." Though Bian's servants had lived here most of their adult lives and were like family, they ate together in the kitchen – never at the dining table. Most meals for Bian Tu were lonely ones, when he did not have his children and grandchildren visiting.

"I thought that today we would visit the municipal gardens, see some of the temples, and have lunch at one of my favorite pinyin restaurants. That ought to be enough for one day," their host told the children. Enclosed by its wall, Tiangong was far smaller than many another city in Hanshu. But it was also the country's foremost tourist destination, and one could spend weeks exploring without seeing everything that was worth a visit.

The children had picked up most of what he had said, but not all of it. "Pinyin?" Gabriel asked. It reminded him of the name of a tree that grew in some of the mountainous regions of the Dominion. But he doubted they would be eating trees. Bian smiled again. Jiao had been kind enough to them, but they had never seen any genuine warmth from him such as his friend possessed.

"Little bites," he explained, holding up his right hand with the thumb and index finger held about an inch apart to show what he meant. "Everything they serve is small, with a few of them on each plate. You order many plates, whatever you want, and at the end of the meal they count the plates to learn how much to charge you."

Again, there had been a lot of words in there Gabriel wasn't sure he'd understood; but he thought he'd gotten the idea. He turned his attention to something else Honorable Bian had said, as he began to lead them down the street toward an area of rampant greenery that could be seen in the distance, some half mile away. That must be the gardens he'd mentioned.

"Honorable Bian, you said we would see… uh, visit… temples. Yes?" Bian nodded. "There are many temples in Tiangong?" Jiao had told the children there were a lot, but had not mentioned that a Temple of the Eight was among them. Nor had he mentioned anything about a temple of Betsalel.

"Another name for Tiangong is 'The City of a Thousand Gods,'" Bian assured them.

"So many?" Berta asked. Her education had included some Kiswa, the tongue most often spoken throughout Palambo, and an overview of the many languages once spoken in the Dominion before Ostden the First had united it into one nation. Thus her facility for languages was better than Gabriel's, and she'd understood their guide had claimed there were temples to a thousand gods here. Considering they only worshiped eight gods in the Dominion, that seemed a little excessive.

Bian smiled deprecatingly. "I have lived here nearly all my life," he admitted, "and I have only counted a few hundred. But there are indeed a great many temples. Here in Hanshu we feel that all of the gods worshiped by mankind are deserving of honor. And here, we have made space to honor them all."

"Then there's a Temple of the Eight?" she cried eagerly.

Now their guide looked discomfited. I let my local pride run away with my mouth, he thought ruefully. This cloak-and-dagger stuff his old friend Jiao had brought to his door was not something he had the skills for. "Uh, yes… of course," he replied. "But it is far away on the other side of the city. As you are from the Dominion I'm sure you would like to worship there. But that will have to wait for another day."

Gabriel gave Berta a meaningful look and murmured to her under his breath in Gasparto: "I'll bet Jiao told him not to take us there. He knows we'd just call Betsalel to take us home." She nodded resignedly. But surely, she and Gabe were of no use to Jiao or his king just staying here in Hanshu. Once they'd arranged for her papa to pay the reward – or the ransom, more like – they would surely be home again before long. And meanwhile, they were in a beautiful exotic city and being shepherded around by a kindly native who knew all the best places to visit. Might as well enjoy the trip! Having a hot bath and wearing new, gorgeous clothing had done a lot to improve her outlook on life.

Gabriel was trying hard to hold on to his resolve not to play into the hands of their captors. But they were being treated well, and he didn't believe they were in any danger. The political repercussions of Berta's being used to extract favors from her father didn't really register on him. He was too young, too inexperienced to understand how the world worked. So he decided to give up and for today at least, just enjoy their outing. Of all the places they'd been since their adventure began, Tiangong seemed the most appealing.

The municipal gardens were amazing. They offered the finest examples of the landscaper's art to be seen anywhere in the world, so Bian claimed – and the kids were inclined to believe him. With their fantastically sculpted flowering shrubs and graceful reflecting pools, they made the Imperial palace gardens in Parat look like an unkempt wilderness.

There were ducks with their well-grown ducklings swimming in the many ponds, exquisite lotus blossoms floating on the surface. Everywhere they looked grew flowers neither of them had ever seen before. And the gardens included a small menagerie – the property of the crown, and maintained at the royal family's expense, but open to the public every day between the hours of nine a.m. and four p.m. It contained a few animals considered exotic in Hanshu, such as giraffes and zebras, as well as many creatures more familiar to the locals but exotic enough to thrill the Gaspari children. There were black and white creatures, clearly some kind of bear, but much smaller than the bears of the Dominion and so adorable with their fuzzy patterned fur Berta just wanted to pick one up and cuddle it.

"I wouldn't recommend that," Bian told them with a laugh. "Xiong looks cute, but he really is a kind of bear. He doesn't eat meat like most other bears, but he could still bite and scratch you. Not a good pet." There were rolling carts selling treats to the visitors strolling through the grounds, and Bian bought them each a strange, gelatinous-looking confection. It was very, very sweet.

"It's made with rice, and with sugar of course," he told them. Their understanding of Hando seemed to be growing by leaps and bounds as they were immersed in it. Jiao had always spoken to them in Gasparto, in which he was very fluent, almost as if he did not want them to learn the language spoken almost everywhere east of the Killtops.

They wandered the wonderful gardens until early afternoon, then walked a few blocks away to the pinyin restaurant Bian liked. The place was huge! Gabriel guessed that at any given time as many as half the people in Tiangong might be visitors rather than residents. That meant there were more restaurants and inns than he was used to seeing – though his home city of Parat was also a magnet for tourists and pilgrims.

They took a round table near a window, with a view out to the south. The children had some experience of Hando cuisine, having been eating the Hando cook's dishes during their days aboard the Piao Qin and in inns nightly since arriving in Dongyi. But most of the dishes here were new to them, and they left it entirely up to their guide.

In rapid-fire Hando, he spoke to the waiter for a couple of minutes. And before long, little plates of food began arriving at their table. Feeling as if they'd embarked on a culinary adventure, the kids tried at least a bite of everything. Most of the offerings were so small that you could devour the entire tidbit in one bite – even if you were very small yourself.

Women with rolling carts laden with more dishes of small treats, and fresh pots of tea, wandered the room offering additional fare to the diners. "Could we have more of those… the little dumplings with the shrimp in them?" Gabriel asked, and Bian smilingly took another plate of them from a passing cart.

As he stuffed another couple of them into his mouth, the boy remarked, "It's a long way from the ocean, here. How do they get shrimp?"

"Ah," Bian said with a smile. He truly was proud of his home city, and of his nation. Showing it off to these young visitors, even if he was treating with them less than honestly, gave him a great deal of pleasure. "These shrimp are not from the sea, but live in fresh water. Centuries ago we of Hanshu learned the art of breeding them in small ponds." Gabriel goggled at the answer.

After lunch they went to visit a few of the nearby temples before making their way back to Bian's house. Temples could be found everywhere in Tiangong – some enormous, some smaller, and some no more than a shrine the size of a closet. But every one harbored a true idol.

As the son of high-ranking clergy Gabriel had thought that he knew a lot about religion. He certainly knew a lot of things that the average citizen of the Dominion did not know, including the significance of true idols, the fact that gods could transport you from one true idol to another, and how daemons came into being. But walking with Berta and Honorable Bian along The Street of the Plum Blossoms made him realize how little he, or anyone in the Dominion, had understood.

There were not eight gods and goddesses – there were dozens, hundreds, deities beyond count! Where the staid citizens of the Dominion had hidden away their daemons, made them arcane beings only accessible to those who had studied as mages, east of the Killtops humanity had embraced every notion of divinity that had ever crossed their minds and made them real.

On this street (the plum blossoms, Honorable Bian informed them, were truly lovely in the spring) there were dozens of temples. And every one of them honored a deity who had been created by man. The majority of these had been created in remote antiquity, some of them before knowledge of the Eight had even reached this region. The mind of man craved gods, and the universe had been configured to provide them.

Gabriel's parents had told him about the One. There was certainly a possibility that he might go into Betsalel's priesthood himself someday – it *was* the family business, after all. From what they'd said the One had arisen at the same time the universe had. But if the One was not the creator, what being was? How could a universe vast beyond imagining just pop into existence?

And by what coincidence had a being capable of providing gods for life forms who needed them also come to be? It was impossible to imagine the universe simply starting without something to start it. But when he thought about it – if some being had created the universe, then what had created that being? It made his head hurt.

The adherents of each deity represented along the Street of Plum Blossoms – indeed, of each deity represented in the entire Celestial City – had done their best to make their temples shine, and draw worshipers. The more worshipers a deity could gather, the greater that deity's powers would be. It was in some ways like a marketplace, with dozens of vendors selling a similar product and every one of them clamoring for the attention of passersby.

Therefore the architecture of the buildings the visitors passed ran the gamut of styles and building materials. Some sought to dazzle the eye with brightly colored tiles and inlays, others to lure you with mystery or convince you of the respectable nature of their church by adhering to long-accepted conventions of conservative design. The overall effect was staggering.

In a smallish temple made of black stone and inlaid with designs inset in lapis lazuli, a worshiper knelt before a plinth on which was mounted a dark idol no more than three feet high. It depicted a woman with four arms, two of which held knives while the others held boons offered to her adherents. "Blessed Danava, come to me," the kneeling woman called. The Destroyer was little known in Hanshu, but she had her followers. And the black goddess was eager that there might become more of them.

She manifested in the idol, growing as tall as she could without grazing the ceiling of the small room. The temple overall was no more than ten feet high, and around twenty feet on a side. "I come, Siu Lan," she purred in the woman's mind. The woman, in her later forties, gazed up in wonder at the black goddess who had come to her call.

"Thank you mistress," she replied humbly. "I am confused. I have been offered marriage by Honorable Sung Shai Lo. I like the man, I must admit, but I do not trust him. Is his offer genuine, or does he only seek to gain control of what was left to me by my first husband?"

In the presence of Siu Lan's adoration and belief, Danava's power soared. She reached out her senses, seeking the mind of Sung Shai Lo. She had taken his image from the mind of her petitioner. As she did so, she was astounded to encounter another image she knew

– one she had expected never to find again. The girl! And the shadow child, her companion, as well!

Bian and the children returned to the house as evening was coming on, tired and hungry but well satisfied with the day's activities. They had had fun together, and there had been experiences Gabriel and Berta, at least, would cherish for the rest of their lives.

They found Jiao Jing there before them, though not by many minutes. Zu Lao was pouring wine for him and providing him with some small appetizers. The rest of them eagerly devoured those, and Bian joined his friend in the wine while Gabriel and Berta had some chilled goat's milk to drink.

Jiao seemed disinclined to discuss his day at the palace in front of the children, so Bian suggested they retreat to his study again. The children were happy to join Zu Lao in the kitchen, where she put them to work chopping vegetables. "Hold it like this," she commanded, demonstrating. "Keep your fingers bent and your knuckles up, so the cleaver cannot add your fingertips to the meal. That's right, good. Now, I need five carrots and three cups of celery…"

In the study, Jiao Jing was showing signs that the wine was beginning to wash away some of his pique. "Did you enjoy the day with the children?" he asked. Bian grinned at him. "It was fun!" he declared. "My grandchildren were all born here and have lived here all their lives. It's not often I get to show *them* something new. But Jurgen and Gerdur's eyes were wide with delight at each new sight. That's what makes children such a joy, really. You see the world fresh through their eyes. Do you get to spend much time with your own grandchildren?"

"I'm afraid not," Jiao said stiffly. He had always left the raising of his own children to his wives, and scarcely even knew his grandchildren. For most of every year, he'd been anywhere from hundreds to thousands of miles away from Tzinshai, traveling the Ivory Road to provide them all with a living. Perhaps, after he had become governor of Tzinshai, he would have the time to get to know his descendants. Now that he was an ancestor, it was probably time.

"So how did it go at the palace?" Bian asked, still feeling jovial after the enjoyment he'd had shepherding the young visitors around his home town. Jiao's expression was forbidding, but he lightened it after a moment with a wry almost-smile. "Better than I'd feared," he admitted, "if worse than I'd hoped. I waited in the seneschal's office for most of the day, wishing that I had brought a chamberpot with me. And later, that I had thought to pack a lunch."

"But Shian eventually saw you?" his friend said with concern. "Not above half an hour before closing," Jiao said. "I had feared I might be pushed off onto some underling, and would be spending the next week working my way up through the ranks before I finally got to speak with someone in charge. But your Shian Tze Din deigned to talk with me at last, and while I of course did not tell him everything I hinted at enough that he was willing to make an appointment for me to speak with King Wang Qian. I will attend him in his audience room at the palace day after tomorrow, at mid-morning."

Chapter 46

Gabriel and Berta woke in the morning, wondering what the day would bring. If Honorable Jiao had to wait until the morrow for his interview with the king, he would be around all day. Would he want to take them out sightseeing, as Honorable Bian had done? They'd talked quietly in their beds last night before going to sleep, and concluded that Bian was an essentially good man who'd been drawn into Jiao's dishonest enterprise by their ties as boyhood friends. That didn't mean they could trust him, though.

"Let's try to act normal and pretend everything's all right," Gabriel suggested. "But if Jiao wants us to go out with him into the city, we tell him we have to go to the Temple of the Eight. See what he says, then we'll know."

"But then what?" Berta asked. "If he admits he just plans to sell us to his king, what do we do about it?"

Gabriel didn't really have an answer. He was convinced that it was essentially *wrong* for grownups to be using kids as pawns in some kind of power game, anxious to spoke Jiao's wheel if he could. But what, really, could they do? Throw a tantrum in the middle of the public square, crying out in their broken Hando that they'd been kidnaped? Even if, somehow, they managed to convince passersby that Jiao was a bad guy, wouldn't they just end up in the custody of the king anyway?

"Well, at least if we stand up to him we'll know him for what he is. We could tell the king he's a bad guy." He sighed. "I don't know," he said finally. "Let's go eat." The black dragon talismans remained in the drawer, as they donned the same outfits they'd had on yesterday.

They found Honorable Bian and Honorable Jiao eating at the table before them, pretty much the same meal as yesterday except that today there were duck eggs that had been boiled and then fermented until they were nearly black. The two Hando men ate them with relish, but the Gaspari kids declined. Jiao's mood seemed to have improved since yesterday evening, and he made an effort to be jolly at the table. For their part, the children made an effort to pretend they were buying his act.

"So," he said jovially, "Tu tells me you went to see the gardens yesterday, and the menagerie."

"Yes," Berta chattered enthusiastically. "They were the most beautiful gardens I've ever seen, and the animals were interesting too. Oh, and Honorable Bian took us to a wonderful restaurant to eat pinyin. Before we go home, I hope we could find someone in Hanshu who would consider opening a Hando restaurant in the Dominion. I'm sure it would be very popular."

"Well," Jiao said, "Honorable Bian tells me that he needs to go to his family's store today to take care of some business matters. But as I have the day free, I could take you for some more sightseeing. It's been quite a few years since I was regularly spending time in Tiangong, but not much has changed. I think I can still find my way around. Would you like that?"

Gabriel and Berta exchanged a glance and then she smiled and said "Thank you, Honorable Jiao. That would be very nice."

It had rained overnight, and the streets had been washed clean. Not that they weren't already far cleaner than the streets in any Dominion city. People in Hanshu seemed to have a greater appreciation of sanitation. The overcast was breaking up as they set out on foot, and it looked like it would be another nice day.

Jiao Jing strode along, taking small steps out of consideration for his pint-sized companions. "So, where would you like to go? There's an art museum, if you're interested, and if I recall correctly there's a place up near the palace where you can borrow a pole and fish for carp in a pond. What do you think?"

Fishing sounded intriguing to both children, who had done a little bit of ocean fishing in the Northern Ocean on excursions there in summer but had never really caught anything. It was quite a climb to the palace, so Jiao hailed a sedan chair to carry them there.

The place was still in business. It included a small park near the wall of the palace compound, where families could stroll around the grounds or have picnics. There was also a casual eatery, and a half-acre pond stocked with carp. The bamboo fishing poles had unbarbed hooks, the idea being that after enjoying the thrill of catching a fish you could release it. Dough ball bait was supplied with the pole rental.

This proved so much fun for the children that Jiao found himself with too much time on his hands – sitting on a bench feeling bored and anxious. He had harbored desires for political power for years, and on having this opportunity handed to him had invested weeks of his time and many pieces of gold getting the children here. Tomorrow morning, he would have his opportunity at last.

But would the king smile on him, and grant him what he wanted? A worst-case scenario, that King Wang Qian might have him seized by the guards and thrown into the dungeon as a kidnaper and would-be extortionist, had crossed his mind. But as long as the king and his guards had no idea where the children were, that seemed unlikely. The danger would come when he actually delivered them. It was not wise to trust kings. Perhaps he could extract his appointment to the governorship first, then arrange to have the kids delivered by some innocent third party?

It was well past lunchtime before Gabriel and Berta, getting too hungry to keep fishing, turned their poles back in at the rental kiosk. They all ate lunch at the on-site restaurant, as that seemed most convenient. The food was not as good as they'd had yesterday, but it wasn't bad. The children filled up on warm steamed buns and crispy spring rolls.

After lunch they began on foot, strolling through the wealthy neighborhoods just below the palace compound. The homes there were certainly something to behold, and some of Tiangong's largest and fanciest temples were there, too. Gabriel and Berta had their eyes peeled for a temple to any of the Eight. They had met all of them in Parat, and likely could beg any of them to be returned there. They saw none, though.

A few blocks later Jiao came to a halt. "We still have a few hours of the day," he said. "Where would you like to go next?" The children exchanged another glance, and it was Gabriel who spoke up.

"We want to be taken to the Temple of the Eight," he said flatly, looking defiantly into Jiao's eyes. The man looked down at him coldly.

"I'm afraid that won't be possible," he said.

"Why not?" Gabe retorted. "Do you have it on good authority that Rajani is lurking there, waiting for us to appear so she can snatch us away from you and sell us to a *different* king?" Jiao's face paled, and his mouth formed a hard line. Berta looked at him anxiously. What if Gabe had pushed him too far?

"You want to go to the temple of the black god, do you?" Jiao said tightly. "Very well. Come along, and I will take you there." He seized each of them by the hand and began striding along down the slope, walking so fast the children had to trot to keep up. Both of them were frightened enough to raise no protest. He wouldn't kill Berta, at least. But this close to handing the children over for ransom, he might think Gabriel's usefulness was at an end.

It was a long walk to the black temple, but Jiao showed no sign of the infirmity of age. Though he was a grandfather, he walked without any stiffness. Nor did he speak to them further until they'd fetched up in front of a medium sized building faced with black stone. It was square rather than circular, with red designs set into the black façade. It didn't look like any temple of Betsalel Gabriel had ever seen, and he'd seen quite a few.

They stepped inside the door, finding the room warm verging on hot inside. The heat was caused by red and orange flames, licking up around the inside walls from channels set on two of the four sides. At the rear was a door that probably led to a room where a priest or priests might live or rest. But there was no one in the main sanctuary. In the center of the floor was a broad pedestal, and curled on that pedestal in a posture of aggression was the idol of the black god whose place this was.

Ling Zao was nearly ten feet long from blunt, bewhiskered nose to spiked tail tip, but thin. He looked more like a serpent with four short, clawed legs than like the dragons the Gaspari children were used to from illustrated folk tales. The Dominion's concept of a dragon looked more like a squat, long-tailed lizard with bat wings, and usually had a pointed beak. The god was completely covered in scales – smoother below, rougher above – and was matte black all over except for the glowing orange eyes. The mouth was open, and even the teeth and tongue were black.

Jiao kept a tight hold on their hands, as if he feared they might run away. They had nowhere to go, and were utterly lost in this foreign city; but his caution was not unwise. Ling Zao was almost as scary-looking as Danava standing there, and their terror rose dramatically when Jiao murmured an invocation and the god manifested before them.

"Jiao Jing," the black dragon hissed. Steam issued from his nostrils and he writhed and coiled but did not leave his pillar. "Long has it been since you called on me. Your gold increases?" "It does, master, and I thank you. It is about these children that I seek your aid. I have given them your talismans, that they might be bound to your power." The children realized that though the god seemed to be speaking in Hando, they had no trouble understanding him.

Ling Zao peered down at them nearsightedly. For a creature that size, his eyes were tiny. "They wear no talismans, my servant. And the boy already bears the protection of my brother Betsalel." Though the origins of the daemon gods were entirely human, they felt a kinship with the Eight – a kinship the Eight would not generally acknowledge.

"What?!" Jiao snapped, turning to Berta and unbuttoning the frogs that held her tunic closed down the front. "Why are you not wearing your talisman? Did I not tell you must keep it on at all times, to hide and protect you from Rajani?" He looked ready to strike her, and Gabriel chimed in.

"It was my idea," he said defiantly. "We figured you put them on us to hide us from Betsalel, who is sure to be looking for us. We took them off yesterday morning, and Rajani didn't show up. We haven't seen her at all, or felt Danava's influence, since we left her back on the Ivory Road in the Gholim lands. She *wasn't* chasing us like you said."

Now Jiao's face had gone red, furious at this betrayal from one to whom he'd shown every kindness. He got a grip on his temper, though. He had not spent a lifetime as a canny trader without learning how to control his emotions. "What did you do with the talismans?" he asked.

"We threw them away," Gabriel ad-libbed. "Tossed them out the window at Honorable Bian's house."

"We'll see about that!" he snapped coldly. "Master, I need these two to behave themselves until tomorrow. Can you... influence them?"

"Without the talismans my power over them is weakened," the black dragon replied. "They are not my worshipers, and the boy is dedicated to the Shadow God. Even with a talisman, I could probably not harm him by supernatural means."

Jiao looked disappointed, but he had a thought. "But while you are manifest, master, are there not other means by which you might coerce their cooperation?" Ling Zao writhed on his platform and hissed.

"Boy," he said, "hold out your hand."

"No!" Berta screamed. "Don't hurt him!"

"You must see and believe," the dark god said, his voice almost a caress. Gabe stuck his hands behind his back and glared stubbornly at the creature. If Betsalel protected him, he couldn't be forced to do anything.

Or could he? Jiao Jing grabbed Gabriel's arm and thrust it forward. He had the wiry strength of his mother, but he was only seven years old. He could not overpower a grown man. Ling Zao inhaled, then expelled a small, tightly controlled stream of flame onto the back of Gabriel's left hand. The boy shrieked in agony as the skin blistered.

Berta was shrieking as well, crying and trying to comfort her friend. And the black dragon was admiring his handiwork with a self-satisfied air. "Oh be quiet, both of you!" Jiao snapped. "It's just a little burn. But you will both be spending the rest of our time in Tiangong locked in your room at Bian Tu's house. I will have to find those talismans, and when I do you will put them on and not take them off again. This is important! If you fail to obey, I will bring Gabriel back here and we will burn him again. Or perhaps my master is hungry, eh?"

Ling Zao did not customarily eat human flesh, preferring to imbibe molten gold. But he was willing to go along with his dedicant's ruse. He opened his mouth in a toothy grin, tongue lolling, and eyed the boy hungrily. "We'll be good, I promise!" Berta said, and Gabriel nodded agreement.

Jiao Jing hailed another sedan chair to return them to Honorable Bian's house. The children sat huddled on the seat opposite him, tear-streaked and cowed. The burn on Gabriel's hand, a circle half an inch across, hurt so much it was all he could do to keep from sobbing.

When they got back to the house Zu Lao tut-tutted at the boy's injury (which Jiao informed her curtly had been the result of a mishap at the restaurant where they'd had lunch, without offering any details). The grandmotherly woman insisted on cleaning the injury and applying a soothing ointment before wrapping the hand in gauze bandages. Whatever was in that ointment, it quickly eased the pain. Gabriel wanted to kiss her for her kindness.

The children were not to join their host and Jiao Jing at table tonight, Jiao informed the housekeeper. She made up a tray for them and the house's only other servant, a man of forty who performed odd jobs that were beyond Zu Lao's abilities, brought it up and handed it to Berta before closing and locking the door again. Jiao had explained to him that the children were being punished for some bad behavior during the afternoon, once again without offering details.

After supper and before it got dark, Gabriel looked out the room's window and spotted Jiao Jing in the yard, down on his hands and knees among the shrubbery and loose mulch searching for the talismans of Ling Zao. He glanced up. "Oh crap!" he exclaimed, drawing raised eyebrows from his companion.

"What?" she asked, perplexed.

"I just realized these windows don't open," he said, pointing. They were of a casement type, hinged on one side with a latch on the other. But at some time in the past, possibly out of fear that Honorable Bian's children might open them and be injured or killed falling from the second floor, the latches had been removed and the casements nailed shut.

"Uh oh," Berta said. "When he gets tired of searching the yard, he's likely to come up here and discover that. Then he's going to threaten to take you back to Ling Zao and burn off your whole arm, or something." Gabriel looked subdued. His hand felt much better, but he couldn't really think of any logical reason why Jiao Jing would hesitate to inflict whatever painful, non-lethal injury he thought would get Berta to cooperate. And he wasn't anxious to see the black dragon ever again. I'll bet Lord Betsalel could totally kick his ass, he thought. I wish he were here!

But it was not until hours later that they had to confront their captor again. As darkness was beginning to fall and he still had not found the missing talismans, he had hailed a small sedan chair and gone off toward the area where the temple of Ling Zao was located. Gabriel and Berta had gone to bed and were asleep when he suddenly burst into the room, an oil lantern in his hand.

He did not notice the nailed-shut windows, now hidden by curtains. But he was nearing the end of his rope. He had found no one in the city, not even at Ling Zao's temple, who could supply him with another two talisman necklaces. Jiao slammed the door behind him, waking the children, and strode between the bed platforms to set the lantern on the night stand between them.

As Gabriel was rubbing the sleep from his eyes, struggling to sit up, Jiao seized him by the throat and lifted him bodily half out of the bed. "All right, you black monster," he grated, his fury getting the better of him. "What did you *really* do with the talismans?" The boy was in shock, clutching at his attacker's hands as he struggled to breathe.

"Stop it!" Berta yelled at him. "Stop it, you're hurting him!" She jumped to her feet and began pummeling Jiao, easily two feet taller than she was, with her little fists. He dropped the boy in a fury and whirled on the girl, who cowered back from him. "Here, they're here!" she squeaked, pointing at the bottom drawer of the nightstand. He ripped it open and saw the two talismans lying within. Aha!

In under a minute both children were once again wearing the talismans of Ling Zao, and had been threatened with dire consequences should they take them off again. "You don't seem to realize that they are truly for your own protection," Jiao said, having gotten his temper under control again. "Do you not know that there is a temple of Danava here in Tiangong? Without these, she or any of a thousand other deities, many of them malign, might cast their eyes on you." The children sat on their beds, eyes downcast. They were thoroughly chastened.

I'd expected the little princess to be spoiled, Jiao mused, but the boy is even worse. Who is he? Some lordling? "As punishment for your misbehavior, there will be no breakfast for you tomorrow. I hope that by as early as midday I will have concluded my negotiations with the king, and you will soon be on your way to the palace. I am sure he will be more than happy to feed you.

Chapter 47

Though Leila and Tevo had rid themselves of the slow horses provided by Lee Ho Sing, it was still more than two full days before they reached Tiangong. The limitations of travel by horse could not be entirely eliminated simply by granting tirelessness to the mounts and their riders. Hunger, thirst, and elimination all required time to deal with.

They entered the city fairly late on the second day, as the sun was going down in a blaze of glory behind the Shan Lings. They galloped up the remainder of the river road, which ended here, and came in through the gates – just two more pilgrims out of the hundreds who had passed through those gates today.

Leila erected a silence bubble, which barely encompassed Tevo riding at her side. She hoped that her quiet words in Gasparto would go unremarked. The two still appeared to be Hando men in their early twenties, rough enough to be anything from laborers to mercenary soldiers. Their mounts were far too fine for such, but they could only hope that fact would go unremarked.

"By the Eight, I hope we can find lodging here!" she said, slowly urging Nimble through the crowds. The city reminded her a little of Namei in Palambo, with its palace atop the hill. But where Namei had been built of concentric circles, each higher than the next, here the circle was only an arc pressed up against the mountainside. The small rushing stream that had been dubbed the official source of the Holy River ran through the middle of Tiangong, cascading from one level to another before spilling out below the city wall.

Neither of them was tired by their long ride, Betsalel's gift giving them the power to go on indefinitely as long as they had food and water – and occasionally, sleep. But psychologically they were both ready for a break. "We need to find the temple of Betsalel," Tevo said. "Once we have him working for us, we should be able to find the kids and take them home in no time."

Leila wasn't sure, though, what kind of reaction they might get asking after the Shadow God. She wasn't even sure that he had a temple of his own here. Given how much competition there was in the god business, in this part of the world, it was likely that the

Temple of the Eight was their best bet. "Let's ask for Belantos, instead," she suggested. "We might get pointed to Betsalel from that, or Belantos himself could guide us."

Belantos, along with Andros and Mulia, were the three of the Eight who were worshiped most universally east of the Killtops. War was a fact of life for millions here. And wherever there was humanity, the god and goddess of masculinity and femininity were of primary importance. Leila felt that her master Betsalel, as the god of death, was every bit as universal; but this view was not widely shared.

So it was that the hard-bitten young man mounted on the tall red Shuang gelding climbed down from his horse and approached a street vendor. He bought a paper packet of some little fried objects that proved to be wheat dough wrapped around seasoned pork, and remarked casually, "Where can we go to pay our respects to Belantos?"

The vendor was used to dealing with pilgrims. This fellow looked like he was probably here to seek employment with the Royal Guard. "The Guard's got their own temple to Belantos up near the top, outside the palace wall," he said. "You just keep going uphill and eventually you'll hit Soldier Street. Can't miss it. Or, holy Belantos is also represented at the Temple of the Eight. That's a little closer, around a mile from here. You need to go up three blocks, until you get to the Street of the Golden Dawn, then turn left until you find the temple on your right. Can you read?"

The supposed thug nodded, and the vendor looked surprised. "You'll see the signs, then, 'Street of the Golden Dawn,' painted on the buildings on all four corners. Just turn left there. The door's open all night." The fellow had been so helpful, Leila had to ask "Where can we get lodging, and stable our horses?"

The vendor considered. "If you're here to sign up with the Royal Guard, they'll give you a berth and stable your horses for you too. They're always looking for strong young fellows, and having your own mounts is a plus. Otherwise, there are quite a few inns along the Street of the Golden Dawn. Can't say which one will have room. Summer's a busy time, you know. Good luck!"

"Thank you," the young thug replied, and remounted his horse. He passed the rest of the fried dumplings to his companion. "Hey, these are good!" Tevo said, devouring them in short order. There'd been very little in the way of hot food on their journey from Xia Gu.

They were soon making their way along the fabled Street of the Golden Dawn. It was situated so that a goodly stretch of it was pointing east, but like all of Tiangong's roads it curved around the mountainside. Perhaps the street naming was random, or a cultural thing that had little to do with a road's particular attributes.

They encountered quite a few inns on the way, but bypassed them – eager to confer with Betsalel after days without being able to. They were brought up short when at last they saw the Temple of the Eight. It was every bit as elaborate as the one in Parat, or the one in Iskand – a large building, faced with pure white stone, and octagonal in shape.

In this case, inlays of the other seven deities' colors had been added to the white for a rainbow effect. The place was lit by dozens of lanterns and torches – and though night had fallen, it was swarming with people. "Shit," Leila remarked inside her bubble of silence, which she'd renewed as they went along.

"Maybe we'd better try to find an inn with space for us," Tevo suggested. "We could get some dinner, and come back here later when it's not so crowded." They could scarcely call the Shadow God and have him make them a couple of new idols while dozens of onlookers were standing around, or actively engaged in worship of the other seven.

Hours later, Nimble and Milacek were happily eating the inn's stable out of its supply of grain. Leila and Tevo, in their disguise as the two muscular young toughs (who mysteriously not only had fine mounts but gold as well – were they robbers?) had eaten a delicious hot meal and even had a short nap. It seemed like forever since they had made love, and the longing was on both their minds; but the time for that had not yet arrived.

It was now past ten, and they made their way invisibly and silently down the Street of the Golden Dawn toward the Temple of the Eight. Many lanterns still lit its exterior, but the doors had been closed and the crowds were gone. Assuming the guise of an elderly

Hando couple and going visible, they pushed open the large double doors that were the temple's main entrance.

Their entry had gone unnoticed. As Betsalel was one of the Eight and his worship was associated with darkness and night, it was usual for temples honoring the entire original pantheon to be unlocked most of the night as well as all day. But while the Temple of the Eight in Parat was staffed twenty-four hours a day, here it seemed that competition had caused the temple to cut down on employees. Any offerings that had been left by worshipers had been taken away and stowed, and the staff had gone to bed. Perfect!

The idols, each around twelve feet in height, ringed the large room in silence. With no one here to call the gods, they remained immobile statues. Joy surging through her at finally reconnecting with her god, Leila fell to her knees and called, "Betsalel! We are here!" She maintained the "old woman" illusion in case there were any unseen watchers, but the Shadow God would know who she truly was.

In an instant the black idol stirred and shrank to a height of six feet, their master's preferred size for interacting with mortals. "Where have you been?" he asked, concern in his dark voice.

"We were set on by thugs hired by the man who is holding the children," Leila said. "They took our idols and threw them to the bottom of a thousand-foot-deep river canyon, I'm afraid."

"Maybe I'll make some new converts among the fish," Betsalel suggested with a smile. He stepped down off his pillar and hugged his two favorite humans to him. He had many to love now, and many who loved him. But these two were special. Without Leila and Tevo, he might have become nothing but a small voice wailing in the wilderness.

"The children are here?" Leila asked. Everything they had done for the past few weeks had been centered on finding Gabriel and Berta and bringing them home, and she was now convinced that they must finally be reaching that goal. Rajani had been left far behind, and Jiao Jing had nowhere else to run. If he sold the children to the Hando king, they would be there to take them back.

Betsalel extended his senses. He was stronger here than at almost any other point east of the Killtops, stronger still with this particular pair of worshipers in his presence. They loved him with all their hearts, and their love and devotion was power. And he was surprised. Gabriel blazed out in the darkness like a beacon, and even Berta was clearly visible.

"They are near!" he cried. "In a house a few miles from here, further up toward the summit of the city. They…" Suddenly the clear vision was gone, ripped away again. Leila and Tevo were looking up at him, entranced. "The barrier!" Betsalel cursed. "It has come down again!"

"Master, what is it?" Leila asked, disappointed. For a moment there she had imagined marching up the hill and just taking their son back by main force. "It is the influence of one of these daemons," the Shadow God explained. "One who's particularly powerful in this part of the world. It's not a true warding such as I can place on a believer, but a talisman of some kind. I think that your Jiao Jing is an adherent of one of these local gods, and has cloaked the children with the tokens of that god. I can still sense them, Gabriel especially, but it is no longer clear."

Disappointment stung, but Leila and Tevo were not defeated. They had been battling one setback after another for weeks, and they had no intention of accepting defeat. "Master, give us new idols to replace the ones that were lost," Leila said. "In the morning, we will find where Jiao Jing has hidden our son."

Chapter 48

In the morning, the children slept in. The traumas of the previous afternoon, and Jiao's late-night visit, had sent them retreating from the world. A sense of helplessness had come over them, as well. They dared not remove the black stone talismans now. Jiao Jing was clearly in favor with his strange god, and they were afraid of crossing him.

So they slept. By the time they awakened, Jiao had already left by sedan chair for the palace, eager for his interview with the king. And they were locked in their room, hungry but denied breakfast as a punishment for daring to confront their captor at last.

There were two chamberpots in the room, but both of them were at least half full and beginning to smell when they found the door unlocked by Zu Lao. She was accompanied by Bian's manservant, who took the chamberpots away and returned them clean while Lao laid out a platter of sweet buns and little pastries, along with a large pot of tea and two delicate porcelain cups, on the room's small table.

"I don't know what Honorable Jiao's problem is," she told them, "but he's not here. I'll be back later for the tray, so just don't tell him I brought you food and everything will be fine!" She winked at them, then departed. They heard the room door being locked behind her.

At the royal palace, more than a mile up the hill, Jiao Jing was ushered into the king's smallest audience chamber. Here Wang Qian still sat a throne, but it was really nothing more than a large and extra-fancy chair. The official throne of the kingdom of Hanshu, which sat in the grand audience hall elsewhere in the palace, stood ten feet high at the back and was cast from solid gold (or so it was claimed), embellished with precious gems.

This room was no more than twenty by forty feet in size, but it still contained a score of royal guards. They stood, spears at the ready, as still as statues with their backs against the walls on the room's long dimension. Two flanked the doorway, and another two stood behind the throne.

Jiao eyed them uneasily, after he had been commanded to rise from the prostrate position he had assumed on first being admitted to the presence of his Imperial Majesty, King Wang Qian the Third.

"Fear not, Honorable Jiao," the monarch said. "All of my secrets, and yours, are safe with the Royal Guard."

Wang Qian was a less than a decade older than Jiao was, a still-vigorous man whose die-straight raven hair hung down past his hips. It was shot with silver now, but it was still hard to believe he was in his late fifties. The Wang dynasty had proven to be one of Hanshu's most successful, and it seemed the line bred true.

Now that his moment was finally at hand, Jiao found his confidence wavering. He could scarcely believe it! For more than twenty years he had been the master of his family enterprise – directing its path to fame and fortune with deft strokes aided by the powers of his master Ling Zao. Yet now, in the face of his Celestial Majesty Wang Qian, he found himself at a loss for words.

Wang Qian smiled. He had often noticed that he had this effect on petitioners. "So," he said, trying to put the merchant at his ease, "Honorable Shian tells me that you have located these missing children who were the subject of Emperor Ostden's proclamation?"

The opening broke through Jiao's paralysis, and he launched into his prepared presentation. "Yes, your majesty," he said. "I recovered them from the woman who had taken them from the Dominion, and brought them here. But they are not just any children. The girl is none other than Emperor Ostden's own daughter, Berta Piastin."

Wang Qian's eyes bored into Jiao's inscrutably. Finally he spoke. "I was aware of this," he said quietly. "I have not met the Gaspari emperor, but we have established diplomatic relations and often correspond by letter. He wrote to me personally to reveal that the children taken were his daughter and her friend, the son of the arch-priest and arch-priestess of Betsalel in Parat. Evidently they are close family friends of the Piastins."

Jiao was stunned. So *that's* who the black brat was! As was the case throughout much of the Dominion, those with darker skin were regarded as a lesser race by the Hando. Not that the milk-pale Gasparis were any better. But clearly the boy was important, important enough to warrant a good ransom. It was a good thing he had not fed him to Ling Zao!

The trader recovered himself. "I had recognized immediately that the children would be of value to your celestial majesty," he said humbly. "At great effort and expense to myself I took them from the Ivory Road all the way by ship from Tongnan to Dongyi, that I might bring them to you."

The king regarded him sardonically. "I see," he said. "And what reward, do you think, might compensate you for this 'great effort and expense'?" Jiao spread his arms, a gesture encompassing his silk-clad body.

"For many years I have traveled the Ivory Road, majesty, bringing the superior goods of Hanshu to the barbarians in the west. But I am getting older, and I long to spend more time at home. I was born in Tzinshai, and my business is based there. No reward of gold or jewels would mean as much to me as the simple boon of being named governor of Tzinshai."

Tzinshai, as well as being one of Hanshu's most important port cities, was the capital of a province that encompassed thousands of square miles of land. Its governorship was a political plum, yet Honorable Jiao had billed it as a minor concession. Wang Qian raised an eyebrow. "Only that?" he said, and Jiao's hopes soared.

The current governor of Tzinshai was an old man, in his mid-eighties, who had long since handed over the running of the province to subordinates. Commanding that he go into honorable retirement and naming Jiao Jing to the post would be the work of a few minutes with a pen.

That the trader was a scheming, grasping bastard who'd put his own welfare over that of a couple of innocent foreign children was not necessarily a mark against his qualifications for the governorship. Wang Qian needed able, ambitious men running the provinces – men who were willing to do what it took to make sure things ran smoothly, and that the crown always got its taxes.

"I do not see why that should be a problem," the king said at last. "And where are these children?" The fears that had tormented him yesterday came back, and Jiao's stomach clenched. But he pushed through them.

"Close, your majesty. Here within Tiangong itself. If your majesty is willing to put pen to a decree declaring me the new

governor of Tzinshai, they could be here for you within two hours."
He wanted to make sure they were cleaned up. A pity about the boy's
burn, but it was too late to do anything about it now.

"Very well," the king said. "I will command Shian Tze Din to
draw up the paperwork. Return to his office with the children, and
the governorship is yours once he has verified their identities. But do
not be too long about it! If you and they are not here within three
hours, the deal is off."

Rajani arrived at the temple of Danava in Tiangong in the early
hours of the morning – which had been the middle of the night in
Ashbat. After her defeat in Khirzai, she had realized that Oghul Khan
would be likely to have her head should she return to him empty-
handed. Instead, she had gone back across the river into Indaya, to
the nearest temple of Danava, and obtained from her goddess not one
but two new idols.

A blessedly uneventful river journey had taken her west to
Ghezh, where she had bought another horse for the journey north to
Ashbat. Oghul had indeed been unhappy with her report that their
prey had been stolen from them; but with Danava in her pocket, the
sorceress had cowed the mighty khan into accepting her claim that
this was only a minor setback. The emperor's daughter *would* be
delivered, as promised. These Gholim horse-lords were so fierce,
such mighty warriors – and a whiff of divine power sent them
scurrying. It was laughable!

It had taken Rajani weeks to acquire her new idols and return to
her employer. Then there had been more anxious weeks of waiting.
The children had to have gone east, else they would have come
within Danava's range again as they approached Khirzai. But what
had happened to them after that? Might they have been found by
Gaspari agents and transported home? If so, she could have Danava
return her to Delai. She would have to stay out of the Khanate for the
rest of her life, and she would lose the reward Oghul had promised
her; but it beat dying in nasty ways as a punishment for her failure.
And then, her goddess had come through.

"When did you sense the girl?" Rajani asked, speaking mind to
mind after exiting the temple.

"It was late the day before yesterday, I think," the goddess replied.

"What? Why did you not contact me sooner?"

"I was in the middle of conferring with another worshiper," the Destroyer answered petulantly. "And when I had given her the information she needed, there was another in Delai. And one in Balore. You are not the only one who worships me, Rajani."

A cold shiver ran through the old sorceress. Her sacrifice of her father to the dark goddess had won her status as Danava's most important priestess of her time. But that had been forty years ago. Was her goddess' support slipping? She would happily make another sacrifice to the Destroyer, if that was what it took to win back her favor. That Gaspari boy, perhaps? The one she'd really like to kill was Oghul Khan, but he was an important patron. She'd have to think on it.

"All right, we're here," Rajani said, dismissing her other concerns. "Where are the children?"

There was a moment's silence, then the goddess in her pocket admitted, "There is some barrier to my sight that has been erected since I saw the girl. Some other god's protection has been laid over her."

"Betsalel?" the sorceress hissed. If the Shadow God had found the children, her cause was lost.

"No," Danava replied. "Some other, an eastern deity from the flavor. The barrier is strong, but not impenetrable. They are off in that direction, to your right and up the hill."

Anxiety about finding the children had Leila and Tevo up not long after dawn. As the two young toughs, they ate breakfast in the inn's common room and then stepped out onto the street. Tevo called Betsalel to the idol in his pocket and they began their search.

The cloaking provided by Ling Zao's talismans was such that they had to stop at every intersection and allow Betsalel to turn, hidden within the pocket, through three hundred-sixty degrees until he had decided in which direction his sense of Gabriel was strongest. It was an ordeal.

Jiao Jing was ushered from the audience room and led by royal guards back along the way he had come to the exit. His mind was alive with excitement. The king had been so receptive to his offer, he had scarcely needed to use any of his finely-honed negotiation skills! Had it been too easy? All of the fears from yesterday came back to him. He had spent much of his adult life being a tiger in the jungle, the man others feared to deal with. But he had never dealt with royalty before. Was he stepping blindly into a tiger trap?

He made his way down the hill toward Bian's house. His old friend had once again gone off to work at Bian Mercantile, fulfilling his job duties. As the head of the family business, he rarely got a day off. By the time he returned from work the children would be gone, and Jiao would be on his way back home to Tzinshai and his new duties as governor – or locked up in a cell in the palace dungeons, for the crime of kidnaping and extortion. He prayed it would be the former.

The sun was high by the time Leila and Tevo, still impersonating the two anonymous young Hando men, approached the house where the Bian family had made its home for generations. "That's it... No! He is gone!" Betsalel said, communicating mind-to-mind from inside Tevo's pocket.

"What?!" Leila cried aloud, unmindful of anyone near enough to hear her.

"That house is where the children were being held," the god insisted. "And just now, as we approached, I suddenly lost the trace. I can no longer sense Gabriel anywhere near."

"That can't be!" she cried, and rushed toward the house's front door. They found it unlocked, slightly ajar, and pushed inside. A few paces down the hall, they found an elderly Hando woman lying in a pool of blood. Her throat had been slashed open by some kind of sharp blade. A cold fear gripped Leila's heart.

"Gabriel?" she cried, standing in the center of the house's ground floor. "Gabriel!" There was nothing but silence. They searched the living room, dining room, and kitchen. No signs of life. Then they took the stairs to the second floor, evidently where all the bedrooms were to be found. In the hall, the found the body of a Hando man in his forties. He had been killed in the same way as the old woman.

Tears were gathering in Leila's eyes. She and Tevo had dropped their illusions – there was no one to see them. Tevo reached out and squeezed her shoulder, trying to comfort her even as his own heart was threatening to tear apart in grief. Had Betsalel lost Gabriel because the boy had ceased to live?

The man lay, his blood still warm, on the carpet outside one of the bedrooms. The door was closed but not locked. They pushed inside and saw a bedroom meant for two children. There were twin sleeping platforms with puffy feather pallets on them, a nightstand, a couple of cabinets for clothing, and a small table with two chairs. Two broken necklaces, with pendants suggesting a small black serpent, lay on the floor. And in the center of the room, standing seven feet tall, was an idol of Danava.

Chapter 49

"Damn, damn, damn that woman to all the hells real and imaginary!" Leila cursed. "We should have killed her when we had the chance!" Both of them felt on the verge of tears. It was a relief, after the trail of blood from the front door, to see no signs that the children had been harmed. But this time, they had missed rescuing them by no more than minutes, perhaps a few hundred yards. It was too frustrating, too heartbreaking. Would they have to begin again from Ghezh?

Just then they heard a wordless cry from downstairs. Someone must have come in through the front door, which they'd left open in their haste to find the children. Without consultation the two went invisible, drawing their daggers, and crept past the body of the manservant to the stairs.

In the front hall a middle-aged man dressed in the garments of a wealthy trader knelt beside the body of the elderly woman, his face white with shock. From his resemblance to Jiao Shao, they knew who he must be. As he rose to his feet and called, "Hello? Is anyone here?" in a voice touched with despair, he suddenly found himself flanked by a young man and woman. They were both shorter than he was, but also decades younger than him and armed with razor-sharp daggers. Their expressions were menacing.

"Honorable Jiao Jing, I presume?" the woman said in perfect, unaccented Hando – though from her appearance, she was no countrywoman of his. Her tones dripped acid, and he shrank away from her menacing dagger. But the man on his other side looked no more friendly.

"I... I am Jiao Jing," he said resignedly. These had to be the two Gaspari agents whose message in Balore had sent him fleeing with the children as fast as their horses could carry them. Somehow they had escaped Lee Ho's band of thugs – but if they could, as it seemed, appear out of thin air perhaps it was more of a surprise they had not caught him the day he'd left the caravan.

"You found our son and his friend on the Ivory Road, and had the opportunity to return them to their families in exchange for a reward that was beyond generous," the woman said through her teeth. Though she was scarcely above five feet tall and slender, Jiao sensed a ferocity about her that made his blood run cold. "Yet you chose instead to run with them for a thousand miles though we had sent word we were coming for them. Would you care to explain *why* you did this thing?"

Merciful gods, she was the dark boy's mother! No wonder she wanted his blood. "Please, mistress, I never meant the children any harm," he said, backing as if he might turn and flee out the open front door. Tevo stepped over and closed it, then took the older man by the arm and guided him down the hall to the kitchen. He shoved him down into a chair.

"You were saying?" he asked, and took another chair at the table. Leila looked around and found a teakettle. The house had a modern oil stove, and she soon had water going for tea. Jiao's fears were beginning to ease, at this. Perhaps they didn't mean to kill him out of hand.

"Truly," he said, "It was always my intention that the princess and your son would be returned home soon, and unharmed. But as a loyal citizen of Hanshu, did I not have a duty to offer my king the chance to gain favor with the Gaspari emperor by being the one to restore his child to him?"

Leila's jaw dropped. Take the missing kids thousands of miles in the wrong direction, as a courtesy to his king? Just doing his duty? The man had enough gall to pickle an elephant! Jiao had fallen silent. He had been so shocked to find poor Zu Lao lying in a pool of her own blood that he had not entirely thought through the consequences of having been caught until just now. Even if these two let him live, and did not drag him back to the Dominion to face charges, he was ruined! How was he to tell the king that the children were no longer in his possession?

Leila and Tevo watched a parade of emotions passing over his smooth face, but were then brought up short when he said, "She was just an old woman! Why did you have to kill her?" They exchanged glances.

"Our god led us to this house as we sought the children," Tevo told him. "We found the door unlocked and the old woman as she is. There is a dead man, younger, lying in the hallway upstairs."

301

Now Jiao Jing's consternation deepened. "The children!" he gasped. "Were they…"

"So far as I know, certainly as I hope, they are still safe. Rajani, the woman you might have heard spoken of as a 'Nima sorceress,' took them and departed with them through an idol of Danava," Tevo explained.

Rajani! Curse it, it was if he was being repaid for using the woman as a bugaboo, an excuse for fleeing toward Tiangong. But how had she come here, how had she… the talismans! "I am a devotee of Ling Zao, the Black Dragon," Jiao explained. "I gave the children talismans of Ling Zao to wear, to shield them from any who might be seeking them using supernatural means."

"Talismans? Do you mean idols?" Leila asked sharply. The water was boiling, and she put a handful of leaves into a pretty porcelain pot and set it to steeping. Jiao looked at her strangely.

"The boy… I never learned his true name…"

"Gabriel. Gabriel Karmarzin," Tevo said shortly. Our boy was smart enough to give this greedy bastard an alias, he thought proudly.

"When I gave them the talismans, which are carved likenesses of the Black Dragon and blessed by the god to infuse them with his protection, your Gabriel asked me if they were true idols. I didn't understand what he meant." Leila pulled her little idol out of her pocket and showed it to him. Then she set it on the floor, and it expanded to six feet in height. Betsalel had been manifest in it since before they had entered the house.

Jiao Jing nearly fell out of his chair. "Lord Betsalel!" he stammered, turning still paler.

"You have much to answer for, Jiao Jing," the Shadow God said coolly. He had already tested and found that, as he'd expected, the man was protected from supernatural harm by the blessings of Ling Zao. But that would not stop him from growing ten feet tall and ripping the trader limb for limb, if it seemed appropriate to do so.

"Go on," Leila prodded him, setting cups of tea around the table. "What about these talismans?" Jiao seized the cup of tea as if it were his greatest earthly desire and took a long, careful sip.

"Gabriel figured out that the talismans were preventing you, with the help of your god, from finding him. Ling Zao said the boy was under the protection of Betsalel, is that right?"

"He is a child of my heart," the god said simply. "I have guarded him since before he was born." Not well enough, the trader thought crankily – but had the sense not to speak the thought aloud.

"While I was at the palace seeking audience with the king my friend Bian Tu, whose house this is, took the children sightseeing. They removed their talismans after bathing and did not put them on again until I had discovered what they had done more than a day later. Gabriel believed that Rajani was no threat, and in truth I had not thought her one. How much of a sorceress could she be, if I was able to take them right past her goddess' nose, and all the way to Tiangong, without her catching us? But clearly I was wrong."

Powerful regret surged through the trader as he considered how badly he'd miscalculated. With any luck Shao and the rest of the Jiao family employed by Black Dragon Imports would not suffer from his blunders. But for him, his political ambitions were dust – and his stellar career as a wealthy merchant as well. Perhaps being dragged back to Parat to face charges for absconding with the children would be better than staying here.

The tea was gone, and Leila and Tevo at least felt the better for it. They stood up, and Tevo took the older man by the elbow again. "Come," he said, "See what your greed and ambition have wrought." The four, Betsalel bringing up the rear, went up the stairs and stepped over the body in the hallway. It was cooling rapidly.

"Rajani did this?" Jiao choked. He'd thought she was supposed to be an old woman, older even than he was.

"More likely Danava," Leila replied sardonically. "From what I know of her, she enjoys using those *kukrisi* of hers. I believe there may still be blood on the blades." She gestured toward the door and they walked in to gaze at the idol where it stood in its dancing pose – one leg raised and all four arms in graceful positions.

"Blood would not linger on the idol once Danava departed from it," Betsalel intoned. He ought to know, though his own true idols did not bear weapons.

"I wonder if she took them to Indaya again?" Leila mused. Jiao looked surprised.

"The children told me Rajani had kidnaped them in Miradil, taking them east in her Nima wagon," he told them.

"She took them in Parat, and got some miles away from the city with them before we caught her wagon," Leila explained. "Then she and they were transported away from there by Danava, leaving an idol behind. We had it taken away and hidden in the Imperial Treasure House vaults. What else were we to do with it?"

"And now we have *this* beauty," Tevo said sadly. "But here in Tiangong, there are probably worshipers of Danava who could call her to manifest." Leila had a sudden idea.

"Jiao Jing, could you call Danava?" He backed away shaking his head, fear on his face.

"In Indaya both men and women worship the Destroyer of Illusions," he explained. "But the black goddess has few devotees in Hanshu, and most of those are women. I've been pledged to Ling Zao since I was a young man."

"We were pretty sure when Rajani and the kids disappeared the last time that she had gone to Indaya, because there were no worshipers of Danava in the Gholim lands," Leila reasoned. "But it's been weeks since we left her there in Khirzai. What if she went back to one of her goddess' temples in Indaya and got *two* new idols, one to leave in the khan's palace? She could have traveled from there to Danava's temple here, assuming it was the goddess who spotted the children when they were out in town without their talismans. The khan could have them in his possession right now!"

Tevo paled at the thought. Everything they had gone through the past weeks, all the hardship and deprivation, and poor little Miri left at home without mother or father – all in a desperate attempt to prevent the Gholim khan from using Berta as a lever against her father. And it had all gone for nothing? No, he would not give up!

"Let's go to the temple of Danava," he suggested. "Maybe we can find a worshiper there, somebody she'll manifest for."

"It is unlikely that she will answer your questions, even if she comes," Betsalel said. Across the Dominion and Palambo, believers were reaching out to him in their prayers. He must go to them, and soon. But this was more important.

"Please stand back," the Shadow God said. They pushed back against the walls of the room, staring fascinated as Betsalel grew until his head nearly brushed the tall ceiling of the room. Not that Danava could not grow to match him, but it was the intimidation factor that counted. She was a couple of thousand years old, the product of human imagination fused with a human soul. He was more ancient by far, created by the One, and counted his believers among nearly two-thirds of the human population.

The Shadow God laid his hands on the black goddess' idol, placing them on the upper shoulders, and spoke in a low voice that somehow reverberated through the soul of everyone in the room. "Danava, come to me. I would have words with you." In an instant the idol writhed, the knife in one hand scraping harmlessly off of Betsalel's impervious flesh.

"Get your hands off me!" the goddess snarled, growing in an instant until she was looking Betsalel in the eye.

He as one of the Eight and she as an upstart eastern daemon had seldom met, but the gods did not forget. "Betsalel," Danava said with almost a purr, as if reasoning that since her attempt to knife him had failed, plan B would be to seduce him with her impressive hourglass figure and gleaming black melon breasts. She was barking up the wrong god. "What is it that you want from me?" It was rare indeed for one deity to call another, but it was only while both were manifest in the physical plane that they could interact with one another.

"I am asking after the whereabouts of your arch-priestess, Rajani," he told her, red eyes locked on her black ones. The black goddess pulled back a little.

"My arch-priestess is no concern of yours, Shadow God," she said coolly. To the onlookers it seemed they spoke neither Hando nor Gasparto nor Hindai, yet their words were understood. "Suffice it to say she is far from here."

Betsalel exerted his will. In a physical contest between gods, even upstart daemons like the djinn Kivuli, it had been proven that neither could prevail. But in this room, in this house, Danava had no worshipers present – while the Shadow God had two whose devotion to him was immense. One of them had given his life for Betsalel's cause, and the other had nearly lost everything in life she had loved.

The black goddess shrank away a little more. "You need not tell me where she has gone," Betsalel said teasingly. "It is the children with her I am more interested in, in any case. Shall we play a guessing game, Danava?" She looked at him blankly, all four arms at her sides and feet planted on the floor a foot apart. Tevo and Jiao Jing could not help being impressed by those breasts. They were bare, and far larger than a man's head.

"Are they perhaps here in Tiangong, at your temple in the city?" Betsalel asked, and Danava smiled. It was not a pleasant expression. "Ah, or in hot, steamy Delai? The monsoon must be nearly over by now..." The smile broadened. "Or, perhaps... might they be in Ashbat, in the khan's palace?" the dark god said at last, and Danava's smile turned to a scowl.

"What if they are, Betsalel?" she asked. "You have no presence there. By the time you and your priests can reach Ashbat, my arch-priestess will have sold them to the khan. She is to use the reward he gives her to build me a temple there, finer than any the world has seen. And she will train acolytes so that my worship may increase among the Gholim. Soon, dark one, I will be more powerful in the Gholim lands than you!"

Talk about the pot calling the kettle black, Leila thought irreverently as she watched this exchange. She knew that her master had long valued her for her wiliness, but she hadn't realized it was a quality he possessed himself. He had neatly goaded Danava into revealing the kids' location. Unfortunately, she was right. The closest they could come to Ashbat through a temple of Betsalel was by returning to Miradil – where they had begun. And then, suppose they found the eastern gates barred against an expected Gholim invasion? Emperor Ostden had not been twiddling his thumbs while they were chasing the children. He had immediately begun to take steps in case the horse tribes came in force.

"Oh, Danava," Betsalel cajoled, "Don't be unkind! Why don't you transport us to Ashbat, so my worshipers can rescue their son? The khan only needs the little princess, surely."

"Transport *you*?!" the black goddess barked a sharp laugh. Leila wondered if such a sound had ever been heard issuing from those frightening lips before. "I must be leaving," she announced next, as if a call from a worshiper had just come in. She left her idol at a height so that her upraised upper arms, with their daggers, would just fit under the ceiling. With a sigh, Betsalel shrank to six feet again.

"I too must go," he said sorrowfully, resting his hands gently on Leila's shoulders and planting a kiss on her brow. Then he shrank to pocket size and she scooped up the idol from the floor, tucking it into her pocket. The old merchant's eyes were wide. He had had plenty of dealings with Ling Zao, but he had never seen anything like *that* before.

Leila looked stricken, but she came back with a tough smile. "That was more than I'd hoped we'd get," she said. Jiao Jing had a thought.

"So it really is true that you can get your god to transport you from idol to idol in the blink of an eye?" he asked. The boy had said so, and the recent conversation with the Destroyer of Illusions had seemed to confirm it.

Tevo nodded. "I doubt that any of the gods, even these myriad daemons you have here in the east, would like it widely known that they can perform this service. They would be deluged with requests for transportation, and nobody would bother to travel by coach or ship any more. But Betsalel will do it for us, as his foremost clergy. And clearly, Danava was willing to do it for Rajani on more than one occasion, even though it forced her to leave a true idol behind."

He gestured at the nine-foot monstrosity, wondering how this Bian Tu guy was going to get it out of his house without cutting out a wall. A flood of sympathy washed through him as he considered the man would return home to find his servants slaughtered, his house invaded by a gigantic black idol, and his old friend vanished. They intended to take Jiao Jing with them and return him to the Dominion to face justice for his crime. Rajani, a murderess, they would kill if they got the chance.

"Mulia transported me once in Palambo while I was on a mission to destroy one of the nests of Makucha Nyeusi," Leila pointed out. "And all of the Eight – well, except maybe Lucia –

307

helped to distribute our proclamation against Kivuli worship. I think the gods can pretty much do for you whatever they feel like doing for their worshipers, whether it's part of their usual job description or not. You were certainly the beneficiary of that, Tevo." She stepped to stand beside her husband and gave him a little squeeze.

He smiled down at her. Seeing Jiao's questioning look, he said "Our lord Betsalel brought me back from the dead around nine years ago, after we freed his principal idol from its confinement in Parat. I'm surprised you haven't heard about it."

"That was *you*?" the trader asked in horrified tones. He had really, *really*, picked the wrong people to mess with. They had a god, one of the Eight, in their pockets – and he had stolen their son!

But maybe there was a way that he could do them a favor, a big enough favor they might be willing to overlook his crime. It wasn't as if he'd harmed the boy – well, just a little… "There are no temples of the Eight, no temples to Betsalel, anywhere near Ashbat," Jiao pointed out. After his years on the Ivory Road, he knew the region better than almost anyone who didn't live there.

"The horse tribes worship mostly Andros, Mulia, Belantos, and that horse god of theirs… Roschig. As they are nomads, they mostly carry their gods around with them – and I suspect few actually worship true idols. I take that phrase to mean that some idols are just statues, and that gods cannot manifest in them?" he asked.

"That's right," Tevo said, without going into details.

"But there are a few cities in the Gholim lands besides Ashbat, or perhaps it would be more appropriate to call them towns," Jiao went on. "Places, in any case, where people have abandoned the herding-and-intertribal-warfare lifestyle and settled down. One such is Khrizan, in the eastern foothills of the Pahadai around two days' ride to the north and east of Ashbat."

Both Leila and Tevo were giving him a "yes, what's your point?" look, so the old trader continued. He'd never put more effort into a sales pitch than he did now. "Khrizan was the site of a gold discovery a couple of centuries ago," he explained. "The veins proved to be much more extensive than originally expected, and a small city has grown up around the mining enterprise. Other minerals have since been found as well. But it is the site of an ancient volcano, and earth's fires are still there not so far below the surface. They have a mountain lake with waters as warm as any bath, and a temple to the Earthquake God, Ling Zao."

"A real temple?" Leila asked sharply, "With a true idol?"

"Ah yes." Jiao Jing smiled avuncularly at her. "I visited the place in my youth, trading my wares for gold and silver, and did my devotions at the temple. My god came to me there, and we spoke."

The two were now eyeing him suspiciously. "And what do you want from us, if you can convince your Black Dragon to transport us to this Khrizan?" Tevo asked. The man was so slick, he could sell sand to the Daregs. He was disinclined to trust him.

"I ask nothing from you, nothing at all," Jiao assured him. "But I hope you will accept my sincerest apology for the worry I have caused you. I had no intention of hurting your boy. The King of Hanshu has accepted my offer to bring him the children, and now that I am unable to do so I must flee Hanshu for my life. I mean to have Ling Zao take me far away from here, perhaps to Jhirga or Urkhrian. Only go and find your son in Ashbat, and leave me be."

Chapter 50

The black goddess, who had temporarily freed her hands of weaponry, set her arch-priestess and the two traumatized children on the floor of a large chamber. Rajani's quarters within the khan's palace at Ashbat were as opulent as any in the ancient place – a remnant of an earlier civilization. The stone complex had half fallen into ruins by the time Oghul Khan had come to power and renovated it to become his royal palace. It lacked most modern conveniences, but the Gholim were not a modern people. And it certainly had grandeur.

The Black Witch's quarters, a gift to her from the khan for previous services, were lined with richly colored Gholim carpets and wall hangings to add warmth to the cold stone that encompassed them. But the children were in no state to appreciate the room's exotic splendor. Berta's lip was trembling, her face a mask of grief. They had thought they had escaped Rajani, but then suddenly she was there – her goddess, knives whirling, killing Honorable Bian's serving man in the hallway before bursting in through the door of their room.

More death threats had been used to convince Gabriel to permit Danava to transport him. Had they known that his parents were minutes away, they would have been even more devastated. Both of them were close to tears, but the old sorceress cared nothing for their woes. These two had led her a merry chase, and it was only by the merest chance that her goddess had found them before the khan decided to take her head off or burn her at the stake for failing to come through on her promise. They *owed* her, she felt, and she was tempted to beat them for running away from her in the first place. But she wanted them coherent (and intact) when she handed them over to the khan.

She put a hand on each of them, as Danava's idol went still again. Off to consult with another of her oh-so-many *other* worshipers, Rajani thought bitterly. She had devoted her life to the dark one, and this was the thanks she got? Though she had to admit, at least the Destroyer of Illusions had come to let her know the children were in Tiangong, and had brought her there, in time to do something about it.

"Come on you two," she growled in Gasparto, "It's time for you to meet the king." They stumbled along beside her, trying to keep up as the old woman practically flew along the corridors of the palace. She'd alerted the khan before leaving for Tiangong that she would have the children shortly, and he was expecting her.

Rajani shoved the children down to their knees, and prostrated herself. One did not stand in the presence of the Great Khan, unless commanded to do so. Oghul was grinning from ear to ear. Just in time to save his khanate from disintegration! Already runners had been sent out to the tribes further afield, though half a dozen of them were already encamped in strength along the road between Ashbat and Ghezh, awaiting his command to march.

"You may rise, Rajani," he said. "And the children as well." He spoke in heavily accented Gasparto, but Gabriel and Berta understood him well enough. "I would know you anywhere, little princess," he went on, addressing Berta. Having gotten back to her feet she had pulled herself up to her full height, chin up, and was glaring at the barbarian overlord imperiously. She most assuredly was her father's daughter!

"But you, boy, who are you?" the khan asked. When Rajani had returned empty handed just a week or so before, she had mentioned that she'd taken a boy, a close friend of the princess, to help make her more cooperative as she transported them to Ashbat. Unfortunately that had backfired on her – for with Gabriel at her side, the princess had had more confidence – enough confidence to keep running once they'd gotten outside of Danava's reach.

"I am Gabriel Karmarzin, sir," Gabriel said. He, too, was standing up straight and looking the Gholim monarch in the eye. "My parents are the arch-priest and arch-priestess of Lord Betsalel in the Dominion. They and our god will be looking for you."

The khan smiled. He seemed to find Gabriel's defiance as amusing, and as non-threatening, as the mock ferocity of a kitten. "They may find me," he admitted cheerfully, "but getting at me before I can slit your throat is another thing. Don't worry, you'll both be going home just as soon as our princess' papa delivers what I want."

"Come closer," Oghul Khan beckoned to the three, and Rajani stepped forward with an arm on each child's shoulder. The Gholim ruler studied Berta. "What on earth did you do to her hair?" he asked the sorceress. Rajani looked annoyed.

"When we were forced to detour to Indaya," she explained, "disguise was required. A pale, green-eyed child with waist length red hair was too conspicuous."

Leaning on one arm of his throne, chin in hand, the khan mused. Then he sat up. "I need to have both of them looking exactly as they did when their parents last saw them," he commanded. "Use your arts to restore her hair to its former appearance. I will have servants find some suitable Gaspari garb for them. This Hando stuff is quite unsuitable. Make sure they eat supper, bathe, and get plenty of rest. Tomorrow, we ride for Miradil."

Oghul Khan dismissed the sorceress and her charges, and sent one of the guards in the room for the seneschal and some other servants. After some had been sent to find and deliver the required clothing, he turned to the palace functionary who did most of the real work.

"Send to the barracks and tell General Yudzhin to mobilize," he instructed. "We will be riding out tomorrow morning, and picking up the rest of our troops as we move south. I'll need two relay riders, the fastest. One will bear the ultimatum we prepared before to the authorities at Miradil, now that the hostages are in hand. The other will alert the tribes encamped along the road to be ready to ride. Our host should reach the gates of Miradil five days hence."

Back in her quarters, Rajani frowned. Perhaps it had been a mistake for her to overplay the extent of her "sorcerous powers," not revealing that all she did was actually accomplished by the goddess in her pocket. How in all the hells was she to make the girl's hair grow long again, and restore its color? It had grown out nearly an inch since she had dyed it, but the dye was approximately permanent. That she'd used on Berta's skin had worn off, but her shoulder-length hair was mostly streaked dark brown.

Well, there was only one thing to do – call Danava. After her experience with asking the goddess to heal her horse, she was loath to risk her position by making any more requests that were outside her mistress' purview. But what choice did she have?

"Holy Danava, I beg you to come to me," she intoned, kneeling before the large idol. In a few seconds the idol writhed, and the black goddess stood before her.

"What is it now, arch-priestess?" she asked in neutral tones; though Rajani detected an edge, as if Danava were somehow… flustered?

"Oghul Khan commands that the girl's hair be restored to its former length and color," Rajani began.

"Am I not the Destroyer of Illusions?" the goddess said coolly. In an instant Berta's hair was once again waist-length, gleaming red. Her skin, which had picked up some more freckles and even a little suntan, was restored to its usual creamy paleness. "Your attempts to disguise her were only an illusion," Danava declared. "Anything else?"

"Thank you, mistress!" Rajani said, sinking to her knees and kissing the goddess' feet. Had she been taking Danava for granted after all this time? Maybe she only needed to increase her devotions, perhaps make some small sacrifices, to become once again the most favored of the black goddess' worshipers.

The idol had already reverted to stone. Feeling a little better – though not much, after the khan's threats – Gabriel grinned at his friend. "You look beautiful, Berta!" he assured her, and she smiled back and hugged him. It was still early morning here in Ashbat, so many miles to the west; but in Tiangong it had been lunchtime and Zu Lao had been killed before she could bring them anything more to eat.

There was a bowl of fruit on the table, apples and early pears, and Rajani saw the children eyeing it with interest. "Go ahead and have some," she motioned to them. "They'll be bringing us some lunch later on, but not for hours yet. And we'll all be spending the rest of today and tonight here in my rooms, so you might as well make yourselves comfortable." The kids dug in.

Chapter 51

They left the sad corpses lying as the three of them closed the door on Bian Tu's house and went out into the street. Jiao had jotted a hasty note to his friend, explaining briefly what had happened and saying goodbye. He expected they would never meet again – something Tu would no doubt be grateful for, after all that had occurred.

"The temple of Ling Zao is to our right, up the hill some distance," he told them as they stood on the walk outside.

"We need to go back to our inn and check out, get our horses," Tevo told him.

"Horses?" Jiao said. "Did your god bring horses from Parat as well?" He looked as if he could scarcely believe it.

"You have noticed that when a god or goddess is manifest in their idol, size is merely a matter of will?" The arch-priest asked him, and he nodded. "The gods can make their believers, and anything those believers wish transported, any size they want as well. Just as Betsalel made himself small enough to slip into Leila's pocket, so – if our lord *had* any pockets – he could make me and Leila small enough to fit into his. But I doubt we would withstand the experience as easily as he does."

Jiao's jaw dropped. Meeting these two had certainly been an informative experience. Perhaps he should become a member of Ling Zao's clergy in Jhirga or Urkhrian, and spend his retirement years atoning for his sins. At least it would be a living.

But what Betsalel could do, was not necessarily within the power of Ling Zao. "Honorable Karmarzin," Jiao said hesitantly. "Have you ever seen Ling Zao?"

"Oh!" Leila gasped. There had been a picture of the Black Dragon outside the offices of Black Dragon Imports in Tzinshai. "He's a serpent-like dragon with short little legs and clawed feet," she reminded her husband. "We might be able to sit on his back and be transported that way, but I don't see how we could get him to carry horses. He has no hands."

Tevo slapped his forehead, then had a thought. "Once we arrive in Khrizan, there will be idols of Betsalel in the Gholim lands. We can leave the horses with the priests at the Temple of the Eight near our inn, and after we arrive at our destination we can get Betsalel to manifest there and carry them to us!"

His wife gave him another squeeze. Though he was a year older their relationship had been lopsided when first begun – she had had vastly more experience and training than he. But Tevo had grown into not only a competent head for Betsalel's church in the Dominion, but a man with a brilliant mind. He wasn't a bad husband and father, for that matter.

So, the three of them went in the other direction, down the hill, and fetched up at their inn. Tevo kept an arm on Jiao Jing while Leila checked out of their room, settled their bill, gathered their packs (which, for the time being, they would wear), and got the stableman to put the tack on their mounts. Nimble and Milacek had spent the past day happily lolling around the stable, content to do nothing much besides eat, sleep, and swish flies. When they had no work to do, their appetites would soon decline to normal and they would seem no different from any other horses.

They walked the horses the few blocks along the Street of the Golden Dawn to the Temple of the Eight, Jiao feeling increasingly apprehensive. Would it occur to these priests of Betsalel that some other of the Eight – Mulia, perhaps – might have a true idol no further from Ashbat than Khrizan? If so, he was probably done for.

"Why do you not simply purchase more horses when you get where you are going?" he asked them, trying to keep them thinking of anything else. It was clear they were extremely anxious to reach their son – but five minutes of careful thought now might save them two days at the end of their journey.

Leila and Tevo exchanged glances. "These animals have been in our family for years," she explained. "The children look on them as members of the family. We wouldn't consider parting with them." Jiao eyed her, then shrugged. Such sentimentalism! She wasn't about to admit the *real* reason these beasts were worth hauling all over the continent.

There were priests at the Temple of the Eight, and after Leila and Tevo called Betsalel to his huge idol there they were more than happy to look after the horses until such time as he would manifest again and carry them off. At Jiao's suggestion they hailed a fast four-seat sedan chair, carried by two burly young men, for the trip up the hill to the temple of Ling Zao.

Leila and Tevo still had plenty of gold, thanks to their foiling of the attempt to waylay and rob them in Xia Gu. The money they'd gotten selling those other horses had helped to swell their coffers, as well – and of course with idols of Betsalel on their person the Shadow God could supply them with as much money as they desired – brought from the palace in Parat. But Tevo beckoned to the old trader to pay the bearers when they reached their destination. It was the absolute least he owed them.

As they walked inside the black temple, admiring the exotic architecture, Leila called Betsalel to her pocket. In case Ling Zao proved to be hostile, they might need their lord's protection against physical as well as psychic attacks, and that he could only provide while he was manifest.

Jiao Jing tossed a handful of coins into the offering bowl, which appeared to be carved of volcanic stone. Then he knelt before the dragon idol as Leila and Tevo stood back to give him room. In truth, the thought that he might request Ling Zao to incinerate these enemies of his had occurred to Jiao. But what good would that do? Once they had departed for the Gholim lands he would be free in any case, and having these two dead would not get him out of trouble with the king. In any case, after meeting the Shadow God, he had his doubts that the Black Dragon could even harm them should he ask.

"Lord Ling Zao," he intoned, "Your humble servant Jiao Jing begs audience." The idol writhed, looping and twisting like a serpent while all four stubby legs with their clawed feet remained firmly on the pillar. Though the pillars of daemons were not brought forth from the bones of the earth imbued with magical power, as had been the case at the Temple of the Eight in Parat, they could acquire that power over millennia of human worship at the same spot. Only the most powerful deities were able to leave the usual resting spots of their idols and wander around freely.

The Black Dragon blew steam from his nostrils. "Who are these with you, Jiao Jing?" he asked in his hissing, purring voice. "Like that boy you brought to me yesterday, they bear the protection of Betsalel. In fact, he is here – in my temple!"

Clearly the God of Earthquakes was not pleased. The ground shook slightly, a little tremor that dislodged a few pebbles from the ceiling and made the human occupants of the temple look around anxiously. Leila hastily bent and set her little god on the floor, whereupon he immediately grew to ten feet in height. If Ling Zao wished to become larger, he would have a hard time keeping all those feet planted on his pillar, and he hissed and blew a gout of flame at the Shadow God as the humans edged back in fear.

"What want you here, Betsalel?" Ling Zao demanded. This was *his* temple, and another god – even one of the Eight, those stuck-up, older-than-thou blowhards – had no business coming here.

"Relax, Ling Zao," the Shadow God replied calmly. He could already sense that the daemon's power – even standing on his pillar – was not as great as his own. Not with Leila and Tevo in the room, and only Jiao Jing on the side of the dragon god. If this temple was staffed with priests during the day, none were now in evidence.

"Your faithful dedicant Jiao Jing has come to ask a favor of you on behalf of my worshipers," Betsalel continued smoothly. "We trespass here only briefly, and if you will grant Honorable Jiao's request we will soon be gone and trouble you no more." The dragon god felt a surge of relief. He did not like the feeling of being the weaker god, especially here in what was supposed to be his seat of power.

"These two priests of Betsalel are in need of transport to your temple in Khrizan, great one," Jiao said. His posture was one of worship and submission but Leila noticed he was standing beyond the range of the gout of fire Ling Zao had sent toward the black god. "If you will do me the favor of carrying them there, I would then ask you to transport me to another of your temples – whichever you like, as long as it is not within Hanshu. I have decided to retire from trading and seek to join your priesthood."

The black serpent ceased his writhing, lifting his sinuous neck up to peer down at the man who had been among his most faithful worshipers for the past thirty years. "Transport... ?" He hissed in puzzlement. Jiao gaped at him. Had the Karmarzins lied? Was this all some kind of cruel joke?

Betsalel stepped in. "Many of the… younger gods and goddesses may not have learned how to do this," he explained. "The ability seems to have been inborn in me and my siblings, but perhaps Ling Zao will need to be taught the technique." He stepped closer to the Black Dragon again, and reached out with his mind. "Little brother, let us speak mind to mind. Will you permit me to show you how you may carry your worshipers from one true idol to another?"

The reply came silently, defensively. Ancient daemons often despised the Eight, but knew in their hearts that they were overmatched by them. "Show me, then!" Ling Zao snapped. "Perhaps this will prove useful to me." The three human onlookers stood watching, wondering what was going on, as the two black gods – one human in form, the other serpentine – stood motionless in silent communion.

Finally Ling Zao spoke. "I have it now," he said. "But how shall I carry these… friends of yours, Jiao Jing?" Jiao was starting to wish he'd never made the suggestion. He could probably have found some other way to escape – from these captors and from the wrath of the king. But it was too late now.

"I, uh… I thought they could sit upon your back, great one…"

An explosion of steam and fingers of flame escaped from the Black Dragon's nostrils, causing all three of them to step backward involuntarily. But then they realized that Ling Zao was laughing. "Dragon riders!" he snorted. "I command you, Jiao Jing, when all of this is accomplished, to seek out a practitioner of pingtan. I would have this story become part of my legend, as it will surely enhance my worship in the world."

Betsalel shrank again and vacated his idol. It was not possible for one god to carry another one through the dimension of spirit in which they dwelt. Leila slipped it back into her pocket and carefully climbed up onto the pillar, straddling a section of the Black Dragon's serpentine back. His scales were far rougher than those of a snake, closer to those of a lizard; but her leather traveling clothes protected her legs well enough. When Tevo had seated himself in front of her he told their "mount," "Thank you most kindly, Ling Zao, for this service. If you like, we will spread word of it in the west when we return home. Now, if you please, take us to Khrizan!"

Chapter 52

Gabriel and Berta awoke early. They'd gone to bed far earlier than usual – partly from stress after the day's events, and partly out of boredom. Rajani's chamber was spacious and well-appointed, but she refused to consider taking them out to explore the rest of the palace, let alone any of the city of Ashbat.

Besides, they were still on Tiangong time. Here it was far earlier. Now it was the crack of dawn and they were wide awake, while their captor slept on. The room had no windows, just a wide door giving out on one of the palace corridors. Gabriel crept over and tried it, but it was locked. In stories Mama had told, the hero sometimes got past locked doors by picking the lock – but he had no idea how that was done, and even if he had he'd be willing to bet the black goddess had cast some kind of spell so only Rajani could open it.

The two of them got drinks of cool water from an ewer that stood on the room's small table, then sat close together on some brightly-patterned cushions that did duty for a settee. The Gholim lifestyle didn't lend itself to heavy furniture. Even the bed was a thick pad stuffed with wool, lying on a carpet on the floor. The children had slept on a pair of similar but smaller pads, brought along with bundles of clothing an hour or so after they'd returned from their interview with the khan yesterday.

"We really need to think about escape," Gabriel murmured to Berta. During the past several weeks traveling with Jiao Jing they'd had their doubts about the man, but it had always seemed as if his intention had been to return them home. Even when they'd learned he was selling them to the Hanshu king, Berta hadn't been too concerned. There were a thousand-plus miles of land between Hanshu and the Dominion, so it wasn't as if there were any border disputes between the two countries.

"He'll send us right back to my father," she'd told Gabriel. "Hanshu is a valued ally and trading partner with the Dominion. King Wang Qian wouldn't do anything to jeopardize that. If he gave father any trouble about sending us home right away, father could just close Miradil to Hanshu trade and put the members of their trade delegation under arrest. I'll bet we'll be home before suppertime, once Jiao Jing gets back."

But Jiao Jing had not returned. Instead it was Rajani who had appeared, and now their worst fears had been realized. They were in the hands of the Great Khan of the Gholim, whose bloodthirsty hordes would just *love* to sweep across the Dominion raping and pillaging and destroying the peaceful way of life its citizens had enjoyed for centuries.

A knock came at the door, and Rajani aroused from her slumber and sat up on her sleeping pad. There was a sound like a key turning in a lock, and a maidservant came in with breakfast tray. Gabriel considered taking Berta by the hand and bolting past her. Perhaps two agile children could run fast enough to escape pursuit, and lose themselves in the palace corridors. It was not an ideal situation, as they would still be lost in a foreign city where no one spoke their language. But at the very least, it would delay the khan's march on Miradil and give help more time to arrive.

But as they stood up and walked toward the door they found a burly guard standing there, a spear in his hands and twin tulwars in his belt. They changed direction and headed for the table, to see what was on the breakfast tray. Last night's dinner had been chunks of marinated and grilled lamb with some kind of greens and a light wheat pilaf – not bad, really.

Breakfast in the Khanate, it seemed, meant sticky little pastries loaded with honey and nuts, more apples and pears, and a pot of tea. There was also a jug of fresh mare's milk for the kids. They thought it tasted funny, but there'd been few enough opportunities to drink milk during the past few weeks. "These pastries are a lot like the ones they eat in Iskand," Gabriel informed his friend. He had spent time in the royal palace there on several occasions, visiting with his grandparents.

Rajani was an old woman, and it took her a while to get moving. She felt a bit anxious. At least the reward she'd requested from the khan, two huge chests of gold, had been delivered by a team of servants yesterday evening after she'd reported that the children were ready for their journey.

This would be more than enough to build the temple to Danava she planned, and start winning new converts to her goddess' cause. Though she was called an arch-priestess, "sorceress" was a more apt term for what she'd been doing most of the past several decades. But now she could spend the rest of the time allotted to her in spreading the word, training new acolytes, and giving the eastern goddess a power base in the Gholim lands. Perhaps if the khan was successful in his invasion of the Dominion, she could even send teams with true idols there to start churches of Danava in that stronghold of the Eight.

But for now, she and the goddess were required to accompany the khan and his hordes on the long journey to Miradil – guarding the children and keeping them in line during that trip until it was time for them to fulfill their role as hostages. Rajani's original suggestion, that the khan curry favor with the Gaspari emperor by "rescuing" the kidnaped children, had been discarded in favor of a more active approach – one that would win approval from the bloodthirsty Gholim warriors under his weakening command.

It remained to be seen how long the Gaspari Emperor could stand by and watch as his daughter was whittled down. Oghul Khan was convinced that all Gasparis were weak as lambs. Without war to keep them strong, how could they be otherwise? He was sure that as soon as he bent to cut the first finger from the child, the gates of Miradil would be thrown open and his hordes could pour in. The gateway between east and west would be in the Khanate's possession, and before winter they would begin carving off chunks of the Dominion to become client states – replacing the Gaspari counts with warlords loyal to the khan as they spread west and north across the land.

Rajani was less sure. The Dominion might not have fought a war in more than a thousand years, but that did not necessarily mean they were weak. Ostden was a young man, and likely a bold one. Ah, time would tell. Meanwhile she needed to eat breakfast and get her two charges ready to go.

Guards accompanied them through unfamiliar hallways to the enormous courtyard where the khan's party was preparing to leave. Another opportunity lost, Gabriel thought. But maybe once they were mounted he and Berta would have the chance to bolt away in the confusion. They still had not seen any Gholim horsemen in action, and had no idea how outclassed they were as riders.

In any case, that idea bit the dust when they got to the courtyard. The khan was already mounted, on a gorgeous dapple gray stallion Gabriel recognized as a Palamban Hisan. It was little taller than the scrubby hill horses favored by the Gholim tribes, but more clean-limbed and muscular. Rajani stood flanking the children, Danava manifest in her pocket to prevent any mishaps. "Excellent, Rajani!" he said with a smile. He had taken her word for it, delivered by a servant, that his orders had been carried out. Gabriel and Berta were clean, brushed, and dressed in the sort of clothing upper-class Gaspari children might wear around the house.

He motioned for them to get on with it, and the guards escorted them up a step to the box of a large wagon. It was shaped roughly like a Nima caravan, but lacked any of that conveyance's charm. It was easily twice the size, as well, pulled by four large horses that appeared to be of the Gaspari breed used for plowing and drayage. There were no windows, only some holes drilled along the sides for ventilation. The single door opened behind the driver's box, and had a stout lock on it.

Gabriel looked at the thing appalled. They were going to ride in that… rolling crate? For five days? Oh, no! The wagon was more like a rolling fortress, plated all around with metal lest it be set on fire. The wood was two inches thick. But as he stepped inside it seemed that some effort had been made to provide comforts as well.

Within, the walls were cushioned and lined with soft fabrics. There were oil lanterns hung on the walls, four comfortable bunks, and an area with cushions to sit on around a low table. At the rear a space had been walled off to provide privacy, with a privy stool, washbasin, and room for changing clothes. The lack of windows seemed like a big problem, but otherwise it was a fairly snug chamber. Probably far more comfortable than spending those five days on horseback, surrounded by thousands of hard-bitten warriors, in a cloud of dust and flies.

But the biggest treat of all was the bookshelf. Someone, somehow, had acquired a small cache of Gaspari books intended for young readers. There was *The Adventures of Dobbin* and several volumes in the Pippa Farstrider series, as well as children's versions of world history and geography. The idea that those five days might be spent doing something more entertaining than enduring Rajani's sour company and threats from her black goddess was almost enough to shake Gabriel out of the despair he felt, when the door clanged shut and he realized that their last chance for escape was gone.

Chapter 53

Jiao Jing had seemed a tricky fellow, but his god dealt with them as promised. Leila and Tevo found themselves astride the writhing dragon's back looking out at a quite different temple than the one in Tiangong. They thanked the dragon god after climbing down, and soon made their way outside. The door had been closed but was not locked.

From the look of the late summer light it was still before noon here in Khrizan. The temple behind them was circular, made of black stone, and surmounted by an onion dome – a style they hadn't seen before. Behind it a little mountain stream leapt and bubbled down a hillside, and beyond that the eastern peaks of the Pahadai rose in snow-capped grandeur where they were not obscured by cloud.

It seemed there was no one in the immediate vicinity, though as a precaution Leila and Tevo had become the Gholim version of the two young Hando toughs they'd impersonated in Tiangong. These might have been the sons of the two Gholim sisters they'd begun as all those weeks ago.

"Khrizan looks an attractive place, at least in the summer," Leila remarked. The season was advancing toward autumn and at this altitude there was already a chill in the air. Probably the entire area would be under several feet of snow in another two months. "Maybe when their mines dry up they can stay afloat as a tourist destination," Tevo mused. "Assuming the Gholim tribes ever achieve that level of civilization."

"I suppose the khan and his 'Khanate' are a step in the right direction," she replied. "Not that I'm anxious to have him succeed." She bent to set her idol of Betsalel on a patch of flat ground beside the stream, which was steaming slightly and smelled faintly of sulfur.

A couple of minutes later they were patting their horses, who had just awakened after their trip from Tiangong. Nimble and Milacek had now traveled via the Betsalel express enough times that they were getting used to the experience – but that didn't mean they liked it. They sniffed at the water but didn't drink any, and when Leila stuck her hand in it she found it quite warm – nearly as hot as the water that came out of their magical taps at home.

It was getting on toward suppertime in Tiangong, and not yet lunchtime here; and neither of them had eaten since breakfast. "I'd really like to get on the road for Ashbat," Tevo said. "But I'm starved! Let's find an inn and have some food, and pick up some supplies for the road before we start out."

"All right by me," she replied. They mounted up and followed a dirt path down the hill toward the cluster of wooden buildings that they took for the center of town. They soon passed through an unmanned gate in a tall log stockade. Leila supposed that with all of the mineral riches this town was supposed to have, raids by bandits must be a concern.

Without a central government until recently, the roads in the Gholim lands were mostly either not paved or at least not maintained. The civilization that had existed here millennia ago was long gone, and most of its works had vanished with it. Here and there you could see a few paving stones beneath the dirt and moss, but there were very few thoroughfares that were up to Dominion standards.

Khrizan boasted one, though. It ran right through the center of town leading from the road running south and east to Ashbat, and terminated at the main mine workings further up in the mountains. Leila and Tevo, as the two young tribesmen, selected what looked to be the largest of the inns in town. It had a small barn out back and they arranged for the horses to be fed and watered while they went inside.

The innkeeper, a toothless hag in her late forties, eyed the two hard-looking young men as they stepped up to the bar and ordered some lunch. The inn offered hot food, a pot of stew that had bubbled over its fire for decades – its contents being augmented from time to time throughout each day. At the moment, it seemed to be brown broth thick with chunks of mutton, onions, turnips, and carrots. And was that barley? Probably.

They ate large bowls of the stuff, sopping up the juices with hunks of flatbread and washing it down with the inn's own ale. The Gholim culture here was different from elsewhere in the tribal lands – these people had built houses and settled down, begun to amass wealth and property. They were slowly turning into a town that wouldn't have seemed out of place in the eastern Dominion.

"So, you boys heading for Ashbat?" The two eyed each other. How had she known? The old woman laughed. "You think you're the first through here? Boys come in to make money working the mines, but you can't keep 'em away from a fight – not while they're young and dumb. As soon as word got here the khan was calling the Horde, all the boys started sharpening up their tulwars."

Tevo grunted around a mouthful of stew, suggesting she was not wrong in her assessment. The woman took a none-too-clean rag and began mopping the bar with it. "You'd better get a move on, then. It's been a couple of weeks since the proclamation went out, and the tribes are marshaling all along the road from Ashbat to Ghezh. You'll be needing to gallop to catch up, or all the fighting will be over by the time you join them."

They bought some non-perishable food from her to eat on the road, and filled their water skins. Then they were soon on their way. Nimble and Milacek hadn't been all that hungry, and they were perfectly content to be moving at a trot until they'd left Khrizan behind.

The paved road petered out not long after they'd left the log stockade behind, and the travelers let the horses move into a comfortable gallop they could maintain for hours while hardly breaking a sweat. It was mostly downhill for the first fifty miles, winding down out of the foothills. They crossed the Tekushi on a heavy wooden bridge that looked as if it had been built in the past decade.

No doubt the river, which drained most of the Pahadai's eastern slopes, would flood and wash it away every few years. But there was enough money in Khrizan to rebuild it each time, preserving their access to the outside world. The Tekushi was navigable for small boats within a few miles of Ghezh, where it spilled into the Huang. But this far north it had far too many rocks in it to make boat travel, or even a ferry, a good idea.

A dozen miles east of the river they came to a much broader though still unpaved road. There were a few towns and villages north of here, but most of the traffic was south – to Ashbat. They were traveling down the center of a broad valley, and there was more agriculture here than Leila and Tevo had expected to find. Clearly, not all of the Gholim were wandering around with their herds all the time.

The road was wide and old paving stones were visible here and there, suggesting it had once been a major highway. Now, though, it looked as if the first winter snows might render it impassable – at least for wheeled traffic. Maintaining their comfortable gallop, they passed many farm carts. With summer almost over, farmers were rushing to take their crops to market.

There were almost no young mounted men on the road, though. "Oghul Khan must have been pretty confident that Rajani would deliver the kids if he sent out a proclamation calling the tribes' warriors together two weeks ago," Leila remarked to Tevo as they slowed to a walk, waiting to get past a knot of traffic.

"He must have been on tenterhooks waiting for her," Tevo replied. "I'd sooner spend my days sitting on a barrel full of live vipers than try to be 'king' over the Gholim. But now that she's come through for him, I suppose they'll all be dashing south as quickly as they can."

"Shit!" she replied, knowing he spoke the truth. She had hoped they might arrive in Ashbat and find the khan still mobilizing his troops, the children tucked up with Rajani in some section of the palace. She *assumed* there was a palace... From what she'd seen of life in this part of the world so far, she wouldn't have been surprised to learn their "Great Khan" made his home in an extra-large stone hut. That would far outstrip most of the local accommodations.

"It's still going to take this Gholim horde the better part of a week to get to Miradil," Tevo reminded her by way of consolation. "It'll be a mob scene. Maybe we can just edge in disguised as some of the khan's guards and winkle the kids out before they know what's happening." She smiled at him, which in her present disguise was an unsettling impression. But in his heart, Tevo saw his beloved wife beneath her seeming.

Hours after dark they came to an inn and decided they must stop for the night. The moon had gone down, and it was becoming impossible to see the road. Besides, they were both getting hungry – and it was sure the horses would be ready for a good meal.

The inn sat on the outskirts of a market village that had grown up between the road and the river, and it was clear from the boisterous crowd they found in its common room that this place was the nexus of what passed for night life in the region. Looking around, the two hard-bitten young warriors guessed that everyone here had probably known everyone else here since they were babies.

Conversation paused and all eyes were on the strangers as they came in and requested a room. They'd already taken their horses around to the side yard, where a stable lad had accepted coin to remove their tack, rub them down, and provide them with as much grain as they cared to eat.

"Need a room," Tevo said gruffly, eyeing the middle-aged innkeeper with an expression that seemed to say "Go ahead, look cross-eyed at me. I dare you." The Gholim of these parts were increasingly more settled, and the older man looked askance at the two young warriors. From their garb and their armament, as well as from their attitude, they were from one of the rougher northern tribes.

Only the tribes with large groups of warriors at a reasonable distance from the Ghezh road had been called to join the Horde – but probably a few young men from every tribe that heard about it would want to join in the fun. It was rumored that the streets of Miradil were paved with gold, and that beyond its walls lay the southern Dominion like a soft, rich, plum waiting to be plucked. Hell, the innkeeper thought, if I were a young man I'd probably want to run off and join the Horde myself.

These two looked dangerous, and outside of their own tribes the Gholim were notoriously prickly and easily angered. He accepted their coin and showed them to a room, and found some food for them in the kitchen though dinner had been served hours ago. They didn't linger drinking with the locals, many of whom were surreptitiously eyeing them, but just went right to bed. Not long after dawn the next morning they were gone.

It was late in the afternoon when Leila and Tevo, still in the guise of the two late-arriving Horde members, came in through the north gate of Ashbat and found themselves in a surprisingly large, thriving city. "I'd half expected yurts," Leila admitted as they trotted along the teeming stone-paved streets. The gate had been sparsely manned and they saw little presence of uniformed guards in the streets – likely most of the khan's armsmen had followed him on the march to Miradil. But there were plenty of ordinary citizens around – housewives, merchants, grocers, butchers, prostitutes...

Sheep, goats, horses, yaks, and even a few camels were being herded through the streets. The city stood on a low rise, marking the southern end of the valley of the Tekushi. The river dipped east here, broadening as it was joined by several small streams coming out of the distant mountains, and curved around the city walls on two sides. The palace, truly a palace if not a patch on either the one in Parat or the one in Iskand, stood nearer the southern end of the city atop its largest hill. The sun, nearing the peaks of the Pahadai to the west, painted its stone walls a golden tan.

Betsalel had informed them as they approached that the children were to the south, but were once again screened by the shielding Danava had erected from the time when they were first taken. Yet this effect seemed to come and go, evidently only operating when the goddess was manifest near the children. He kept picking up Gabriel's location for a short period of time, then losing it again.

If Danava were near the children, Rajani must have gone along on the trip south as well. Perhaps the khan intended her to be the children's babysitter and watchdog until it was time for them to be paraded as helpless captives before the walls of Miradil. But Leila still wanted to check at the palace. Might Rajani have left something behind, some item or clue that would help them to defeat her?

Getting into the palace proved easier than they'd expected. They arrived in the guise of new recruits, anxious to join the Horde, and found only servants and a few older military personnel around. Everyone else had gone south. The one-armed gate guard directed them to hitch their horses in the courtyard, and go in through the door and down the hall to where they would find the recruiting sergeant. Oghul Khan's efforts to knit his people into a nation had included providing his "troops" with a uniform of sorts, like the one the gate guard was wearing.

Footwear and trousers were at the option of the individual soldier, as was the shirt you would wear beneath your jacket. But each soldier wore a short military jacket with braid sewn onto the front, plus a stiff wool cap with a badge of rank on it. Once inside the door, Leila and Tevo had a brief consultation and decided to go see the sergeant.

He proved to be a fat man in his late fifties, missing three fingers from his left hand. It was beginning to look as though nobody was minding the fort at Ashbat but old men, green boys, and cripples. He was delighted to see them, having been signing up additional recruits for the Horde in twos and threes all day long as stragglers from the more remote tribes got the word. These two, at least, looked as if they might be competent killers.

They made their marks on a piece of paper saying they had signed up to join the Horde and would obey the orders of whichever commander they were assigned to. Then they were told that the khan and his party had just left yesterday morning. As two mounted men should be able to make much better time than a thousand of them with baggage train and camp followers, the sergeant expected they should catch up with the growing Horde by no later than tomorrow evening. And good luck.

Leila and Tevo committed the uniforms, with the badges showing their rank of *strelezh* (the lowest, basic rank in this newly formed army) to memory. Then they stashed them behind a pile of wooden crates in a corridor. They would now be able to appear as members of the Horde whenever they wished, but their own clothes were far more comfortable. The uniform jackets sized for the two strapping six-footers wouldn't have fit them, in any case.

Within a bubble of silence in the corridor, Leila told Tevo "I want to go see Rajani's quarters. I'm pretty sure she must be Oghul Khan's court sorceress, so she probably lives in the palace when she's in town. From what the sergeant there said, we'll have no trouble catching up with the Horde." Tevo looked around them.

"It's an awfully big palace," he said. "Any idea where Rajani's quarters would be?"

"Probably not too far from the throne room," she mused. Then she said, "I have an idea. Go invisible, will you?" Giving her a questioning look, Tevo did as she'd asked. The next instant Rajani stood there before him, as she had looked when they saw her in Khirzai – maimed hand and all. The wooden crates, which seemed to be full of some kind of military supplies, were not huge. Each one was square, around eighteen inches on a side and no more than a foot tall. They were heavy enough, though, as Leila found when she lifted one down from the stack beside her.

"Ungh!" she said, getting a better grip. "Hope I bump into a servant who knows Rajani soon." She carried the box with her, moving deeper into the palace complex, heading in what appeared to be the likely direction of the throne room. Leila had had a lot of experience of palaces in her life, and they all seemed to have a similar logic in their layouts. Tevo, invisible and moving in a bubble of silence so his footfalls would not be heard, trailed her.

They had been walking like this, twisting and turning almost at random, for three or four minutes when Rajani walked around a corner and nearly collided with a youth of around fourteen, dressed in the livery of the palace servants. He nearly jumped out of his skin. "The Bl... Mistress Rajani! You're here!" he sputtered.

"So it would seem," the old sorceress said sardonically.

"But... but, I saw you leave yesterday, in the wagon with the hostages! How..." The dark woman peered up at him with a gimlet eye, burning into his soul.

"I have my arts, and I go where and when I please," she said sharply. She thrust out the box. "Here, carry this to my quarters."

He took the box, staring at it as if he'd never seen such a thing before. "But... your quarters..." the boy gestured with his head back down the corridor she had just come from. Oh, crap.

"I was looking for someone to carry it for me!" Rajani snapped. "The damn thing was getting heavy. Come on, let's go!"

The boy was too cowed to wonder how it was, if the Black Witch's powers were all they were rumored to be, she would be wandering the corridors of the palace looking for someone to carry her box for her. Surely such a mighty sorceress could simply translocate herself, and whatever wanted carrying, straight to her room? But he said not a word, thinking only as he walked along with her trailing behind him that he hoped she was not going to turn him into a sand lizard, or cause his manhood to shrivel up and fall off. He'd recently discovered he was quite fond of it.

After a few more turnings they arrived at the door. Leila and Tevo had not been more than a few hundred yards away from it, but there was certainly nothing on the outside to announce that within dwelt the black sorceress. The kid was still holding the box and looking at her expectantly. Oh, right. Rajani would not likely leave her quarters unlocked. "Betsalel, the door please?" "Yes, beloved," came the amused thought. There was a click, and the door swung open. The old woman strode inside, looking neither right nor left, and pointed to the small table in one corner of the large room.

"Set it there," she said sharply, "and then go. You will not see me again."

"Yes, mistress," the boy said miserably, and nearly ran from the room. Tevo had to sidestep hastily to avoid being stumbled over. Betsalel closed and locked the door again, and Leila and Tevo stood taking in the quarters of the woman who had stolen their son.

The room was dominated by a large, ominous idol of Danava. It was unlikely she could manifest for either of them, and probably *would* not manifest for Betsalel even if called. The Destroyer of Illusions had come out the loser in their last encounter. But the sight of the idol still gave them the creeps.

Betsalel joined them at his customary height of six feet, and surveyed the room. Leila was hoping that his divine sight might detect something the old sorceress had hidden. But other than the idol, he found nothing occult about the room. There were no signs that the children had been here, the servants having removed the extra sleeping mats and cleaned the room as they'd been getting ready to leave yesterday morning.

"What's in those two big chests against the wall by the bed?" Leila asked, walking over. Unsurprisingly, they were locked. The Shadow God raised an eyebrow. "Gold," he said. "A very large quantity of gold. Rajani's payment from the grateful khan for a job well done, I would imagine."

"Can you make it vanish, like you did that Kivuli idol in Namei?" she asked spitefully. Whatever else happened, it would do her heart good to have Rajani receive nothing for her criminal efforts.

"Yes, I suppose I can do that," Betsalel said thoughtfully. "But it would be a waste. Could not such riches be used to help provide more services for my temples?" Gods were always concerned about their believers – the more worship they got, the more power they had.

"But you would need to pick up the chests and transport them to Parat," Leila pointed out. She was getting anxious to be on their way. "And if/when Rajani comes here, she will know immediately they are gone. What if she blames the palace staff, and brings down her wrath on them?"

"That lock is not one that a common thief could open," the god replied. "I tell you what. I will carry the chests to my temple in Parat, empty the contents on the floor, and return here with the empty chests. Once they are locked again, it will be a mystery to her what became of the contents."

"All right," Leila said, biting her lip. Betsalel grew larger, hefting a chest on each shoulder, then only an idol stood there. It was not above three minutes later, during which time she and Tevo searched the rest of the room, that the idol's posture changed and the god was there once again, the chests on his shoulders.

He set them carefully down in exactly the places where they'd stood before. They seemed heavier than they should be. "Did you put something else in them?" Leila asked, curious. Betsalel smiled.

"Stone from the temple floor," he explained. "When next I manifest there I will repair the damage. But I spoke with Maks and explained what I was doing. He was quite pleased to get the gold."

I'm sure! Leila thought. Maksim, once an impoverished street urchin and later the Karmarzins' household servant, had joined the priesthood a couple of years back and was doing well in it. Few people in Parat had as much experience with the Shadow God as he did.

"I think we're done here," she told the god and her husband. "Let's be off after the Horde, shall we?" "I'll leave one more little present for Rajani," Betsalel remarked. Before shrinking and departing his idol he dropped a tiny object, no larger than a grain of sand, to the floor near the idol of Danava. With the sorceress' locks on the door to this chamber, no one would be sweeping or mopping until her return.

Chapter 54

The sergeant at the palace in Ashbat had been unaware of the special talents of the two new recruits' horses. They caught up with the khan's small army (unlike most armies, consisting almost entirely of light horse) in the wee hours of the same night.

By now most of the campfires had died down to embers, there being no need to keep them going for warmth here in late summer. The warriors who had accompanied the khan and his generals from Ashbat had joined the Kazhakim tribe's contingent of riders, who had been encamped at a waypoint a day's ride south.

Most of the men were sleeping now, many of them having passed out after drinking, tale-telling, and fighting with their fellows for hours beforehand. The Great Horde of the Khanate was not an army in the sense that historians from Hanshu or the Dominion would recognize. Professional soldiers knew how to inflict death and horror on a scale far grander than anything these tribesmen could achieve.

For the Gholim tribes fighting, killing, and blood feuds were a cultural lifestyle – a hobby, almost. A way for men to prove their manhood, for tribes to prove their ferocity and right to survive. But even blood feuds didn't mean you went in and slaughtered your enemy, killing every man woman and child as you destroyed their possessions and left their lands incapable of supporting life for another century. More likely you would kill all the men of fighting age, rape all the women, carry off some plunder along with a few children, and leave your enemies to get on with their lives so they could return the favor in a few years.

Mounted on their quick, tough little horses, the tribal warriors were masters of guerrilla warfare. They could sweep in like lightning, mowing down their opponents with tulwars and their deadly horse-bows, then be gone again before conventional forces could muster a response. It was not for them to become a massed army, facing another massed army across a battlefield and fighting them toe-to-toe. They wore no armor, and lacked the kind of discipline that would prevent chaos from descending as soon as the first arrow was loosed.

Yet Oghul Khan intended that these young tribesmen he had gathered would become such an army. They had come to his call, each of the five closest and most numerous tribes sending as many warriors as wanted to go. The promise of rich plunder from Miradil and the lands of the west was too good for any able-bodied young tribesman to pass up. He had started with over a thousand riders, and now more than two thousand were encamped. By the time they reached Miradil, it would be a horde indeed.

Leila and Tevo, a.k.a. Koblin and Zirghei Aliyev, slowed their horses to a walk as they came in sight of the encampment ahead of them. The moon had gone down a little while ago, but there was still enough glow from campfires and torches to enable them to see that the massed riders and their mounts, supply wagons, and so forth were spread before them. They completely blocked the road for more than a mile, and occupied the land on either side of it for a considerable distance.

Almost surprisingly, the khan had set sentries around the camp. Considering Oghul had been acclaimed the leader of all the Gholim tribes and they were deep in the Khanate's territory, Leila wondered whom they were guarding against. Perhaps it was just for form's sake, something he'd gotten out of a book. She was beginning to suspect that this Oghul Khan was a man unlike any leader the tribes had seen in centuries.

A pair of sentries standing in the center of the road some fifty yards north of the encampment held torches up and commanded them to stop. They saw a pair of similar-looking young men, black-haired and brown-eyed, their faces a deep bronze from hours spent outdoors. They were wearing the uniforms of the Great Horde, and expressions of pleased excitement.

"I told you we could catch them if we hurried, Zirghei," the older one said.

"But we missed dinner, Koblin!" the younger complained. The sentry on the left, who might have been their first cousin, grinned.

"A little late answering the call, eh?" he asked.

"Father wouldn't let us leave until after slaughtering time," Koblin said ruefully. Tribes further north would thin their herds before the cold set in.

"Go on ahead," the left-hand sentry told them, "and find a place to lay your bed rolls. We'll be mustering to march again first thing in the morning, but you should be able to catch a few hours' rest." Seemingly there wasn't much organization to this place, no formal companies with a command structure, no rosters. Leila had never been a scholar of military history, but even to her this seemed so haphazard she wondered how Oghul Khan thought he could possibly succeed.

They had to move off to the edges of the road, picking their way along until they came to a steep hillside. South of Ashbat the Tekushi ran through a narrower valley, with the foothills of the southern Pahadai across the river to the west and hills climbing higher until they became small mountains eastward. The hills formed a barrier to the Horde east of the road, and unless Leila and Tevo were going to climb up into them in the dark they would have to wait until morning to move closer to the front.

They guessed Oghul Khan would have Rajani and the children close beside him, riding in the van. He wouldn't want them out of his sight. But there were more than a thousand horses and sleeping warriors between him and them. Betsalel confirmed it – the children were to the south of them, about a mile away. Danava was apparently not manifest now, as her arch-priestess was no doubt asleep. But so were the children.

"I can come to Gabriel in his dreams and command him to wake if you want, Leila," the Shadow God suggested.

"It'll be dark so he probably wouldn't be able to see anything to share with you," she pointed out. "Let's just find a place to get some sleep." They'd been eating trail food from their packs as they road, but the horses were hungry. They found a flat patch near the Horde's northeastern edge and stripped the saddles and reins from the horses so they could crop what remained of the late summer grass. Nimble and Milacek would not wander off.

Morning came far too early. Koblin rubbed the sleep out of his eyes and rose to his feet, scratching and looking around him. He'd slept in his uniform jacket, and it was rumpled. He left it that way. His younger brother was soon on his feet as well, and they rolled up their bedrolls and stuffed them into their packs. The horses, hungry after their long gallop and wishing for some grain, had moved further afield in their quest for fresh grass to eat. But they would come when called. For now, though, they needed to find a campfire and get some breakfast.

The Horde seemed to have been organized into loose companies, all of whom ate together around the same campfire and answered to at least one officer. In most cases these companies had been put together by whichever tribe the men came from, their leaders chosen before they set out to answer the khan's call. But Koblin and Zirghei weren't the only stragglers, and when they came up to the nearest fire circle where cooks were spooning out a thick grainy porridge, they were welcomed in without any questions being asked.

After breakfast they slipped away again, tending to their horses. Most of the riders here had brought at least two horses, resting one while riding the other on the long journey from their tribes' territories to the mustering point. With Nimble and Milacek no spares were needed, but Leila and Tevo were anxious not to draw attention to this fact. After they were mounted again, they began weaving their way through the milling crowds, trying to edge closer to the front without drawing attention to themselves.

The entire horde was soon underway, and at a pace little faster than a caravan could muster. Huge wagons drawn by draft horses were loaded with food for the troops and their mounts, horseshoes, tulwars, bows, and arrows. The Great Horde employed no washer women, as Gholim warriors saw no need to wash their garments while they were riding to war. Leila schooled Tevo on how to add a whiff of stale sweat to his illusion. Though without having bathed after days of hard riding, it would soon be no illusion.

The vast majority of the Horde's riders were mounted on the scrubby little hill horses the Gholim preferred; but fortunately Nimble and Milacek were not the only Gaspari horses in the crowd. They might have been forced to extend their illusion to their mounts, a tricky affair while worming their way forward, if they had been the only warriors mounted on horses three hands taller than the average. But the big Gaspari animals – imported at great cost from west of the Pahadai – were a status symbol to some. Some Gholim tribes had even begun breeding them, using Gaspari stallions to add muscle to their own herds. Any who asked were told proudly that these two had been bred by their father.

It was nearly noon when they finally got close enough to the front to see the vanguard. It was there that the Great Khan rode on his Hisan steed (a surprise to Leila, who had seen no such animals since coming east of the Killtops) amid his most trusted lieutenants. The kid at the palace yesterday had mentioned that Rajani and the children had gotten on a "wagon," and she'd been looking forward to seeing her precious boy for the first time in more than a month, sitting on a bench seat in the kind of high-sided wagon the supplies were hauled in. No doubt the khan thought it too dangerous to have his hostages mounted on horses of their own.

But there were no women, no children to be seen at the Horde's leading edge as it moved sedately down the Ghezh road. And no wagons like the ones at the rear. Just one enormous, lumbering, armored box mounted on three axles with heavy cartwheels, drawn by a team of four draft horses. From where Leila and Tevo sat their horses, a hundred yards back and off to the east, there were no doors or windows to be seen.

By the Eight, it was a wheeled fortress! A portable treasure chest carrying the khan's two most valuable possessions – *their* son, and the daughter of Emperor Ostden! Leila felt a wry trickle of satisfaction as she considered that at least the sorceress Rajani was also locked up inside there. How were they even able to *breathe*?

Inside that rolling fortress, the temperature was starting to rise. They had the shutter flaps over all the vent holes open, but the silk cloth screening those holes reduced the air flow. On the plus side, it kept out the flies and most of the dust as well. Several thousand horses and their manure had turned the Horde into a mobile fly paradise. Likely farmers along the strip between the Tekushi and the road would have enough fertilizer to last them for years.

The day had barely begun, and already Rajani was in a foul temper. She should have just taken her chests of gold and had Danava transport her to Delai, abandoning her plan to build a temple in Ashbat. The hostages were just a couple of seven-year-old brats. Oghul Khan could have hogtied them and thrown them over saddles for the trip to Miradil, and it would have been fine with her. But no –

he demanded that she accompany the Horde, providing her sorcerous aid to his plan for the conquest of Miradil and the Dominion beyond it.

She was stuck inside this creaking, rattling, foul-smelling prison cell with them twenty-four hours a day, not even allowed outside to stretch her legs or get a breath of fresh air. It was intolerable! The rift that seemed to have grown up between her and her goddess was another source of irritation. She was almost afraid to call Danava at all, let alone request that she stay manifested in her idol, maintaining the shield that hid them from the boy's parents.

Danava had confessed that she had come to Betsalel's call, and might have unintentionally revealed that Rajani and the children had been taken to Ashbat. She was convinced that there was no way they could come here in less than several weeks, the Shadow God having no temples within the Gholim lands. But Rajani had developed a healthy respect for the abilities of those two and their dark god, and she wasn't so sanguine.

She took the little idol out of her pocket and set it on the floor. Danava disliked having to remain manifested in an idol smaller than a full-sized human woman – such as her soul had once inhabited, but so long ago she had forgotten what it was to be truly human. "Mistress, come to me, I beg," the old woman said humbly. Gabriel and Berta were lying on their bunks, reading some of the books that had been provided.

Danava manifested and looked around. She disliked these cramped quarters, but had endured worse during the weeks it had taken for the "Nima woman" Rajani to travel to Parat. "It will soon be very hot in here, mistress," her arch-priestess remarked. "I fear for my own health and that of the children, if we are forced to endure these conditions for long."

Danava considered. Such things were outside her purview, and she had found her attempted healing of Rajani's injured horse a few weeks ago unpleasantly taxing. But she didn't want the old woman to die on her! No person living today was so attuned to her mysteries, despite what she'd said. And Rajani had promised her goddess a great new temple with new worshipers, new acolytes being trained to carry on Danava's mysteries. That was important, a goal worth working for. After her recent experience with Betsalel, the goddess was feeling in need of a confidence-booster.

The black goddess concentrated, and fresh cool air flowed through the wagon's interior. She had discovered the same spell by which Betsalel had provided climate control to Leila's little house in Namei, but did not know how to make it permanent. "Thank you, mistress!" Rajani cried in relief, falling to her knees and kissing Danava's feet. A little shot of energy flowed through the black goddess at the surge of worship. She was even getting a little from the children, though that was really just gratitude.

"I can maintain this while I am manifest," she warned her arch-priestess, "but I fear the effect will soon wear off when I am not here." Rajani didn't reply, just gave her a pleading look. "Of course, I will stay with you as much as I can," the goddess said graciously. It would require no more than a few minutes at a time to go to the aid of other supplicants, and she could pick and choose which prayers to answer.

Her four arms waving gently in their dance, Danava cast her awareness out. They were at the head of a great company of mounted warriors, she realized. As a warrior goddess herself she enjoyed being in the midst of them. A pity that Belantos was the one most warriors in this part of the world turned to! What victories she could provide them, what feasts of blood, if only a fraction of those beyond these wooden walls were her believers!

Suddenly a beacon blazed in her mind, not that far away behind them. Not a burst of light, but of darkness – shadow, illusion... Betsalel! "Rajani, there are two among this host who bear the protection of Betsalel," Danava warned silently. "They are the same two who were there when I spoke with the Shadow God in Tiangong, a man and a woman. I believe the woman is the dark boy's mother, whom I saw in Parat. The man was with her when they caught us on the road after taking the children. And now they are mounted on horses that also bear the dark one's touch, though I am not sure how. The humans are shrouded in illusion, but I can see them clearly."

"Can you strip this illusion from them, so that all men may see them as they are?" Rajani asked eagerly. She could rid herself of her dogged pursuers once and for all, if they were taken in the midst of the khan's army. He'd have their heads off in a moment, if she gave the word. That the god they carried with them could protect them from all harm and whisk them off to any of his temples should they be hard pressed didn't immediately occur to her.

After making an effort, Danava reported "No, I cannot. Piercing their illusion is my nature, but the illusion itself is a thing of Betsalel's and his power is beyond mine." Damn! Well, it was worth a try. This morning the goddess had been more cooperative and forthcoming with her favors than had been the case since that incident on the Ivory Road weeks ago.

Rajani made her way to the wagon's door, mounted in the front up a short flight of steps to the driver's box, and shouted through the ventilation slit. "Hey!" she called out, "A word!" The wagon driver was flanked by an armed guard, and the latter turned around.

"What is it?" he asked in neutral tones. He didn't like being around the Black Witch, as everyone in the palace called her (but never to her face). But he wasn't about to sass her, either.

"My arcane arts have revealed that there are spies traveling with the host, and they are quite near this wagon!" she said, annoyed to be speaking through a slit. Why couldn't they just open the door and let her out? Even their meal trays were delivered and returned through a small hatch in the bottom of the door, kept latched except when in use.

The guard was alarmed. "Spies?" he stood up on the driver's box and leaned on the top of the wagon, scanning the host behind him. All he saw was hundreds of nearly identical young Gholim warriors, all in the same uniforms and riding horses. A few horses were taller than others, but there was nothing to suggest that any were not what they seemed. "I see nothing out of the ordinary," he reported.

"Danava has alerted Rajani that you are near," Betsalel informed Leila and Tevo silently. "She told the guard there are spies here, and now he's looking to see if he can spot you. Don't do anything to draw his attention." Koblin and Zirghei rode along as before, glancing around no more and no less than any of the other riders in the Horde. Since the tall Gaspari horses' strides were longer, there was a greater number of them here near the front than there were further back, and they did not stand out.

Rajani sighed. How were they to root out two spies cloaked in illusion, from among thousands of mounted warriors? The woman, Gabriel's mother, had made herself into a dead ringer for Berta, even though she was far taller than the little girl. Clearly, they could take on any appearance, or disappear entirely. On the other hand, they could scarcely get to her and the children locked as they were in this armored box. "Warn me if they come closer or try anything, mistress," she told her goddess, and sat back down.

Chapter 55

Leila and Tevo eased back, encouraging Nimble and Milacek to move more slowly, and gradually they fell further back in the host until Betsalel informed them that he no longer sensed Danava's eyes upon them. "She is not eager for us to meet again!" his voice commented in their minds, tinged with amusement.

The Horde moved along at a fast walk, which was the best pace they could maintain without outdistancing the star of the show – the wagon with the khan's hostages inside. With their power of tirelessness, Leila and Tevo could probably have beat them to Miradil on foot. But for now they just hung back, keeping their eyes and ears open as they tried to hatch a plan for freeing the children.

Not long after they'd returned to the outskirts of the sprawling, many-legged beast that was the Horde, a halt was called. No fires were to be made, but water troughs were pulled from the wagons and filled so horses could drink. There were a few small rivulets coming down out of the hills, but this was a dry land once you got away from the Tekushi. Men drank from their water skins and ate cold rations they carried with them, relieved themselves. The grass around the stopping spot would be dead and reeking of ammonia within a few days after the host had departed.

Soon they were on the move again, Leila and Tevo communicating silently with each other through their link with Betsalel. "That box they're in looks awful," Leila said sadly. The thought of everything her beloved son had had to endure these past weeks, all because they had not thought to watch him more carefully… but no. He was a strong boy and a smart one, a child with skills. There had been no reason for them to fear he would be snatched from among friends at the Gathering, the less so with Berta's loyal guard in tow.

"I sensed that Danava has made some alterations to it," Betsalel said. "It may not be so uncomfortable as you fear."

"But how can we get them out?" she asked. They had expected to be able to creep close, invisibly, and just spirit the children away – not break them out of a rolling prison cell.

"We must wait until night," the god replied. "When Rajani sleeps, it is likely that Danava will go elsewhere. Then we may be able to approach more closely."

"Could you just become enormous and rip the box apart?" Tevo suggested.

"I fear the children might be injured were I to do that," came the reply.

As the sun was dipping near the peaks of the Pahadai to the west, the road swept around a curve and they beheld the next meeting place. They could smell it as well as see it – the hundreds of warriors, along with twice that many horses, had been here for days awaiting the arrival of the Horde.

There seemed little the would-be rescuers could do until well after the camp had gone to bed, so they had let Betsalel go his way. The dark god was clearly committed to helping them save Gabriel and Berta from being used as the khan's political pawns; but he had thousands, perhaps millions, of other worshipers now and they needed him too. In the meantime, while there was still plenty of light, Koblin and Zirghei found another small company of tribesmen who didn't mind a couple of strangers joining them. The Horde had become even more chaotic as those already riding mingled with those who had awaited them, and everyone was inclined to assume that whomever they met was just like them: along for the ride, and looking forward to a good fight and plenty of plunder at the end of it.

The two slightly grim-looking young men tethered their horses to the rail that had been set up nearby. Functionaries were already working their way through the camp pushing carts, providing fodder and water for the horses. Others brought food supplies, which were passed over to whichever member of the company had been designated as tonight's cook. And as they sat around the fire waiting for the camp stew to boil, skins of fermented mare's milk were passed around the fire.

Leila found the stuff revolting. She'd have much rather had a nice red wine, with the stew of goat and leeks that was simmering over the fire. The Horde had brought along flocks of sheep and goats to provide fresh meat as they rode, for the land could not long support such a large force. Koblin, on the other hand, gleefully drank from the skin and then passed it to his brother. Zirghei, younger and eager to do whatever his big brother could do, drank more and then passed it along. The man he passed it to didn't notice that the skin seemed no emptier than it had been.

There was a hiatus in the drinking as the meal was served. Every rider provided his own tin plate and spoon, and was expected to clean it himself after eating while washing the cookpot fell to whoever had cooked the meal. There was a piece of flatbread for each of them, to wipe the last of the juices from the plate; but that was all. Not much for an army that marched on its feet, but Leila supposed that with the horses doing all the work of getting from point A to point B, the men needed little more.

Besides more fermented mare's milk, of course. As the evening wore on there was tale-telling and boasting, and the singing of battle songs specific to the tribe this group had come from. They had all known each other since childhood, and other under circumstances they might have resented the two strangers in their midst. But this was a special undertaking, an exception to the usual rules, and a carnival atmosphere prevailed.

Whores appeared, strolling through the camp from fire to fire and offering their services to any who had the coin. One older man (that is to say, closer to Tevo's age) took a girl up on her offer, and they went off hand in hand in the direction of a nearby supply wagon. Once you got away from the fires, it was pretty dark out there. Tonight, though, the moon rose late and would be in the sky for most of the night.

Around the sprawling encampment plenty of fights were breaking out – usually within, rather than between, the different tribal groups. You were more likely to have festering resentments against people you lived your life with, than against people you'd only just met. The Aliyev brothers mostly kept to themselves, letting others do the talking and staying out of trouble. While the two carried enough armament to assure they came out the victors in any squabbles, the tulwars they carried were as illusory as their six-foot frames and their uniforms.

With all the drinking going on there was a constant stream of men making their way to the latrine trench to relieve themselves.

When Leila had to go, she stumbled off into the darkness and then vanished, carefully winding her way through the crowds and reappearing as one of the female camp followers. In addition to prostitutes, many constituents of the Horde had brought along wives to cook for them – eliminating the necessity to elect a member of their company for that duty and probably improving their diets as well.

Finally, sentries came through the camp announcing that it was lights-out. Torches were extinguished, fires allowed to die down, and the men were expected to lie down and go to sleep. They'd all be rising before dawn tomorrow to set off, now nearly five thousand strong, on the next leg of their journey.

Koblin and Zirghei laid their bedrolls down not far from one of the supply wagons, and soon appeared to be sleeping. They had almost two hours to wait, to be sure that most members of the throng they had to pass through were sound asleep. Conditions were so crowded that a bubble of silence would always contain at least one person who was not supposed to hear them.

As it grew darker Leila and Tevo went invisible, and began stuffing spare clothing from their packs into their bedrolls until they gave, to the casual eye at least, a semblance of being occupied. The khan's "army" was run in such a haphazard fashion it seemed unlikely anyone would notice or care if two anonymous riders were not in their beds; but better safe than sorry – and it gave them something to do.

Soon silence had settled over the camp. All the little night creatures for miles around had been driven away by the massive human presence here in the lower valley of the Tekushi, and the only sounds were snoring, the occasional burp or fart, and gentle murmuring between sentries as they tried to keep each other awake.

They called Betsalel to their idols, allowing them to speak telepathically with each other through the god's mind. "Time to move, I think," Leila said hopefully. She was getting more anxious by the minute. Would they be able to winkle the kids out of their prison under cover of night?

"Careful not to step on anybody," Tevo warned unnecessarily. The moon was well up on the eastern horizon, and bright enough that their dark-adjusted eyes could make out the sleeping forms littering the ground in every direction. Since they'd been keeping well back out of range of Danava (or so they hoped), they had close to a mile to walk to reach the horde's leading edge and the wagon where Rajani and the children slept. Meanwhile Betsalel monitored the wagon, and reported that Danava's shielding was currently off.

Inasmuch as Danava and Rajani knew they were here, and they knew exactly where the sorceress and her goddess were as well, it hardly seemed to make sense for the Destroyer of Illusions to maintain that shield – especially since she could apparently only keep it in place while she was manifested in her idol inside the wagon with Berta and Gabriel. But whatever reason she had for doing so, it was useful for her adversaries – it gave Betsalel an easy way to sense when she was not present.

Their progress was slow, and another hour of careful creeping from bare patch to bare patch had passed before Leila and Tevo came within sight of the wagon. And they were not happy with what they saw. The entire southern edge of the encampment was a blaze of light, torches mounted on poles stuck into the ground every few feet while armed sentries patrolled between them. The wagon was fitted with six sconces, and each of these held a burning torch.

The torches made it quite easy to see the eight armed guards standing around the wagon with their backs to it, arms crossed and eyes alert for any sign of intruders. While it had seemed unlikely that the khan's guards would be able to find the spies Rajani warned them of amid the thousands of riders in the Horde, they had taken her warning seriously. If, as she said, the spies in question were seeking to take the khan's hostages away from him, they had no need to search for them in the chaos – just mount a stiff guard on the wagon so no one could get in.

"So much for using a pry bar to break open the door," Leila said silently. She was staring in frustration at the hard-faced guards with their dual tulwars. She and Tevo between them might be able to take out four before the alarm was raised, but there was no way they could eliminate all of them without drawing the notice of the other several dozen in the immediate area. Shit!

"I will go see if it's possible for me to get in," Betsalel said. Leila bent and set her little idol down on the ground. The Shadow God was as invisible as they were, so they could not see him as he grew to the height of a cat and scurried silently across the thirty feet of bare ground between them and the wagon.

Betsalel had given his arch-priests the power to erect a bubble of silence around themselves; but the power he took for himself as he made his way to the wagon stopped sound from reaching anyone less than half an inch away from his small body. He slipped easily through the space between two of the guards, who noticed nothing, and strode beneath the wagon.

The thing appeared to have been new-built for the purpose, and by carpenters who knew what they were doing. Even the underside, supported on its three heavy axles, was sheathed in metal against the risk of fire. There were no cracks.

Among his other attributes Betsalel was the god of sleep and dreams, and he could certainly have caused all of the guards around the wagon to fall asleep. Any sentries patrolling nearby would sleep as well. But here in the heart of the Gholim lands, far from his centers of power, he would not be able to send all of the sentries to sleep. Some would see the others fall, and there would be a huge stir. There must be some other way!

The enshadowed god shrank still smaller, and began climbing up one of the wagon's wheels like a bush baby. But from atop the wheel he could see that even the little vent holes in the sides had been covered over by heavy wooden shutters for the night. And the smooth metal covering the sides offered no handholds, in any case.

Balanced on the wheel, he grew until he was tall enough to step across to the driver's bench. The door was heavily barred and locked from this side, and on the inside as well, he could tell. But as he quested inside with his mind, he suddenly rebounded against a barrier. Danava had returned!

"An intruder!" came a voice from inside the wagon. The guards turned at their posts, surrounding the wagon facing inward now – and saw nothing. As one of them climbed up onto the box to check the door Betsalel, tiny again, dropped to the ground and ran – silently and invisibly – back to where Leila and Tevo awaited him.

"The wagon is a fortress indeed," the Shadow God said in their minds. "I am wondering if it might be better to wait until we arrive at Miradil. When Rajani and the children are taken out of the wagon to be displayed to those on the walls, there will be many chances that are not available to us now."

He went visible long enough for Leila to scoop him up and return him to her pocket. Then she and Tevo, still invisible, began walking the long way back to their bedrolls. There would not be much sleep for them this night.

Chapter 56

Leila was not happy about waiting, though she could see Betsalel's point. Breaking the kids out of an armored box surrounded by alert armed guards would be a desperate act. And as the Shadow God formulated his plans, she had to agree that his idea seemed more likely to achieve success without anyone getting hurt.

But traveling with the Horde was an ordeal – one that became worse every day as another one to two thousand unwashed warriors and their manure-producing mounts were added to its numbers. She and Tevo were beginning to develop a certain amount of respect for Oghul Khan – the man seemed to be achieving something that seemed impossible, forging these drunken, testosterone-poisoned, unschooled young warriors into something like an army. Not to mention having arranged for them to make the five-day trek from Ashbat to Miradil without starving to death or stripping the surrounding countryside bare.

Since they'd abandoned their efforts to get close to the wagon where the children were being held, they were at least free to hang back – *far* back – behind the main body of the force, avoiding some of the worst of the noise and confusion.

The Horde's third night was spent in the caravan camping grounds along the Huang, near Ghezh. Tethering their horses for the night, Leila and Tevo slipped into town. The arrival of the khan's army had nearly wiped out trade in the crossroads city, with caravans staying away and ordinary citizens afraid to go out lest they be accosted by drunken soldiers.

But discipline in the camp was good enough that very few Horde members actually came into town. The Karmarzins donned the appearance of the same young Gholim couple they had posed as while staying here weeks before, had a delicious meal, got their laundry done, took hot baths, and made sweet, passionate love before drifting off to sleep in a large, comfortable featherbed in Ghezh's finest hostelry. The innkeepers were glad of their custom.

Unfortunately they had to get up before dawn and rejoin the Horde before someone started wondering who those two big horses belonged to. "Back to the salt mines," Leila groaned, as they walked back to camp. Soon the Aliyev brothers, seeming a bit more cheerful than usual, were hunkered around the campfire with their fellows, eating bowls of porridge.

This day the Horde was strung out for hours moving through the bottleneck of the long stone bridge across the Tekushi, a short distance north of its confluence with the Huang. The land beside the mighty river was narrow, and the congestion persisted through the rest of their journey. As the throng of warriors camped for the night the Ivory Road was completely blocked, from riverbank to escarpment, for a distance of several miles.

Koblin and Zirghei had been slowly moving forward during the day, staying far enough from the wagon that Danava would not become alarmed at their presence but wanting to be sure they could *reach* the wagon when it was time. They spent the night less than half a mile back from the vanguard, sleeping near the escarpment to the north.

The day dawned on what would be the Horde's last day of travel before reaching Miradil. It had taken on the last of the tribal groups called to join it at Ghezh, and now consisted of nearly nine thousand men, twice that many horses, and nearly a thousand non-combatants who were driving wagons, handling supplies, or performing other useful services for the mighty Gholim warriors.

Betsalel warned them not to try getting any closer to the front during the day. Half a mile seemed to be Danava's practical range here – after all, she had only Rajani nearby to supply her with strength. And she seemed to be staying around more than she had when they'd first joined the Horde – her barrier remained in place for almost the entire day.

It was early evening when the Horde arrived at the walls of Miradil, the sun sinking behind the fortress. Here there was a little more room to spread out, and the rear of the column pulled up closer to the front. They remained out of bowshot from the walls, which rose seventy feet above the surface of the Ivory Road.

Miradil was well-garrisoned, and it seemed likely that Ostden had had enough warning of the Horde's march that more guards would have been brought in. So as the host made camp for the night trenches were dug and sharpened stakes placed, lest there be any late-night attempts to sally forth and free the hostages. It appeared Oghul Khan had been reading some books. These military tactics in no way resembled the Gholim tribes' usual way of fighting.

Now, instead of being at the very forefront of the Horde as it had been each night since leaving Ashbat, the wagon with the hostages was a hundred feet back. Between it and the walls were rows of men on foot with bows and spears, riders with tulwars and horse bows. And all eyes were turned to the west.

Two hours after lights-out, Leila and Tevo were once more on the move toward the front. Betsalel had reported that Danava was absent for now. He hoped that if he did not reach out as he had done, she would not know he was close even should she put in a surprise appearance. It had been a mistake to try to probe the wagon's interior.

The circle of empty space around the wagon, provided to assure that no one could sneak up on it without immediately being spotted by the guards, made things easier rather than harder for the Shadow God as he scurried silently between two guards and into the blackness beneath the wagon. He sensed Danava was not present, and acted swiftly.

Betsalel had known Gabriel since the moment when the infant soul that had formerly inhabited the djinn Kivuli had fled into the embryo Leila bore in her womb. That soul had seen much strife, but never had Betsalel detected any sign that its months as an evil daemon had tainted it in any way. The child Usafi had been a victim, and in willingly giving up the status of a god to be reborn as Gabriel Karmarzin he had regained the life, the promise, that had once been stolen from him by his uncle, the cruel and power-mad Mauaji.

Reaching out with a slender thread of power straight into the child's sleeping mind, the Shadow God entered Gabriel's dreams. The boy was anxious about what the coming day would bring, and in the dream he was armed and armored, trying to defend Berta from a swarm of Gholim riders who all had four arms – each wielding a tulwar.

Betsalel appeared, striding over the ground. The battlefield was gray and nebulous, showing no landmarks. He rose treetop high and scattered the black warriors like so much chaff. Then he scooped

Gabriel and Berta up in his strong, loving, hands and lifted them so he could look them in the eyes.

"Lord Betsalel!" Gabriel gasped, his face shining with relief. He didn't think he could possibly have held out against all those four-armed warriors for long. "You came for us, I knew you would!" The dream landscape changed, and Betsalel was once again no more than six feet tall. The three of them were relaxing in the gardens of the Imperial palace in Parat, amid warm summer breezes laden with the scent of roses.

"Gabriel, I truly am here with the khan's army before the gates of Miradil," the black god told the little boy. "I am speaking to you in a dream, so that no others may hear. Do you understand?" Gabe's eyes widened, but his expression was one of delight.

"Cool!" he said. The news that his parents were near, and that the god he'd known as a sort of fond uncle was with them, had renewed his hope.

Betsalel went on, as Berta sat on the grass and watched. She was not sharing the dream, but was always in Gabe's thoughts. "Tomorrow morning they will bring you out to display you to those who watch from atop the city walls," he said. "The khan will deliver his ultimatum, and he expects that Berta's father will yield to his demands in order to save her life. But we will rob him of his triumph. And you are going to help."

"What do I need to do?" Gabriel asked eagerly. He had felt so powerless all these weeks, just baggage being dragged from one place to another by a succession of untrustworthy adults. The chance to actually take some action filled him with excitement and glee.

The dream Betsalel put a hand to his side, barely pinching the flesh. "Hold out your hand," he told Gabriel, and dropped something into it. It was black, contrasting with the dark boy's pale palm, and no bigger than a grain of rice. He peered at it with his sharp young eyes. "It's an idol!" he exclaimed. "A teeny tiny idol!"

"And a true one," the god explained. "Before you were born, your mother helped to revive my church in Palambo with such tiny seed idols. When I manifest in one, I can make it whatever size I need. And when you are shepherded out of your prison tomorrow, as they prepare you to fulfill the role they intend for you, you will find

355

these tiny idols scattered on the driver's box outside the door. I will put two on the driver's box, on the side of the door opposite the hinges, and more on either side of the small ladder that leads down from the box to the ground."

"What do I do with them?" Gabriel asked, all business.

"You need only collect one of them," Betsalel replied. "I don't know exactly how the khan expects to display you and Berta, so you will have to decide where to put one. Should he choose to have you stand on the driver's box of the wagon, you will need to do nothing. If he takes you somewhere else, you will need just to drop the tiny idol to the ground beside you. When the moment is right, I will take you two away to Miradil."

Chapter 57

Koblin and Zirghei Aliyev, seemingly as gung-ho for plunder and conquest as any other of the thousands of bloodthirsty young men in the Horde, nonetheless ate supper and sacked out for the night far toward the rear of the host that was spread out from the riverbank to the cliffs across the Ivory Road east of Miradil. They and their chance comrades were roused before it had gotten fully light, instructed to prepare themselves for what was anticipated to be a triumphant march through the opened gates of the city followed by a short, bloody battle with its defenders.

But instead of pushing forward to get closer to the front, as many were trying to do, the brothers discreetly edged backward – moving slowly to the east until they were near the eastern edge of the encampment. Then they, and their horses, vanished.

Leila and Tevo, maintaining their invisibility and extending it to their horses, climbed down off their mounts and took their packs. They might still need some of the items in them, before this day was out. Then Leila set her little idol on the ground, and it remained invisible.

Betsalel grew, putting a hand on each of the horses and sending them to sleep on their feet before shrinking them. They rapidly got smaller until he could carry one in each hand without becoming too large for the Temple of the Eight in Parat. Then he, and the sleeping animals, were gone. For a split second an enormous idol of Betsalel dominated the road behind the host. But it vanished again almost immediately, and any who saw it must have taken it for a hallucination.

Minutes elapsed. It had probably taken Betsalel a while to deal with returning the horses to their original size and getting someone at the temple to take them in hand. Everyone at the Temple of the Eight knew the Karmarzins, and knew these horses. They would be hitched outside the temple to await their masters, or else someone would take them up to Shadow Manor to be stabled at home.

Tevo, who had his hand on the idol to include it in his shadows, suddenly felt the cold stone quicken beneath his fingers and begin to shrink. He stepped back, and Betsalel cloaked himself in shadows as he shrank to six feet in height. As he was the source of his arch-priests' shadow power, they were not invisible to his sight.

"Something else occurred to me while I was taking the horses to Parat," he told them silently. Tevo and Leila were standing close together, and he touched each on the shoulder. "I am conferring on you the power to speak so that all within sight will hear you clearly," he told them. "Who knows, perhaps it will prove useful to you in your ministries. But I will be otherwise occupied when we begin, so you must do this for yourselves."

Leila was tickled. Superpowers, collect them all! She thought whimsically. Although the collection of powers granted to her and Tevo by Betsalel was certainly an odd one. Trying out this new power would have to wait until the moment when it was needed, however.

That done, Betsalel shrank the rest of the way until he was small enough to fit into Leila's pocket again, then went visible. Even in daylight, the little matte-black idol with its tiny red-jeweled eyes was not easy to spot, and he commanded her "Pick me up, beloved. I'm just in front of your right foot."

Leila scooped him up, then she and Tevo – still invisible – turned toward the west. The mass of Gholim riders filled almost all the space between them and the trenches that had been dug last night, but some way back from those trenches was a large clear space.

Leila pulled binoculars from her pack and peered through them. "It looks like carpenters are knocking together some kind of construction down there next to the wagon," she told Tevo silently. Betsalel extended his awareness for a closer look. The trenches were nearly a mile to their west.

"They are building a platform," he told them. "I suspect that they plan to display the children on it. They must be certain the hostages are visible from the walls."

"You warned the emperor and empress not to worry?" Leila asked.

"Lisabet has become a worshiper," the Shadow God told her. "I have been keeping her informed of all that has gone on during your pursuit of the children, and she was very relieved to learn you had caught up with them. I didn't tell her all we planned, but promised her the children would be taken to the Temple of the Eight in Miradil when we make our move. She and Ostden are on the walls now, watching through binoculars, but will hurry there as soon as they see that we have been successful."

"As soon as," not "if," Leila thought with pleasure. It was a good plan, and it should work. And if unforeseen circumstances arose, as they had done over and over and over again since Gabriel and Berta were first snatched, there were backup plans. Here before the walls of Miradil, Betsalel had more than just two worshipers feeding him power. She resolved to keep calm and assume that everything would come out all right. But if they were just now building the platform, there would probably be hours of waiting ahead. She and Tevo tossed their bedrolls down on the ground, and sat on them.

The waiting was driving Gabriel crazy. On the one hand he felt as he imagined a condemned prisoner might, waiting for the executioners to come and lead him to the gallows. And on the other, he was bubbling with excitement and anticipation of the moment when he would grab up one of those tiny idols Betsalel had promised him, and the Shadow God would whisk them away.

He imagined Lord Betsalel growing as high as the walls of Miradil. He would sweep the khan, and Rajani, and all those stinky Gholim warriors away with a wave of his hand, and just lift the children over the walls into the arms of their waiting parents. But breakfast had come as usual, and that was hours ago. When were they going to get started? Gabriel burned to tell Berta about his dream, and about what was going to happen so she wouldn't be afraid. But the confines of their rolling prison were too small for him to say anything to her without the risk of Rajani hearing. And anyhow, he didn't really want to try to explain to his friend how he knew it had been a real sending and not just a stupid dream. She didn't know Betsalel the way he did.

Finally, when Gabriel was about ready to jump out of his skin, there came a rattling at the door. It was being unbarred and unlocked from outside. There was a bar and a lock on the inside as well, one that apparently only Rajani could open. The door had been opened a couple of times every day since they'd been locked up in here, taking out the chamberpot and replacing it with a clean one. Meals came through a slit in the door that was usually covered with a locked flap, just as the air holes were covered at night.

After unlocking the door for the guards Rajani moved back, behind the children. "All right you two, time to leave," she said sourly. Inside she was thinking "Praise Danava to the highest! I will never go back inside this stinking box again!"

The goddess, manifest within the little idol in Rajani's pocket, replied silently with an amused, "Thanks, dear."

Gabriel urged Berta to go first, stepping in behind her as they moved up the aisle and to the open door. They could see a pair of guards waiting on the other side. There were a few short steps up to the level of the driver's box. Rajani would have to stoop going through the doorway, but that wasn't a problem for the kids.

Augh, the sunlight! After days cooped up inside the box with only candles, lamps, and the least little bit of filtered daylight, the late morning sun shining in from behind them and reflecting from the pale stone walls of Miradil was like a knife through Gabriel's eyes. He stood on the driver's box blinking and rubbing his eyes, trying to get them working so he could look to the side for the little black idols. But before he could do so, Rajani prodded him from behind.

"Get a move on!" she demanded. She was as stir-crazy as they were, and anxious to breathe fresh air again. Not that the air in this encampment of more than ten thousand horses was exactly "fresh." Before Gabriel could even glance at the bench the guard on the left side of the wagon, where the ladder down to the ground was, had seized him roughly by the elbow and was pushing him over to where another guard stood on the ground, waiting to take him off the wagon.

"I can climb down by myself!" he demanded as the man held out his arms. The guard shrugged. He had kids of his own, so he knew what they could be like. Let the boy show everybody how grown up he was. Gabe stood with his back to the guard and put his feet on a rung of the ladder, while his hands were on the platform where the wagon driver's feet would rest. He felt something small and hard lying on the smooth wood, and in an instant he had palmed it!

Berta had been lifted down by another guard and was already being led, held by her left elbow, to a raw-looking wooden platform that had been built beside the wagon. It even looked like the gibbet Gabriel had seen a picture of in one of his history books, except there was no pole for a noose to hang on. It was maybe twelve feet wide, six feet deep, and four feet high – enough to put anyone standing on it well above the sea of warriors massed before the walls of Miradil.

Near the forward edge of the platform, which had a low railing around it, some heavy chains with manacles and leg irons had been firmly attached to the wood. Uh oh. The guard with Berta seemed to be searching her, making her open her hands, checking that she hadn't slipped anything into her pockets before chaining her to the platform.

Yow! As the guard held his left elbow and chivvied him to the platform, Gabriel pretended to cough. Being a well-bred boy, he of course covered his mouth with his hand. And a moment later, the tiny idol of Betsalel was lodged between his cheek and the gums on the rear right side. He climbed the platform and submitted to the same search Berta had endured before being chained up, and Rajani came up to stand at the far end. No doubt she had Danava manifested in her pocket, ready to sound the alarm if Betsalel showed up. Gabriel hoped the god, and his parents, had come up with a good plan.

Finally all was in readiness. The walls above them were thronged with watchers as Oghul Khan mounted the platform to stand at the children's right. "All right, Rajani," the khan told the old sorceress quietly. "I require your assistance so that all may hear me." They'd discussed this before, and Danava had assured her she could produce the effect as long as she was manifest nearby.

The khan stepped toward the front of the platform and his voice boomed out, speaking passable Gasparto. He was probably the most educated, and the most ambitious, man his tribe had produced in a dozen generations. "People of Miradil, Emperor Ostden, and Empress Lisabet," he began. Everyone within sight of him heard his words – but the vast majority of his Horde behind him could not understand them. Only a few of those he addressed knew the details of his ultimatum, a written copy of which had arrived here days ago. Now all would learn of it.

"I have tried for more than a year, using peaceful diplomatic means," the khan went on, "to acquire for my Khanate the same rights and privileges which other nations enjoy, free admission to Miradil so that we may trade with the Gaspari Dominion, and space within the city for a trading enclave. As this was denied to me repeatedly, I have regrettably had to resort to more… direct means of achieving my goals."

On the walls above, Empress Lisabet was staring fixedly at her daughter through a pair of the finest binoculars available in the world. Her precious baby, long red hair blowing in the wind, standing there straight and brave beside her little friend. Oh Betsalel, please, come through for us! She prayed silently.

Oghul Khan continued with his public address. "You see before you Berta Piastin, only daughter of the emperor and empress of the Gaspari Dominion. And beside her is Gabriel Karmarzin, only son of the arch-priest and arch-priestess of Betsalel within the Dominion – and grandson of the king of Palambo." How did he know that? Gabriel wondered. He was sure he had never told Rajani, let alone the khan, anything about his Bapa Vandao. But he supposed kings had their own ways of getting information.

"As these children are under my control, my demands have now changed," the khan went on. "You will open the gates of Miradil to me and my warriors. You will lay down your arms, and cede to the Khanate ownership and control of Miradil, its operations and revenues. Taxes collected on goods passing through Miradil will henceforth be the property of the Khanate. The Dominion is a large and rich land, and my people have far more need of these resources than you do."

There were gasps and mutterings atop the wall, but the sound didn't reach those on the ground. Was this man insane? Oghul Khan continued. "If these demands are met, your children will be returned to you safe and unharmed once the ink is dry on the paperwork effecting the transfer of ownership. However, if the gates are not opened to us within one hour from now" – the khan pulled out an expensive pocket watch – "I will remove a body part from each of the children. A finger, an ear, perhaps a nose? My sorceress stands by to assure that the wounds will be healed so the children will not bleed to death. At least not immediately. But they will be maimed for life. This will continue every hour until the gates are opened. I suggest you do it now, and spare these innocents the pain that will come to them unless you act swiftly."

This time the murmur of outrage from the watchers above was loud enough that Gabriel and Berta could hear it from where they stood on the platform. The late summer sun was almost overhead, and it was getting hot out here. Gabriel glanced to the side. Berta was looking stricken, her freckles standing out stark against her pale cheeks. "It's all right, we're going to get rescued," he murmured to her under his breath. The Horde hadn't understood what their khan had said, but they were cheering anyway – waving their tulwars in the air and calling out their warbling battle cries. So it was unlikely anyone besides Berta had heard him.

Berta reached over and took Gabriel's hand, squeezing it and giving him a wan smile. She probably thinks I'm just saying that to make her feel better, Gabriel realized. I hope she's wrong... The chains permitted them to move a little bit, but not more than a foot in any direction. Gabriel twisted around and saw that Rajani was starting to look uncomfortable. She was an old woman, after all. It was probably a strain for her to be standing on her feet, but no cushions had been provided. The Gholim didn't seem to go in for chairs, he'd noticed.

Meanwhile a palace functionary of some sort, a man the khan had brought with him from Ashbat to see to his personal needs, had come up and ceremoniously presented his boss with a sharpening steel. Oghul Khan produced a gleaming jeweled dagger with one curved, tapering edge about a foot long, and began ostentatiously sharpening it. Clearly, he meant the onlookers to assume that he was getting ready to start lopping bits off the children if his demands weren't met. Gabriel wished he could believe it was just for show. But from what he'd seen of the Gholim culture he was sure the khan would do exactly as he said. So now, Lord Betsalel, he prayed silently, would be a really good time to get us out of here!

Suddenly there was a roaring sound from the rear. The riders had been sitting their horses and idly looking around, waiting for the signal to move forward and take over Miradil. Those afoot at the front had been looking up at the walls, wondering how long it would take the Gaspari emperor to admit defeat. There was no one directly in front of the platform now, as Oghul Khan had wanted the emperor and empress to have an unobstructed view of their little girl as she stood in chains awaiting mutilation.

Gabriel and Berta were the only ones in the host who could not rotate completely around to stare in disbelief and wonder as two enormous figures suddenly appeared. They were a mile away, at the very rear of the host, yet they towered above it and were plainly visible to everyone in it. Their voices were heard as well, even by those on the walls of Miradil.

The kids were able to crane their necks around enough to see what was going on, though, as everyone else's eyes were riveted on the huge apparitions to their east. And every person there recognized the likeness of Andros, god of all things manly; and Belantos, god of war.

Gabriel immediately realized that the figures must be an illusion created by his mother. He had seen her become monsters plenty of times, though appearing as *two* enormous gods at once was a good trick. So were the booming voices, which seemed to fill the air. But the gods spoke in the language of the Gholim, not in Gasparto.

First one, then the other god bellowed out curses on the assembled tribesmen. "It is the part of a man to protect children, not to torture or harm them!" cried Andros. Belantos took up the refrain, "There is no honor for a warrior to win his battles by trickery, or in coercing his enemies by threatening his children. Shame!"

Gabriel glanced around, and every eye was on the enormous gods. Quick as a wink, he spat out the seed idol and dipped his knees, setting it on the platform between him and Berta. No one paid him any attention, and the gigantic gods continued to rant.

Rajani was staring at the apparitions as hard as anyone. She'd never had any truck with the Eight, having been raised from early childhood in the mysteries of Danava. Could Andros and Belantos truly appear out of thin air? And why should they care whether the

Gholim Horde was behaving honorably? Bad things had been happening for thousands of years, and the gods had rarely gotten upset about the situation.

Only a few seconds had passed when Danava spoke in her mind. "That is an illusion created by the mother and father of the boy," she said.

"Is Betsalel with them?" Rajani asked sharply, and as silently. She had greatly disliked her one encounter with the Shadow God.

After a moment the goddess replied, "No. I do not sense him there. Seemingly he has granted these powers to his dedicants so that they may serve him, even when he is not present." How, how could he do that? Danava had been a goddess for thousands of years, and it was a trick she had never learned. The knowledge rankled.

Gabriel was still expecting the tiny idol he'd set down carefully at his feet to grow huge, carrying him and Berta off. He was astonished when, instead, their chains vanished into thin air and everything around them became enormous. Then he recalled how Danava had shrunk them before carrying him, Berta, and Rajani off to Delai. Betsalel must be making them the size of ants!

As Rajani continued to stare in wonder at the illusion of the ranting gods, wondering what her opponents hoped to gain by this mummery, the goddess suddenly cried out in her mind. "He is here! Betsalel, right beside us..." Rajani whirled. A diversion, she should have realized!

But where the chained children had stood there was nothing. No dark god, no children, no chains. They had vanished! Her wordless cry alerted Oghul Khan, and he turned to find his hostages gone. He glared at the Black Witch in fury. "You! What have you done?" Rajani started back, drawing her idol out of her pocket and setting it on the rail of the platform.

"I did nothing!" she protested. "It was the work of those..." she gestured toward the towering figures of Andros and Belantos, and realized that they had vanished as suddenly as had the children.

"You bitch!" Oghul gritted, stepping toward Rajani wielding the razor-sharp dagger he'd intended to use on the children. "Guards! Take her!" he commanded. But as he stepped closer, intending to slash the Black Witch's throat for her perfidy – or at least for her failure to prevent his hostages from being taken from him – the black goddess Danava rose to a height of seven feet and hopped nimbly down off the rail. The khan recoiled.

His guards, braver or more foolhardy, came rushing in and met death as the Destroyer filled all four of her hands with the deadly, divinely sharp *kukrisi* that were her signature weapon. They sliced through tulwars, shields, armor... flesh, and muscle, and bone. In moments the platform was awash in blood, strewn with the corpses of those who had tried to get at Rajani.

Oghul Khan gaped at the carnage. What was this monstrosity the Black Witch had conjured? He was an educated man, but he had never heard of Danava. He turned and fled, and a thousand Gholim riders close enough to the platform saw him go. Their rage turned incandescent. "Coward! Liar! False khan!" The warriors' disappointment at seeing the promised plunder ripped away from them was replaced with a burning desire for revenge. Moments after the khan had mounted his silver stallion and attempted to flee, he was swarmed under.

Leila and Tevo were aghast. The chaos that erupted as the word came from the front that the captives had vanished and the khan had fled was beyond anything they had imagined possible. As soon as they had dropped their gigantic illusions they went invisible and began sprinting east, moving north as well in the hopes that, if they could just reach the cliff, they would be out of the worst of the fighting. They were now wishing they'd kept the horses – though if they had, their plan would have left the poor beasts stranded and possibly dead.

On the platform, Danava found no more enemies opposing her. The khan's retreat had left the rest of his guards disinclined to pursue the fight. Indeed, some of them were now chasing their former leader – in hopes that joining the throng seeking his death would make people forget they had been his supporters.

The black goddess took her arch-priestess into her arms, and in a split second only the seven-foot black idol stood upon the platform. Nobody noticed, unless it was some of the watchers up on the walls of Miradil. A few minutes ago they'd all been anxiously waiting to see whether the khan would carry out his threat, wondering if

Emperor Ostden would give in and hand them all over to the tender mercies of the Gholim Horde. Now, they watched in fascination as the "army" imploded, breaking into tribal groups and fighting amongst themselves. It was entertainment they could happily have watched for the rest of the day.

In the Temple of the Eight in Miradil, more than a mile from the eastern walls, the enormous idol of Betsalel came to life. Almost before Gabriel and Berta could notice, they were once again their normal sizes and being gently set down by the Shadow God. Priests of the temple stood by ready to receive them. "Your parents know that you are here," one told Berta. "They will come for you before long. In the meantime, come into our quarters and we'll offer you refreshment."

To Gabriel, Betsalel said "Your parents and I have some unfinished business. But we will be with you shortly." "Thank you, Lord Betsalel," the boy responded formally. But his grin was as bright as the full moon shining in a midnight sky.

Chapter 58

Leila and Tevo had not yet reached the cliff wall when Betsalel manifested in the idol contained in her pocket. To their left, the battle of Gholim against Gholim raged. Seemingly, they were not yet ready to become a nation and were demonstrating that fact in the bloodiest way possible.

"The children are safe at the Temple of the Eight," the Shadow God informed them. "Let me down, and we'll be on our way." They seemed in no immediate danger, invisible as they were and with the fighting taking place at least fifty yards to the west. She set the tiny idol on the ground. Betsalel grew to a height of eight feet, and gathered Leila and Tevo into his arms.

"The khan?" Leila asked, before they were transported. "Gone, I think," the god replied. "At any rate he will never again lead his people."

Rajani found herself in her familiar quarters in the palace at Ashbat. Her mind was full of rage and despair. Destroyed, utterly destroyed! The khan's gold would be small enough compensation for the disaster that had befallen her plans. She had been thinking of those plans lovingly for weeks, turning them over in her mind as she became more and more convinced that the position of arch-priestess at the new temple of Danava in Ashbat would be the perfect way to finish what life remained to her.

Now all was in ruins. She would take her gold and go back to Delai. Mayhap the goddess would grant her a position of prominence at her temple there, and she could still work to acquire new acolytes. But the disappointment, the destruction of all her plans, was a bitter taste in her mouth. Those cursed Gasparis! They had scotched her in Khirzai, and even though she had come back to fool them in Tiangong they had somehow done her in again. She still did not understand how.

Danava remained manifest in her idol as Rajani hurried around the room, gathering up a bundle of things she would need to take with her. Clothing, jewelry, trinkets she'd amassed during her years as the khan's court sorceress. After putting the bundle on the floor near where the goddess stood, she went over into the corner near the bed and considered the chests of gold. She gave one a tug. No, it was ridiculous. They were far too heavy for a single human to move. Danava would have to shrink them for transport. And better the gold stayed in the chests they'd come in.

Rajani moved back toward the center of the room, intent on requesting Danava's aid in dealing with the chests of gold. Suddenly a black shape erupted from the floor, no more than five feet from where the black goddess stood. Betsalel! And his arch-priest and arch-priestess, as well! How…?

Danava whirled, cold fear like a knife in her heart. Their last encounter had not gone well, but she was prepared to fight him with everything she had. Betsalel had no weapons – when he killed, he did so with a thought, not a knife. And that would not work against another god or daemon, or against any human who bore another god or daemon's protection. But here in this room he had two believers – powerful believers – to Danava's one. The Shadow God flexed his power, and a weapon appeared in his hand. It was an enormous club, all black and somehow fuzzy around the edges. When he swung it at his adversary, there was a wash of shadow and a low-pitched moaning sound like the groan of a dying behemoth.

Danava fought back with her *kukrisi* as Leila and Tevo approached Rajani. "You stole our son," Leila told her. They had come as themselves, at the last.

"You terrorized him for weeks, and put him through untold hardships," Tevo said.

"He was just along for the ride!" Rajani screeched at them, drawn dagger in her left hand. With two fingers missing, she no longer trusted the grip of her right. Each of her foes were holding a pair of daggers, and she suspected these were not the only ones they had.

"You should be thanking me I did not just kill him outright!" the sorceress declared. From her point of view, keeping Gabriel alive had been completely optional. Why were these insane dedicants of Betsalel being so vindictive? They continued their approach, backing her into the corner where the chests of gold stood. "I treated him kindly!" Rajani cried. "I never intended either of them harm!"

Now there was a familiar tale. Leila wondered where Jiao Jing was now. Had he truly exiled himself to some remote province, there to live out his life as a priest of Ling Zao? Across the room, Danava had rediscovered the fact that the Shadow God, manifested in his idol, appeared to be impervious to harm. Her *kukrisi* skittered harmlessly across his supple black flesh – so like her own in appearance – though the blades would cut through steel or stone.

The black goddess, despite the unwieldiness of her extra pair of arms, was more nimble. But she could not harm Betsalel, and with every sweep of that club he was coming closer to striking her. "Yield to me, Danava," he urged her. "You cannot defeat me." Yield? That was ridiculous! She was an immortal goddess, and he could not destroy her. If he struck her with that club, he would only damage the idol in which she was currently manifested. She thought. But did she truly know? What ancient, secret powers might the Eight possess? She could not reach her arch-priestess, backed into a corner on the far side of the room beyond the looming Shadow God. Danava fled.

In an instant, the protection that had shielded Rajani from physical attack vanished. Despairing, she pulled her second dagger from its hidden sheath, holding it as best she could and standing with her back against the chest she believed held an uncountable treasure in gold. Her black eyes dared her opponents to come near, but they had no need to. A second later a dagger sprouted from the sorceress' throat, another from her breast. With a faint moan, she collapsed to the floor.

Epilogue

Summer had gone, but a last glimmer of golden weather still lingered on. The throng gathered in the gardens of the Imperial palace in Parat were dressed in light clothing, warm sun beating down on them as all eyes were fixed on the stage that had been set up for this event. Later there would be a Grand Ball in celebration, but first there was to be this public ceremony.

Busara and her children had returned to Palambo briefly after Leila, Tevo and Gabriel had come home; but they were back – this time with Vandao joining them. As members of the family, they'd been given seats on the stage while the rest of the spectators were in chairs that had been set out on the lawn.

Vandao, now in his early forties and with a lot of silver creeping into his black hair, watched with pride as his daughter and her husband came forward to stand in front of Emperor Ostden the Fourteenth. Empress Lisabet, their daughter Berta, and their little son Aleksei stood beside him.

Miriam (who looked little like her namesake, but was still utterly adorable), was sitting with her aunts and uncle. They and Busara had been her whole family for more than a month while Mama and Papa were gone, and she'd bonded with them deeply. They all watched as Leila and Tevo, clad in clothing they would never have dreamt of a decade before, rose and walked to the center of the stage to stand before their monarch.

"Leila and Tevodar Karmarzin," Ostden began with the greatest formality. Betsalel, manifest in a tiny idol inside a small lace-embellished pouch at Leila's hip, had volunteered to provide him with the ability to be heard by everyone watching. "Your efforts on behalf of the people of the Gaspari Dominion, and of my family and me in particular, are beyond any that history records. Without what you two have done, our beloved daughter might be dead – or the Dominion in ruins. You have earned the gratitude of all the Gaspari people." The Dominion held many ethnic groups who were emphatically not Gaspari, but in a sense every citizen of the Dominion might be considered so.

371

Leila and Tevo inclined their heads graciously. They'd been told that they were to be honored in front of this gathering of every noble that could be gathered during the weeks that had elapsed since their rescue of the children. That was pretty much every count in the Dominion, with assorted family members brought along for the occasion. If the two former thieves stopped to think about it, it was enough to make their heads spin. Even Count Friedrich of Oester, son and successor to the late Count Wilhelm, had come.

The Imperial Seneschal stood beside the emperor, holding up a case. He opened it and Ostden removed a gleaming gold necklace on which an elaborate gold medallion hung. The Order of the Gaspari Dominion had been created centuries before, but no one had received it in living memory.

Of course as the man Tevo had to be the first to have the medal hung around his neck. But Leila didn't begrudge him the honor. The teenage thief whose abilities she'd disparaged nearly a decade ago had given rise to a man who was worthy of every honor that could be given. And she was next.

Ostden addressed the crowd again, his ringing voice reaching all the way to the back rows. "The Order of the Gaspari Dominion is the highest honor our nation has ever bestowed," he said. "But it is not enough to repay you for the service you have rendered. After consultation with the Grand Assembly, it has been decided that the title of Duke of Parat will be resurrected."

Leila and Tevo stood motionless, staring at Ostden in disbelief. There had last been a Duke of Parat more than a thousand years ago, when the king of Gaspar was just beginning his march to conquest. With Parat the empire's seat, and the counts providing local rule to the empire's many regions, there had been no need for dukes here.

"The title of Duke of Parat," Emperor Ostden declared with a twinkle in his eye, "is primarily an honorary one. The duke, or his duly appointed representative" – a sly glance at Leila – "will of course have a seat in the Grand Assembly. There are certain lands and revenues associated with the title, and the Karmarzin family will be added to the Imperial archives as the holders of that title henceforth. Other than that, I expect you" – a gesture at Tevo – "and the duchess" – a wave at Leila – "to be in attendance at all of the best parties in Parat from now on."

As the new Duke and Duchess of Parat wilted on the stage, flabbergasted, the crowd went wild. It was a gathering of the nobility, and the nobility loved to see worthy individuals welcomed to their exalted ranks. Leila, who had grown up regarding the nobility as parasitic scum, was now confronted with the knowledge that she'd just become what she had always hated. A few moments later, she realized that she had been let in the front door. The entire structure of the Dominion's aristocracy was now open to her – from the inside, where there were no stone walls and no locks. This was going to be fun!

The End

www.ingramcontent.com/pod-product-compliance
Lightning Source LLC
Chambersburg PA
CBHW061309170626
46817CB00001B/116

* 9 7 8 0 8 9 6 2 0 0 2 3 4 *